Other books by Peter Grant:

The Laredo War Trilogy:
1 – War To The Knife

The Maxwell Saga:
1 – Take The Star Road
2 – Ride The Rising Tide
3 – Adapt And Overcome
4 – Stand Against The Storm

Memoir:
Walls, Wire, Bars And Souls

Forge
A New Blade

Book 2 of The Laredo War trilogy

PETER GRANT

Fynbos Press

ISBN: 0692461981
ISBN–13: 978-0692461983

Cover art by Luca Oleastri:
http://www.innovari.it

Cover image supplied by Dreamstime:
http://www.dreamstime.com

Cover design by Oleg Volk:
http://www.olegvolk.net

This book is dedicated to my sisters,
Elizabeth, Frances and Margaret.

Contents

Laredo: March 27-28 2851, Galactic Standard Calendar

PRISON CAMP #3, NEAR THE SMALL TOWN OF CARISTO

The twilight was deepening as the two figures walked slowly around the perimeter track. The warning wire five meters inside the triple-layered fence was strung at knee height, marking the outer limit of the furrow worn in the dirt by the prisoners over the past several months in their aimless anticlockwise circuits every day. To cross it without permission was to risk being shot by the guards in the towers at each corner of the small compound. Even if they weren't feeling trigger-happy, any such transgression would earn the offender ten days on bread and water in solitary confinement. Considering the sawdust consistency and flavor of the prison camp bread, that was bad enough.

Gloria patted Jake's hand as it rested lightly on her right arm. "I know it's frustrating, but there's nothing we can do with the level of technology available here. If the Bactrians had been able to treat your injuries properly – not to mention quickly – it would have made a difference, but most of their medical supplies had been destroyed, and their facilities were swamped by thousands of their own wounded soldiers and civilians. Prisoners of war were low on their priority list. By the time they got you to an operating theater, all they could do was extract the remains of your eyes and clean up the scarred sockets. They couldn't even fit glass eyes, because that would have meant removing the scars and bio-engineering smooth sockets, and they didn't have the time or the facilities for that."

1

Jake rubbed the bandage over his empty eye-sockets. "It's still frustrating to know that on a more advanced planet they could give me back artificial vision at least, if not clone new eyes."

"Yes, but they're not going to ship a prisoner of war to Bactria or Neue Helvetica or anywhere else to incur that kind of expense – not unless we tell them your real name, of course."

Jake grimaced, and lowered his voice to a whisper. *"Careful!* Don't say that too loud, in case a guard's listening over a parabolic surveillance mike. No, we've got to let them go on thinking I'm just Captain Jake Smith, a supply puke who got conscripted into our last big operation because of a shortage of warm bodies. If they ever find out who I really am, they'll try to use me to put pressure on my son, sure as we're standing here."

"I doubt Dave knows you're alive."

"Not yet he doesn't. At least he's raising all kinds of hell for Bactria at the United Planets – or rather, reading between the lines of their propaganda, that's what he seems to be doing."

She sighed. "I *wish* we had more accurate information about what he was up to!"

"It'll be something interesting, I guarantee you. I –"

Her gaze had gone to a particular bush about forty meters outside the perimeter fence, as it always did when they passed this point. She tensed as a momentary, very faint pinprick of blue light flickered at its base, almost invisible unless one knew where to look for it. A few seconds later a tiny dark object arced silently upward from the bush at high speed. It hit the hard earth inside the fence, bounced three times, then rolled gently underneath the warning wire and a meter or two into the compound. The guards in the towers about fifty meters to either side gave no sign that they'd noticed anything, which didn't surprise her. This technique was tried and tested.

She patted Jake's hand on her arm to interrupt him, then spoke very softly, hardly moving her lips. "A message ball's just been launched into the compound. It's landed about twenty meters ahead of us. You know the drill."

"Say when," he murmured.

"Stand by... almost there... *now!*"

Jake pretended to trip over his own feet, clutching at Gloria's arm for support, stumbling sideways into her. "I'm sorry!" he called plaintively as he went to his knees. "It's these damned eyes. If I can't see my own feet, how the hell do I know where to put them?"

She toppled forward and to the left, reaching out with both hands to break her fall. Her right hand closed over the tiny ball. "It's all right, Jake. I understand."

"Yeah, but I hate it when I hurt you!"

"It didn't hurt much." She pushed herself to her feet, brushing dust and dirt from her clothing. In the process the little ball disappeared into a pocket. She reached down to Jake and helped him stand once more, speaking a little louder than usual for the benefit of any guard who might have trained a security camera with its parabolic microphone on the disturbance. "I think we'd better get you inside. You're tired, and when you get tired you're always more off-balance than usual."

"I guess so."

The guard in the nearest tower watched them as they cut across the compound to Hut Number 3. As they disappeared inside, she wondered idly whether the woman would take the man into her bed that night to help him relax – then shivered at the thought of a lover with empty, scarred eye-sockets looming over her, pawing at her body that he couldn't see. *Ewww!* No, if that woman had any taste at all she'd look for a sighted partner instead. There were several dozen other rebel prisoners in the compound who'd doubtless be more than willing to oblige her, particularly given the ratio of thirteen men to one woman inside the wire. Besides, despite being the oldest person in the camp, she was not unattractive.

Gloria led Jake slowly down the corridor to her room and through the door. He felt his way along the wall to her lower bunk and sat down as she drew the curtains, then took the tiny ball from her pocket. He listened to the crinkling of paper as she unscrewed the rubber-coated halves of the steel sphere and opened the message inside.

"It says George Charlie Tango," she read, her voice rising with excitement. "That means we've heard from off-planet at last! Charon wants us to listen for him at zero-two-hundred."

"*At last!* It's been almost a year since our big fight, with no direct word what they were up to."

"I guess we'll find out later tonight. Who is Charon, anyway? Do I know him?"

"You know better than to ask that. What you don't know can't be tortured out of you or given away by accident."

"Yes, but it's so damn *frustrating!* I know you military people have several projects you're working on, but no-one will tell me a thing!"

Jake was unmoved. "That's the way it should be. I'm not party to all of them either."

"*Jake Carson!* You can be so *exasperating* sometimes! I chaired the Council of the Resistance, dammit! Even my husband took my orders as such, and he was our Commanding General! Now I'm the only civilian leader left. I'm just a spare part, basically ignored in military affairs. It's as if all my past accomplishments count for nothing at all anymore. How do you expect a person like me to feel about that?"

He sighed. "I guess I hadn't put myself in your shoes. I can see your point, Gloria; but facts are facts. We have to deal with the situation we're in now, not the one we were in this time last year, nor the one we may be in this time next year. You led the Council of the Resistance. I commanded a regiment. Neither of them exists any longer. Both of those roles are behind us now. We've got to do what we can, with what we have, where we are."

"But what *can* we do? What can we accomplish? We can't affect *anything* rotting in here!"

"I'm not so sure about that – but I can't say any more about it either."

"Why not? Am I any less trustworthy now than I was last year?"

"No, not at all. It's simply a basic principle of security. What you don't know you can't reveal – whether because you want to, or because you're tricked into it, or because it's forced out of you. The fewer people who know a secret, the more likely it is to stay a secret. That's just the way it is."

~ ~ ~

At 01:45 the following morning they walked slowly down the dark, deserted corridor, lit only by a few dim night lights spaced far apart, to the corner room at the end of the hut. It was designated as a recreation room. A shelf on one wall supported a selection of readers, loaded with whatever books their captors had decided did not pose a security risk. They'd all read most of them by now, forced to do so by sheer boredom if not out of interest.

They didn't switch on the light, preferring to leave the room in darkness. She kept watch at the window while Jake ran his fingers over the reader devices, selecting a medium-sized unit with a keyboard and a smaller one with only a few selector buttons. He carried them over to a table beneath the window and set them down.

Gloria put her writing pad and pen on the table, picked up the smaller reader, pressed three buttons in a complex sequence of keystrokes, then held it out in front of her as she walked around the little room. Her circuit complete, she did another while holding it down towards the floor, then a third pointing it up towards the ceiling. "Looks like they're not listening," she murmured.

"Good." Jake lifted a flowerpot from its drainage dish on the table. "Any water in there?"

"A little."

"OK." He picked up the dish and emptied it into the flower pot, tapping it to remove as much moisture as possible, then turned it upside-down and set it on the table once more. Sitting down, he deposited the flowerpot on the floor.

Gloria took the chair next to his, putting down the reader and pulling the inverted drainage dish towards her. She bent low and sighted along two of the four raised bumps on its lower surface, lining them up precisely between a nick on the edge of the table and a mark on the windowsill. Satisfied, she picked up the larger reader and laid it carefully in a slight depression on the inverted dish. To the untrained eye it looked like a simple flaw, a hollow in the clay, but it held the reader firmly in a specific orientation. Daylight would have shown its top aimed directly at the peak of a distant hill, but in the darkness nothing was visible outside the window.

"It's aligned," she told Jake.

"Good." He produced a simple pair of wired earbuds, plugging them into a socket in the reader. They were normally used to listen to music without disturbing others who wanted to read, but tonight they'd serve a far more important purpose. He pulled on the buds, separating the wire connecting them a little more, then handed one of them to her. She placed it carefully in her ear as he did likewise with his bud.

Jake held out his hand, and she placed her pen in it. He uncapped it and used the point to pick carefully at the spacebar of the reader's keyboard. After a few attempts the bar came loose from the clips holding it at either end. He removed it, revealing two black dots on the gray plastic case between its two clips, then returned the pen to Gloria, who poised its tip over the nearer of the dots. They waited in silence, glancing frequently at the timepiece on the wall.

At 02:00 precisely, a tiny diode on the top of the reader glowed red. A voice crackled over the earbuds. "Sink me the ship, Master Gunner – sink her, split her in twain!"

Gloria clicked her fingers in frustration. "That's... who is it, dammit?"

"Tennyson," Jake replied. "It's from 'The Revenge'. The response to that challenge is from Macaulay's 'Horatius'."

"Trust an egghead to use *poem* challenges and responses!" She nudged his arm impudently with her elbow.

"A lot of military men like martial poetry. Besides, I'm betting ancient verses from England on Old Home Earth are the last thing the Bactrians are likely to recognize."

"I've got to admit, it's not a bad idea. Go ahead." She pressed gently on the black dot with the point of the pen.

Jake leaned over towards the microphone – the other black dot. "And how can man die better than facing fearful odds, for the ashes of his fathers, and the temples of his gods?"

There was a brief pause, then, "This is Charon, over."

Gloria replied, "Persephone to Charon, go ahead. Peleus is with me. Over."

"Charon to Persephone and Peleus. There's a hell of a lot to tell you. Are you ready to take notes? Over."

She pulled the pad closer. "Persephone to Charon, ready, over."

"Charon to Persephone, here goes."

The voice talked for almost half an hour. Even using abbreviations and writing as fast as she could, Gloria was forced to interrupt several times and ask the speaker to slow down or repeat something. At last he came to the end of his narrative. "That's the story so far. Now we come to orders for future operations. Over."

Gloria raised her eyebrows, glancing across at Jake. *"Orders?* What makes Dave think he can issue orders to us?"

"We made him Commanding Officer of all off-planet Laredo forces, remember? And he's now the President Pro Tem of our Government-in-Exile as well. I'd say that gives him more than enough authority."

Her lips tightened. "Yes, after those bastards murdered Vice-President Johns!" She was silent for a moment, struggling to control the fury that had been bubbling inside her since they'd learned that news. "Still, that only gives him authority *off*-planet." She ignored Jake's sudden frown as she depressed the 'Transmit' button once more. "Persephone to Charon, go ahead, over."

"Charon to Persephone, this is a verbatim transmission of Mercury's words. I quote: 'If the Council of the Resistance is still operational and free of enemy restrictions, I respectfully request that they subordinate all their future activities to the plans I've outlined. They should not do anything that would interfere with them. If the Council is no longer operational or its surviving members are subject to enemy restrictions of any sort, I issue the following orders to the remainder of the Resistance and the citizens of Laredo. I do so in terms of the authority conferred upon me by my orders from the Council of the Resistance last year, and also as President Pro Tem of Laredo's Government-in-Exile under the authority of the Great Seal of Laredo, in terms of the Declaration of Emergency filed by Laredo with the United Planets prior to the Bactrian invasion. Under no circumstances is any Laredo citizen to say or do anything that might be used by Bactria to undermine or counteract the policies, actions and plans of Laredo's Government-in-Exile, particularly since the latter will have very few opportunities to discuss or co-ordinate its future actions with anyone on the planet. In particular, any co-operation with Bactrian military, diplomatic or political efforts against the Resistance or the Government-in-Exile is absolutely forbidden. I hereby authorize the Resistance to execute anyone disobeying these orders, if that becomes necessary.' End quote. Over."

Gloria's jaw dropped in astonishment. She managed to gather her thoughts sufficiently to say, "Persephone to Charon, please wait."

She looked at Jake. *"Well!* Your son's on a tear, and no mistake! Ordering *everyone on Laredo* to obey him, just as if he were President – and

7

encouraging the Resistance to execute our citizens! Who the hell does he think he is?'"

"Gloria, he *is* the President of our Government-in-Exile. He has the right and the authority to issue orders like that."

"Yes, but only to our *off-planet* forces!"

"No. You're flat-out wrong." Jake's voice was hard, remorseless. "Our Declaration of Emergency specified that in the event of his death or capture, the powers of our President would transfer to the President Pro Tem of our Government-in-Exile until we can hold free elections to replace him. Also, Dave qualified his message. If the Council is still operational and free of restrictions, he *requested* its co-operation. Well, it's no longer operational, and its only surviving member – you – is a prisoner of war. Under those circumstances he's issued his orders. I agree he's being hardline, but if I were in his shoes I'd probably do something similar. He's obviously afraid that the Bactrians may look for a way to 'divide and rule' by persuading the Resistance on Laredo to go along with them in some way. If we do, they can use that at the United Planets as an example of how the Government-in-Exile is out of touch with people here, and should therefore be ignored."

"But it *is* out of touch with us! This is the first time we've heard from it, or from him, in almost a year! What if I – if we – don't agree with what Dave's doing?"

"That's irrelevant. We handed him the responsibility, remember? He's taking the ball we gave him and running with it. We have no right to complain, even if we don't like the direction he's going or what he has in mind – which he hasn't told us anyway except in the broadest possible outline, obviously for fear the Bactrians might learn enough to cause problems for him. Personally, I don't see anything wrong with his intentions."

She struggled to find words. "I – I don't..."

"Gloria, you're feeling left out, ignored, slighted at being excluded from the decision-making process. I don't blame you for that – it's only natural after having held such authority – but you've *got* to understand and control that reaction. It's wrong. You no longer have any authority, because the Council of the Resistance is defunct. You mustn't try to oppose Dave just because he's exercising *his* authority. He doesn't even know you're alive."

"The Council may be defunct, but I retain the title and authority of its Chair and I won't let anyone take that away from me! Dave doesn't know *you're* alive either, remember? You're his father, not to mention his senior in rank! How do you feel about him issuing orders to you?"

Jake's brow furrowed in concern. "Gloria, in the absence of a Council you have no authority. *Period.* That's just the way it is. We admire and respect you for all you've achieved, and we'll continue to listen to your advice, but you never had the right to issue orders on your own – only in the name and with the consent of the Council. As for Dave issuing orders, I can hardly object. I'm under military discipline, as he is, and we both understand the situation."

"And you don't mind that?"

"That's irrelevant. I'm a prisoner of war – not to mention blind! There's damn all I can do to further our cause from in here. It's up to him and his little band now."

"And how can he and a handful of soldiers hope to accomplish all he's laid out?"

"I don't know, and neither do you, but he obviously has a plan in mind. It's up to him."

She struggled for a moment to find more objections that would hold water. "You may – *may!* – be right, but it grates me to be ignored like this!"

Jake softened his tone. "He's not doing it deliberately, Gloria. He's doing his best from hundreds of light years away, without any opportunity to co-ordinate his actions with you or any of us. There's nothing you can to do influence events from in here. Even if an opportunity arose to do something, unless you know what he's up to, anything you do might interfere with his efforts. He wants you – he wants *all* of us – to stay out of his way. Under the circumstances, I think he's right."

"Well, I don't!" She depressed the button once more. "Persephone to Charon, are you still there? Over."

"Charon to Persephone, still here, over."

"Persephone to Charon, thank you. Please acknowledge Mercury's order. Have you already passed all the information previously agreed? Over."

"Charon to Persephone, yes, I have. Over."

"Persephone to Charon, that's good. Please additionally inform Mercury that we will attempt to comply with his wishes unless circumstances make that impossible or inadvisable. In that case Persephone reserves the right to take whatever steps she deems necessary at the time. She will do her best to liaise with him if possible, but if this is not feasible she will act on her own initiative and authority as she sees fit. Over."

"Charon to Persephone, understood, Ma'am, but I respectfully point out that the Council of the Resistance no longer exists. Your authority died with it. Furthermore, anything you say or do is affected by your status as a prisoner of war. By definition, you're under duress. On both counts, that means Mercury's order is binding on the Resistance. I've already so advised our surviving members on the outside. Over."

"Persephone to Charon, I have not surrendered my authority as Chairperson of the Council even if it's currently non-functional. I *will* act in terms of that authority if necessary. Mercury doesn't have the right to take that away from me. Over."

There was a pause, then, "Charon to Persephone, I respectfully submit you're wrong about this, and I will advise Mercury of the facts of the matter and my opinion. Over."

Gloria bit her lip to avoid saying something that would disrupt relations with their most reliable outside contact. She settled for, "Persephone to Charon, understood. Please advise Mercury of my position as I've stated it to you. Over."

"Charon to Persephone, will do. Anything else? Over."

"Persephone to Charon, negative. We'll circulate this news to the others, and —"

She paused as Jake tapped her arm. "I want to say something to him," he whispered.

She depressed the button again. "Sorry about that. Stand by for Peleus."

Jake bent over the microphone. "Peleus to Charon, please tell Mercury that I agree with his position on current and future plans. I do not agree with Persephone's view that she retains her authority as Chairperson of the Council even though it's now defunct, but I'm not in a position to do anything about that because she isn't subject to military discipline. I urge him to try to coordinate with her as often as he can to avoid complications. Furthermore, in my capacity as senior surviving military officer of the Resistance on Laredo, I confirm all Mercury's orders, current and future, unless and until I instruct otherwise. Finally, Operation Phoenix is to be pursued with all possible urgency. Pass that on to all our remaining cells, please. Over."

Gloria fumed as he spoke. She'd been sorely tempted to interrupt the transmission to prevent him continuing, but knew that if she'd done so she would have destroyed her relationship with Jake. He could order everyone else in the camp to ostracize her – or worse, if it came to that.

"Charon to Peleus, copied and will comply, over."

"Finished?" she asked Jake ominously.

"Yes. Go ahead."

"Thank you," she said icily. "Persephone to Charon, let's hope Mercury gets in touch again soon. That's all from our side. Over."

"Charon to Persephone, I've no idea when the next contact will be. I'll convey your additional information to Mercury's messenger. This is Charon, signing off."

As Gloria put the cap back on her pen, she snapped, "I hope you're satisfied! What is this 'Operation Phoenix', anyway?"

"That's on a need-to-know basis; and no, I'm not satisfied if you're going to get all pissy about this," Jake retorted. "Sorry, Gloria, but you're way out of line."

"*I refuse to accept that!* As its surviving Chairperson, I can reconstitute the Council anytime I please!"

"No, you can't. It was never a statutory body. President Wexler established it as a temporary team of advisers to his office, and he personally selected its members. After his death we kept his Council in being as a symbol of civilian control over the military, but that was always a temporary stopgap until we could hold elections again under our pre-war Constitution without any outside interference. Sorry, but that's the way it is."

"And if I decide to reconstitute the Council anyway? What if I ask you to be a member?"

"You can't, Gloria, and I'd refuse any such offer as being invalid from the start."

She gaped at him in utter astonishment. "You can't mean that!"

"Gloria, there *is* no Council anymore! It no longer exists! Get used to that!"

"I absolutely *will not* accept that! I retain my authority as Chairperson, and I'll use it if necessary against anyone who tries to stop me!"

"And just how will you do that? Who are you going to issue orders to? Who's going to obey them? I promise you, none of the Resistance will. They take orders through our military chain of command alone – meaning me at the top on-planet, and Dave off-planet. Also, remember Dave's second order to the Resistance. Disobey that, and you'll make yourself a target."

She stared at him, aghast. "Do you mean to tell me you'll issue orders to kill me?"

"No, I won't. After all we've been through together, you know better than to ask that. However, the rest of the Resistance will know of Dave's order by now, and those here in the prison camp will know of it as soon as I tell them later this morning. I don't know which of them might decide to act against you, but I've no doubt that if your actions violate Dave's orders, one or more of them probably will."

She thrust herself to her feet. "In that case, you can tell them from me that I *refuse* to be subject to a military authority I've never sworn to accept! I won't be bound by your notions of the right thing to do. If I see a better way forward, I'm damn well going to take it!" She stormed out of the room without waiting to offer him the guidance and support of her arm.

As Jake gathered up the readers, returned them to the shelf and replaced the pot in its drainage dish, he was deeply troubled. He gathered up the notepad and pen she'd left behind and felt his way slowly down the passage, counting doors with his fingertips until he came to his room.

~ ~ ~

"D'you think she means it?" The speaker was a tall, thin man wearing a faded utility uniform.

Jake heaved a sigh. "I honestly don't know, Major Tredegar. I wish I'd understood before how frustrated she was feeling at having lost her former position of authority. Of course, none of us had any certainty that we'd survive our assault on Banka, and none of us expected to end up as prisoners of war like this. Prior to that fight the Bactrians had executed every prisoner they took. I still don't know what caused them to change that policy, but it's at the root of our problem today. If none of us had survived Dave would have pretty much a free hand. As it is, we're going to have to figure out a way forward. I don't want anything to happen to Gloria because of this – out of respect for her husband, if nothing else."

"If Brigadier-General Aldred were still alive, you know he'd throw his authority behind your son as well, Sir, and order his wife to do the same," Lieutenant Kubicka pointed out.

"Yes, but he died in the assault on Banka – right in front of her, as it happened."

Sergeant-Major O'Connor mused, "I wonder if that has anything to do with the vehemence of her reaction last night, Sir? Perhaps she feels that because she nearly died with him, and was part of his final assault, she's got the right to continue his work, even though his authority was military rather than civilian."

"I just don't know, Sergeant-Major." Jake considered a moment. "I suppose all we can do right now is to try to assure her that we continue to respect her as an individual, even though her official position expired with the Council. Do please make that last point clear if she tries to persuade any of you to support her. We can't allow her to divide us."

"Of course not," Major Tredegar agreed vehemently, "particularly given that Dave is at last in a position to move ahead with plans to take the war to Bactria. New ships, new weapons, new crews – he's got some very ambitious plans. I hope he's not reaching too far."

"He's *got* to reach as far as he possibly can, Sir," Sergeant-Major O'Connor pointed out. "With only fourteen survivors of the group he led from this planet, he's going to have to hire a hundred mercenaries for every one of them if he's to get anywhere. I've no idea where he's going to find enough trustworthy people, let alone the money to hire them, and that's without even thinking about ships and missiles."

Jake nodded. "It's a tall order, but his message sounded confident. The Resistance ended up like an old, worn-down, broken knife. He's planning to forge a new blade for it – for us."

"I just hope he doesn't try to rescue us, to add us to his forces," Lieutenant Kubicka said in a worried tone. "He can't know about the trap the Bactrians have prepared for him if he does."

Jake couldn't resist a glance towards where he knew the window lay, even though he couldn't see the hilltop beyond it. They all knew where the hidden missile batteries and laser cannon were sited, ready to ambush any rescuers. Their surviving colleagues on the outside had watched them being emplaced, and plotted their positions.

"He'll know about it as soon as Charon's news reaches him," he pointed out. "That's another reason I instructed Charon to pass the word to accelerate Operation Phoenix. If an opportunity arises, we want as many people as possible to be ready for action." He stretched as he rose from the table around which they were sitting. "All right. You now know as much as I do. Pass the word to your people as discreetly as possible. It's going to be frustrating as hell sitting here twiddling our fingers and toes while waiting for something to happen, but that's all we can do right now."

Neue Helvetica: April 20 2851 GSC

NEW GENEVA, CAPITAL CITY OF NEUE HELVETICA

Dave nodded to the receptionist at the front desk of the Laredo Embassy. "Morning, Sally. How are things?"

"Fine, Mr. President. And you?"

"All parts taking an even strain," he said as genially as possible. He'd long since accepted that trying to get her to use his name instead of his title was a losing battle. He still didn't feel like a President, even though he'd unwillingly fallen heir to the title and position the year before. At least her efficiency compensated for her punctiliousness.

As he passed her desk she added, "Mr. Baumgarten said he needed to see you, please, Mr. President."

"Very well, I'll stop at his office on the way to mine."

The Head of Security was at his desk. He was a man of medium height, powerfully built, dressed in a tailored business suit. Dave frowned as he saw him. He was cleaning a disassembled pulser laid out on his desktop.

"What's up, Mike?"

The man looked up, then came to his feet. "Morning, Sir. We have a problem." He nodded at the door, and Dave closed it behind him before sitting down.

"What is it?"

"You remember the watchers we noticed last week, Sir? They're back – twice as many of them as before. I've just come from the local cop shop, where I greased a couple of palms and got them to run our surveillance pictures through their database. Five came back with matches. Seems they're minor operators for the Gesellschaft."

"That's the umbrella organization for organized crime here, isn't it?"

"Yes. Its name translates as 'The Society'. It's something like the Cosa Nostra used to be on Old Home Earth."

"Huh. I thought they existed only in movies and cheap novels."

"No, they were real enough. They probably still exist in some form. That sort of organization never completely goes away."

"All right. What do we do about them?"

"That's the problem. My contact warned me to tread carefully. If this has been ordered from high up in the Gesellschaft, they'll have cover. They own some city politicians, and they can afford to pay the cops a lot more than their salaries to look the other way. Since I'm paying him to give me information on the side, I guess he's living proof that at least some of them are on the take."

"Yeah. The problem remains; why are they here? This is a relatively quiet neighborhood. There's no likely target here but us, and only one source would be willing to hire the Gesellschaft to keep an eye on us."

Mike seemed to hesitate, then make up his mind. "It might not be just surveillance. There have been cases where other crime groups – gangs, families, even internal Gesellschaft rivals – have been wiped out. I mean, no survivors. According to my contact, each time it seems his bosses didn't much care. 'Good riddance to bad rubbish' was the way he put it."

"So you think we might be in their sights?"

"I can't think of any other reason why they'd be here, Sir."

"I agree. Who's in charge, and where do we find them?"

Mike's eyebrows shot up. "May I remind you that you're an accredited diplomat now? If you take the law into your own hands, you'll endanger your entire Embassy's diplomatic status. That's what got the entire staff of the Bactrian consulate expelled as *persona non grata* last year, after they tried to mess with you."

"You're right, of course." Dave's voice was uncompromising. Despite his words, Mike knew he wasn't about to let the matter rest.

"Er… Sir, you hired Argos to provide embassy and residential security. We're quite happy to do anything of that nature, including defending your premises and people against intruders, but…"

"I won't ask you to do anything that violates local laws. I know Argos is bonded and insured in the Lancastrian Commonwealth. If you did anything like that, it'd cost you millions in local fines and probably lead to the Lancastrian authorities shutting you down, even though Neue Helvetica is many light-years away from the Commonwealth."

"That's about the size of it, Sir."

"I presume you're still willing to gather information for me?"

"Of course, Sir, particularly if it involves potential threats to your security."

"Good. Here's what I want to know…"

~ ~ ~

"Sorry I'm late," Dave apologized as he stepped into the conference room. "Something came up."

"We reckoned it was something like that, Sir," Captain Bill Deacon replied with a smile. He was sitting next to his brand-new wife of only three days, the Embassy's press secretary Elisabeta, who was leaning against him.

"You two look just as sickeningly happy as Tamsin and I must have looked last year," Dave told them with a mischievous grin as he sat down next to his wife. She chuckled as the newly-weds blushed simultaneously. "Any news from Manuel, Elisabeta?" Her brother had been instrumental in getting them all off Laredo the year before, despite all the Bactrian occupiers could do to stop them.

"Yes, Sir. His latest letter arrived yesterday on the weekly dispatch vessel from Lancaster. He sent his congratulations on our marriage and apologized that he couldn't be here. He says you'll learn what's been keeping him so busy very soon now. He teased me that it'll be a wedding present for Bill, among others, but not so much for me. I've no idea what he meant by that."

"Oh? I wonder if that has anything to do with a message that was waiting for me this morning from the Lancastrian Commonwealth's

Ambassador to the United Planets. He wants me to visit him as soon as I can arrange it."

Her eyes sparkled. "It might be related, but I really don't know."

"Oh, well, I'll find out soon enough. The good news is that we've heard from the agent we sent to Laredo. He was able to communicate with a group of senior Resistance prisoners, including my father and Gloria Aldred."

"*Prisoners?* Your *father? Gloria?*" Deacon sat up with a jerk. "But they're dead, surely? The Bactrians haven't taken prisoners of war for two years or more!"

"It seems they've changed that policy. Let me give you our agent's report."

Dave spoke for almost half an hour, his audience listening hungrily to the first real news they'd had from their home planet since they went into self-imposed exile a year before. At last he sat back. "So that's it. I'm amazed that the Bactrians didn't execute their prisoners after the Banka operation, or the others they took during the following months. I don't know what prompted the change in their policy, but I'm very glad it happened! At least some of our best friends and most experienced comrades are still alive. If we can figure out a way to free them, they'll be an invaluable asset."

"Isn't that precisely what the Bactrians want us to do, Sir?" Captain Deacon asked. "From the sound of the defenses they've erected on hilltops around the camp, and the reaction force only a few kilometers away, they're hoping to sucker us into something like that, then wipe us out."

"If we did it their way, sure – but we're not going to. I suspect that's why my father initiated Operation Phoenix. All the surviving members of the Resistance on the outside are combing through those released from slave labor camps – another new Bactrian policy for which I'm profoundly grateful, even though I've no idea why they've changed their approach. Whenever they find someone with any military background, or the right attitude and a willingness to learn, they're recruiting them into cells and training them as soldiers. By the time another year's passed they expect to have enough to form several battalions. If those people on the ground can disrupt the defenses while we move in from orbit, we might be able to rescue all of them in one fell swoop."

"What about their families?" Tamsin wanted to know. "Will the Bactrians retaliate against them?"

Dave smiled at her. "I don't know, so if it comes to that I think we should plan to rescue their families as well."

A rustle of surprise ran through the meeting. "That'll mean ferrying several *thousand* people up to orbit, putting them aboard a ship or ships capable of accommodating that many, and taking them to a planet that's willing to accept that many refugees, Sir," Staff Sergeant Bujold pointed out dubiously. "That's a hell of a tall order, not to mention a bloody expensive operation."

"True. That's why we won't even consider it unless and until we're sure we can do all those things. Of course, a lot will depend on what happens on the planet."

"How soon will we be in contact with them again, Sir?"

Dave shrugged. "It cost us over a million Neue Helvetica francs, mostly in bribes, to smuggle our messenger onto a freighter going there, equip him to communicate with the surviving members of the Resistance using our backdoor satellite channels, and get him back here with his information. We can't afford to do that too often, both financially and in terms of the risk of exposure. If the Bactrians ever find out how we're doing it, they'll shut down our only channel of communication at once. I hope to try again late this year or early next year."

"What have they done about Orbital Control?" Tamsin asked. "Did they replace the space station we blew up?"

Her husband grinned. "Yes, they did, with an old, worn-out five-million-ton freighter, one of the biggest in space. She was apparently beyond economical repair, but that didn't worry the Bactrians. They bought her cheaply, took her to Laredo, limping along, holding her systems together with string and plugging the holes with chewing-gum, and parked her in orbit. Her bridge and accommodation have been converted into the new OrbCon, while her holds are being used as transient accommodation and orbital warehouses. They're parking a lot of supplies aboard her and ferrying them down as required, rather than keep them all on the surface where the Resistance can get at them. They're also spreading them among three or four smaller depots planetside, instead of one huge base like the depot we destroyed in the Battle of Banka."

"What about Mrs. Aldred, Sir?" Staff Sergeant Higgs asked. "If she's going to be difficult, what might that do to our efforts here?"

"I don't know. She doesn't have any actual authority anymore, but she was used to exercising it. I can understand her frustration. Unfortunately, if she insists on trying to influence events, that might play right into the Bactrians' hands. They'd like nothing more than to be able to point to a divided Laredo leadership – even if Gloria isn't officially a leader any more – and use that to undermine our efforts at the United Planets."

Now it was the Captain's turn to shrug. "I suppose we'll just have to cross that bridge when we come to it. There's nothing we can do about her situation from several hundred light years away, so why lose sleep over it? We'll deal with any problems as they arise, just as we've always done so far." There was a murmur of agreement from the others.

"You're right," Dave sighed. "Very well, people. You know as much as I do about the situation on Laredo right now. If any of you have any ideas on how to exploit or make use of any aspect of it, let us know. We've got a busy couple of days ahead. Captain Deacon and I will attend tomorrow morning's session of the UP inquiry, then tomorrow afternoon there's the sentencing phase of former Ambassador McNairy's trial."

Something very like a snarl ran around the table. "I hope they hang his ass out to dry!" Higgs exclaimed viciously.

"We all hope so. He's been convicted on first class felony charges, which should get him a minimum of ten years in jail followed by automatic exile on a prison planet for the rest of his life."

"Let's hope they pick a really nasty one for him," Deacon muttered.

"I'll second that." Dave stretched, then stood. "Very well, people. We've all got more than enough to do. Let's get on with it. Bill, stay behind for a moment, please."

There was a general bustle as the meeting broke up. Dave stroked Tamsin's cheek as the others filed out. "How are you holding up this morning, love?"

She smiled up at him. "OK so far. The morning sickness isn't as bad this time as it was the first. I'm scheduled at the clinic next week to have the baby transferred to a gestation pod, and after that things will get back to normal within a couple of days."

"Thank heavens for pods! I really can't afford for you to be out of action for any length of time."

"You can't afford any of us to be out of action, darling." She heaved a sigh. "We're spread so thin it's just not funny." She grinned suddenly. "I don't know why you're complaining, though. I seem to recall this is all your fault!"

Dave tried – unsuccessfully – to adopt a look of injured innocence. "Hey, you co-operated!"

"Huh. That's *your* story!"

Grinning, he threw up his hands in mock-surrender. "Yes, it is, but a guy can't win an argument like this." He sobered. "Speaking of being spread so thin, that's about to get much worse when some of us head off-planet. Still, there's no help for it. We've got a war to organize."

"Yes, and I've got my part of it waiting for me." She rose to her feet. "I'll leave you two to talk in private."

After she'd gone out and closed the door, Dave sat down again. "Bill, we've got a problem. The watchers are back, and they're bad news." He summarized what Mike had told him. "It's obvious who's hired them. I think we're going to have to teach them a lesson. They've got to learn that it's not worth taking Bactria's money, because we're too dangerous a target."

"I'm with you on that. What's the next step?"

"I've asked Mike to find out more about them. I'm a little concerned that after they killed other people, the police reaction seems to have been to shrug their shoulders and be happy that there were less bad guys around."

"Yeah. That suggests either the cops are being paid off, or they're using them as surrogates. They may even be encouraging them to keep the really nasty bad guys under control. That would mean less competition for the Gesellschaft, less fuss in the press about crime and an easier life for the cops. The politicians can even point to reduced crime statistics when it comes to elections. I guess the powers that be aren't going to be very happy if we deal with them too harshly."

"Right first time. Here's what I have in mind. See what you think."

He described his idea, and the Captain chuckled. "It'll be just like old times on Laredo when we were planning to raid the Bactrians. I'll get right on it."

"Thanks. Try to set it up as quickly as possible. We don't know their timetable, and I want to disrupt their plans before they can put them into effect."

"Will do. Good thing we made friends with the Special Forces Squadron last year. I reckon the Sergeant-Major will be open to a little horse-trading."

"I think so too. You've got enough of the equipment we'll need?"

"I have." Deacon gave a feral grin. "What's even nicer is that most of it used to be Bactria's. I bribed the shipping crew who packed up their offices and homes after the Consulate staff were kicked out at twenty-four hours' notice last year. They let me look around. They didn't know what the cases were, but I recognized them at once. I took them all."

Dave shook his head in disbelief. "Why they smuggled them in through the diplomatic bag system is beyond me. That was probably the Consulate's Security Service representative being paranoid. I won't object, because it means they were there for us to find. One point, though. On Laredo they used lethal neurotoxins only – no antidote. D'you think they'd have been dumb enough to bring that here?"

"Ye Gods, I hadn't thought about that!" The Captain's face was momentarily aghast. *"Surely* they can't have been that crazy! They *must* be using the regular stuff that comes with an antidote… surely?"

"Better find out before it's too late."

"You got that right!"

Neue Helvetica: April 24 2851 GSC

LANCASTRIAN COMMONWEALTH EMBASSY, NEW GENEVA

To Dave's surprise, a receptionist escorted him not to Ambassador Delamere's office, but to a small conference room on the second floor of the Embassy. The Ambassador was already there, along with two men he didn't know. They wore civilian suits, but he instantly recognized that they weren't at home in them – just as he still felt after wearing a military uniform for so long.

"Good morning, Mr. President," the Ambassador greeted him courteously. There was genuine pleasure in his eyes as he offered his hand. Dave returned his handshake equally warmly. They'd built up a relationship of mutual respect over the past year.

"This is Commodore Wu of our Fleet's Bureau of Intelligence," he introduced the shorter of the two people with him, an older man with vaguely Oriental features. "This is Lieutenant-Commander Steven Maxwell, Commanding Officer of one of our communications frigates. He brought Commodore Wu to this meeting."

"Pleased to meet you," Dave acknowledged as he shook hands with them, thinking, *Why is Maxwell at this meeting if he's just a chauffeur? No. He's got to be more than that.*

"Commodore Wu is here to discuss business about which I have neither the need nor the desire to know anything, so I'll leave him to tell you more." There was definitely a mischievous twinkle in the Ambassador's eyes as he headed for the door, closing it behind him.

"Coffee, Mr. President?" Wu invited, gesturing to the pot waiting on the sideboard, accompanied by cups, creamer and sweetener.

"Thank you. Shall we dispense with the diplomatic niceties among ourselves? I may be 'Mr. President' to the Ambassador, but in military circles I'm still Major Carson. That puts me at the same rank as you, Lieutenant-Commander Maxwell, and far junior to you, Commodore."

"As you wish."

They helped themselves to coffee. As he was stirring in sweetener, Wu asked, "I understand the trial of your former Ambassador to the United Planets ended recently. I know he was convicted, but what was the sentence?"

"It was as expected – ten years at hard labor on a prison planet, followed by permanent exile there." Dave gave a short, humorless laugh. "He deserves the death penalty for helping to plan the attack on us at the spaceport, when Vice-President Johns was murdered. Trouble is, we couldn't prove his involvement, so we couldn't charge him with that - only with stealing the contents of her bank account an hour later."

"At least he won't be troubling you again."

"If he does, I'll deal with him myself rather than leave it to the law!" Dave knew that raw anger was suffusing his voice, but couldn't help himself. Vice-President Johns had been killed in the moment he'd reported to her after their arrival at Neue Helvetica from Laredo. The memory was still raw and painful.

They sat down around the small table. "Let me start at the beginning," Wu said. "You launched an appeal for assistance in cash and in kind when you took over as President Pro Tem of Laredo's Government-in-Exile last year. May I ask how successful that's been?"

Dave shrugged. "I suppose it's no secret that the sums actually donated don't come close to those pledged. We were promised almost five billion Neue Helvetica francs by the interplanetary community, of which we've actually received about one-point-eight billion – including a very generous two hundred and fifty million from your own Commonwealth, for which my most sincere thanks. We had six hundred and sixty million francs in our planetary reserve account when I took over. After our expenses over the past year, we currently have about two-point-two billion francs available." He didn't think it was necessary to mention the President's private account he'd established for clandestine, off-the-record projects, into which he'd deposited the proceeds from the sale of the uncut diamonds and other assets he'd brought from Laredo last year.

"That would be enough to buy you just one modern destroyer, fully equipped and armed, and pay its operating expenses for six months," Wu pointed out gently.

Dave grimaced. "You said it! I've got to start buying ships, but I'm at a loss as to what to buy and where to find them, to say nothing of arming them once I've bought them."

Wu smiled. "BuIntel has been looking into that very closely for the past few months. The Lancastrian Commonwealth is very much in favor of your efforts to encourage minor planets to establish some sort of mutual defensive relationship. We've had to support too many United Planets peacekeeping missions to such planets, at a very considerable cost in money and equipment – and sometimes in the lives of our personnel as well. If your efforts bear fruit they should reduce the need for such operations, which will be very much to our advantage. Therefore, we're going to offer you a great deal of covert support to take back Laredo, in the hope that you'll then be able to further develop your proposed interplanetary defensive alliance."

Dave tried to control the excitement swelling within him. "I'm very grateful to hear that. What sort of support did you have in mind?"

"For a start, our armed forces are amongst the largest in the settled galaxy. We have about fifteen hundred vessels in the active Fleet, both in service and undergoing routine maintenance and overhaul, and a similar number in our Reserve Fleet – older warships and auxiliaries in long-term storage that can be reactivated in emergencies. Every year we scrap thirty to fifty ships from the latter, replacing them with vessels from the active Fleet that have been supplanted by new construction. That means we have a steady supply of used equipment – fusion reactors, fire control systems, missile tubes and so on – that are often still in perfectly good order, but no longer required because they're a generation, or two, or three, behind our current systems. We usually salvage components from them or sell non-sensitive equipment on the open market, but we can also install them in other hulls, including any ships you might obtain."

"What about the costs involved in doing the work?"

"We have our own Fleet dockyards, with thousands of robots for construction and maintenance. In time of peace, adding a little extra work isn't something we'll worry about. We can lose that in the petty cash column of our budget. Furthermore, we have thousands of engineers and technicians in various stages of training. It's to our advantage to give them real work to do instead of just make-work training assignments. We'll supervise them very closely, of course, to ensure that the work meets our high standards: but by using them to upgrade and refit your ships, we'll actually improve the quality of our instruction, so we won't charge you for their services. That's already been discussed and approved by… those in a position to do so. I won't be more specific, for obvious reasons."

Dave grinned. "Understood. I can only say that I'm very grateful indeed. I've been pricing major overhaul and refurbishment costs, and even for merchant vessels they're pretty steep – ten to fifteen million francs for a typical half-million-ton tramp freighter. To convert one into what the Bactrians call an 'armed merchant cruiser' would be far more costly. Would your surplus equipment include missiles and laser cannon?"

Wu shook his head. "Weapons are the one thing we can't provide, because interplanetary treaties restrict their sale and they can be easily traced back to the supplier. We're willing to install any weapons you obtain from other sources, of course; and once Laredo's free again, we can sell or donate weapons to it in the same way as we would to any other friendly planet."

Dave's face fell. "That's a blow. They're hard to come by, because most reputable sellers don't want to do business with a Government-in-Exile that appears to be losing a war. Those that are want very high prices for them. Unless and until we can show successes against Bactria, and attract more donations, we're going to find it very difficult to get what we need."

"I understand Lieutenant-Commander Maxwell has some ideas about that, but for various reasons I haven't asked him about them. He's a man with an inquiring mind and a great deal of initiative, which is why I brought him with me this morning. He also has… shall we say, useful contacts that we can't officially use or recommend as a Fleet. If you and he should come to a meeting of minds during a private discussion, I won't know anything about it, of course."

"Ah. I see... I think." Dave grinned at Commander Maxwell across the table, who returned it impishly. He decided he was probably going to like his Fleet counterpart.

Wu nodded. "Let's just say that senior BuIntel officers can't answer questions from politicians concerning something we know nothing about, provided we can *prove* we know nothing about it – under truth-tester examination if necessary. That... avoids complications, you understand?"

"I do. All right. Leaving aside the question of weapons, then, what sort of ships do you recommend we buy?"

"I'm glad you asked that. Let me show you."

Wu took a small device from his pocket. He pressed a couple of buttons to synchronize it to a three-dimensional holographic display that sprang to life above the sideboard against the far wall.

"What do you know about the Bismarck Cluster?"

"It's a group of seven planets about six hundred light years from Neue Helvetica," Dave replied. "They were settled by various German regions and corporations during the Scramble for Space, and developed into a local political union over time." He grinned suddenly. "I've had to learn a lot about the makeup of the settled galaxy since I arrived here. If you'd asked me that question a year ago, I wouldn't have known what you were talking about."

"I can understand that. The Commonwealth's built up close commercial ties with the Cluster, to the extent that some of our planets have economic treaty relationships with them. We also maintain good military-to-military relations with their armed forces, exercising with them from time to time and conducting joint anti-piracy operations."

He brought up a picture of what looked like a freighter on the display. It was longer and narrower than the fat-hulled merchant ships Dave had so far researched. "Lieutenant-Commander Maxwell found out about these ships, so I'll let him tell you more about what you're seeing."

Maxwell sat forward. "This is the Bismarck Cluster Fleet's *Bavaria* class assault transport," he began, "with a net register capacity of about three hundred thousand tons. They built eight of them fifty years ago. They were constructed to military specifications with stealthy reinforced hulls, two reactors and high-performance drive systems. They can cruise at a quarter of light speed, only a little slower than modern destroyers, fast enough to operate with a Fleet if necessary. Each is also equipped with four laser cannon to defend against incoming missile fire."

He frowned. "Trouble is, they're too small for the job they were built to do. An assault transport's supposed to carry enough cargo and supplies to support extended military operations far distant from base facilities. That's why our own assault transports are almost twice as large. They can load far more supplies and many more supporting services – personnel or hospital pods, for example, plus artillery, counter-missile batteries and drone squadrons to deploy with ground forces. The Bismarck Cluster Fleet found it had to use two or three *Bavarias* for an operation instead of one or two larger transports, which was sometimes very inconvenient – not to mention expensive. That's why they built only eight *Bavarias* before canceling the rest of the class and designing larger ships. However, they kept the *Bavarias* in service and used them for training and internal transport duties. That's pretty light work, so they're still in great condition.

"They've finally taken the decision to remove them from service. Instead of transferring them to their Reserve Fleet, they're going to strip them of military equipment and dispose of them, because they don't think they'll have any further use for assault transports that are half as big as they should be. However, they're smaller than most tramp freighters and have less internal cargo space thanks to their military construction and compartmentalization. They're also more expensive to operate, thanks to military-grade systems that don't use standard commercial spares and need more sophisticated dockyard maintenance. That means merchant shipping companies won't want them. They'll end up selling for their scrap value after their usable systems have been taken out – probably no more than five million Lancastrian Commonwealth credits apiece."

Dave nodded thoughtfully. "That's certainly a very attractive price, particularly for military-grade ships; but what about their systems? It's no good if we buy hulks in the Bismarck Cluster that aren't capable of traveling under their own power to wherever your shipyards can re-equip them."

"That's where we come in," Commodore Wu assured him. "We can talk to our counterparts in the Cluster. We've helped each other out on more than one occasion in the past. I think we can arrange to bring the ships from the Cluster to wherever we refurbish them for you. We'll take off their equipment as we replace it with our own, and ship it back to the Cluster for disposal. What's even better from our point of view is that we're about to scrap several old battleships of the *Legion* class. Each has four fusion reactors, fifty per cent more powerful than those in the *Bavaria* class ships but small enough to fit into their reactor spaces. Their gravitic drives and capacitor rings will also be suitable for installation in your ships, as will some of their other systems."

"The news gets better and better! So how many of the Cluster's ships should we buy?"

"I'm going to suggest you buy all of them," Maxwell said. "There are several reasons for that. First, if you put in a bid for the entire class of ships through a front company it looks convincing to outside observers, as if they're being bought in a job lot for scrap. If the ships are later identified in your service, the Cluster can claim they must have been illegally re-sold by the company that purchased them. It won't exist anymore, of course, so tracing the sale will be impossible. Second, the ships should be in good condition, but there's always the possibility that one or more may have been damaged in service. That sort of thing can only be identified by an in-depth inspection, which is difficult and expensive. If you buy all eight and we find a hull that isn't worth refurbishing, you'll have another available to replace it. Third, you're going to need crews. You can hire mercenaries of dubious provenance and reliability, but there's a better alternative. You may be able to swap ships for crews, saving a bundle and getting more reliable people into the bargain."

Dave frowned. "Who would want to provide crews in exchange for old spaceships?"

"I'll come to that in a moment. The fourth reason is that your ships may suffer damage during operations. You may not have access to a dockyard where they can be repaired quickly. If you buy all eight ships, you'll have another available to replace the damaged one. Finally, we can provide spares for the systems we install, but structural spare parts may be hard to come by for ships like these – they're not commercial vessels, after all. If you buy all eight, you can cannibalize one or more of them – perhaps one unsuitable for refurbishment – for structural spares if necessary."

"You're making a lot of sense. If we can get a good price for them all, I'll go for it."

Wu added, "You might want to consider hiring one or more retired senior Fleet personnel to serve as advisors on how best to employ your ships. We can probably introduce you to a few suitable candidates."

"That also makes sense," Dave agreed. "What about the crews?"

Maxwell grinned. "What do you know about Gandaki?"

"That's the planet of the Gurkha mercenaries. I've looked into hiring them, but their rates are very high – too rich for our blood."

"That's not surprising. They're probably the best in the settled galaxy – the only mercenaries we've cleared for operations with our Fleet and member planets of the Commonwealth. In fact, we think so highly of them we've based some aspects of our Marine Corps training on their standards."

"High praise indeed."

"Yes, it is. Anyway, as part of the grant of their planet to them by the Bihar Federation, they were forbidden to form their own System Patrol Service or compete in merchant freight services with other planets of the Federation. They've chafed under that restriction ever since. They've managed to obtain concessions in other areas, but Bihar's remained adamant that they don't want Gurkhas expanding into spacefaring. I found out about that when I worked alongside them on the planet Rolla a few years ago. In private conversations with Gurkha officers I learned they'd love to find a way to train some of their people as Spacers and set up their own merchant freight line, perhaps even have their own warships and provide mercenaries to crew spaceships in due course. The problem's been how to get that started without arousing the suspicions of the Bihar Federation, which has meant they can't do anything in their own system. That's where you – and we – come in."

He paused to drink the last of his coffee. "If you have ships to offer them, we can outfit them with new systems – weapons too, because the Commonwealth has a treaty relationship with Gandaki. We just won't tell anyone about it until it's too late for the Bihar Federation to prevent it; a *fait accompli*. We can arrange with Rolla, one of our planets, to allow you to base your ships there while the planet's System Patrol Service trains your spacers and Gandaki's, and helps to bring the ships to operational readiness. I've worked closely with their SPS, and I can assure you their standards are very good indeed. You'll have to pay for their assistance, of course, but I think with Commodore Wu's help we can arrange for that to be provided at a reasonable cost.

"What this means is that we can offer Gandaki the opportunity to get their hands on a couple of military-grade ships free of charge, fully refurbished, armed and equipped for service. We'd also train several hundred of their people as Spacers. In return they'd be required to provide enough people to crew your ships for a fixed period – say, a minimum of two to three years. Your funds would be used to purchase all the ships, buy weapons and cover operating expenses for your vessels, and pay Rolla to train Spacers for both Gandaki and Laredo. You'll also probably set up a very good long-term relationship with Gandaki by helping them get around the restrictions the Bihar Federation imposed on them. How does that sound?"

"It sounds very fair," Dave said slowly, brow furrowed in thought. "I'll have to look into the actual numbers, of course, but if they're within reason I see no reason not to do it."

"It'll be a lot cheaper than hiring your own military-trained spacers, particularly given issues with quality," Maxwell pointed out. "Any Gurkhas will be high-quality by definition. They won't be experienced Spacers, but they will be experienced and highly disciplined soldiers. That's more than half the battle won right there. They can add Spacer skills without too much problem."

"True. I presume we'll need some experienced officers and senior NCO's as well, though."

"Yes, you will. You can hire them yourself – Rolla might make available some of its retired personnel – or we'll arrange introductions to firms on Lancaster that act as agents for retired Fleet personnel. We can make sure you get good people, although they'll be expensive."

"Quality always is. I don't mind paying for it, as long as I can afford it and I get my money's worth."

"Then you won't have a problem. I'd say you're looking at fifty to eighty million Lancastrian Commonwealth credits to buy the ships and get them to one of our dockyards. Refurbishment will be on our tab. Routine operating costs will be about a million credits per ship per month for those actually in service, plus the cost of non-Gurkha personnel, and you'll probably pay Rolla four to five million per operational ship in terms of training their crews and providing base facilities while doing so. Weapons are going to be your most expensive purchase, of course."

"That's my cue to disappear," Commodore Wu said lightly as he stood. "I definitely shouldn't know any more about what Lieutenant-Commander Maxwell has in mind. That way I can't be made to answer questions about it."

Dave and the Lieutenant-Commander stood with him. "I can't tell you how much I appreciate all the help you've offered this morning," Dave said as he offered his hand. "What will be the next step, please, Sir?"

"If your associates approve of our proposals, you'll have to spend a couple of months traveling to various planets to set up everything. I'll make Lieutenant-Commander Maxwell's communications frigate available for that. He'll tell you more about it. Meanwhile, I'll arrange the purchase of the ships from the Bismarck Cluster. One of your associates will have to set up a company on another planet to act as a front for the transaction, and provide the necessary funds."

"It'll be time and money well spent. I'm sure they'll approve. Thank you, Sir."

They sat down again as the Commodore closed the door behind him. Dave said, "So what about those weapons, Commander?"

"Call me Steve, if you like. We're the same rank, as you pointed out earlier."

"OK, thanks. I'm Dave."

"Good. I'm limited in what I can tell you right now, but let's just say that we – or, more accurately, I – have contacts in certain organizations that... shall we say, aren't very strict in observing interplanetary treaties governing the transfer of weapons. Some of them can best be described as downright criminal. I'm pursuing certain options that might lead to a number of anti-ship missiles becoming available to you. It'll take a few months before I can tell you more. In the meantime, there's a very good option for laser cannon. Ever heard of Marano?"

Dave frowned. "It's where Bactria bought its corvettes and the Satrap's yacht, as well as a bunch of other weapons."

"That's right. Marano makes a pretty wide range of military equipment, from warships to missiles to assault shuttles. They sell them to anyone who's got the cash to buy them, asking very few questions – just enough to stay within United Planets arms export guidelines, and sometimes not even that for cash customers."

"Uh-huh. Money talks."

"As always." They exchanged a cynical grin. "Their weapons aren't the latest or highest technology, but they're workmanlike and of acceptable quality. Among other things, they make a self-contained laser cannon barbette that can be fitted to any ship with a sufficiently strong structure and enough reactor power. That includes the *Bavaria* class transports, of course. They aren't too expensive – about two million apiece, including all associated systems – and they can be integrated with any fire control system."

"Sounds good. Will they sell them to us?"

"Not directly. Don't forget that Bactria buys weapons from Marano too, so they won't want to offend a valued customer. I therefore suggest you use a broker to make an anonymous purchase."

"How do I find one?"

Steve took a folded sheet of paper from his pocket and handed it over. "I'm given to understand that any of these three firms on Marano will arrange the purchase for you, obtain a forged end-user certificate in the name of a third party, and have your weapons loaded aboard a freighter of your choice. They'll charge a premium of anywhere from fifty to a hundred per cent, so play them off against each other to get the best deal. By using them, Laredo's name won't appear on any sales documentation. You can conduct initial negotiations and put down a deposit by message, but you'll have to go there to pay in full, in advance, in bearer bank drafts or hard assets."

"All right. How many will we need?"

"I'd suggest twenty. That'll give you enough to equip four of your ships, plus four spare units. You won't want to arm more than four initially, because you won't be able to afford enough crew members or missiles."

"That sounds logical. Thanks."

Steve sat back. "You may be interested to learn that Bactria's talking to Marano about repairing the two corvettes you damaged at Laredo last year. They're not mobile under their own power, so Marano would have to collect them using a special ferry. Personally I think it'd be cheaper to replace them with new ships, but I guess they have reasons for doing it their way."

"You seem to know a lot about what Bactria's doing."

"Not directly. BuIntel is keeping an eye on Marano, which happens to be talking to Bactria."

"All right. I won't ask awkward questions."

"That's good, because I won't be able to answer them!" They chuckled softly together.

"Two more questions. What do assault shuttles cost? I think we'll need some for boarding operations and any planetside excursions."

"They're expensive. Marano's basic model – you know them; Bactria manufactures a variant under license – costs about fifty million apiece. The more advanced ones like ours run double that or more."

Dave made a *moué* of distaste. "We certainly won't be able to afford many at those prices."

"You may not need to buy any. Gandaki has assault shuttles. They might agree to provide a few as part of their deal with you, or at least lease them to you at reasonable rates."

"That's good to know." Dave hesitated. "The second question may sound weird, but remember I'm just a ground-pounder, not a Spacer. Did you ever read how our people used assault shuttles to ram Bactrian ships?"

"Yes, I did. Commodore Wu gave me some background material that described it. They took out two Bactrian troop transports when they invaded, and the Satrap's yacht during your escape last year. Your pilots were very brave people indeed."

"They were. That started me thinking. The kinetic energy released by a head-on collision between those masses at those velocities exceeded even that of a thermonuclear warhead. I read that many powers, including the Commonwealth, convert old main battery missiles into targets for use during training. They retain guidance and maneuvering systems, but lose the ability to carry warheads. They're very low-cost; under a million francs apiece, compared to many times more than that for a brand-new missile. I suppose that's because their initial cost was amortized long ago. They're freely available, because they're not classified as weapons. I figured that if we launched them as kinetic energy missiles, to hit a Bactrian ship and damage it through the collision alone, it might be as effective as those assault shuttle collisions."

Steve looked at him with sudden respect. "You're absolutely right. They'd have to be fitted with updated guidance systems to be able to home on a target and score a direct hit. That's not an easy thing to do in the face of modern defensive fire and at space combat speeds. Bomb-pumped laser warheads can be detonated ten to fifteen thousand kilometers from the target and lace it from bow to stern with laser beams, making them much harder to intercept. Still, if you launch a barrage of, say, fifty or sixty target missiles against a corvette like Bactria's, armed with only forty defensive missiles, at least some will get through her outer layer of defenses. Unless she has lots of laser cannon for point defense, some of them should reach her."

"The Bactrian corvettes have three or four laser cannon, I understand."

"They'd be lucky to hit all the missiles closing in at high fractions of light speed. I think your idea is a good one. Even better, if you manage to get some nuclear-tipped regular missiles, you can launch an initial wave of target missiles to soak up the enemy's defensive fire. They may get most of them, but then they won't have enough interceptor missiles left to deal with your second wave carrying nukes and bomb-pumped lasers."

"D'you think your Fleet will sell Laredo several hundred target missiles?"

"Probably not that many, but as you say, there are far fewer export controls on missile targets than on missiles themselves. They're available from many planets. If you ordered twenty here and thirty there, you could build up a useful stock over the next year or two. We can modify their electronics and integrate them all with your fire control system."

"Great! That moves up the priority list, then. What's the next step?"

"Over the next two to three months Commodore Wu and I will be making arrangements in our respective ways. I'll be back here in about three months to collect you, then we'll spend two months traveling to various planets before I return you here. After that there'll be an ever-increasing amount of travel for you and your associates as everything comes together."

Dave sighed. "I can see I'd better find a communications frigate of my own as well. How much is a used one?"

"That's not a bad idea, but they're expensive to buy, costly to run, and you don't have a trained crew for one yet. I'd let that ride until you've got enough money to buy one and enough spare crew members to operate her. If you need one in a hurry, you can charter one."

"Fair enough." Dave came to his feet. "Thanks for everything so far. You've given me a lot to think about."

"I'll look forward to your company on board my ship in a few months' time. I want to hear all about Laredo's war with Bactria. You were there from the start, weren't you?"

"Right from the beginning – and, please God, I'll be there at the end as well!"

Neue Helvetica: April 27 2851 GSC

NEW GENEVA

"That's the place," Bill said softly as they turned into Lagerstrasse. The street lights gave an orange cast to the buildings lining it.

"Looks pretty nondescript, just another workers' lunch counter," Dave murmured as they passed the target building.

"Yeah, but that's just the cafeteria up front. The warehouse behind it is where everything happens. They park their cars on the lower level, then take an elevator. The upper level's the most opulent private club on the planet, if rumor's correct."

"We'll see for ourselves soon enough. When do they start arriving?"

"Most of them are already here. Don't turn your head, but a swanky runabout's just turned in behind us. He's... yes, he's turned off into the side street next to the warehouse. The entrance is at the rear."

"Security?"

"Ten people in and around the warehouse, including a team in the cafeteria when it's open – it closes at twenty. The staff in the club are probably armed as well."

"Can we handle them?"

"Is the Pope Catholic?"

Dave grinned. "I guess that was a silly question. They may be good crooks by local standards, but they can't hold a candle to the kind of enemies we faced on Laredo."

"Yeah, Bactria's Security Service makes the Gesellschaft look like a church choir on Sundays. Don't worry. Rusty Higgs and his team can handle anything they try."

Captain Deacon turned into another side street. "We're five blocks away here, outside their surveillance zone." He expertly steered the car through a narrow gap between the doors of a derelict warehouse, its few intact windows grimy, panels missing from the roof. The car's lights illuminated a small group of men waiting against the far wall, where three vehicles were parked facing outward. Bill turned the car around, reversed it to park next to them, and they got out.

"Everything's ready, Boss," Bujold told them with a smile. "Rusty's keeping an eye on them until you say the word."

"Good. No trouble infiltrating the place?"

"None. They've got pretty good security against things that walk on two legs, but that won't help them tonight. I guess they've never had to deal with anyone like us before."

"It's a good thing for us they haven't!"

Another man whistled admiringly as he looked at what Dave was wearing. "Camo fatigues, body armor, webbing, a fancy pistol – you're loaded for bear, Boss."

"Yeah, we never had it this good on Laredo, did we?" Grins and headshakes. "The Sergeant-Major was worried in case I mussed up his gear, so we upped the ante. We're paying him ten cases of beer to borrow it instead of five. That eased his mind real quick." Laughter.

"What's he drink, Sir?"

"Anhalter Bock. It's expensive, but I reckon it's cheap at the price to be able to have this stuff. It'll help to convince the Gesellschaft we aren't bluffing."

Hopefully, "You didn't bring any of the beer with you?"

"What do you think this is, a Founders Day barbecue on Laredo?" More laughter. "Just remember to keep out of sight until the bad guys are out of it. We don't want them to realize that we're not all wearing this stuff. Come on, let's go."

Deacon remarked as they started walking, "That was a stroke of genius, Sir, going to Neue Helvetica's Special Forces squadron soon after we arrived and offering to show them some of what we learned the hard way on Laredo. They were real grateful."

"They sure were. Neue Helvetica's military has a very limited budget for training with foreign forces, and they tend to spend it on their Fleet rather than their Army. That's why I made the offer. When the Squadron saw us demonstrate what we used to do on Laredo all the time, they were hooked right away – and we made some real useful friends, like Sergeant-Major Gerhardt."

"Yeah. He came through for us tonight, in spades."

~ ~ ~

"You all set?" Dave asked Staff Sergeant Higgs as he moved up beside him on the rooftop.

"Ready to go, Sir." Higgs indicated the four consoles in front of him. "Over the course of the last two days I've sneaked the nanobugs and flitterbugs into each location one by one, whenever I came across an open door or window. No-one noticed anything. I've moved them into position under and on top of furniture and inside light fittings. They're ready when you say the word."

"How many of the big shots have arrived?"

"They said all eight were in town, and eight luxury cars have arrived."

"That should be all of them, then. Guards?"

"Three on the perimeter, Sir." He indicated their positions on a roughly-drawn diagram as he spoke. "Four more have just left the cafeteria up front, now that it's closed. They'll join three others inside the warehouse."

"How many of them will be in the club itself?"

"Three or four, usually – the rest look after the vehicles and offices downstairs. There's also a manager, two hostesses, two cooks and two assistants in the kitchen, and seven wait staff and busboys. I'll bet some of them do double duty as extra guards if needed. Each couple came with a bodyguard of their own, who usually doubles as their chauffeur. Three brought an extra bodyguard."

"What are they up to now?"

"The aperitifs and soup have been served. The fish course is coming out now."

"We'd better not let them eat too much. The watchers in the street had just eaten when we chilled them. They vomited their guts out when they woke up."

Higgs made a face. "Can't have been good for the carpet."

"What carpet? We knocked them out, drove their cars around to the rail yard, dumped them there, and put the watchers in a freight car with some water and emergency rations before we administered the antidote. They're probably pounding on the sides right now, trying to get out."

"As long as they stay locked up long enough for us to do our job here."

"They will. We used nanoglue on all the doors before the train pulled out of the yard."

"Wait – you put them on an *actual train,* not just in an empty car?" Higgs' face was alight with glee.

"Yes. I've no idea where it was going, but it took the main line south. At mag-lev speeds even a freight train can be half a continent away by morning. Sooner or later someone'll find them and call a wrecking crew to get them out. That'll be interesting, because we left them stark naked with no ID, money or comm units."

Higgs spluttered with laughter. "Let's hope they're headed somewhere warm!"

"Yeah. All right, let's get this show on the road. How – no, I won't ask questions. You know these things better than I do. I'll just watch. You do your thing."

"Thanks, Boss." Rusty glanced at the other console operators lined up on the roof beside him. "Everyone ready?" A chorus of muted affirmatives came back. "Right. Hein, take out the perimeter guards and those in the warehouse."

Dave found the assault intensely frustrating. He wasn't using virtual-reality goggles to show him what the nanobugs and flitterbugs were seeing through their lenses, so he was dependent on what little was visible to the naked eye. From his position on the rooftop he could see only one guard, halfway down the alley running alongside the target building. In the gloom no movement was visible except the man's slow pacing, his head turning alertly from side to side, scanning from the ground to the rooftops – until he suddenly staggered, reached out a hand to the wall beside him for support, shook his head violently, then crumpled noiselessly to the ground. A few seconds' pause, then two dark figures emerged from further up the alley. They hurried down to him, picked up his limp figure and half-carried, half-dragged him back to the place where they'd emerged. They disappeared from sight around a corner.

"That's it, Sir," Rusty murmured, eyes invisible beneath his goggles. "We've taken out all seven ground-level guards."

"Just like that, huh? No noise, no fuss?"

"None, Sir."

"Okay, I'm impressed. What's next?"

"We take out the big shots and everyone else upstairs, Sir."

"Go for it."

Rusty nodded absently, eyes already focused into his virtual reality goggles. He maneuvered the ten nanobugs and flitterbugs under his control to the edge of their hiding places, positioning each of them where it had at least one enemy target within range. He knew that his colleagues would be doing the same alongside him, preparing their bugs to strike simultaneously. The views reflected in his goggles were sometimes disorienting, distorted by looking through the fine gauze of a tablecloth overlay or inverted because the bug in question was clinging upside-down to the edge of a table or serving trolley. He lined up all of them, one by one, and locked each in on its designated target. It would fire one of its drug-laden needles into its victim, then stand by to fire its second barrel if necessary.

"In sequence, confirm when ready," he muttered.

"Console Two, ready."

"Console Three, ready."

"Console Four, ready."

"Console Five, ready."

"Console One, ready," he affirmed. "On my mark... stand by... three, two, one, *mark!*"

~ ~ ~

Dave looked around the bottom level of the warehouse. Over against a wall stood a row of posts supporting chain-link wire storage cages. One of them was much larger than the others.

"That big cage over there should be large enough to hold all our guests of honor."

"You got it, Sir."

Grunting with the effort, they dumped the men draped over their shoulders onto the plascrete floor of the cage. Dave waited while more bodies were carried in, until eight men and women, all in expensively tailored evening dress, were lined up on the floor. He administered the spray-injected antidote, then left the cage as they began coughing, spluttering and choking their way back to consciousness. As he did so, the others in the team set up several powerful lights in a line along the front of the cage and plugged them into wall sockets. As Dave padlocked the gate behind him, they switched on the lights. The eight struggling victims were suddenly bathed in brightness, forcing them to shade their eyes as they looked up, rendering everyone standing behind the glare invisible and unrecognizable.

Dave waited until he was sure they'd all regained their senses and those worst affected by the neurotoxin had stopped vomiting. At last he said calmly, in the German he'd learned with the aid of hypno-study since arriving on Neue Helvetica last year, *"Guten abend, damen und herren."*

The eight were suddenly alert, heads and eyes turning as they hunted for the author of the voice. "Wh – who are you?" one of them spluttered. "How dare you –"

"Shut up!" Dave's voice cracked like a whip as he stepped forward into the light, all their heads swiveling to look at him. He gave them a moment to look, then said, "You know who I am."

Eight heads slowly nodded. If looks could kill, he thought irreverently, I'd be dead right now.

"You made a mistake. You took Bactria's money to spy on us, then take action against us when they said the time had come. That was a fatal error of judgment – or almost fatal. You're still alive… for now."

"Ja – because you are afraid of us! You don't dare to kill us!" one of the men snapped.

Dave shook his head in mock-sadness. "How did someone as stupid as you end up as a member of the *Lenkungsausschuss?* This 'steering committee', as you call yourselves, is supposed to regulate the Gesellschaft and provide wise guidance to its followers. An idiot like you would lead everyone straight to Hell in a handbasket, you *dumbass piece of SHIT!"* He bellowed the last words, and his audience couldn't help recoiling in shock. He had to fight down a grin. They probably hadn't been spoken to like that in years. He made a mental note to remember the translated version of the insult. The German *'Trottel stück SCHEISSE!'* sounded much more impressive than its Galactic Standard English equivalent.

"Observe." Dave held out his right hand, palm upwards, and waited. Within seconds there came a faint rustling sound. A tiny insect-like metallic creature descended out of the darkness, mechanical wings fluttering, and landed on his hand. He walked closer to the wire and held it up for his audience to see. "Do you know what this is?" Some heads nodded, some were shaken. "It's a flitterbug. Its crawling cousin is called a nanobug. See the twin tubes beneath its glass 'eyes'? They fire neurotoxin-laden darts. That's what put you out for the count tonight before we brought you down here."

All the heads were nodding now. One of the women said, "I remember now... I saw a movement out of the corner of my eye, something small, then I felt a sting at the back of my neck." Her hand went to the place. "Was that one of those darts?"

"It was." Dave reached for the spray injector at his belt and held it up. "Consider yourselves fortunate that we used a temporary paralyzing agent instead of a lethal poison. This is the antidote. We injected you with it once we got you down here. Your partners, the club staff and all your security people are still unconscious." He held out his hand again. The flitterbug took off and disappeared into the darkness behind the floodlights as he returned the injector to his belt.

"We infiltrated this place with no trouble at all, and brought in enough flitterbugs and nanobugs to take care of everyone. You never even saw them coming. Tell me, dumbass," looking at the man who'd snapped at him earlier, "what was to stop us killing you all? Why should we be afraid of you after we've penetrated every one of your defenses so easily?" The man glowered, but made no reply.

"Perhaps killing does not come easily to you?" another woman asked half-mockingly.

"*Ha!* Let me remind you of Bactria's claims about our big assault on Laredo last year. They say they suffered over twenty thousand casualties, including twelve thousand dead. The team under my command killed well over four hundred that day alone. How many people has your most dangerous, most lethal enforcer killed for you? Ten? Fifteen? Twenty? I've personally killed more than that during a single battle; and in three years of constant, unrelenting warfare I saw plenty of battles and firefights. No, ma'am. Killing doesn't bother me *at all.*"

She nodded slowly. Her face had gone pale.

"Then why have you spared us?" another man asked slowly.

"Because I have a more important mission." Dave paused to let that sink in, then went on, "I've just demonstrated I could have killed you tonight as easily as snapping my fingers. I can do so at any time in the future. However, you know what happened to the Bactrian Consulate last year. They were found to be in violation of their diplomatic status, and all their people were expelled. I don't want that to happen to us, so I'm trying to avoid doing anything that might cause it. Note that I said *'trying'*. If I have to act, I will, and I won't let anything or anyone stop me. I decided to first show you how vulnerable you are, in the hope that it might – *might* – make it unnecessary to kill you. That's what this is all about.

"Be in no doubt of the danger you're in. I know all of you, and what's more, I know every generation of your families, from great-grandparents to great-grandchildren. I know all their names, where they live and work, everything I need to target them. If you make it necessary for me to come back, I'll wipe out your entire bloodline – every one of you." He took a printed photograph from a chest pocket of his black combat jacket. "For example, here's little Hans. He's your grandson, right?" He held it out towards one of the men in the cage, who stared at the picture, then nodded. "Note the background. He's standing in front of his school. If I'd meant to harm him, he wouldn't have come home today."

Slowly, his lips pressed tightly together, the man nodded. "But *we* also know *you,*" he pointed out, suppressed fury grating in his voice. "Fourteen of you arrived on Neue Helvetica last year. You all live together in apartments above your Embassy. We can find you as easily as you can find us."

"But you don't know where the others are."

All eight heads jerked upright, eyes fixed on Dave as the man demanded, "What others?"

"We had thousands of fighters on Laredo. What makes you think we were the only ones to escape?" There was a sudden stillness in the cage. Dave grinned ferally. "More than fourteen left the planet with my team." *True,* he thought to himself. *Three were killed in action before we departed the system.* "Others have done so since then." *True – as prisoners being taken to Bactria for special interrogation.* "You've no idea how many have joined us since our arrival, coming down from orbit in ones and twos and blending into the population." *None – but you don't know that, and it sounds entirely plausible.* "With

44

the United Planets headquartered here, there are so many transients and temporary residents on Neue Helvetica that it's impossible to keep tabs on them all.

"You also have no idea how many locals are backing our play." He drew the pistol from the holster at his waist and held it up, careful to ensure that his extended trigger finger covered and concealed the serial number. "Notice the stylized gold eagle engraved on the slide. You all know what that means. This is a Neue Helvetica service pistol. Where do you think I got it, and these combat fatigues, and this body armor and web gear? They're all current military issue on this planet. Civilians can't buy them, so the fact that my entire team has access to them demonstrates that we have powerful allies." *Just as long as you don't see any of the rest of us, and realize that my entire team has access only to the gear I'm wearing right now. Once I return it later tonight, we won't have any – but you don't know that.*

Dave returned the pistol to its holster, the rasp of steel on polymer clearly audible in the stony silence. "We've been very careful never to allow you, or anyone else, to follow us when we meet with our comrades and friends. The proof of our success is that every one of your watchers was taken out tonight before they could warn you that some of us had left the Embassy. Don't worry, we didn't kill them; you'll get them back eventually, although they're going to have a rough time until then. Who do you think took care of them while we were still inside? *You don't know,* and what's more, you'll never find out." He didn't bother to explain that it was the work of more flitterbugs, flying down from the roof, controlled by a console in the building, aided by the warm evening that had led the watchers to partly open the windows of their vehicles for comfort's sake.

"You can target us, yes; but if you do, those we leave behind will *Wipe. You. Out.*" His voice was ice-cold, deadly. "Let's use an old-fashioned term from the dawn of the Space Age. We'll call it Mutual Assured Destruction."

He paced slowly back and forth in front of the cage. "This is the first, last and only warning I'm ever going to give you. *Verstehen sie?*" The last words were uttered in a gravelly rasp, and all eight listeners nodded jerkily.

"You will do the following. First, you'll withdraw all your watchers and never try to monitor or follow us again by any means. Second, you'll deliver to the Embassy by noon tomorrow everything Bactria paid you to do their dirty work, plus suitable compensation for the trouble you've caused us. I leave the amount to you, but I point out that it will be a sign of whether or not you've taken this warning seriously. Be sure I'll respond accordingly."

More nods, emphatic ones. Money, like violence, was a language these eight men and women understood very well.

"Third, you'll eliminate at once the Bactrian agents who contacted you, in such a way that we know you've done it. I suggest appropriate news headlines – a tragic accident, perhaps? Fourth, you'll keep a watchful eye for any further Bactrian attempts to… inconvenience us. As and when you learn of them – and there *will* be more, I'm sure – you'll inform our Embassy about them. I want to know *everything;* who's behind it, their names, their pictures, where they live and work, the whole lot. I, or my deputy in my absence, may ask you to deal with them for us. If we do, we'll pay you half a million francs for each person you kill at our request, plus a suitable bonus in difficult cases." Their eyes widened. "Yes, it will be profitable work for you. We're reasonable people. We don't mind paying, provided we get value for our money." Nods of understanding.

"All that will make up for your mistake in targeting us. If you do all those things, I won't trouble you again. We'll be gone from this planet in a few years, and you can continue with your affairs as if we'd never met. However, I *strongly* advise you not to forget this evening. We can get to you anywhere, anytime. You can't build or buy enough defenses to stop us, so don't waste your money. Your bribed policemen and bought-off politicians won't be able to help you either, just like they couldn't help you tonight."

Dave shook his head. "You probably think of yourselves as hardened criminals, but you don't even *begin* to understand what 'hard' means. I'm willing to bet that my wife has killed more enemies than all your enforcers put together – and she's killed only a small fraction of the number I have. My comrades in arms have all done the same. Underestimate us again at your mortal peril."

He took a folded piece of paper from his pocket and passed it through the wire to the nearest man. "This combination will open the padlock. Don't enter it into the lock for at least the next fifteen minutes. You'll hear us walk out, but the flitterbugs will still be here." The eight in the cage looked up and around nervously. "They'll be under the control of other members of my team from their consoles outside. After fifteen minutes they'll be gone. You won't be able to hear them fly away, so don't try to move before the time's up."

He took the spray injector from his belt. "Do any of you know how to use this?" Two of the prisoners nodded. "Good." He laid it on the floor outside the cage, along with three ampoules of a clear liquid. "There's enough antidote here to inject everybody. They won't feel good when they wake up, just like you didn't. Some may vomit. Don't worry, they'll recover."

Dave looked at them all one last time, staring each of them in turn straight in the eyes.

"Don't. Make. Me. Come. Back."

He turned on his heel and walked into the blackness on the far side of the blazing floodlights. The eight, staring after him, heard other footsteps join his as they receded into the distance. A door on the far side of the warehouse opened… then closed… and then there was silence.

Bactria: April 29-30 2851 GSC

THE ROYAL PALACE IN SODIA, CAPITAL CITY OF BACTRIA

The Satrap stared out moodily over the city. Both of Bactria's moons were in the sky tonight, casting a pale ghostly light over the buildings spread out as far as the eye could see. The central business district was agleam with lights, looking much prettier than its blocky utilitarian architecture appeared during the day.

A rustle of cloth came from behind him. He turned as Zeba pushed through the curtains onto the small private balcony, smiling as she saw him. She'd changed into a pale blue flowing gown, softening her face and body, making her appear much more feminine and desirable than her official, uniformed *persona* as Captain Yazata of the Satrap's Bodyguard.

"Hello, Rostam," she greeted him, walking over and reaching her face up to his. He leaned down and kissed her lips slowly, lingeringly.

"Hello, darling. I'm very glad to see you. You're a breath of fresh air after that persnickety delegation from the House of Nobles."

She frowned. "Are they still giving you a hard time over me?"

"You bet they are! The old guard simply can't accept that I won't knuckle under and let them push me around. For generations the Satrap has allowed the nobles to choose his bride. They've swapped the position around every generation between half a dozen of the most influential families. I've upset their entire historical applecart, and they can't get used to it."

She giggled. "I've never forgotten their faces the day you announced to the House that you were going to marry. First, incredulity that they hadn't been told long before and allowed their say in your choice of bride; then greed and avarice as they waited to hear which of the noble houses you were going to favor; and then outrage when you announced you'd ennobled *me*, and we were already engaged!"

Rostam shrugged, but he couldn't keep the grin off his face. "Well, the constitution is quite clear – the Satrap must marry a member of the nobility. I simply sidestepped it by making a new noble."

"Yes, but that hadn't been done in over a century."

"It was high time, then! We *have* to break the stranglehold of the old guard. They've operated a 'closed shop' for generations. They don't know it yet, but after our wedding I'm going to publicly announce that the ranks of the nobility will again be opened to those who faithfully and loyally serve Bactria. I'll ennoble half a dozen prominent people right away to prove I mean business."

Her face fell, and she put her hand on his arm. "Do please be careful. There's already immense resentment that you accepted the traditional resignations of all your father's officeholders, instead of rubber-stamping their continuation in office. Elevating new nobles will set at least half the House firmly against anything and everything you want to accomplish. Some of them are already angry enough with you that this might push them over the edge from grumbling into outright disloyalty."

Her fiancé threw up his hands in disgust. "Most of them are already set against everything I want to do. What have I got to lose?"

"Hmm… I suppose, when you put it like that, you've got more to gain by bringing in people who'll act as counterweights to the stick-in-the-muds."

"That's the way I see it. You're also not taking into account the enormous support I've had from the House of the People after ennobling you. I know you're embarrassed by it, but they regard you as one of their own who's slapped the nobles right in their snooty faces. You're a hero to them." He grinned as she blushed. "I'm going to use that support, just as I'm going to use the newly ennobled members of the Upper House, to help push through my budget reforms for the next year. The traditionalists will hate my proposals, so that's the only way I can see to get it done."

She nodded thoughtfully. "You'll be finalizing the military budget outline tomorrow, right?"

"Yes. The War Council will consider the final offer from Marano, decide on the most essential expenditures in the light of the new threats facing us, and work out how to pay for them. There are going to be plenty of sore losers." He shook his head. "Anyway, that's enough of politics for tonight." He put his arm around her and hugged her close, and she leaned into him. "Only one more week and we'll be married. Then you can live in this apartment openly, instead of having to sneak in the back way in order not to offend traditionalists."

She giggled again. "Yes. Heaven forfend that the Satrap actually *enjoy* making love to his wife, and she to him – especially when she isn't even his wife yet! That would be *untraditional!*"

"Indeed. Shall we break with tradition yet again, darling?"

"I thought you'd never ask."

She reached up and kissed him lingeringly, her breath coming faster as his hand rose to caress her breast. She pressed herself tightly against him as he led her back inside.

~ ~ ~

MINISTRY OF WAR, SODIA

Rear-Admiral Stasanor looked down through the rain-streaked glass. "At last! Here comes the Satrap's motorcade."

His deputy, Commodore Eschate, chuckled. "Ever since he took up with Captain Yazata – sorry, I mean Lady Zeba – he's been running late in the mornings. One wonders whether that's merely a coincidence, Sir."

Stasanor tried to look severely at his subordinate, but couldn't keep a grin from hovering on his lips as he said, "Make sure you don't say that any louder. I'd hate to see you dismissed – or worse – for the crime of *lèse-majesté.*"

"With respect, Sir, I think the Satrap has enough of a sense of humor that he'd merely laugh."

"Perhaps he would, but our opposite numbers in the Army would not."

Eschate's smile was replaced by a scowl as he glanced at the two Generals on the other side of the room. "True. They're prickly enough as it is over our proposals. They're going to do all they can to cut us off at the knees, Sir."

"Yes, they are. Their service has hogged the lion's share of the budget for so long it seems like the natural order of things to them. They can't get it into their heads that the threat's changed. The same goes for the Security Service." He nodded discreetly towards the two black-uniformed figures talking to the Generals. "It's always gotten whatever it wanted, and to hell with other fiscal priorities. What's more, they haven't forgiven the Satrap for taking away their status as an independent Cabinet-level office and subordinating them to the Ministry of War."

"Let's hope the Army and the SS don't work together to derail our proposals. If what we hear from Neue Helvetica is accurate, we don't have much time to prepare."

The two looked at each other in grim agreement as they heard the sound of footsteps approaching down the long corridor. They moved to their seats as the Satrap came in, accompanied by four bodyguards under the command of his fiancée. Everyone snapped to attention as he walked to the head of the conference table, his bodyguards fanning out behind him against the wall.

"Thank you, gentlemen. Be seated, please."

The six uniformed men, plus the Minister and Deputy Minister of War, moved to the table and sat down. There was a rustle of papers and a series of beeps from electronic units as they prepared themselves. Servants poured coffee and offered biscuits under the eagle eyes of the Satrap's bodyguards, then discreetly left the room.

Satrap Rostam sipped his coffee, then set the cup down in its saucer. "I call this meeting of the War Council to order. Minister, please inform us of Marano's final offer."

"Yes, Your Majesty." The Minister of War stood and began pacing the floor. "They're refusing to lower their prices any further. They say they've already cut them as far as they can afford. I don't believe that's true, not for a minute, but they know we're hurting for hard currency. They're the only supplier we can find that's prepared to accept concessions for asteroid mining in part exchange for weaponry. That means they can afford to drive a hard bargain."

"Such is life." The Satrap shrugged. "We'd probably do the same if our situations were reversed. Go on."

"Yes, Your Majesty. Their surveyors state flatly that our two corvettes damaged during the fighting last year are beyond economical repair. They suggest that we scrap them, salvaging what parts we can, and buy two new or refurbished ships from them. They're prepared to offer us two corvettes from their Reserve Fleet, modernized and upgraded to match those we already have in service. Each will cost three-quarters of the price of a new vessel."

Rostam frowned. "Rear-Admiral Stasanor, what does the Navy have to say about that?"

"It's daylight robbery, Your Majesty, but I don't see that we have much choice in the matter unless the Ministry accepts our alternative proposal – which, quite frankly, I'd prefer."

"Minister?"

"Your Majesty, I agree that the Navy's proposal to buy a squadron of eight heavy patrol craft would greatly improve their coverage of our system. However, they won't be able to travel to Laredo under their own power, because they can't hyper-jump."

General Demetrias interrupted, his voice icy with disapproval. *"Where* did you say?"

The Minister rolled his eyes. "I'm sorry, General – I meant Termaz, of course. You'll have to excuse me. We referred to the planet by its original name of Laredo for years until it was renamed just last year."

Rostam interjected, "I don't mind the occasional slip of the tongue, Minister. Please continue."

"Thank you, Your Majesty. As I was saying, the heavy patrol craft would be limited to the defense of this system unless we ferried them to Termaz aboard freighters. On the other hand, I understand the Navy believes they would actually increase its flexibility, because for routine patrols one of them can replace a corvette in the Bactria system, freeing the latter to proceed to and from Termaz under its own power if necessary. Admiral?"

"That's correct, Minister," Stasanor agreed. "Each patrol craft carries the same military-grade sensors as a corvette, although only half the number of missiles. We currently have only three corvettes in active service. We lost two at Termaz last year, and as always, some ships are out of service at any given time. When we had eight corvettes we used to keep four on duty, one on standby giving liberty to its crew, one preparing to re-enter service after maintenance, and two undergoing shallow or deep maintenance. With only six of them left we've had to go to a three-up, three-down arrangement, which frankly can't provide adequate coverage of both the Bactria and the Termaz systems even with the assistance of our three remaining armed merchant cruisers. Eight heavy patrol craft will transform the situation. We can keep four patrol craft in active service here and two corvettes on duty at Termaz. Two more of each class of ship will be on standby, ready for action if required, and the final two of each will be undergoing maintenance."

"But why do you need so many warships?" General Demetrias expostulated angrily. "Why not convert more freighters into armed merchant cruisers? They're *much* cheaper than corvettes or patrol craft!"

"Yes, General, they are, but they're also much less capable. They sufficed to patrol the Termaz system in order to prevent contact between the rebels and their Government-in-Exile, but they'll be hard pressed in actual combat. They have only one-third the speed of a warship, so it's much more difficult for them to intercept or catch up with another spaceship, as we saw last year at Termaz with the escape of the rebel delegation. They carry less capable weapons and sensors than a patrol craft, despite vastly out-massing it, because they don't have sufficient reactor power to keep them all in operation; yet they need a crew two to three times as large. Finally, they're built to merchant ship standards, much flimsier than warships, less able to withstand high-stress maneuvers or absorb battle damage."

"It seems to me your corvettes at Termaz didn't absorb battle damage very well last year – and they were warships!"

The Rear-Admiral pressed his lips firmly together to prevent himself saying something he'd later regret. Beside him, Commodore Eschate interjected, "That's hardly fair, General. The corvettes found themselves facing a salvo of missiles from a supposedly friendly space station at point-blank range. They had no warning, not enough time to go to General Quarters, no opportunity to deploy their defensive weapons or mobilize their damage control teams. They were caught completely off guard, just as your troops were at the Arena and throughout the city of Tapuria at the same time. I seem to recall they also suffered more than their fair share of battle damage."

Now it was the turn of the General to tighten his lips in frustration as Eschate's counter-thrust sank home. His point was unanswerable. The Satrap's father and predecessor on the throne had died at the Arena while nominally under Army protection. He'd only escaped thanks to the efforts of then-Lieutenant Yazata.

Rostam raised his voice. "We're not here to score points off each other, gentlemen. We're here to decide on the short-term defensive priorities of this nation. Kindly keep that in mind." He looked around the table until he was sure they'd taken the point, then nodded to the Minister. "Please continue."

"Thank you, Your Majesty. I think the Navy's point is that more warships, even smaller ones, would allow them to conduct more intensive patrols and avoid being caught off guard again as we were at Tapuria. It would also allow them to more effectively engage enemy ships, which are likely to be armed merchant cruisers because that's probably all the rebels can obtain or afford."

"That's correct, Minister," Stasanor agreed. "In the absence of hard intelligence as to the enemy's intentions, we have to assume the worst and prepare for it. I hasten to add that's not a dig at our Security Service colleagues," nodding to the two black-uniformed figures. "I know it's very difficult for them to get information about our enemy's intentions and actions after the closure of our consulate on Neue Helvetica."

The two SS Generals frowned bleakly. It had been the ill-advised and completely unauthorized actions of their representative at the consulate that had led to its closure and Bactria's diplomatic disgrace at the United Planets. The repercussions of that disaster, plus the SS's intelligence failure on Termaz, had led directly to its five most senior officers being summarily retired and their department being downgraded, something they still bitterly resented.

"We don't even know whether the rebels have actually bought any ships yet," one of them objected. "There may be no threat at all."

The Satrap shook his head. "I can't agree. After all, it was your department that reported to us that some of them were undergoing Spacer training. They can't be doing it for the sake of light entertainment. Clearly, they expect to need it; and that means they intend to obtain ships. I agree with the Navy that they probably can't afford more than armed merchant cruisers similar to ours, but we know they raised a lot of money from sympathetic nations after the assassination of their President Pro Tem last year. Admiral Stasanor, what does a typical merchant freighter, similar to those we converted, cost on the used market?"

"An old half-million-ton tramp freighter would run... oh, perhaps a quarter of a billion bezants at current exchange rates, Your Majesty. That's before conversion costs, of course."

"And according to the Security Service, the rebel delegation on Neue Helvetica has access to something like a hundred times that amount. I'd say that's enough for a couple of squadrons of armed merchant cruisers, wouldn't you?"

"Indeed it is, Your Majesty, although I think they'll struggle to afford enough weapons for them. Missiles and fire control systems are very expensive and hard to come by. There's also the difficulty of finding enough trustworthy spacers to crew them. Mercenaries are notoriously unreliable, except for a few of the top outfits that charge correspondingly high fees for their services. I think they'll go for fewer ships to begin with – probably one or two, no more than three or four."

"I agree. Even with fewer ships, I expect they'll launch attacks on our space-based commerce and industry as soon as they can. How long do we have, do you think?"

"I expect they'll be ready by mid to late next year, Your Majesty. If I were in their shoes and had that sort of money at my disposal, I could have two ships and their crews ready by then – even faster than that, if I had access to a fully-fledged military dockyard."

"Then that's what we'll assume. Minister, what's the Navy's total shopping list from Marano?"

"Your Majesty, should I assume the purchase of two more corvettes, or eight heavy patrol craft?"

"Assume the patrol craft for now, and let's see what the numbers look like."

The two flag officers exchanged a private look of intense satisfaction.

"Let's see… There's the cost of the ships themselves, of course, each with two laser cannon. Each patrol craft mounts a main battery of twenty offensive and twenty defensive missiles, the same types used on our corvettes. That's a hundred and sixty of each for a squadron of eight ships, plus one full reload for each ship, which totals three hundred and twenty. Then there's the need to upgrade our existing missiles. They –"

"What do you mean, upgrade our existing missiles?" Major-General Pamir exclaimed angrily. "What's wrong with them?"

The Minister looked at the Navy officers. "Gentlemen?"

Eschate said mildly, "General, there's nothing 'wrong' with them, just as there's nothing 'wrong' with your assault shuttles. However, a few years ago the Army insisted on a very large budget allocation to upgrade them all, on the grounds that their electronics were one to two generations out of date. That's precisely the problem with our missiles. When we got them thirty years ago along with our corvettes they were state-of-the-art, but their electronics are now two generations out of date. We can't upgrade them in our workshops, because they've never been equipped to that level of sophistication. Instead we'll buy enough modern missiles to re-equip two corvettes, then send their old missiles to Marano to be upgraded. When they come back, we'll exchange them for the older missiles in two more corvettes and send the latter to be upgraded, and so on. Over the course of about two years, we'll bring all our existing missiles to the same standard as our new weapons."

"Oh… well, I suppose that makes sense," the General conceded sourly. "You can't economize by doing one corvette at a time?"

"That'll take much longer. We're concerned that time may not be on our side."

"A very valid point," the Satrap agreed. "Please continue, Minister."

"Thank you, Your Majesty. One hundred and sixty offensive missiles plus the same number of defensive missiles for two corvettes – one war load plus one reload per vessel – makes our total initial requirement four hundred and eighty of each type. They'll be loaded into twenty-four missile cells, each holding twenty of each type of missile, forty in all. Each patrol craft carries one cell, while each corvette carries two. There'll be the usual complement of spares for each ship, specialized tools, maintenance equipment and instructions and so on. The total cost for ships, weapons and equipment, including delivery charges aboard a special Marano ferry because the patrol craft can't make the trip under their own power, will be about sixty billion bezants."

Both Army Generals and the Security Service officers erupted from their chairs. "Impossible!" "That's *ridiculous!*" "You're insane!" *"Out* of the question!" Their explosive complaints overlaid each other in an angry barrage of sound.

Satrap Rostam surged to his feet. *"SILENCE!"* He glared at the offending officers. "Resume your seats at once!"

"But, Your Majesty –"

"At once!"

Slowly, reluctantly, the recalcitrant officers took their seats. Rostam waited until they had done so, then said very quietly, "I remind you for the last time: we are not here to fight for the needs of our respective services against those of others. We are here to consider the *overall* defense needs of the Satrapy of Bactria. If any of you forget that again, I shall instantly relieve you of your command, revoke all your military awards and send you into retirement in disgrace. Do I make myself clear?"

He looked at each officer in turn until he'd got a nod, a "Yes, Your Majesty," or some other token of compliance. They knew he wasn't bluffing. They'd all witnessed how he'd brought the hammer down on the Security Service the year before, and they weren't likely to forget it.

At last he looked at the Minister. "Please continue."

"Thank you, Your Majesty. Sixty billion bezants is an inflated price, but as I said, Marano's in a position to drive a hard bargain. It'll dwarf all our previous military capital expenditures. To afford it we'll have to drastically curtail other purchases. Perhaps General Demetrias should go into more detail about his needs."

"Thank you, Minister," the senior General said curtly, without looking at him. "Your Majesty, we have several critically important requirements that simply can't be delayed. We urgently need a hundred and fifty more assault shuttles, to replace those destroyed or damaged beyond repair at Tapuria last year and others that have been completely worn out by operations on Termaz. We also need to replace the anti-aircraft missile batteries, armored cars, artillery pieces and an enormous quantity of stores and supplies lost in the fighting in and around Tapuria. The total cost will amount to not less than fifty-five billion bezants, possibly sixty. Over and above capital expenditure, we need to recruit thousands more troops to replace those lost at Tapuria. We can't rely on conscripts – they don't serve long enough to be given sufficient training. In fact, I'd like to suggest that we extend the period of conscription from two years to three, to allow us to rectify that."

"And what will be the impact of that extension on Bactria's economy, General?" The Satrap's tone was clearly skeptical.

"That's for the bean-counters to work out, Your Majesty." The General waved his hand dismissively. "My priority is the combat readiness of the Satrapy's armed forces."

"Not quite, General. You're responsible for the combat readiness of the *Army*. Rear-Admiral Stasanor does the same for the Navy, and Lieutenant-General Gedrosia for the Security Service."

Demetrias nodded stiffly. "I stand corrected, Your Majesty."

"General Gedrosia, what are the capital expenditure requirements of the SS?"

The black-uniformed officer replied, "We have yet to replace all the equipment we lost in the destruction of our headquarters on Termaz, Your Majesty. That included a great deal of computer equipment and electronic surveillance gear, a large quantity of weapons and other items. Total costs are likely to approach eight billion bezants. We also need to recruit approximately a thousand staff to replace those killed in Tapuria. As General Demetrias has pointed out, we can't use poorly-trained conscripts for many tasks. I'd like to support his call for an extension of the period of conscription to help overcome that problem." The Army officer nodded his thanks to his SS counterpart.

"Thank you, General. Let me summarize." The Satrap looked around the table. "We face capital expenditure requirements from all arms of service totaling approximately one hundred and thirty billion bezants, over and above operating costs. This has to come out of a defense budget that has never before exceeded fifty-five billion bezants in a single year, even when we fought a war to occupy Termaz. Over and above that, there's the question of more than half a *trillion* bezant's worth of infrastructure – a space station, Termaz' entire traffic control system, dozens of buildings and public works, and so on – that were destroyed by the rebels last year. Clearly, something's got to give. We can make the case to the House of Nobles and the House of the People for an increase in defense spending, but we can't possibly ask them to triple or quadruple it *and* rebuild Termaz' infrastructure as well. They'll reject that out of hand."

There was a gloomy silence around the table. Major-General Pamir eventually asked, "Wasn't that the point of offering asteroid mining concessions in exchange for weaponry, Your Majesty – to reduce the amount of actual money required?"

"It was," the Minister confirmed, "but the value we place on an asteroid mining concession will be a lot higher than its valuation by Marano. We're in a difficult situation. Marano can demand enormous concessions from us, knowing that we can't do without what they alone are willing to provide in exchange for payments of that nature."

Rostam looked around the table. "I think we have no choice but to give priority to the Navy's needs at this time. The immediate threat facing us is likely to be space-based, after all. There's been little or no rebel activity on Termaz since last year's disaster – correct, General Demetrias?"

"Yes, Your Majesty, but that doesn't mean it might not begin again at any time!"

"True, but there's no evidence to suggest that. We haven't sent additional units to Termaz for a year now, instead funneling replacements to build up the units already there. Frankly, that's been a waste of money. They're sitting there twiddling their thumbs with nothing to do. I think it's high time we drastically cut back the number of troops on the planet." He held up a hand to still the General's outraged, inarticulate squawk of protest. "It's time to face facts. We aren't currently facing armed combat there, we're unlikely to do so for the foreseeable future, and we're in a budget crunch. We have to balance what we'd *like* to do against what we actually *need* to do and what we can *afford* to do. Right now, those three elements are in conflict with one another. We have to bring them all into line with reality.

"As for capital expenditure, I agree that the Army and the Security Service can't be starved of it entirely, but they've enjoyed priority for the past two decades or more. It's time for them to temporarily step back to allow the Navy to upgrade its ships and weapons. That will also allow us to withdraw from Termaz many of the units currently awaiting re-equipment. Not only will that allow us to delay the purchase of that equipment, it'll also save the huge costs involved in shipping it to Termaz and later bringing it back here. All those factors will greatly reduce the pressure on our Defense budget and the Treasury."

"I agree, Your Majesty," the Minister said firmly. "We've got to cut our coat according to our cloth, and right now there simply isn't enough cloth for the coat we want."

"Very well. The Navy gets priority this year on capital expenditure. If we can pay for most of its needs using asteroid mining concessions, it will free up funds to buy more equipment for the Army and the Security Service in the medium term. I ask the War Council to vote on that proposal now. All those in favor?"

The two Admirals, the Minister and the Deputy Minister raised their hands.

"All those opposed?"

The two Army Generals raised their hands, as did the two from the Security Service.

"The vote is evenly divided, four to four. I cast my deciding ballot in favor of the proposal, which is therefore approved." The four Generals scowled and opened their mouths in unison to object, but the Satrap held up his hand remorselessly.

"Minister, you'll go to Marano personally to conduct the final negotiations. I authorize you to offer them even more than they ask for, up to and including exclusive mining rights in Termaz' asteroid belt for a period of five to ten years – the shorter the better, of course." Everyone around the table sat up with a jerk. The mining rights in the former Laredo system were in the sole gift of the Satrap, and so far had never been assigned to anyone.

"There's a condition attached to my generosity. We need those ships and weapons as quickly as possible. The mining concessions are our carrot, but we need a stick as well. It's this. We'll pay a minimal amount as a deposit on our order. Offer ten per cent at first, and don't go higher than twenty no matter how hard they bargain. Marano must deliver our entire order aboard one of its ferries, to arrive here at Bactria by not later than the first of July next year, Galactic Standard Calendar. Until that date, no concessions will be signed. Marano will retain ownership and possession of the shipment until our Navy has inspected it and agrees that everything's there in good order. At that point we'll sign the mining concessions, after which Marano will transfer ownership of the shipment to us and offload it. If they don't deliver everything on time, they don't get the concessions. What do you think?"

The Minister smiled. "They'll hate it, Your Majesty, because it puts them under enormous time pressure. Still, if our offer is lucrative enough I think they'll accept the deal. They won't be able to afford to turn it down. The only problem I foresee is that their factories and shipyards may not be able to produce everything in so short a period, even using robotic construction and assembly. After all, they'll have other orders to fill in the same time frame."

"Then they must take ships and weapons from their Navy, refurbish them to new condition, and supply them to make up for what they can't produce in time. They can replenish their own stocks later – after all, they aren't facing any immediate threat that we know of. As Commodore Eschate pointed out, time may not be on our side, so let's do all we can to speed things up."

"I think that approach might work, Your Majesty."

"Good.". He looked at the Generals. "If they accept the deal, that'll free up money in the defense budget to address some of your capital expenditure requirements. We'll discuss them further at that stage. I won't consider extending the term of conscription until we've conducted an in-depth analysis of its impact on the economy. I'll have that put in hand at once, with a view to making a decision as soon as its findings are available. However, that'll take some time."

"Thank you, Your Majesty," General Demetrius said grudgingly.

Rostam rose to his feet. "Then I declare this meeting of the War Council closed."

He watched as the officers gathered their papers and electronics, put them into their briefcases, and made for the door. Behind him Captain Yazata motioned with her head to the bodyguards. They followed the officers to the door, going out into the corridor to form a protective screen before the Satrap emerged.

He glanced at her. "I think that went as well as could be expected."

She grimaced. "You've alienated the Army and SS Generals almost completely. I'd look for trouble from them if I were you."

"What sort of trouble?"

"They may genuinely believe you're a threat to the safety and security of Bactria, even though they subconsciously mean you're a threat to their own positions of influence. I don't think they can separate the two realities in their minds any longer. If so, anything's possible, particularly if they get together with some of the disaffected nobles."

"Then we'll just have to be doubly on our guard, won't we?"

Bactria: May 5 2851 GSC

ENTERTAINMENT DISTRICT, SODIA

A discreet knock came at the door to the private dining-room. Those inside halted their discussion in mid-sentence as they looked up. A moment later the door was opened and a tall figure stepped inside. The host rose to greet him as the door closed.

"Good evening, General Gedrosia. Thank you for joining us at such short notice."

"It was my pleasure, Wazir Khanoum. An invitation from so important a noble has the force of a Royal command as far as I'm concerned."

"I'm honored that you feel that way. Please be seated."

The SS officer sat down next to General Demetrias. The two shook hands warmly, then returned their gaze to their host.

"Now that we're all here, we can begin. I've taken the liberty of ordering our meal in advance. I know this restaurant and its menu very well, so I hope you'll trust my judgment as to the courses. Waiters will bring them at intervals, then leave us undisturbed so we can continue our conversation."

He clapped his hands. The first course, a savory fish soup, was laid before each guest, then the waiters withdrew.

"Before we proceed, may I ask whether we're certain that this restaurant is secure?" Demetrias asked.

"It is," replied the Wazir confidently. "I own it. Its staff have all been carefully selected and rigorously vetted before being trusted to work here. We can speak freely."

"Excellent! Thank you, Wazir. Your thoroughness is very encouraging."

"It's my pleasure. Now, to business. I trust you were all as... as *nauseated* as I was by this morning's spectacle? I can't bring myself to refer to it as a 'wedding'."

Gedrosia looked as if he were hard pressed not to spit in his soup. "It was disgusting! How the *mithrayana* priests could restrain themselves from throwing hot coals over the Satrap and his... his *consort* to punish their blasphemy, instead of offering them the traditional ashes to mark each other's foreheads, I simply could not understand!" The others murmured their angry agreement.

"I see we're all of one mind. That's gratifying. It means we share the same values... values I fear our present Satrap honors more in the breach than in the observance. That being the case, the question arises as to how we should act in order to... safeguard and preserve those values."

There was a long silence. They all knew that to go further down this road bordered on, if not actually crossed the line into treason.

Major-General Pamir was the first to demonstrate the courage of his convictions. "In so many words, Wazir, you're asking us to consider how the Satrap might be... controlled... or even replaced, if necessary."

There was an intake of breath around the table, but no-one objected. Khanoum looked approvingly at the Army officer. "Thank you for expressing our problem so succinctly, General. That is precisely why I asked all of you to join me tonight. I am not without influence in the House of Nobles. I think I can guarantee the support of at least a third of them for any such effort, and the tacit acceptance of another third. The Satrap alienated many of us by elevating this... *Yazata*... to the nobility." He spat out her name as if it were a virulent curse. "It's not that we object to our ranks being enlarged, of course. Looking around this table, I see six *outstanding* candidates for elevation." His half-dozen guests preened slightly, glancing at each other. "However, you've all proven yourselves fit for noble rank through long and faithful service to the Satrapy. This Captain may be courageous, but she's far too young to qualify."

"She's also dangerously ambitious," General Demetrias growled. "She helped save the Crown Prince's life, sure enough, but luck had much more to do with that than skill or courage. As soon as he was safe, she abused his natural gratitude towards her by insinuating herself into his life and daily routine to an ever-increasing extent. It's no wonder the poor boy's become infatuated with her. He doesn't have the experience to understand how a worldly-wise woman is manipulating him. All he can see and think about is her body – which is admittedly attractive and would naturally obsess a young man, particularly if she knows how to use it. He can't see the devious, twisted mind inside it."

"An excellent point, General!" the Wazir exclaimed. "Our concern over the present situation isn't disloyalty at all. In reality, it's an expression of our higher loyalty to the Satrapy as a whole, regardless of the present incumbent of the throne. He's simply unable to see how he's been led astray. It's up to us, who know better, to... put the situation to rights."

"One hopes that it won't be necessary to replace the Satrap," SS Colonel Arachosia observed thoughtfully. "If he could perhaps be... restrained, removed from the pernicious influence of that woman, given more suitable advisers to help him reach the correct conclusions and assist him by implementing them instead of his present misguided policies, he could continue as Satrap indefinitely, not so?"

"Most certainly!" Khanoum assured him.

"But what if he doesn't agree to be restrained?" Army Colonel Ferghan wondered.

"That would be... unfortunate," the noble admitted. "Only one of the Blood Royal can succeed him. There are at least half a dozen contenders who would vie to replace him if anything were to happen to Satrap Rostam. That would be a most difficult and complicated situation for our country. We would have to assess the candidates very carefully, and decide among ourselves who should be... discouraged... from seeking the throne, and who is most deserving of our support."

They all knew, without having to be told, that he really meant they'd auction off the throne to the candidate who promised them the most. If he failed to deliver on his promises, he'd be replaced in his turn. This would not be the first time something of the kind had occurred in Bactria's history.

The last member of the party set down his spoon on his plate with a sharp *clink!* of metal on crockery. "All right, let's stop beating about the bush. We all know why we're here. What's the next step? What are we actually going to *do* to resolve this mess?"

Khanoum smiled genially. "We'll have to move slowly and carefully, Major Kadeh. All of us are too valuable to the Satrapy to take needless risks." Vigorous murmurs of agreement came from his guests. "You of all people should know the need for caution. You are, after all, a member of the Satrap's Guard, and therefore potentially the most exposed of any of us." He glanced around. "I should add that I invited the Major to join us despite his more junior rank because, if direct action should become necessary, he may be in the best position to initiate it. His cousin was the late and greatly lamented Colonel Kujula, martyred on Termaz last year, who was one of my confidants. It was he who assured me that the Major is absolutely trustworthy." The others nodded approvingly.

"Let me summon the waiters to serve the next course. Once they've departed, I'd like to offer a few proposals for your consideration."

~ ~ ~

SATRAP'S PALACE, SODIA

The curtains were pulled back and the windows and double doors to the balcony were open, allowing the cool night air to flow freely through the bedroom. They laid together, spent, perspiration cooling on their skin, letting the afterglow wash over them.

At last she stirred next to him. "That was... spectacular. Thank you, darling."

"It was special for me, too. What was different this time? It was as if you were even more... involved than you usually are. It can't be just because we were married this morning."

She smiled in the darkness. "No, it's more than that. I had the doctor cancel my birth control a couple of weeks ago, and adjust my hormone balance. I'm fertile tonight."

He sat up with a jolt. "You mean...?"

"Yes. You need an heir, Rostam. No – the *Satrapy* needs an heir. If anything happens to you, there are half a dozen potential claimants to the

66

throne. If they start fighting among themselves, it might develop into a civil war. I want to bear you a child as soon as possible, so that any rebellious spirits who might be thinking of replacing you with someone more... compliant... find that's no longer an option." She sat up and hugged him. "That's why tonight was different for me. It was... deeper, somehow... more intimate. It's almost like I can feel your seed taking root inside me."

He was speechless for a moment as he hugged her. "I... what can I say? Thank you, darling."

"Oh, it was *very* much my pleasure. Yours, too, I seem to recall!" They laughed softly together.

He lay back again, pulling her down into the crook of his arm. "While you look after that side of the future, I'm going to do more myself. You read the most recent report from Prison Camp Three on Termaz, didn't you?"

"Yes." Her voice was suddenly thoughtful. "It looks like that female doctor we captured at the Arena is suddenly at odds with the others. She seldom talks to them, and then only as briefly and coldly as possible."

"Uh-huh. Her husband was the rebels' military commander, and she chaired the committee that ran the Resistance. Her influence has probably been curtailed since her husband's death; she may no longer be head of that committee, if it even exists any more. She's obviously intelligent – I mean, you don't get to be a doctor unless you've got at least *some* smarts. I wonder if we could use her to crack open the rebels' united front behind their Government-in-Exile?"

"Hmm... you may be onto something there, darling. What do you have in mind?"

"I think I'll have her brought here. I'm not sure she'll talk to any of our military officers, but I was thinking that you, as a wife and – hopefully – mother-to-be, could approach her on the basis of 'we women have to make peace because men can't be trusted to do so'. What do you think?"

"That goes back to humanity's oldest myths. Remember Lysistrata?"

He chuckled. "She led the women of ancient Greece in a sex strike until their men made peace, didn't she?"

"So the legend says." She hugged him. "I'm not threatening *that*, you understand?"

"I should think not! You'd infuriate the House of Nobles even more than they are already!"

"It wouldn't work. They have so many mistresses and consorts that they're sure to find some strikebreakers among them," she sniffed, drawing renewed laughter from her husband. "Anyway, it's worth a try."

"Good. Let's put arrangements in hand. Next, I don't know if you're aware of it, but the Satrap's Guard has always included a special surveillance section."

"I've heard of it, but I'm not cleared for it."

"We'll fix that first thing in the morning. A couple of months ago I tasked them with keeping a much closer eye on potentially disaffected nobles. If any of them have ideas about moving in on me, I'd like to have as much advance warning as possible. I'd like you to take over monitoring that side of things. I'm so busy I might miss a potential threat, but I know you'll spot one if it arises."

She shivered. "You're so... matter-of-fact about it. We're talking about your *life*, dammit!"

"Yes, we are; but I learned an important lesson from your friend Captain Dehgahn last year, and from General Huvishka as well. Remember how the Captain volunteered to hold back the rebels while we escaped? He was already badly wounded. The General said to him, 'Die well,' and he replied, 'I'll do my best.' When you think about it, that duty is laid on all of us, isn't it? I've never forgotten a line in an ancient play from Old Home Earth. 'A man can die but once; we owe God a death, and let it go which way it will, he that dies this year is quit for the next.' My tutor used to quote that at me as an example of a Satrap's final duty to his people."

She raised up on one elbow and stared at him. "You sound almost morbid, darling. You aren't having premonitions of doom, are you?"

He laughed. "No, I'm not. I'm just very well aware of the risks confronting us for the next couple of years, until I've consolidated authority in my hands and cut the old guard down to size. I'm not prepared to cower under their threats. I'm going to stand tall and confront them. I don't see any other way to turn things around here."

She nodded slowly. "I don't either... which makes it even more important to give you at least one heir as quickly as possible. In fact, I may transfer the first to a gestation pod as early as possible, then try to conceive again even before our first child reaches term, so as to have another ready, just in case."

"Now who's being morbid?"

"Hey, you started it! I'm trying to be as realistic as you are. I knew what I was getting into when I agreed to marry you."

"Yet you still said 'Yes'. I love you for that."

She twisted around and eased herself on top of him. "I love you for a lot more than that. Shall I demonstrate? After all, if we want a baby soon, we're going to have to work at it."

"Uh-huh. Practice makes pregnant."

"Oh, *you!*"

He caught his breath. "Did you know that you move delightfully against me when you laugh like that?"

"You mean like this?"

"Oh, yes... *just* like that... yes..."

Laredo: July 11 2851 GSC

PRISON CAMP #3, NEAR CARISTO

"No change?"

Jake sighed. "No change. She's as cold and distant as ever."

"Must be hell living next door to her, never getting a civil word out of her."

"I do my best to treat her as I've always done. If she doesn't want to respond, it's on her, I guess. It's not that we've decided to ostracize her. She's chosen to isolate herself."

"Here she comes now."

"Where's she going?"

His aide watched as Gloria stepped down from the door of the mess hall. "Looks like she's heading for the perimeter track. Must be wanting to walk a while."

"Given the way the breakfast porridge sticks to your ribs, maybe she's trying to shake it down."

The other grinned. "Could be. Speaking of that, I could do with a walk myself. Want to join me?"

"Why not? Just don't get too close to her, or she'll accuse us of crowding her again."

They paced out three circuits of the perimeter track, just two more walkers among several groups enjoying the morning sunshine before the heat of the day became too great to bear.

Jake tensed suddenly. "D'you hear that?"

"What?"

"That rumble. Sounds like the reaction thrusters of an assault shuttle."

"Can't hear it… no, wait a minute, there it is. You know, your hearing's gotten a lot sharper since you lost your sight."

"Compensation, I guess. Can you see it?"

"Not yet… now I can. It's coming from the direction of Banka, heading this way. Hey, it's dropping lower. Wonder if it's going to land here?"

"We'll soon find out."

The bored prisoners watched as the assault shuttle circled, then touched down on the small landing pad laid out behind the administration buildings beyond the triple fence of the prison camp. A brown-uniformed officer and a female civilian walked down the rear ramp and turned towards the building housing the office of the Camp Commandant.

"What rank is he?" Jake asked, his voice fretful. "Do you recognize him?"

"No, I can't see him clearly from here, but the Camp Adjutant has just braced and saluted him."

"That's not saying much. Any officer who rates an assault shuttle to come here, instead of slower and less impressive transport, has got to be field grade at least."

"Yeah. They've just gone into the Headquarters building."

"Maybe we'll find out what they're up to in due course. Let's get back to walking."

Slowly the prisoners began pacing out their unchanging circuits once more, just as they did every day. The unusual distraction of the shuttle's arrival had been welcome, but the tedium of prison camp life was eternal, or so it seemed.

They hadn't done more than a couple of circuits when the loudspeakers suddenly crackled to life. *"All prisoners are to return to their quarters at once. I say again, all prisoners are to return to their quarters at once. Remain there until you are informed that normal routine can resume."*

"What the hell?" Jake wondered aloud.

"I don't know, but I guess we'll find out."

"Yeah. Steer me back to my room, will you, Griss?"

"Sure. This way."

Jake sat down on his lower bunk. He normally enjoyed the privacy of not having a roommate in the bunk above, but at times like this, when he couldn't see what was going on outside and had no-one to tell him, it grated.

His thoughts were interrupted by the clump of boots in the corridor outside. He recognized them. They were worn by the guards who periodically shook down their rooms, looking for contraband. They marched past his door and stopped at the room next to his. Through the door he recognized the voice of one of the Sergeants of the guard.

"Mrs. Aldred, Ma'am? You're to come with us, please. There's someone to see you in the Commandant's office."

"See *me?* Who?"

"I really couldn't say, Ma'am. I was told to fetch you. That's all I know."

"Oh, very well. I'll come."

He heard her footsteps as she walked through the door of her room into the corridor outside, closing it behind her. He jumped to his feet as she and her escort walked past his door.

"Gloria! Be careful!"

She didn't answer him. Instead the footsteps died away down the corridor until he heard the door at the end of the hut open, then close. Silence descended.

He sat down again on his bunk, his mind whirling. Was this what he'd feared ever since Gloria had begun her self-imposed and very public estrangement from the military prisoners?

~ ~ ~

The Sergeant snapped to attention in the door of the Commandant's office. "Mrs. Aldred is here, Ma'am."

A pleasant contralto voice replied, "Thank you, Sergeant. Send her in, please, then close the door."

Gloria walked inside to find a woman of about her own age facing her. She wore a smartly tailored business suit. Her face was open and... if one could ever call a Bactrian face 'honest', Gloria admitted, she looked honest.

"Good morning, Doctor Aldred. I'm Doctor Surkh, one of the personal physicians to the Satrap of Bactria and his wife."

Gloria's eyes widened. "Good morning, Doctor. I must admit, you're just about the last person I'd expect to see in a prison camp on Laredo!"

Surkh laughed, her voice merry. "I didn't exactly expect this assignment myself! Her Majesty asked me to undertake this mission because I'm a doctor, like you are. She hoped that our relationship might be more professional than adversarial."

"I see," Gloria said slowly. "What sort of 'mission' is it?"

"I'm to bring you a message from Her Majesty. What happens after that is up to you. Please, sit down." As Gloria did so, she took a holographic display unit from her briefcase and placed it on the desktop. "Here's Her Majesty's message." She pressed a button.

A three-dimensional image flickered to life above the desk. It revealed an attractive young woman wearing a long flowing gown. She walked towards a chair and sat down, the camera following her movements and zooming in on her face as she looked into the lens and began to speak.

"Doctor Aldred, today I may be Lady Zeba and the wife of Satrap Rostam, but a year ago I was simply Lieutenant Yazata of the Bactrian Army. I was a low-ranking aide to General Huvishka when your forces attacked the Arena in Tapuria – I'm sorry; you would refer to it as Banka, I suppose. I'm afraid the change of names has confused many of us, on both sides.

"I was one of those who helped get the Satrap clear of your initial assault. We fought our way through the changing-rooms and corridors beneath the Arena. Eventually I was ordered to take the Crown Prince and find a place to hide. Your forces didn't locate us, but they did find and kill his father and those with him. I understand your husband and the others in the assault party were then killed by our forces. You have my condolences. As women, I think we have an altogether deeper and more profound sense of loss over the death of those we love. Men never seem to feel it in the same way that we do, in our wombs."

Gloria closed her eyes. *Oh, yes!* she thought with a pang of mental anguish. *How often I've heard these military men talk with pride about someone 'laying down his life for his country' – but their wives still mourn, and their children still weep, and nothing can ever completely fill the void they leave behind.*

"You've lost your husband and children during the war between our nations. I haven't lost any blood relatives, but I've lost comrades in arms who were dear to me, and my husband lost his father. I think both of us understand the cost of war at a visceral level. I can't change the past, just as my husband can't either. He didn't start this war, and he wasn't consulted about it. From the moment of his father's death, he's sought to begin reconciling our two nations. You have personal experience of that. He immediately stopped his father's policy of executing captured prisoners of war, and overrode Security Service opposition to the change by having their senior surviving officer on Termaz – I mean, Laredo – executed. He also arranged for you to be given medical supplies to treat your wounded. We're both grateful that you offered to help treat our civilian casualties as well. I'm sure some of them survived only because of you.

She sighed. "We now face a situation where the militarists and traditionalists who've previously controlled this nation's policies are temporarily in retreat; but they're not defeated, and they're trying to claw back the influence they've lost. They're bitterly opposed to my husband's attempts to reduce expenditure on the Army and the military occupation of your planet. They're making it as difficult as possible for him to implement domestic reforms that might, over time, transform our nation's outlook from bellicosity to a more... rational approach. Sadly, his efforts don't appear to be reciprocated by your Government-in-Exile, which is now comprised of former military people. They appear to have the same perspective on the conflict as our military leaders.

"That's why I'm sending you this message. My husband is not a soldier and has never been one. He wants both Bactria and Termaz – Laredo – to be free of hatred, violence and savagery; but he's stymied at present by entrenched military interests on both sides. It's going to take time and hard work to overcome their resistance. Terrible atrocities and tragedies have been perpetrated and suffered by both sides, I don't deny that; but unless we interrupt the cycle of reflexive, reactive violence that seems to govern us all at the moment, how will we ever find peace?"

She was silent for a moment, gazing straight into the camera lens. "I need an ally on your side. I need someone I can talk to as a woman and a human being, not a military automaton. I need someone who'll mobilize the supporters of peace on her planet to work with the supporters of peace on my planet. I dare to hope that as a doctor, you'll understand what I'm talking about; and I dare to hope that you may be willing to take a risk and join me in this effort.

"You don't know me, and have no reason to trust me. That's why I asked Doctor Surkh to convey this message to you. She can talk to you as one medical professional to another, which I hope will allow you to interact with mutual respect. I've told her to answer your questions as honestly as she can. Many of them can only be answered if we meet face-to-face, of course. I can't come to you, because my husband needs my active help and support in working for peace. Besides… I'm expecting our first child." She dimpled, and Gloria could almost feel the anticipation and pleasure radiating from her. "I therefore invite you to visit me on Bactria to discuss what we might achieve together. If you agree, Doctor Surkh will escort you here as my honored guest. You will no longer be treated as a prisoner of war.

"I'll leave you to talk with her. I truly hope I'll see you soon. Thank you for listening."

Gloria bowed her head, feeling moisture welling up in her eyes. She could think only of the pain of losing, first her children, then her husband. The hatred of the enemy engendered during the years of war seemed pitifully stupid now that she'd been reminded that the other side had lost just as much, and suffered precisely the same pain. Could she… *dare* she… respond?

The visitor watched her in silence, giving her time to think. At last she asked gently, "Is there anything more I can tell you right now?"

Gloria shook her head. "I… I don't think so. Her Majesty put it very well. I… I just don't know what to do. I…"

The tears flowed suddenly, freely. Doctor Surkh rose from her chair and crossed swiftly to Gloria, hugging her gently, and she couldn't help reciprocating. Both women leaned into each other for a timeless moment of shared grief and sympathy.

At last Gloria wiped her eyes with the back of her hand. "I'm sorry. I must look frightful!" She looked around in vain for something with which to dry her face and eyes.

"Hold on." Surkh disappeared through a side door, to emerge almost immediately with a damp facecloth and a hand towel. "I got these from the

Commandant's private restroom." She handed them to Gloria, one after the other, and waited while the prisoner cleaned herself up.

"Thank you," Gloria said at last, handing back the towel.

"It was nothing." Surkh put the cloths on the desk and sat down again on the edge of her chair. "What do you think?"

"I… I've been alone and isolated for so long it's hard to think straight. There are all sorts of warning lights flashing in my mind… but the Lady Zeba is right. On an emotional, maternal level, this goes beyond thought. Intellect and logic helped get us into this mess, after all! I… I think I have to try. I don't honestly know whether I can bring myself to fully trust any Bactrian, but I suppose plenty of you think the same about us by now. I… I've got to at least *try.*"

"Thank you," the visitor said simply. "I'll take you back to Tapuria with me in the assault shuttle that was placed at my disposal. There's not much in the way of fashionable clothing for civilians on this planet – at least, not yet – but there are a few shops set up for the families of administrators and bureaucrats. We'll get you some better clothes, and get your hair fixed up as you like it, and spend the night at the transient quarters. Tomorrow morning we'll go up to orbit. Our ship will leave for Bactria tomorrow afternoon."

"What about my things?"

"I'll have the guards escort you to your room to pack."

"No!" Suddenly Gloria couldn't stand the thought of going back inside the wire. "If we're going to shop in Banka – I mean, Tapuria, as you call it now – there's nothing I need to bring with me. All my clothing is old and worn-out, anyway."

"Oh, you poor thing! Didn't they give you *any* creature comforts?"

"In a military-run prison camp? You must be joking!" They laughed shakily together. "Oh – there is one thing. I don't want to see him, but could one of the guards take a comm handset to Captain Jake Smith? He's in the room next to mine. I'd better tell him I won't be coming back, at least for a while."

"I'm sure we can do that. Let me talk to the Commandant. Please excuse me for a moment."

"Thank you. Oh – one more thing." She hesitated. This would cross a line, perhaps irrevocably… but she could think of no other way to stop the hard-liners from interfering. "Please ask whoever takes him the handset to also remove all the book readers in the library at the end of that block. They should be confiscated and destroyed."

"Book readers?" The other's voice was mystified. "Is there something wrong with them?"

"I can't say any more at present. Just do it… please?"

"Of course. Anything you say."

~ ~ ~

Lieutenant-Colonel Amu said briskly, "Certainly, Doctor. I'll have a comm set taken to the prisoner at once. The guard will dial my office code when he gets there. Please answer the call as normal, then Mrs. Aldred can speak with Captain Smith."

"Thank you, Colonel." Surkh smiled gratefully at him, turned, and hurried out of his temporary quarters.

He looked at the Adjutant. "Take the handset yourself, then go to the library and get those readers. If she wants them removed, that implies they're a danger to her if they stay there. I can only presume that's because they use them to communicate with the outside."

"Communicate using *book readers*, Sir? How is that possible?"

"I don't know, but that's the only possibility I can think of. If they warn their compatriots that she's going to co-operate with the Satrap, they may try to kill her. We'll send the readers to the Security Service in Tapuria. I bet their tech experts can find out how they work. Get them all."

"Yessir!" The Captain seized a comm unit from his desk and bustled out.

I think I'll mention that possible threat to the Security Service myself, right now, the Lieutenant-Colonel mused, picking up the desk handset. *They may be able to use the information to help convince Mrs. Aldred to co-operate. If that works, they'll owe me. They might even help me get a posting out of this hell-hole and back to civilization!*

~ ~ ~

Jake looked up alertly as the tramp of heavy footsteps came down the corridor. They stopped outside his door, and someone knocked. He heard the voice of the Camp Adjutant say curtly, "Captain Smith?"

"Here," he replied, standing up.

The door opened. "Mrs. Aldred wants to speak with you over this comm unit. Hold on a moment." He heard a code being entered on the keypad. After a brief pause, the Adjutant said, "Stand by for Captain Smith." He placed the unit in Jake's hand. "Go ahead."

Jake raised it to his face. "Captain Smith here."

Gloria's voice came through the earpiece. "Jake, I'm leaving. The wife of the Satrap sent me a message. She needs help to work for peace. I... I can't *not* respond. This is too important. I'm going to try to help."

"Gloria, you *can't!* This is a trap! They're trying to divide the Resistance!"

"No, Jake! I don't believe you. I think you're stuck in the same old military rut you've all been stuck in for years. You can't see the wood for the trees any more. I've got to break out of that mold and work towards something new. You can't see it, and the others can't see it, and Dave and his people off-planet can't see it, but I can. I've *got* to do this."

"Gloria, no! That's an order!"

Her voice turned icy. "You have no authority to order me to do anything. It's the other way round. As Chairperson of the Council of the Resistance, *I* order *you* to do some serious thinking! If you come to your senses you might one day become part of the solution, instead of being part of the problem as you are now!"

There was a sudden *click* as she disconnected the call. Jake called uselessly, "Gloria!", but he knew it would do no good. He was overwhelmed by a sudden wave of despair.

He was still gazing sightlessly at the handset when he heard the footsteps of the Adjutant returning from the library at the end of the corridor. The man said, "I'll take that. Hang on a moment." He heard him shuffling something in his hands, something that clicked together like plastic casings, and he suddenly realized with a surge of horror what Gloria had done.

"Are those our book readers?"

"Yes. I'm confiscating them."

"But... but why? How are we going to read anything?"

"That's your problem. We're going to send them to the Security Service, to see what's going on inside them."

Jake felt the Adjutant take the comm unit from his suddenly shaking grasp, then he turned and walked away down the passage.

~ ~ ~

As the roar of the assault shuttle's reaction thrusters faded into the distance, the loudspeakers crackled. *"Resume normal camp routine. Resume normal camp routine."*

Jake sprang to his feet and opened the door. Up and down the corridor he heard the noise of his comrades doing the same, heading for the door at the end of the block.

He shouted, "Griss! *Griss!*"

From down the corridor he heard his aide. "I'm here, Jake. What's up?"

"Come here, *quickly!*"

His assistant hurried up. "What is it? You sound... what's wrong?" He'd just caught sight of Jake's expression.

"No time to explain. Get word to Major Tredegar at once. Emergency meeting of all leaders right away in his room. As soon as he's started spreading the word, come back and lead me there. *Hurry,* man!"

~ ~ ~

"I'd hoped against hope... but when I saw her go aboard that shuttle, I knew," Tredegar said sadly. "She wasn't restrained or confined at all. She was walking with another woman. They were laughing and talking like it was old home week."

"Yeah." Jake's voice was heavy, redolent with sadness. "Telling them about the book readers was the worst of it, from my point of view."

"At least it's not as bad as it would have been four months ago, Sir," Lieutenant Kubicka pointed out. "You had the foresight to arrange a backup way to communicate."

"Yes, but it's slower and less certain than what we've lost. When's the next scheduled linkup?"

"Tomorrow afternoon at fourteen, Sir. It's supposed to be a brief test, but I guess we can make it a full session if we have to."

"We do. I'll prepare a message giving details of what's happened. My aide or I will give it to you tonight. For the information of those in this room only, I'm going to activate Operation Delve at once." There was a hiss of indrawn breath from everyone in the room. "I want that put into action as quickly as possible."

"But, Sir… where will we go?"

"I don't think it'll be 'we', Major. I think it'll be 'you'. There's one final acid test that will tell us whether Gloria's actively turned traitor. That's if she tells them who I am. If they learn I'm the father of our current President Pro Tem, they're going to come for me. They'll want to use me to put pressure on him. If they take me away, you'll know; and if they do that, you've got to assume they'll try to use all of you in the same way, even though you aren't related to any members of our Government-in-Exile. That means you've got to take a chance on getting away and hiding wherever you can. Don't stay here where they can get their hands on you anytime they want. Some of you may die during the escape; others may be killed later trying to avoid recapture. Those are necessary and acceptable losses. We can't let the enemy hold us hostage to threaten our leaders and influence how they conduct the war."

"I understand, Sir." Tredegar's voice was firm, and was echoed by a chorus of agreement from the others. "We'll do as you order."

"Thank you, Major." Jake hesitated. "If they try to use me, I'll do my best to stop them any way I can. I don't expect to survive. Tell my son, will you, if you ever get the chance? I'd like him to know what happened one day, if that's possible. I *will not* allow them to use me as a tool against him and what he's trying to accomplish."

There was a catch in Tredegar's voice. "We… we'll tell him, Sir."

"Thank you all very much." Jake's sightless, forever dry eye sockets could not see the tears in those of his comrades as they looked at him with pride and sorrow. "I know you'll do your best, just as I'll do mine."

Laredo: July 12 2851 GSC

TAPURIA SPACEPORT

Gloria laughed as she saw the cutter waiting on the hardstand, its white color and that of the second cutter next to it contrasting sharply with the dark earth shades of the assault shuttles lined up on either side of it. "It looks like a toy compared to these hulking great shuttles."

"It's no toy, Ma'am. It can hold as much as they can. It just looks smaller because it isn't armored, and doesn't have stub wings to carry weapons," the pilot explained as he walked beside them. Behind the group a work party tugged a cart loaded with half a dozen suitcases. Gloria had taken full advantage of the expense account provided to Doctor Surkh. She'd completely restocked her wardrobe. She hadn't owned so many clothes since before the war.

"You'll have to replace most of these when we reach Bactria," the Doctor had warned her, sniffing disapprovingly at what she regarded as the abysmally poor selection available in the shops of Tapuria. "We have a much greater variety there, and much better quality too."

"Look at it this way," Gloria had explained, giddy at her first opportunity to shop in a civilized fashion for over four years. "I'm making up for lost time."

"I'm sure you are! We'll do our best to give you plenty more opportunities to do so."

"What's the second cutter doing here?" Doctor Surkh asked the pilot. "I thought we only brought one down."

"They sent another down very early this morning to pick up a few last-minute passengers and some additional luxury foods for our guest, Ma'am."

"Oh, you shouldn't have bothered!" Gloria exclaimed automatically.

"Nonsense. We *want* you to feel spoiled," Surkh insisted. "Heaven knows you've had little enough opportunity for that since this damned war started!"

They strapped themselves into their seats as the pilot supervised the work party stowing the suitcases beneath a cargo net. He cocked his head to listen, then called to them, "The other cutter's just started her reaction thrusters. If you look out the rear ramp, you'll see her lifting off. She'll reach the ship a few minutes ahead of us."

"Thank you," Gloria replied.

Neither she nor Doctor Surkh were able to look directly at the cutter parked next to theirs, so they didn't notice its pilot hurrying down the rear ramp after activating a pre-programmed set of instructions in the flight computer. He got into a utility van, which drove away as the autopilot closed the cutter's rear ramp and increased power to the thrusters. The empty craft lifted off.

Gloria and her hostess craned their necks to watch as the cutter appeared in the aperture of the rear ramp, climbing rapidly as it headed for the spaceport boundary. It rose higher... higher... then a column of smoke and flame suddenly soared from a clump of trees about a kilometer outside the boundary. It streaked upwards and slammed into the cutter with a flash and blast that echoed across the spaceport. The small craft staggered in mid-air, then tumbled, twisting and writhing as it fell. It smashed into the ground just inside the boundary fence and exploded into flames.

"What the...?" Doctor Surkh exclaimed in horror.

"*Rebels!*" the pilot yelled, his face red with fury. "They must have shot it down! That was a missile trace! They were after you, Ma'am!" He stared straight at Gloria.

She went white with shock. "But how... No! That can't be possible!"

"What else could they be shooting at, Ma'am? We were the only cutter scheduled to lift off this morning! No-one knew about the other cutter

82

because it wasn't on the flight schedule. It was a last-minute arrangement. They *must* have wanted to hit *you!* Nothing else makes sense!"

Gloria could only stare at him, her mind frozen. He tugged at her belt buckle. "Come on, Ma'am! Until they've dealt with whoever that was, we aren't going anywhere. Let's get you out of this cutter into the terminal, where you'll be safe."

Numbly she allowed him to lead her down the rear ramp. Doctor Surkh followed, also pale with shock. They emerged into a scene of organized chaos as an emergency response platoon rushed onto the hardstand and climbed into two assault shuttles. As soon as they were all aboard the shuttles lifted off, reaction thrusters roaring deafeningly, and headed at full blast for the place from which the missile had been launched. As they crossed the spaceport boundary their plasma cannon began to fire, cutting through the trees around the firing position, sending more flames and smoke into the sky. A fire engine and ambulance rushed towards the crash site, sirens wailing.

"Come *on!*" The pilot urged them towards the glass doors through which they'd so recently emerged. "Let's get you back inside until they've got things under control!"

Two levels above them, a black-uniformed Colonel of the Security Service gazed down at the hardstand. "Make a note," he murmured to his aide. "Give that pilot a bonus for good acting. He's very convincing."

"Yes, Sir."

The officer raised his eyes to the missile launch site in the distance. "The response team is putting up a good show. Commend the platoon and its commanding officer in my name."

"Yes, Sir."

"Now let's see whether Lieutenant Syr is as good an actress as she claims." He adjusted the volume on a speaker standing on a table next to them.

Two levels below, as the pilot led Gloria and Doctor Surkh through the glass doors, a woman dressed in Army Lieutenant's uniform rushed up to them. "Did anyone get out?" she begged the pilot, her voice impassioned.

He straightened and saluted. "I'm sorry, Ma'am, but I didn't see anyone get out. From the force of the impact, I don't think there'll be any survivors."

"Oh, *damn* this *bloody* war to hell!" She leaned against the glass, hands raised to cover her eyes, tears suddenly streaming down her face.

Gloria couldn't help instinctively reaching out to touch her. "Did... did you know anyone aboard that cutter?"

"My platoon sergeant was aboard. She'd just finished her term of enlistment, and was going home to be discharged. Her husband and their two children were with her – a five-year-old girl and a three-year-old boy. They're all..." She couldn't continue.

Gloria stood frozen, her mind a jumble. *This is what Lady Zeba meant! This is the sort of mindless violence that we've got to stop! Two more innocent children are dead! How many more must die?*

The pilot patted the Lieutenant's sleeve helplessly. "I think that missile was intended for Doctor Aldred here. Our flight was the only cutter listed on the schedule this morning. They could have shot at any one of a dozen shuttles that have already lifted off, but they didn't. They waited for a cutter. They *must* have been after her."

"But *who?* Who would murder innocent kids just to get at a civilian doctor? *Why?*"

Gloria was suddenly suffused with rage. *The pilot's right! Someone* must *have decided to kill me rather than allow me to be part of a peace initiative!* Without realizing she was thinking aloud she blurted out, "It must have been Jake! He's the only one who could have set it up this quickly! *Damn* you, Jake Carson!"

"Jake Carson?" The officer stared at her. "Who's he?"

"He's..." She suddenly recollected herself, and tried to recover. "Oh, I don't know. I've no proof, no evidence. I don't even know where he is these days." She turned away, feigning confusion. *Have I given away Jake's secret?*

The Lieutenant snapped, "If you ever find out, let me know. I'd love to hear his explanation of why children's lives count for nothing!" She turned on her heel and stalked away.

Gloria dropped her gaze to the floor to hide the gleam of relief in her eyes. She didn't notice that once she was a safe distance away, the

Lieutenant took a handkerchief from her pocket and wiped most of a noxious, tear-inducing liquid from her hands and cheeks, then headed for a restroom to clean her skin more thoroughly with soap and water.

She didn't suspect anything, Gloria reassured herself. *I haven't given anything away!*

Two floors up, the Colonel's eyes gleamed. *"Jake Carson!* She must mean the man we know as Captain Jake Smith!"

"I don't understand, Sir," his aide ventured.

"He's the only person named Jake in that prison camp. Who else could she mean? If so, he's the father of the rebels' President Pro Tem – the head of their Government-in-Exile. We thought he'd been killed in the big assault on Tapuria last year. We must bring him here at once to interrogate him. Once we've confirmed his identity, we'll send him to Bactria. Let's see whether his son's still so aggressive after he learns we've got his father at our mercy!"

~ ~ ~

PRISON CAMP #3, NEAR CARISTO

Jake was walking the circuit with Major Tredegar when his companion suddenly stiffened. "A group of guards has just come boiling out of their barracks like the Devil himself is after them. They're forming up in front of the Commandant's office."

As if to echo his words, the loudspeakers blared. *"All prisoners are to return to their quarters at once. I say again, all prisoners are to return to their quarters at once. Remain there until you are informed that normal routine can resume."*

Tredegar asked, trepidation in his voice, "Do you think...?"

"I fear so." Jake held out his hand. "It's been an honor to serve alongside you, my friend. Remember what I said. Make sure that message gets through this afternoon."

"I'll supervise the semaphore myself, Sir. Go with God."

"And God bless you. You're in command now, Major Tredegar. Look after our people."

There was nothing more to be said. Jake waited for Griss to find him, then allowed his aide to lead him back to his room. As they reached it, he said quietly, "Griss, stay in your quarters, no matter what. Don't resist or make a fuss."

"But, *Sir* —"

"No buts, Griss. This is my swan song, and it's a solo part. I've got to sing it by myself."

"Yes, Sir." He could hear the tears in his aide's voice. "I'll sing my own song one of these days. I'll make sure to mention you in it."

"Thanks. I'll try to provide my own escort across the river, but in case I don't succeed, I'll be obliged if you'll kindly do your best to top up its ranks for me."

"Will do, Sir."

Jake held out his hand, and Griss shook it. "All right. Be off with you."

His aide unexpectedly hugged him. "Goodbye, Sir."

The rush of prisoners subsided, and the building was silent for a few moments; then the door to the compound opened. The tramp of heavily-booted feet approached his door, followed by a knock.

"Captain Jake Smith? Or should I call you Lieutenant-Colonel Jake Carson?" The voice of the Commandant was mocking. "Your presence is required in Tapuria at once."

"I'm coming," Jake said steadily. He opened the door. At once his hands were seized, he was spun around, and his wrists were handcuffed behind his back.

"May I ask what threat a blind man poses to you, that you have to treat him like this?" he asked quietly, offering no resistance.

"I'll turn you loose when we have you safely belted into your seat," Amu promised casually.

"Thank you, Colonel, but may I ask that you please cuff my hands in front of my body until then? I can't see, after all, and you must have noticed how I sometimes trip over things – even my own feet. If my hands are in front, I can at least break my fall."

"Oh, very *well!* Sergeant, do as he asks."

"Yes, Sir." A guard repositioned his hands and refastened the cuffs. As he did so, Jake pretended to lose his balance and bumped into him. *Okay. His pulser's on his right hip, in an open-topped holster. If the angle's right...*

"What about my clothes?" he asked.

"I don't think you'll need them. More will be provided in Tapuria if necessary."

"Very well. Would someone please hand me the pocket Bible on my table?"

"Why? You can't read it, after all."

"I used to read it daily until I was blinded, Colonel. Even now, it has sentimental value. My late wife gave it to me." Jake thought, but didn't add, *at the start of this war, just before she was killed.*

"Oh, all right. Sergeant, get it for him."

"Yessir." The Sergeant picked up the little book and handed it to Jake, who slipped it into his chest pocket.

As they led him down the corridor, the Colonel said, "I must admit, I'm surprised you're taking this so calmly."

"What do I have to fear?"

"You... what do you mean?"

"I fought for years before finally being disabled in combat. I've seen my friends and comrades die all around me. My wife and two of our children are dead. I've got nothing left to lose, so why should I be afraid?"

"You have another son to lose."

"No. He's in my heart always. He knows that, and so do I. If we don't meet again in this life, we'll meet across the river." Jake laughed as he remembered their parting the year before. "We've even discussed what drinks to order when we get there."

"I suppose your faith must be a comfort at a time like this."

"It's always a comfort, Colonel. It's also a heck of a responsibility."

The Commandant shrugged. "I've never seen it that way, but then, I don't believe in anything I can't see, smell, hear, touch or taste."

"I'm sorry to hear that."

"I'm not! We'll be taking my personal airvan to Tapuria. It's the fastest transport we have around here."

"Oh?" Jake said casually. "I'd have thought you'd prefer something more comfortable than an airvan. Most I've seen have had two seats for the pilots, plus two long hard benches or folding seats running down the sides of the load compartment behind them."

"No, mine's much more comfortable. It's got four rows of seats, two singles for the pilots up front and three three-person bench seats behind them. We'll put you in the second row with the Sergeant. I'll be in the back with another guard, so don't try any tricks!"

"How can I, when I can't see what I'm doing?" Jake asked, trying to sound reasonable. Inwardly he was smiling. *Yes, I remember that configuration. Once I know where I am in relation to the sides of the airvan, I'll know near enough where the other seats are, and the people in them. I don't need to see them.*

The crunch of gravel beneath his shoes gave way to smooth plascrete. They passed through the inner and outer gates, then turned right. Jake knew they were heading between the wire and the Administration building to the flight pad where the shuttle had landed yesterday. He felt the blustery wind ruffling his hair. It would make handling the airvan more difficult at low speeds and altitudes. That meant the pilot would probably fly it by hand until they reached calmer air higher up. He wouldn't have to worry about an autopilot at first.

As they drew near the pad, he heard the rasp of rubber on plascrete as the airvan was towed out of its garage. "Hold it, please, Sir," the guard beside him cautioned, pulling gently at his sleeve. "They've got to open the door for us."

"Thanks." Jake knew his voice from previous encounters. *I'm sorry, Sergeant,* he thought. *You've always treated me like a human being. It's a pity it has to end like this, but that's war. May Almighty God have mercy on your soul... and on mine, too. I'm going to need it.*

There came the sound of a door opening. "Mind your head, Sir," the guard cautioned, and pulled him slowly forward until he could feel the edge of the seat. "Slide right over, please, Sir. I'll take this side once you're in."

"Thanks," Jake said again as he entered the airvan. *Good. You'll be on my left, so your pistol will be between us.*

He listened carefully, trying to position them in his mind's eye as the Commandant and another guard slid into the rearmost bench seat. *That means the row immediately behind us is empty. They won't be able to reach across it to grab me after they're belted into their seats. They'll be beyond arm's length.*

A single pilot climbed into the left front seat, the airvan swaying gently as its suspension absorbed his weight. As he belted himself in, he asked, "Tapuria, Sir?"

From behind Jake the Commandant replied, "That's right, as fast as you can. They want us there yesterday!"

"Understood, Sir. I'll climb to two thousand meters, to get above the headwind blowing at low altitude. Up there we'll have a tailwind that'll speed us along. We should get to Tapuria in just over two hours from now."

"Very well. Let's go."

The pilot activated the power pack, checked the weight gauge, adjusted the angle of the blades of the airfans, then warned, "We're lifting off." He poured current to the electric fan motors. With a whine and a sudden unsteady lurch the airvan left the ground, dipping and wavering in the stiff breeze. The pilot turned it to face into the wind, then increased power. The vehicle began to climb steeply.

Jake asked, "May I have the cuffs removed, please, Sergeant?"

His escort glanced over his shoulder. "Is that all right with you, Sir?"

"Yes, go ahead."

The Sergeant took a key from his pocket and unlocked the cuffs. As he did so, Jake contrived to slip them over his wrists awkwardly and dropped them on the floor on his right side, farthest away from the guard. "I'm sorry, Sergeant!" he exclaimed. "That was very clumsy of me. I can't see to pick them up, I'm afraid. Can you get to them?"

"Sure, Sir. Hold still a moment while I reach over your legs."

Jake waited on tenterhooks until the guard bent forward across his knees, reaching down for the cuffs. His right elbow snapped up, then came down hard on the man's neck, stunning him for a moment as his left hand snaked out and grasped the butt of the pulser in the Sergeant's holster. Flicking the safety strap off, he drew it, twisting it around as his right hand came over to grab the butt and his left moved to a support position. He lined it at where he judged the pilot's seat to be and fired six fast shots, spacing them left to right. A cry of pain rewarded his efforts as the airvan suddenly lurched violently, twisting in mid-air.

"What the hell are you – NOOOOO!"

He heard the Commandant's futile shriek of panic behind him as the airvan flipped over onto its back and, inverted, fell out of the sky. His blindness spared him the sight of the ground rushing up at them, the racing fans driving them down to destruction.

The airvan hit almost at the same angle as a steep downward slope, scraping along the ground. It tore itself into a thousand pieces as it tumbled over the rugged terrain, throwing its occupants and their seats clear of the fuselage, ripping their seatbelts off, breaking their bones against the rocks, shredding their flesh against the scrub and sandy soil. Jake screamed as agony slammed into him like a giant fist... then everything went black.

He seemed to wake a timeless interval later. Slowly, the unbearable pain began to ebb. In the darkness that was all he'd been able to see for so long, tiny specks of light began to appear. They multiplied until there seemed to be thousands of them, shining like stars in the firmament.

He seemed to feel a small boy's hand in his, and hear a wondering voice ask, "How many stars are there, Daddy?"

He smiled fondly at the happy memory of days long past. "As many as the grains of sand on the seashore," he'd said to little Dave.

"How many is that?"

"I don't know. No-one's ever counted them all."

The boy's face had set in determined lines. "Someday *I'm* going to count them!"

Looking at the stars above him now, he knew there were far too many to count. He squeezed the boy's hand and tried to tell him that, but Dave slipped from his grasp. He tried to call out to him, but he couldn't see him or feel him any longer, and the glow of the myriad stars was coming together, flowing down, pouring into a single glimmering golden stream of light. It grew stronger... brighter... and suddenly he knew with an aching certainty in his heart that his wife and their two youngest children, killed in the destruction of Banka years before, waited for him on the other side.

He let go of the last of the pain that held him back, and plunged forward joyfully into the gleaming river.

Rolla: September 15 2851 GSC

BEAUMONT, CAPITAL CITY OF ROLLA

"You're something of a hero on this planet, aren't you?" Dave asked.

Lieutenant-Commander Maxwell shrugged as they walked down the street. "I happened to be the man on the spot when a pirate came calling a few years ago. It was the luck of the draw."

"Yes, I've heard all about it – but after you killed him, you went on to train their spacers to a hair. When his son came looking for evens the following year, they were able to pound hell out of him and send him packing."

"All I did was train them. They handled all the hard work themselves."

"You're too modest. The Gurkhas on Gandaki also spoke warmly of you. You seem to have built up quite a reputation among a pretty diverse selection of people and planets."

Steve flushed. "Like I said, it's mostly been the luck of the draw. I've been in the right places at the right times."

"Oh, all right. If you don't want to talk about it, I won't embarrass you by asking any more questions."

"Good, then I won't have to run away blushing."

"*Ha!* That'll be the day!"

Steve changed the subject. "Here we are."

He led the way into the Commonwealth Embassy to Rolla. A security guard signed them in and led them to the office of the Military Attaché.

"Good morning, Commander, Major," Lieutenant-Colonel Bonham greeted them, smiling as she rose to offer her hand. "I hope your negotiations with Rolla have been fruitful?"

"They have," Dave assured her. "Gandaki will provide the equivalent of a full battalion of its mercenary troops, ostensibly under contract to Rolla to help with its security and train its own PSDF troops, as they've done before. In reality they'll be contracted to Laredo's Government-in-Exile, and be trained as Spacers by Rolla's System Patrol Service. The SPS will also provide basing facilities for our ships in orbit around one of the outer, disused planets, out of the way of other traffic. Laredo will pay Rolla for its assistance. I'm very grateful to you for handling the preliminary negotiations on behalf of BuIntel and smoothing the way for us."

"It was our pleasure," she assured him. "Speaking of BuIntel," looking at Steve, "the latest dispatch boat entered orbit this morning. It brought a personal eyes-only message for you, if you'll go to the Communications Desk to sign for it."

"Thank you, Ma'am. Dave, if you'll excuse me for a moment?"

"Sure."

They passed a few minutes in small talk until Steve returned. He paused inside the office door. "Ma'am, may I please use the Embassy's secure room to discuss something with the President Pro Tem? I'll also need disposal facilities for an eyes-only dispatch when we finish."

"Of course." She rose. "I'll sign you in. There's a shredder with burn facility inside."

"Thank you, Ma'am."

As they sat down in the small room, shielded against any known form of electronic monitoring or surveillance, Dave asked, "What's up?"

"You'd better read this before I say any more."

Steve handed him a sealed envelope, addressed to him by name. Dave opened it and read.

> Dear Mr. President Pro Tem,
>   Please destroy this letter after reading it.
>   I respectfully wish to remind you that Lieutenant-Commander Maxwell is an officer of the highest probity.

You may trust and act upon anything he has to say to you, or not, as you see fit.

It was signed by Commodore Wu.

Dave looked up, frowning. "This is rather mysterious. Commodore Wu simply says I can trust you. I already knew that, so why the reassurance?"

Steve held out his hand for the letter. "Because something's come up that may get you the missiles you need; but you're going to have to delve deep into the murky side of the settled galaxy to get them, and pay out a lot of money without a guarantee of a return." He took the letter, plus one he took from an inside pocket of his uniform jacket, and walked over to the secure shredder. He passed both documents through the blades, then pressed the 'Burn' button, watching through a glass window as flames consumed the shreds of paper until nothing remained of them.

"You'd better tell me more," Dave said.

"Let me give you the condensed version now. If you agree to my proposal, we'll have an opportunity to talk at greater length on our way to our next destination, but we'll have to send some urgent messages within the hour to the dispatch vessel before it leaves for Lancaster. There's one condition. Everything we discuss in here is absolutely, totally confidential. You'll never disclose it to anyone, not even your wife or your closest associates. It's literally a matter of life or death, because the organization I'm about to describe doesn't take kindly to being publicly discussed."

"That serious? All right. Based on Commodore Wu's letter and my experience of you, I'll agree to that."

"Thank you. Have you ever heard of the Dragon Tong?"

"Only that it's some sort of criminal organization."

Steve suppressed a chuckle. "That's a bit like comparing the Laredo Resistance to a Boy Scout troop. The Tong is widely regarded as the most dangerous interplanetary criminal organization in the settled galaxy." Dave's eyebrows rose. "Through a long series of events that needn't concern us now, I came into contact with them. They consider themselves under an obligation to me.

"As you can imagine, an organization like that can do all sorts of things an intelligence service like BuIntel might find very useful. We learned something recently that gave me an idea, but I couldn't broach it to you immediately. I had to get permission from my superiors. Their message to me said I couldn't do so as a Fleet officer, because this is far beyond anything BuIntel is allowed to do. I'm therefore talking to you now in my personal capacity, not as an officer of the Fleet, and any decision you make must be taken with that in mind."

"This sounds more intriguing by the minute! Yes, that'll be OK."

"Good. We've learned the size and scope of Bactria's latest weapons order from Marano. They're buying eight heavy patrol craft plus a full outfit of missiles and reloads for them, including extra missiles to upgrade a couple of their corvettes. In total they're ordering four hundred and eighty main battery missiles, most with thermonuclear and bomb-pumped laser warheads, and the same number of defensive missiles."

Dave sat up with a jerk. "They must be paying a fortune for them!"

"Well... sort of. They've paid fifteen per cent up front in cash. The balance will be paid on delivery by means of asteroid mining concessions, including exclusive rights in the Laredo system for the next decade."

Dave's face suffused with blood. "The *bastards!* Who the hell gave them the right to... no, that's a stupid comment, isn't it? Bactria controls the system right now."

"Unfortunately, yes, it does. The key is in the timing. Marano has to deliver everything to Bactria by the beginning of July next year, or lose the mining concessions. They're working day and night to produce everything, and refurbishing some of their own patrol craft and missiles to make up for what they won't be able to manufacture in time. Their deadline to load everything aboard one of their specialized ferries is the first of June next year."

Dave grinned unwillingly. "They're going to be busier than a one-legged man in an ass-kicking contest to make that deadline."

"Yes, they are. Let's get back to the Tong. If you agree, I'll approach them with a proposal. If they hijack the ferry with all those weapons on board, and offload its cargo at a rendezvous with one or two freighters, that will get you the missiles you need to equip your ships. The shipment will be split three ways. You'll get two-thirds of the missiles. They come in cells of forty missiles, twenty offensive and twenty defensive, so you'll get sixteen cells. BuIntel will fit them into some of your *Bavaria* class ships, and integrate them with the fire control systems we're giving you from our old *Legion* class battleships. If you put three cells into each of four ships, plus a similar number of the target missiles we've been buying for you here and there, that'll give you the firepower equivalent of four destroyers. Each ship will be as fast as anything Bactria has, and be far more powerful in terms of weight of battery. With me so far?"

"I sure am! What happens to the rest of the missiles?"

"Those will go to BuIntel, along with four of the eight patrol craft. They're small warships designed for local patrols. They can't hyper-jump, so they'll be no use to you in an interstellar campaign, but we can use them for… let's just call it 'special operations'. BuIntel will have no official knowledge of their origin, of course. It'll enter them on its books as payment in kind for dockyard work performed for an unnamed ally – namely, preparing your ships, installing the Marano missiles and the target missiles in them, and integrating everything into your fire control systems."

Dave nodded. "That sounds fair to me. What will we do with our four patrol craft?"

"I reckon you'll use them to patrol the Laredo system once you've taken it back. Don't forget, the assault transports will be expensive to operate. For routine duties it'll be much cheaper to use patrol craft. You'll have a missile cell for each of them. I'm sure you can buy more from Marano or elsewhere once the war's over, or take unused cells from your bigger ships for them."

"All right. What's the third part of the split?"

"That's the ferry itself. They're very specialized vessels, designed to load other spaceships and carry them between stars. They have to cater for very wide variations in the mass and bulk of their cargo. They have huge ballast tanks and other adaptations to ensure longitudinal stability no matter what they carry, otherwise a hyper-jump would be unsafe. That makes them very expensive ships. The Tong will take the ferry to another planet, where they'll alter its appearance, re-register it, and either sell it or use it in the course of their own activities."

"So it'll be payment to them for their help?"

"Partly, but not completely. They'll only get the ship if the plan works. They'll have to go to a great deal of trouble and expense to set this up, so they'll want to be paid for that in advance. I figure you'll need to offer them a hundred million Commonwealth credits – perhaps more if they insist on it, although I think I have enough influence with them to keep the price down. That's less than a twentieth of what those missiles would cost if you bought them at commercial prices. However, you may lose it all if anything goes wrong. There are no refunds in this business."

Dave stared at him for a long moment. "You say I'm not allowed to discuss this deal with anyone?"

"No."

"Then how the hell am I supposed to ask my Council to give a hundred million credits to some anonymous organization I can't identify, for a purpose about which I can say nothing?"

Steve grinned. "I'm willing to bet you can be persuasive if you have to."

"I'll have to be, won't I? Let me think."

Dave was silent for several minutes, staring at the table. Eventually he looked up. "I'll go ahead and do this without consulting with the others. There's no time. Once I explain in broad outline, even without going into detail, I think they'll agree; and if they don't, I have a secret account for clandestine projects on which I can draw. I brought an extra twenty-five million Neue Helvetica francs with me in bearer bank drafts in case of need, over and above the funds to pay for the laser cannon. I can use them to give the Tong the equivalent of twenty million Lancastrian Commonwealth credits as a deposit. I can send the rest to any account on any planet they designate once I get back to Neue Helvetica. Do you think they'll accept that?"

"If I assure them you're good for the money, they will."

"Thanks. With sums like this being bandied about, I understand why Commodore Wu felt it necessary to remind me that you're trustworthy!"

"He didn't want you to suspect that I was trying to siphon a hundred million credits out of your pocket and into mine."

"No danger of that!"

"No... but in the interests of full disclosure, I've got to admit there *is* something in this deal for me. It's not money – it's revenge. It'll benefit you and BuIntel as well, I hasten to add."

"Oh?" Dave's eyebrows rose again.

"Remember what we were discussing earlier, about how Rolla saw off an attack by Constandt de Bouff a few years ago?"

"Yes, when he tried to lob asteroids at Beaumont. *Bastard!* Reminds me of what Bactria did to our capital city, soon after they invaded. They crashed a spaceship into it at full throttle – wiped it off the map. My mother, brother and sister died in the fireball."

"I'm sorry," Steve said very sincerely. "I guess you can understand how angry I was – how angry everyone on this planet was – when Constandt tried to do something similar to this city."

"I sure can!"

"After we drove him off, Rolla put a reward of two hundred and fifty million credits on his head, dead or alive, subject to him being delivered here and his identity confirmed by DNA analysis. It includes a full pardon for any and all previous offenses to everyone who helps get him. It's been officially endorsed by the Commonwealth, making it valid and binding on all of our member worlds, but we couldn't get the rest of the interplanetary community to sign on. That takes a United Planets resolution. No-one's claimed the reward yet. Constandt's dropped out of sight, but we keep getting tantalizing hints through informants that he's still out there. I want to use this operation to force him out of wherever he's hiding."

"What do you mean?"

"What if the hijackers of the Marano ferry were to 'accidentally' let it slip to the crew that Constandt de Bouff was behind the job? They'll release them in a lifeboat before disappearing with the ferry, so they'll spread the word as soon as they reach safety."

Dave began to laugh. "Oh, *boy!* Marano will be baying for de Bouff's hide. It'll protest to the United Planets, where Rolla will be ready to remind everyone that there's a honking great reward already out there for him. If the Commonwealth calls in a few favors, and Marano does the same, they might get the UP to ratify Rolla's reward and pardon as binding throughout the settled galaxy. If they do, every member nation will spread the word about it."

"That's the idea. Right now de Bouff obviously has places where he can hide, almost certainly using a false identity. He's done it before. However, if the UP passes that resolution his picture, DNA profile and other identifying information will be *everywhere*. Every criminal will know that by ratting him out, they'll get a free pass for every crime they've ever committed, and be able to make a fresh start with enough money to do whatever they like. De Bouff will have to run for his life. He'll never be able to feel safe anywhere again."

"Couldn't happen to a more deserving guy, if you ask me."

"You said it! I want that bastard's hide! He and his father caused the death of a man who took the place of the father I lost when I was five. I've never forgotten him. It's because of him I'm making it a priority to fight piracy whenever and wherever I find it."

"I can understand that. Hey, if we can tack that onto this deal, I'm all in favor."

"I'm glad to hear it, because it'll also give us the best cover story we could possibly want. If everyone's blaming de Bouff – which they'll be very willing to do, given his reputation – they won't suspect the Dragon Tong, or Laredo's Government-in-Exile, or BuIntel. Even if you're later found to have some of the missiles and patrol craft, you can claim to have bought them on the open market. Of course, you didn't know they were stolen, and you'll have authentic-looking documentation from the seller." Steve raised his eyes heavenward, trying – unsuccessfully – to look innocent and pious.

Dave started to laugh. "That's a great fringe benefit. All right, we'll do it."

"Thank you. I'll get a couple of messages off by tonight's dispatch boat to Lancaster. One will tell my boss that we'll be taking a bit longer on this trip than previously planned. Another will be to a contact, asking the Tong to set up a meeting with you on Marano to discuss this operation. If they accept the job, you'll pay them a deposit there and forward the balance to an agreed destination."

"You won't be at the meeting?"

"No. Because I'm a Fleet officer, I can't be seen to actively help organize a crime. Don't forget, that's what this is. Legally speaking, it's piracy."

Dave laughed again. "So you're committing piracy to help bring a pirate to justice? That's rich!"

"Yes, I suppose it is."

"All right. What's next?"

"We're heading for Vesta to take a look at your ships, which are being modified and upgraded in a very private area of the Fleet dockyard there. After that we head for Marano, where you'll meet with the Tong, as well as make the final payment for your laser cannon turrets and arrange to collect them in due course. How are you going to do that?"

"I've been wondering about that. I don't want to use one of our converted assault transports. I'd rather no-one got a look at them just yet. I'm thinking of buying one or two tramp freighters. They can go anywhere and load anything without questions being asked. We can use them as tenders to supply our fighting ships at a rendezvous in space. What do you think?"

Steve grinned. "I think it's a great idea. Good ones, about half a million net register tons, will cost twenty to thirty million credits each on the used market. As well as being anonymous, operating them will provide good training for your spacers while they wait for your converted ships to come on line. Why not set up a holding company right here on Rolla? Register yourself as its owner using the name on one of your off-planet false ID's, and use that ID only for that purpose from now on. You'll need a local partner to manage corporate affairs for you, but we can ask the System Patrol Service to recommend a trustworthy lawyer. You can have a broker at Vesta keep an eye out for a couple of good ships, buy them, and send them here to be re-registered in your company's name. They'll be right on the spot for your trainee spacers to use."

"That's a great idea! I can use funds from my clandestine account to do all that, because I won't be able to discuss it with the rest of the team until I get back."

"Good. We'll get all that done, get a good supper planetside, then head back to the ship. After that it's hi-ho for Vesta, Marano, and your new life as an interstellar criminal."

"I can hardly wait!"

Bactria: October 19-20 2851 GSC

SATRAP'S PALACE, SODIA

"Soldiers of Bactria! You can be proud of all you've achieved on Termaz. You return as heroes! We, your grateful people, welcome you with open arms. We know that the service you've rendered to the Satrapy on another planet will be renewed and intensified now that you're back home, ready to pass on all you've learned to a new generation of soldiers."

Zeba grinned tolerantly as they watched the news vid. "Rostam's made that speech, or something like it, at least once a month recently. He must be getting awfully bored with it." She clapped her hands twice, and the holographic display flickered and went out.

Gloria couldn't help smiling at her hostess. "At least he looks like he means it. He's not like some politicians I've known, smiling into your face while slipping a dagger between your ribs, metaphorically speaking."

"Oh, he's very sincere! We've brought back over five thousand troops so far. Coupling that with those we didn't send after the Battle of Tapuria – the Army wanted ten thousand replacements, but my husband authorized only half that number – we've already reduced our forces on Termaz to about twenty thousand, of which a third are combat units and the rest support personnel. That's more than enough to control such a peaceful planet. With your help, we'll have them down to half that number by this time next year." She shook her head. "I can't imagine saying such a thing while I was serving there, but things have changed remarkably since the big fight in Tapuria."

"I think that's largely due to you and your husband," Gloria said sincerely. "You're really working hard to change things. I wish your husband had succeeded to the throne a long time ago! It might have prevented an awful lot of bloodshed."

"Perhaps. We'll never know." Zeba shook her head. "Enough of that. We've got to deal with what is, rather than what might have been. Do you think you'll be able to attract support for your program?"

"It'll take time. So many people lost loved ones during the war years that it's left a residue of grief, hatred, bitterness and suspicion. One can't overcome that overnight."

"No, of course not, but do you think anything can be done in the short term? The longer we leave such attitudes unchallenged, the more they'll become entrenched and the harder it'll be to uproot them later."

"You're right. I'm going to start by looking for kindred spirits. I think I may find some among those living in and around Banka – I mean, Tapuria. They aren't its original occupants, of course; they're former slave laborers brought there to help clean up the ruins. Even though they'll bitterly resent the way your occupation authority treated them, I think they'll listen when I point out that your husband is responsible for their improved conditions. They've had more contact with your people than those in isolated areas, and they'll have learned that there are good and bad among them, just as there are in any group. If I can find some who'll focus on the good, and try to persuade others to do the same, that'll be the thin end of the wedge. I don't know that we'll ever persuade the diehards, but you have the same problem with some of your reactionaries, don't you?"

Zeba's lips pursed in bitter frustration. "They're not so much a problem as a curse! They have a lock on public opinion among the traditionalists, not least because they control a lot of news media. You've seen the sort of propaganda they're putting out. They're very careful not to attack the Satrapy as an institution, but the current occupant of the Throne is another matter. They keep comparing his policies to those of his most famous and popular forebears, always to his detriment, even when the so-called 'facts' they portray are mostly made up out of whole cloth."

"I've seen how upset they are over Rostam's budget this year."

"Oh, they're frothing at the mouth! He not only gored a lot of fiscal sacred cows, he downright slaughtered several of them!" They giggled.

"I got the impression that the House of the People was more supportive of his reforms than the House of Nobles."

"It is. His emphasis on reducing taxes and cutting expenditure is precisely what they've been wanting for years. Unfortunately, the nobles control a lot of heavy industry that relies on state expenditure, particularly defense, so Rostam's cutbacks mean they're hurting. They're passing on the pain by laying off workers and cutting what they buy from small businesses, so that adds to the groundswell of resentment."

Gloria shook her head. "It's still hard for me to comprehend a privileged class that's basically lorded it over the people as a whole since this place was colonized."

"Our founders wanted to 'recreate the glories of the ancient Bactrian Empire', as they put it. I think it was an impossibly romantic and utterly impractical idea, but they were determined and they had enough money and support to found this nation. If the historical record is correct, we've evolved into something very different to the original – but don't tell the nobles that! It would be the ultimate heresy!" They laughed together softly.

"Let's get back to your program," Zeba said at last. "I don't expect rapid progress at first, but please keep me as fully informed as possible. The Navy will allow you to deliver confidential dispatches directly to their ships' Commanding Officers. They'll hand them over to my representative here. That will hopefully stop the Security Service or anyone else interfering with them. We'll have a direct channel of communication. I'll send you regular updates on what I'm doing as well. I won't be forming a political party, of course, but I'll try to organize a social movement that will mobilize public opinion in support of peace and political reform. I'll probably have to work more slowly than you do, because of not wanting to increase antagonism to my husband's reforms."

"I'll do all I can to back you up on Termaz." Gloria was sometimes surprised at how easily she'd come to use the Bactrian names for her planet and its capital city. It had been much less distasteful than she'd initially feared. "As soon as we have enough support I'll announce the formation of a political party, independent of the Resistance, and call for local elections so we can have a voice in how our planet develops in future. If Rostam will then publicly agree to hold them on the basis of my request, that'll give me a lot of credibility among potential voters."

"You know the Resistance isn't going to like that one little bit?"

Gloria shrugged. "They've already tried to kill me. I'm sure they're going to try again. My husband died for what he believed in. Why should I be exempt from the same risk?"

Zeba's eyes softened. "I can only admire your courage."

"It's not courage. It's fatalism born of despair. If we let things go on as they have for years, we're going to see an awful lot more dead on both sides, and many more widows, widowers and orphans. I've seen too many already. It's time to make an end."

"Yes, it is." Her hostess rose to her feet. "I suppose I'd better let you go. Your baggage is already on the way to the spaceport. A shuttle of the Satrap's Guard will fly you up to the ship. You'll be back at Termaz in about twelve days."

They hugged each other warmly. Gloria looked into her eyes. "You take care. I don't want all our plans derailed because you or your husband get assassinated by disaffected nobles!"

"And don't you let the Resistance shoot you. Martyrs are all very well, but they can't get much work done!"

~ ~ ~

The insistent ringing of the bedside comm unit roused them from an exhausted sleep. Rostam rolled over and peered at the time display. "It's two in the bloody morning!" He snatched up the handset. "What the *hell* is it at this ungodly hour?"

He listened for a moment, then sat bolt upright, eyes suddenly wide. "I see. Go on... How long until she reaches orbit?... *No!* Under *no circumstances whatsoever* is that material to be transmitted over any circuit! Quarantine the entire crew on board until further notice, and hand-deliver the entire Diplomatic Bag to me personally as quickly as possible... Yes, I know the Foreign Ministry will be upset. Tell them they can complain to me personally... Very well. I'm sure I don't have to tell you to discuss this with no-one. Don't enter this call in the log, and delete any recording of it... Thank you. Goodnight."

He replaced the handset slowly, brow furrowed. Beside him Zeba stroked his back. "What is it, darling?"

"We've got trouble," he told her grimly. "You remember the book and documentary that the Laredans were said to be working on at Neue Helvetica?"

"Their project to document our so-called 'atrocities' on Termaz? Yes, I'd heard rumors about it. Is it out at last?"

"It's not only out, it's more serious than we could have imagined in our worst nightmares. They have vid footage of an astonishing number of things, including what they allege is the deliberate destruction of their capital city when we dived a spaceship into it at one-tenth of light speed."

"But that was an accident! It was the crew's fault! They tried to escape by slingshotting around the planet, and miscalculated their trajectory!"

"That's what we were told at the time. It's what I've always believed. However, the Laredans have in their possession what they claim is an original message from Major-General Strato to Brigadier-General Aldred, threatening to destroy Tapuria – Banka, as it then was – unless he surrendered immediately. They also claim to have recordings of intercepted radio conversations in which some of our senior officers discuss the strike. Finally, as if those weren't bad enough, they salvaged vid recordings from a number of security cameras and other devices that were running in Tapuria at the moment of its destruction. Apparently some of them are utterly horrifying. They've included excerpts in the documentary."

His wife looked aghast as she sat up. "But… were we lied to? Did that really happen?"

"I… I just don't know any more. I always believed the official version, but if that evidence is genuine…"

They looked at each other in stunned silence. At last she said quietly, almost desperately, "What if it *is* genuine? What will that mean for Bactria?"

"Disaster," he said simply. "Calamity. Ruin. Think of any word meaning 'catastrophe' and it probably applies. The rebels appear to have kept some of the evidence confidential until their book and documentary were ready, so as to maximize its impact. Now they've made it all available to the United Planets inquiry into what we did on Termaz – not just copies, but originals. According to the dispatch boat's captain, the book and documentary are selling like hot cakes and already spreading to other planets. He brought copies – we'll get them in a few hours. Soon they'll be all over the settled galaxy. If the UP declares that the evidence is authentic, the result's a foregone conclusion. Bactria's going to be a stench in the nostrils of decent people everywhere, and we're almost sure to be charged with crimes against humanity by the UP General Assembly. If so, mandatory sanctions will probably follow."

"What about direct action against us?"

"I don't know. The UP may not be able to muster the votes or the budget to support that, but it can – it probably will – call on its members to recognize and support the rebels' Government-in-Exile. That'll open up massive new sources of funding and equipment for them. What's more, if the sanctions against us are strict enough, sooner or later our ability to respond will be crippled."

"How long do we have until the hammer comes down?"

He shrugged. "Probably a year or thereabouts. It'll take the inquiry at least another six months to publish its findings and refer them to the General Assembly, which will take as long to decide what to do about it and pass a resolution. Our Ambassador to the UP will try to delay everything through procedural motions, objections and so on, but those can only slow down the process, not stop it."

"So we'll have time to receive our new ships and missiles from Marano?"

"Gods, I hope so! If not, we'll be hard pressed to defend ourselves against whatever the rebels have in mind. They've gone very quiet on the military front – too quiet. They've *got* to be up to something, but the SS can't seem to find out a thing."

"What happens next?"

"I'll watch that documentary over lunch with the War Cabinet. We'll have to decide what to do about it. You heard me tell the Watch Commander at System Control not to permit transmission of its contents over any circuit. The Gods bless him for having the sense to call me directly on the hotline! I'll have to see he's commended for that. We'll try to embargo the material until we can figure out how to deal with it – and of course we'll do our best to stop it reaching Termaz. It would undermine everything we're trying to achieve through Doctor Aldred."

"Oh, Gods, yes! Thank fortune she left yesterday morning! If she'd learned of it before she returned to Termaz, it might have derailed all our careful work with her over the last three months."

"Let's make sure she doesn't learn about it for as long as possible. Let her talk herself into a public position from which she can't withdraw without destroying her own reputation. That'll force her to quibble about its accuracy rather than attack us. We can use that to our advantage, not just on Termaz but at the United Planets as well."

She stood up. "I can't sleep now. I'm going to start putting down some ideas on how I can minimize the damage from my perspective – and I want to watch that documentary, darling. I know I'm not a member of the War Cabinet, but I'm sure you can make an exception for me."

"For something like this, consider it done."

She hesitated. "When word of this gets out – as it'll inevitably do sooner or later – it's going to outrage the conservatives in the House of Nobles, isn't it? They're going to demand you denounce it as a lie from beginning to end."

"Yes, they are. If I don't, they're going to mobilize against me with everything they've got. In particular, they'll insist that our original report on the destruction of the rebel capital was true and the rebel allegations are lies, no matter what evidence is presented. Too many of their own members, or their sons and daughters, were part of our invasion force. They daren't let them be tarred with the brush of complicity in crimes against humanity."

She nodded soberly. "If they're going to be that angry, you're going to be at even greater risk; so I want to take an additional precaution." She explained what she had in mind.

He looked at her for a long moment. "You really think that's necessary?"

"I don't know, but I'd rather do it and never need it than need it and not have done it!"

"You have a point. All right. Go ahead."

~ ~ ~

"Chief Sergeant Indic reports as ordered, Your Majesty!" The crash of the NCO's boots on the marble floor rattled the old-fashioned sash windows in their frames.

Zeba smiled at him. "At ease, Chief Sergeant. It's good to see you again."

"And you, Ma'am. It's been a while."

She couldn't help grinning. Such familiarity to the Satrap's wife from a commoner would have horrified most people, but then-Staff Sergeant Indic had been the personal bodyguard to the late General Huvishka. It wasn't his fault he'd been excluded from the General's party at the Arena. He'd been vociferously grateful for her efforts to protect his boss, even though they'd ultimately been unsuccessful. As he'd comforted her later, "Sometimes the conditions are against you. Sometimes the enemy's just too good or just too strong. Sometimes you're screwed no matter how well equipped and trained you are or how hard you fight. The Arena was all of those things."

He'd been injured in the same battle. At her recommendation, Rostam had appointed him to the Satrap's Bodyguard before returning to Bactria, and asked him to nominate a score of combat veterans to accompany him. Together with others recruited since then, they'd worked wonders in reinvigorating, retraining and transforming what had become, by default, a largely ceremonial force into something much more combat-capable.

"How's the training going?" she asked as she motioned to a chair in front of her desk.

"It's going well, Ma'am. They're not bad material – just improperly trained and poorly prepared for combat. Until we shook things up, their main focus was on drilling sharp and looking smart, but neither of those things ever won a battle. Some of them just couldn't take the pace, and transferred out. Others decided they wanted to learn how to stay alive, particularly after we showed 'em some battle vids from Termaz. I'd say more than half the Regiment's in good shape now, and we're whipping the rest into line as fast as we can. It was a real good idea of yours to give us a training base far away from towns and cities. They can't slip out for a beer. They have to concentrate."

"I know that's giving you plenty of opportunities to train in open terrain, but what about urban combat? That's a more likely scenario for the Satrap's Guard."

"It is, Ma'am. A few of us put our heads together. We're building a town in one corner of the training base; houses, shops, offices, even part of the Royal Palace. Instead of handing out punishment PT or extra drill sessions for making mistakes, we assign offenders to the building squad." They grinned at each other. "It's all simulated, of course, but it looks real enough for the purpose. We're already running fire teams through parts of it. As soon as it's finished we'll start working with squads, then platoons, then companies. I don't think it'll be big enough to put a full battalion through it, but we'll do what we can with what we have."

"I'm very glad to hear it. Now, let me get to the point. I've got a problem. It affects the Royal Family at the moment, but it might affect this entire nation if things go wrong. I need the best man I know to handle it. That means you."

He grimaced. "It already sounds like I'm not going to enjoy it, Ma'am."

"I think I can guarantee that, so I'm not going to order you to accept. If you'll volunteer, I'll be eternally grateful to you, but it's going to be your choice."

"Sounds fair, Ma'am. What's the job?"

She rose from behind her desk and began to pace slowly back and forth. "You know the protocol for a birth of a royal child?"

"Yes, Ma'am. They discussed it on the news when you podded your firstborn a few months ago. The transfer has to be witnessed and attested by two members of the House of Nobles, two from the House of the People, and two priests from the High Temple."

"That's right. It was pretty embarrassing, I can tell you, having to be naked from the waist down on a delivery table in front of them while the doctor removed my uterine lining and transferred it to the gestation pod." She paused, stared at him, and burst out laughing. "Why, you're blushing!"

"I guess I am, Ma'am. It's pretty embarrassing just having to hear about it!"

She shrugged. "It's been done that way for a long time. I'm told that a couple of centuries ago, a Satrap became impotent before he could father a child, and tried to pass off the baby of a friend of his as the Royal Heir. They found out about it a few years later when the kid got sick, and his DNA profile didn't match his parents. If it hadn't been for that he might have become Satrap. The witnesses are there to guard against that, as is the DNA swab taken from the fetus at the time of transfer. It's compared to the parents' DNA in front of the witnesses, to prove that the kid's theirs, and the results are kept on the child's permanent medical file. When it's grown to full term, another swab is taken and the results compared to guard against any switch having taken place."

"They really do go to a lot of trouble." Indic sounded impressed.

"Yes they do. Another aspect of that is a special guard detail that's appointed to watch over the fetus as it grows to term in the clinic, and then during infancy. It goes on to form the basis for an expanded security detail when the child is old enough to need one."

"Yeah, I saw the orders appointing a dozen of our people to the guard detail for your first child. They're stationed at the clinic for the duration."

"That's right." She sighed. "What I'm going to say to you now is utterly confidential and off the record, Chief Sergeant. If you ever talk about it without my permission, I'll shoot you myself. Clear?"

"Clear, Ma'am."

"Very well." She spent a few minutes explaining the growing resistance to her husband's reforms, and the upsurge in reports of plots against the Satrap. "We're doing our best to keep tabs on the situation, but we probably haven't identified all the disaffected groups. I'm pretty sure there may even be some officers of the Satrap's Guard who aren't exactly happy with him."

Indic scowled. "Tell me who they are and I'll see about arranging a 'training accident', Ma'am."

"I might just take you up on that. Anyway, to cut a long story short, we believe there's a genuine risk of a coup attempt – perhaps more than one, if the first one fails. There may also be attempts to kidnap or kill our first child, even prior to term. If there's no direct heir when the Satrap dies, it opens the throne to other claimants. There are at least half a dozen with similar degrees of consanguinity. That means…"

"Yeah." The Chief Sergeant's voice was flat, deadpan. "That might mean civil war if none of them will back down in favor of someone else. It's happened before."

"That's right. I – my husband and I – want to prevent that at all costs. We want to ensure that even if something happens to both him and our firstborn, we have a backup plan." She took a deep breath. "That's why I'm pregnant again."

"But, Ma'am, your first child isn't even born yet!"

"I know. This is all very unusual and irregular. However, if we can transfer this foetus to a gestation pod, using witnesses we can trust to keep their mouths shut, and guard it in a very secret place, it'll succeed to the Throne if anything happens to its parents or older sibling."

He sat down again slowly, rubbing his chin thoughtfully. "Y'know, that's pretty sneaky. It's not a bad idea at all. You'll certify the birth in the normal way, but keep it confidential at first, announcing it when you think it best."

"That's right."

"What if you aren't around to make the announcement? Sorry to be so blunt, Ma'am, but…"

"No, you're just being realistic. There'll be all the usual witness statements and DNA evidence."

"And if others call the witnesses liars, and something happens to the DNA records?"

"I see you're thinking along the same lines we are. We'll defend against that in two ways. One will be to take certain trusted priests at the High Temple into our confidence. If necessary, they'll announce that the Temple was aware of the birth and certify the child as genuine. The other is to have a very special guard detail to look after the infant in its gestation pod until it's born, then protect it as it grows. We may have to keep it secret for some time if the risk is very high, so we need someone we trust absolutely to raise and command that unit; someone who can and will use his initiative and combat experience to do whatever it takes to protect the line of succession.

"Uh-oh. Why do I suddenly get the feeling that a target's just been painted on my ass?"

She laughed aloud. "Oh, it's so *refreshing* to hear real soldier-talk for once, instead of having to listen to so many pompous primping courtiers! Yes, Chief Sergeant. I'm asking you to accept that burden. I don't trust anyone else to do this job. I need the best."

He heaved a long-suffering sigh. "I was right, Ma'am. I thought I wasn't going to enjoy this, and now I've heard about it I already hate it …

but because it's you asking, and because I reckon Major-General Huvishka would have wanted me to, I'll do it."

"Thank you," she said simply. "I'm more grateful than words can say." She grinned. "There are compensations. For a start, traditionally the commander of a royal infant's guard has to be a Major."

"Oh, no!" She was startled by the vehemence of his reaction. "Dammit, Ma'am, I'm no officer! A lot of 'em are noble sprogs, way better educated than I am and used to high society. I'd feel right out of place in the Officer's Mess. I wouldn't be able to talk to them, relate to them… no, Ma'am. I'm an NCO, and that's what I'm going to stay."

She looked at him for a long moment. "I can see you really mean that. I might point out that I'm from commoner stock, not the nobility, and I managed as an officer, but that's beside the point. Very well; I won't insist on your accepting a commission, but I'm going to twist the Regulations until they beg for mercy. They lay down that a Major has to command a guard detail like this, so I'm going to have my husband promote you to Sergeant-Major. That way a Major *will* be in command – just a hyphenated Major instead of the sort the Regs have in mind."

He began to laugh. "Dammit, I like it, Ma'am! It'll cause a fuss, though. That's a two-step promotion for me. Some of the other senior NCO's may be uptight about it."

"I daresay you can sweet-talk them into a better mood," she suggested, an impish grin on her face and a twinkle in her eye.

"Sweet talk, eh? That's something I can honestly say I've never heard in the Army, Ma'am – apart from now, that is." They laughed together. "Still, I can be *real* persuasive if I try."

"I just bet you can! Select a dozen people for your guard detail – anyone you want, and more than twelve if you think you need them. I know the Regs list desirable attributes for the job, but I want you to pick men and women who also have combat experience and battlefield smarts; people who you'd be willing to trust with *your* life if necessary. If things go to hell in a hand basket, you may have to get the baby to safety in unknown circumstances. There may not even be a safe place to get to. You may have to move fast and think on your feet. I want everyone in your team to be able to do the same if necessary. As far as equipment's concerned, make a list of everything you think you might need. I'll see you get it as quickly as possible."

"Sounds good to me, Ma'am." He hesitated. "Some of 'em won't want this job. If I can offer the carrot of a promotion to go with it, like you offered me, that'll help."

"Pick your team, bring me their names, and I'll guarantee them all a one-step promotion right away. If you want one or two to get more than that, we'll see what can be done."

"Thanks, Ma'am. That'll make things much easier. It won't bother you that we won't have an officer in command?"

"I'll have *you* in command. That's the most important thing as far as I'm concerned. At a later stage, if things quiet down, we can appoint officers you trust to lead the team; but you'll help choose them, and have the right of veto over the final selection. What's more, the Satrap will personally sign the promotion warrants for your entire team. That'll make them Royal Appointments, so no-one will be able to be demoted below that rank or discharged from service without the Satrap's approval. It'll be a little bit of extra job security for everyone."

"They'll like that, Ma'am. When do we start?"

"The transfer to the pod will take place next week. You'll have to be on duty at that time, and from then onward."

A look of horror dawned on his face. "I won't have to actually *watch* it, will I, Ma'am?"

"The Commanding Officer of the guard team is supposed to be there, but if you think that's too much you can pick a female team member to stand in for you."

He heaved a huge sigh of relief. "Thanks, Ma'am. I know what to do when people are shooting at me, but watching *that* would be just too much!"

~ ~ ~

The narrator's voice intoned, "And so a dark and savage conflict continues. The blood of more than half Laredo's pre-war population continues to cry out for justice... so far, without response... but the day will come."

The image of the ruined city of Banka faded to black. Music swelled, a sorrowful lament for the dead, as the credits began to roll. After a few seconds Rostam clapped his hands twice, and the recording shut off. There was a deafening silence in the room. The War Cabinet sat frozen, most of its members still staring at where the now-inert holographic display had been projected.

Eventually Rostam stirred. "All right. We've seen it. Your thoughts?"

The Foreign Minister shook his head. "Your Majesty, quite frankly my initial reaction is to tender my resignation and return to my country estate. Maybe I'll try my hand at farming again. I'm certainly not going to be able to do you much good in the interplanetary arena for very much longer."

"That bad?"

"Your Majesty, if the rebels raised a fleet of warships and sent it into the Bactria system to destroy our entire space-based economy, all our asteroid mines and the Space Elevator and our orbital factories and power satellites and communications network, and then bombarded vital planetary installations like dams, harbors and bridges from orbit with kinetic projectiles... if they did all that, they *still* wouldn't cause as much damage to us as this documentary will inflict. Producing it and the accompanying book was an absolute masterstroke of diplomacy. If the evidence they cited in the documentary is ratified as genuine by the United Planets..."

"So to put it in a nutshell, Simar, you're saying we're screwed?"

"That's not a very diplomatic expression, Your Majesty, but yes, that's about the size of it. In a year or two we'll probably be under interplanetary sanctions. The rebels may even gain access to real warships now, not just converted freighters, because the UP is almost sure to call on its members to offer them support." He twisted in his chair to look at the Minister of Defense. "I know you weren't in office at the time, Griga, so I'm not blaming you; but I have to ask how it's possible that our military could have committed such inhuman atrocities. Even worse, if they did so – which, on the basis of what we've just seen, I presume they did – why in the name of all that's holy didn't they destroy the evidence? That failure has handed the rebels more than enough rope to hang us. The late General Strato might as well have gift-wrapped it with that damn fool ultimatum to his rebel counterpart! Of all the idiotic, mindless, *imbecilic*..." He threw up his hands in disgust and despair.

Rostam asked, "What if we can find some former rebel leaders on Termaz to quibble about the documentary's claims? They might argue it was produced from a partisan perspective, or overstates the extent of the problem, or something like that. We obviously won't be able to get away with denying that atrocities took place, but can we mitigate their impact on public opinion in that way?"

"It's not a bad idea, Your Majesty. It probably won't be enough to stop sanctions being approved, but it might be a useful argument against excessive severity or military enforcement. In almost half the cases where the UP's imposed sanctions, an embargo was enforced by military patrols, basically shutting down interplanetary commerce to the nation concerned. That would cripple us, and of course it'd make our position on Termaz completely untenable. If we can produce arguments from known rebel leaders claiming that things there aren't as black as they're being painted by their Government-in-Exile, that might help us avoid or mitigate that degree of enforcement."

The Defense Minister nodded vigorously. "That's a very important point, Your Majesty. If we face embargo, we'll have no choice but to begin evacuating all our people from Termaz right away. It'll take six months of shuttle trips by every available freighter to bring back all our people, military and civilian, and another six months to return all the equipment we've sent there."

Rostam frowned. "Even if that becomes necessary, we also need our freighters to maintain normal interplanetary trade. We can't afford to shut that down in order to evacuate Termaz."

"Then we'd have to charter more freighters from somewhere, Your Majesty. Let's hope it doesn't become necessary." He paused. "What worries me most, even more than the thought of sanctions, is that our people were officially assured that our armed forces had caused minimal casualties among the civilian population of Termaz. The vast majority of them were blamed on the accidental crash of a spaceship and 'indiscriminate fire' by 'poorly trained' and 'inept' defenders. It now seems those assurances may have been lies from beginning to end – yet I'm supposed to supervise the armed forces that issued them. *How can I trust our Generals any longer?* Most of them were actively involved in the campaign there, and were promoted to their present ranks and positions as a result of that experience. My initial inclination is to dismiss the lot of them, but if I do that, they're bound to intrigue against you and spread disaffection throughout the armed forces. I don't know how to deal with this."

"That makes two of us," the Satrap replied grimly

"Won't they claim that they were following the orders of your grandfather, the late Satrap Tepe, Your Majesty?" the Foreign Minister asked. "I don't know whether his private archive contains any references to such incidents."

"Neither do I, but rest assured, I'm going to find out! If I find anything to suggest that any of our senior officers knowingly carried out such attacks, I'll court-martial them. However, I can't do so without evidence; and my grandfather was a canny old bastard. He'll have taken good care to ensure that posterity can't point a finger at him for anything that may have happened on Termaz. There may be no surviving evidence of atrocities in the Royal Archives. Griga, I want you to check Defense Ministry archives as well, but you may find the same problem. If so, we'll be at an impasse."

"Why not use the evidence the rebels have provided in their book and documentary?" the Defense Minister suggested.

Rostam laughed, a short, bitter sound. "Can you *imagine* the fun defense counsel would have in a court-martial, challenging the accuracy and admissibility of evidence provided by an enemy who's still engaged in hostilities against us? The charges would be dismissed on the spot."

"I take your point, Your Majesty."

"So what *can* we do about the Generals, Your Majesty?" the Foreign Minister asked.

"Right now, I don't know, Simar. I just don't know."

~ ~ ~

ENTERTAINMENT DISTRICT, SODIA

The conspirators sat in stunned silence as the final moments of the documentary played, and the credits rolled. Khanoum shut off the recording with an impatient gesture.

"Filth! *Lies!*" he grated furiously. "How can they expect anyone to believe such nonsense?"

The Army and SS Generals looked at one another silently. At last the black-uniformed General Gedrosia said slowly, "I profoundly regret to inform you, Wazir, that it isn't nonsense. Most of those allegations were true."

The nobleman gaped at him in real shock. "The destruction of their capital?" The SS officer nodded. "The wiping out of civilian communities suspected of harboring rebels?" Nod. "Working tens of thousands of slave laborers to death?" Nod. "But... but *why?* Why were we not told?"

"You were told as much as the late Satrap Tepe would allow us to tell you, Wazir. We were under strict orders never to discuss the truth, even amongst ourselves."

His colleagues nodded in unison. "Those were our orders, too," Demetrius averred. "I was only a Brigadier-General at the time, so I wasn't party to everything that went on, but after I came back here on promotion I tried to raise the matter with my predecessor. He cut me off at the knees – refused to talk about it at all and threatened me with a secret court-martial and the end of my career if I disobeyed. He told me that's what Satrap Tepe had ordered."

Khanoum sank back into his chair, shaking his head. "If... if those were your orders, I can understand you obeying them... but how could the Satrap deceive *his own nobles?*"

"With respect, Wazir, I think you're missing the point." Major Kadeh spoke politely, but firmly. "There's an old saying: 'three can keep a secret, if two of them are dead'. In a matter as sensitive as this, I don't think the late Satrap Tepe would have dared disregard that." There were vigorous and approving nods from all the senior officers. "Just look at the damage this will probably inflict on us now that it's come out. The Satrap wanted to avoid that ever happening; and I suspect the only way he could think of to do that was to prevent *anyone* from learning the truth."

"I suppose you're right. Thank you for reminding me of that."

"There's more, Wazir." Kadeh sat forward, looking around earnestly at each of the others in turn. "We must tread even more lightly and carefully in our preparations, because these disclosures make us more vulnerable. If we act against the Satrap before this news becomes public, when it comes out we'll be accused of having done so to avoid punishment for our part in these acts. That would destroy our credibility at once."

"But if it doesn't come out on Bactria, that won't matter," Colonel Arachosia reminded him. "You told us the Satrap wants to keep this news tightly held."

The Guardsman snorted. "Oh, come *on*, Sir! I managed to make a copy of the documentary this afternoon, to bring to our meeting tonight. I'm not the only person in the Royal Palace with that level of access. If I did it, how many others have done the same by now? I'll bet a year of my salary against an hour of yours that by the end of this month, a hundred people will have seen the documentary. By the end of the year, I'll be astonished if the number isn't over a thousand. Sooner or later it'll become common knowledge."

"He's right," General Demetrias said abruptly. "By the way, Major, we're very grateful to you for risking your safety to make that copy and bring it to us tonight." A rumble of agreement ran around the table. "By doing so on the same day the Satrap and War Cabinet learned of its existence, you've given us time to prepare counter-measures in case they try to use it against us."

"How could they do that?" the Wazir asked, puzzled.

"The documentary identifies dates, times, places and the names of those in command during various alleged 'atrocities'. That will help narrow down the search of anyone looking through our own records covering the same period. We know the Satrap's archives were scrubbed of all reference to such matters. I was involved in doing the same to the Army's and Defense Ministry's records. I presume something similar was done at the Security Service?" He looked inquiringly at General Gedrosia, who nodded wordlessly. "Good. However, we kept a confidential archive in a backup location containing all of our deleted material, for future reference in case of need. I think we'll now have to destroy that entirely to prevent its discovery, even at the cost of losing historically important material."

"I'll make sure we do the same," Gedrosia agreed. "It's a pity, but it can't be helped."

"What do you think this will mean for our plans, Wazir?" Major-General Pamir asked.

Khanoum frowned. "It means nothing good in the short term, I fear, but it may prove very useful in the longer term. Think about it. This is undoubtedly going to cause enormous harm to Bactria. The Satrap and his

Cabinet will do whatever they can to counter that, but it's unlikely to make much of a difference. Whoever's in charge over the next two to three years is going to be blamed in at least some measure for the resulting economic hardship. We don't want that to be us. Therefore, we may have to let matters run their course, allow the Satrap to be blamed for whatever ensues, then act to 'rescue' Bactria from the mire into which she will have sunk by then. In that way we'll appear as saviors rather than traitors to the vast majority of our people."

"A very good point indeed, Wazir," Major Kadeh said slowly, reflectively. "We might want to take that further. We might be well advised to avoid destabilizing the Satrap and his Ministers in the short term. After all, as you say, we want them to remain in power, to take the blame for problems that arise. We might even assist them in critical areas – indirectly, of course, and very discreetly – in order to make sure there's still an adequate infrastructure to support us when we take over."

"And those, too, are very good points, my friend," the Wazir praised. "General Demetrias has already thanked you for bringing the documentary to us tonight. Now you've made another valuable contribution. I think I must express my appreciation in concrete terms. I have an estate on the coast, about ten kilometers outside Sodia. It's a comfortable manor house on a headland, surrounded by a few hectares of woodland and an inland farm. It's yours, my dear Major, along with sufficient funds for its upkeep. I'll have my lawyers start the transfer paperwork first thing in the morning."

Kadeh flushed. "Thank you very much, Wazir, but that's not necessary."

"On the contrary. Rewarding good and faithful service is *always* necessary," the nobleman said firmly. Another murmur of approval and agreement ran round the room.

Looking around at the traitorous team he'd assembled, the Wazir thought, *Keeping the Satrap in power to take the blame is all very well, but ultimately he'll have to go. He's not malleable enough to accept our direction for long, no matter how strong our hold over him. I'll have to start considering potential successors, to see who'll prove most amenable to our direction when the time comes.*

His thoughts were interrupted by General Gedrosia. "Should I renew efforts to target the rebel delegation on Neue Helvetica? Their last attempt failed when the team was killed in a car accident. I only found out about that last week – we had no-one else there to report it to us – so I'm in the process of assembling a new team to replace them. It'll take time to smuggle them onto the planet, but when they finally get there they can try again. If we assassinate some of the rebel leaders, that should disrupt the activities of their Government-in-Exile for some time. That will help the Satrap and his Ministers to deal with the threat they pose."

Demetrias said approvingly, "I think that might be very useful, provided we don't risk another Consulate-type debacle."

"I'll order my team to make no mistakes." He took a printed photograph from his pocket. "I sent a team to Marano as well. The Navy asked us to keep an eye on the progress of our arms order and make sure they don't try to fob us off with substandard refurbished equipment. Yesterday I received this from the leader of my team there." He passed the photograph around the table. "It was taken at a restaurant on the Elevator Terminal orbiting the planet."

Pamir stared, then gasped, "That's the rebel President Pro Tem!"

"Indeed it is; and why do you think he was at Marano?"

Three voices spoke as one. "Buying weapons!"

"Precisely. Marano sells arms to almost all comers, provided they have money. My agent reported that Carson met with a representative from a major weapons broker. He saw a sheaf of papers change hands, presumably interplanetary bearer bank drafts."

"What has he bought?" the Wazir asked, his voice angry.

"We don't know yet, but my people are doing their best to find out."

"Then by all means let's remove him from the equation, and as many of his colleagues as you can manage. Do you think your team on Marano can target him if he goes back there?"

"I'll send orders to them at once. They may be able to bribe the weapons broker to arrange a suitable rendezvous where they can get at him. Such men are seldom honest."

"That's a good idea. Did you ever find out more about what happened to his father?"

"Regrettably, no. The Army report stated simply that the airvan in which he was a passenger crashed in rough terrain soon after takeoff with the loss of everyone on board, probably as the result of high winds in the vicinity. They didn't conduct autopsies because most of the bodies – it

119

would be more accurate to say 'body parts' – were badly mutilated. The recovery party simply gathered them up and disposed of them on site using crematory bags. I wasn't happy about that – I'd have liked our investigators to have access to them and the wreckage, to see if they could learn anything – but unfortunately that wasn't possible in the time available. The heat of summer made it impossible to store the bodies in the absence of mortuary facilities. They buried Carson at the prison camp, and our people at the War Memorial outside Tapuria."

"A pity. It would have been very useful to be able to use the rebel President's father as a lever against his son."

"I'm considering whether we might still be able to do that. After all, he probably doesn't know yet that his father is dead. On the other hand, there's no indication that he knew his father was still alive. He may have assumed he'd died in the assault on Tapuria last year."

The Wazir nodded. "Well, if you kill him the point will become moot. I presume you won't bother the Satrap with that suggestion?"

"Why should I? He doesn't trust us, and we don't trust him. I'll act in what I believe to be the best interests of Bactria – after discussing them with you, of course. I know you all have those interests at heart."

"Thank you, General. You're very considerate to include us. Is everyone agreed that a few dead rebel leaders will be useful to our cause?" Heads nodded around the table. "Then please proceed with your plans. Let's consider ways in which the rest of us can implement Major Kadeh's very useful suggestions."

Laredo: December 14-19 2851 GSC

PRISON CAMP #3, NEAR CARISTO

Major Tredegar glanced around casually. His team were all in position, apparently standing casually in random positions around the prison camp yard, but in reality covering all sides of a carefully calculated area. For the benefit of the guards they pretended to talk with friends, bounced a ball off the hard dirt, did physical exercises, or simply sat and read a book.

He checked his timepiece. One minute to go. Casually he reached up and adjusted the knitted cap covering his head. Now, instead of being level, it slanted slightly to one side, covering the top half of his right ear. He turned in place, apparently looking up at the hills all around the camp. As the prisoners noted his cap's new position, they paid extra attention to their duties.

Right on time, a small disturbance appeared in the rocky soil a little to the right of center of the designated area. Three of the watchers instantly signaled as they'd been trained – pulling at their ear, rubbing their nose, scuffing their foot. A thin dirt-colored rod showed itself for an instant above the soil, then was as quickly withdrawn.

Tredegar sighed with relief. It looked as if Operation Delve had been entirely successful – so far, at any rate. He pulled his hat straight as he turned towards the perimeter. He'd walk around the warning wire for a few circuits while his team carefully estimated angles, paced off distances, and made sure they could pinpoint as accurately as possible where the breakthrough had occurred.

~ ~ ~

"I passed the coordinates by semaphore, Sir," Lieutenant Kubicka told him in a low voice over supper that evening.

"They acknowledged?"

"Yes, Sir. Look for them at midnight on the sixteenth. They'll have a wire laid and ready."

"Thanks be to God! It's been so long!"

"With a little bit of luck, Sir, it won't be much longer."

~ ~ ~

The Major opened his bedroom door ten minutes before midnight, and looked down the corridor of his hut. Two watchers at either end gave him the high sign. They, and others watching covertly from the windows of their sleeping units, had not detected any roving Bactrian snoopers entering the compound. The duty watch were relying, as usual, on armed guards in the corner towers and electronic sensors monitored from the guardroom, sited to detect and monitor every movement inside the wire and listen for the tell-tale sounds of tunneling, in case the prisoners tried to dig their way to freedom through the rocky, unwelcoming soil.

He closed the door and turned to the primitive wood-burning stove set against the wall. No fire had been built in it tonight, despite the chill, and the stovepipe leading up the wall had been disconnected. Swiftly he and Lieutenant Kubicka went to either side of the stove, grasped its handles and lifted it carefully, moving it off the tiled platform and setting it down to one side.

Kubicka knelt and inserted a knife blade into the crack at the edge of the tiles at the bottom corner of the platform. He scraped away the camouflaging layer of carefully ingrained dirt, then levered gently. A wire loop emerged. He pulled it upright, then did the same at the other three corners before folding the knife and returning it to his pocket.

"Ready, Sir."

Tredegar moved to the other side of the tiles. They each inserted their index fingers into two loops, then lifted. The carefully prepared slab rose out of its socket, revealing the ground beneath the floor of the hut, which was raised about half a meter above it on pier-and-beam foundations.

Tredegar grinned as they carefully set down the slab next to the stove. "Good thing the Bactrians didn't want to waste money on plascrete slabs for mere prison camp buildings. They left us room to work down there."

They waited, watching, their hearts pounding with excitement. At the stroke of midnight the soil beneath the opening was suddenly disturbed. The same dirt-colored rod they'd seen in the compound two days before rose a few centimeters above the soil, then stopped as if waiting for something. Tredegar picked up one of his shoes from the floor, reached into the opening and tapped the rod gently with the heel; twice, a pause, once, another pause, then three times. At once the rod disappeared back into the soil.

Again they waited. The next disturbance came almost immediately. More soil and small stones were pushed aside as a larger rod thrust upward. It emerged from the now wider opening with a screwing motion, then was withdrawn, only to be replaced within a minute by a black plastic cap atop what looked like a narrow plumber's pipe. It rose out of the ground and stopped. Tredegar reached down, unscrewed the cap and took out a small comm handset, a wire trailing behind it into the pipe. He adjusted the volume of the small speaker to a lower setting before pressing the 'Transmit' button. Softly he intoned, "Long was the morn of slaughter, long was the list of slain."

As he released the button, Kubicka whispered, "Sounds like Kipling, Sir."

"It is. It's from 'The Grave of the Hundred Head', about a firefight on Old Home Earth before the Space Age. The response should be from Siegfried Sassoon's 'Absolution'."

They listened until they heard, crackling softly through the speaker, "War is our scourge; yet war has made us wise, and, fighting for our freedom, we are free."

"That's it!" Smiling, Tredegar pressed the 'Transmit' button again. "This is Leonidas. Go ahead, over."

"This is Charon. It's great to hear your voice, Sir! Over."

"Less of the 'Sir' – stick to code names; but it's good to hear yours too. What's our status? Over."

A chuckle came over the wire. "It was just as Peleus suspected, God rest his soul. They only have anti-tunneling sensors around the fence line, planted ten meters deep. They can pick up digging sounds within a radius of twenty to thirty meters in all directions. That's enough to detect the sort of shallow tunnel you'd have to make to dig your way *out* of there, but not nearly good enough to pick up laser rock-cutters carving a tunnel *in* at a much greater depth. That allowed us to slip through their outer ring of sensors, five clicks out, and avoid all their drone and satellite reconnaissance. Once we were under the middle of the camp, we were far inside the zone where the microphones would hear us cutting a narrow channel upwards to reach you like this. They're going to have egg all over their faces when this goes down. By the way, where did we come out? Over."

"You couldn't have been more precise. You're exactly on target. Over."

"That's thanks to your team of observers. By triangulating on our test probe, they told us exactly where we were and how to adjust our final digging angle. Computer calculations are all very well, but it was great to be able to confirm we hadn't missed by more than a few centimeters. Over."

"I can understand that. Please convey my thanks and congratulations to whoever ran the calculations, and the miners who dug the tunnel. They did an outstanding job. Now, what's the schedule? Over."

"The tunnel's already beyond the far side of the wire. The upward shaft is in progress, and should be finished tomorrow. One more day to touch it up and we'll be ready to go. The last couple of meters of rock and soil will be left for the main event, of course. The team is ready for action. Have you completed your training for everybody? Over."

"We've discussed everything in theory, but of course we haven't been able to practice anything. Over."

"That's good to hear. Given the experience level in there, you should be fine. Base Bravo reports they're all set as well. Everything will happen simultaneously at both places. I'll sign off and let the rock-cutters get back to work. Cover the hole on your side, and let's do this again two nights from now at the same time for a final update. We'll make our move the following night. Over."

"Thank you. We look forward to seeing you. Is transport organized? Over."

"Yes, it is, including secure bases for everyone. We've been busy out here. Over."

"It sounds like it. Very well, we'll look for you two nights from now. Leonidas out."

Tredegar switched off the handset and replaced it in the pipe before screwing the cap on again. He tapped it three times with his shoe, whereupon it was withdrawn into the soil once more, leaving a hollow. Tredegar took a small stone that he'd picked up out on the compound and laid it carefully inside the hollow, then flicked loose dirt over it with his fingertips. To the uninformed eye the surface of the soil now looked completely natural once more.

"All right, that should do it. Let's put the stove back."

They replaced the slab, lifted the stove back onto it, and reconnected the stovepipe. Kubicka built a fire, commenting with a grin, "It's all very well using the stove to conceal our new comms setup, but it gets infernally chilly in here when we can't light it!"

"Never mind. Soon it won't matter anymore."

~ ~ ~

It was cold three nights later when the Sergeant of the Guard rousted out four of his detail. "Come on, come on, it's almost twenty-two. Get out there and relieve the four tower sentries, so they can come back inside and warm up. You'll be relieved at twenty-four."

Muttering, moaning and complaining, the four put on their heavy winter-issue outer garb and straggled out into the cold air. Their leader, a Corporal, snapped, "All right, that's enough whining! Straighten up and try to look like soldiers, damn you!"

"Huh! You're just a bloody conscript, same as we are, so don't get so jumped-up and full of yourself!" one of the soldiers retorted.

"You –"

Whatever the junior NCO was planning to say died unspoken as dark figures materialized all around them. Bayoneted rifles were trained unerringly in rock-steady hands, the points of the blades touching their navels. A voice whispered, "Make a sound and all of you die right now. Keep quiet and don't move, and you might live to see the dawn."

The four froze in their tracks, mouths agape in astonishment and fear.

"That's good. Stand real still. Squad!"

Four men moved forward. Stepping behind the sentries, each removed the fur hat and greatcoat from the soldier in front of him and put them on himself.

"On your way."

The four moved off in the direction the guards had been heading. The Corporal recovered himself enough to turn his head and look after them, only to feel the prick of a bayonet point in the small of his back. "Not a sound!" a voice warned quietly but savagely. He nodded slowly, carefully, trying to convey as sincerely as possible his heartfelt desire to keep the intruders happy.

"All of you follow me *real* slow and careful. Any noise and you won't live long enough to regret it, let alone make another."

The raiders escorted the four soldiers out of sight behind the Administration building. Meanwhile, the four who'd taken the sentries' places marched around the perimeter. Only the four corner guard towers were manned at night, the others standing vacant until dawn. As the party arrived at the foot of each of them, one of their number detached himself from the group and pressed a button at the base of the tower to let the guard on duty know that his relief had arrived. As he climbed the ladder, the others in the relief party went on around the wire. As the security hatch in the base of each platform was unlocked and the replacement was admitted to the guard post, he pulled a handgun and commanded the startled sentry to freeze, or else. Caught completely by surprise, none resisted. They were soon lying face-down on the floor, hands behind their heads.

In the guardroom, the Sergeant glanced at the time display on the wall and frowned. The newly relieved tower sentries should have returned by now. He muttered, "What's holding up those buggers?" as he brought up another report on the terminal and began to check off the computer-generated boxes. "I'll have to –"

He was interrupted as the door opened at last. "What kept you?" he demanded without raising his head as the tramp of boots filled the guardroom.

"Mice," came the sardonic reply.

The Sergeant looked up angrily, about to verbally blast the disrespectful soldier from pillar to post, but the profanities died in his throat as he found himself looking down the bore of a bayoneted rifle. The other guards were also frozen in place, held motionless by the menacing weapons of the black-clad masked men in front of them.

"We're from pest control," the man in front of him continued. "We're here to deal with an infestation. That would be you."

"W – What do you want? You can't get away with this!"

"Want to bet?" The Sergeant was silent. "No, I guess you don't; but I suggest you start hoping and praying that we *do* get away with it, because if we don't, you'll die first. *Clear?*" The last word cracked like a whip.

"Y – Yessir!"

"Stand up real slow and careful. Pretend you're very old and very frail, with bad arthritis."

The NCO obeyed, taking no chances whatsoever. He knew no-one learned to hold a rifle so absolutely rock-steady without a corresponding ability to place its rounds where they'd do the most good – or harm, depending upon one's position in relation to the muzzle.

"We're going to flex-cuff all of you, search you, then lock you in the cells until we've taken over the rest of the buildings. Don't get any ideas about twisting or snapping the flex-cuffs, because the edges are lined with nanowire. You'll cut your hands off at the wrists if you try. As for you, Sergeant, before you join your guards in the cells you're going to hand over all the keys and account for all the ready-use weapons and equipment. If you all co-operate and don't do anything stupid, you'll all live to see the dawn."

~ ~ ~

The camp residents waited on tenterhooks in their blocks. Everyone had been warned what was about to happen, and exhaustively briefed about their part in proceedings.

At last the loudspeakers crackled. *"It's done! You're free again!"*

Black-clad figures swung open the main gates. Cheering loudly, the exultant former prisoners of war poured out of their blocks, rushing towards their rescuers. The replacement tower guards gathered up night vision equipment and weapons, then climbed down and escorted their captives in the same direction.

Major Tredegar had to force his way through excited groups, hugging friends from the outside whom they hadn't seen for well over a year, exchanging news, asking for information about other people. At last he emerged through the gates to see a small group of black-uniformed men waiting for him. They snapped to attention as he approached, and their leader saluted.

"Good evening, Sir. I'm Captain Barger, but you knew me as Charon. All secure, Sir."

"Outstanding! You've all done a magnificent job tonight. Any casualties?"

"None on either side, Sir. The off-duty guards in the barrack blocks didn't want to give up, but we sent in one of our flitterbugs as a demonstration. That convinced 'em real quick."

"It would convince me, all right, if I were in their shoes. Let's break up old home week and get the groups organized. We have a hell of a lot to do before dawn."

It took half an hour to divide the former prisoners of war into their prearranged groups, equip as many as possible with rifles from the prison camp armory, and issue new warm winter clothing to everyone. Most of the prisoners and those who'd freed them drove away in the direction of the reaction force base. They took with them most of the vehicles in the camp, leaving behind several heavy transporters and twenty people.

Those who stayed conscripted some of the former guards to load the transporters with everything in the camp that might be useful – uniforms, weapons and ammunition, spare parts, electronics, bedding, web gear, rucksacks, ration packs and dozens of other items. That done, the prisoners were herded into one of the barracks and secured with flex-cuffs. Those in the guardroom were brought to join them, while the camp's officers and senior NCO's replaced them in the cells.

The leader of the raiding party stood in the doorway of the barracks and raised his voice to get the soldiers' attention. "Listen up! You people changed tactics last year. Instead of killing everyone you caught, you began taking prisoners. That's why you're still alive tonight. You didn't kill our people, so we're not going to kill you."

A rustle of relief ran through the guards. Some of them remembered how things had been on Laredo up to the year before, when to be captured by either side was the next best thing to an automatic death sentence.

"You're crowded in here, but you'll just have to endure it until a relief force arrives. They'll be on their way as soon as Headquarters realizes that no calls or messages to this place are being answered. Don't get ideas about breaking out of this building to send a warning. Look." He held up a flitterbug in his hand. "D'you notice the black band around its middle? That means it's a Security Service flitterbug. We captured lots of 'em last year when we took the SS Headquarters Building in Banka – what you call Tapuria. Before we blew it to hell, we loaded 'em onto our vehicles and brought 'em out with us. Some of 'em will be flying around outside as soon as we leave."

He looked around the room. "Anyone leaving this barracks is going to be targeted, and these old-style bugs still use darts carrying a lethal poison. There's no antidote, unlike the new version that only knocks you out. Get that through your heads. If you leave this building, *you die.* We've programmed the bugs to fly off into the bush after a while and hide themselves; but you don't know when that'll happen, so don't take chances. Stay in here like good little soldiers and wait for your rescuers to arrive. By the time they get here, it'll be safe to come out. Yes?"

A Sergeant had stepped forward. "What about the relief force? They're just up the road, five clicks away. They may get here much faster than that. The bugs will kill some of 'em for sure."

"They've got problems of their own. They're going to be needing rescue as well."

"Aw, *shit!*"

"Wait until I've left. I don't want to have to smell it." The raider's sally drew reluctant laughter from a few of the guards. "One more thing. We're letting you live tonight; but if you come after us, now or later, we won't be so merciful. We can kill you more easily than you can kill us. Look at the statistics since you guys invaded. We've killed lots of you for every one of us who died. This is our planet. We know it like the backs of our hands. We're fighting in our own back yard.

"Most of you are only here until your term of conscription is over. If you keep your heads down, you might live to go home again. We've got plenty more of these flitterbugs, and tonight we've captured lots more rifles, mortars, missiles and a bunch of other stuff, not just here but at several other bases. We're as well equipped as you are now. We aren't going to come after you unless we have to, so don't you come after us. If you're ordered to look for us, as soon as you get out of sight of your officers find a hidey-hole, get into it and stay there. Brew up some tea, have a meal, read a book, play cards, whatever. If anyone tries to force you to fight, make sure they have an accident or die in combat. After all, if one of your officers is shot with one of your own service rifles you can always blame us, because we use them too. Don't let anyone push you into hunting us, because if they do, *you'll* be doing the dying – not them. Remember that."

He stepped back through the doors, closed and locked them, then jogged to the leading transporter. His people grinned at him from the other vehicles as he passed.

"How long to the new entrance?" he asked the driver as he climbed into the cab. "I haven't been there before."

"Thanks to this spiffy new road the Bactrians built, less than two hours. The last half-hour will be off-road over rocky ground that'll hide our tracks. After we get underground, another hour. Those miners used their laser cutters to carve some really useful long-distance access tunnels. We don't have to expose ourselves so much to drones or satellites, and we've angled and booby-trapped all of them in multiple places. No-one's going to sneak up on us through them."

"Good. Let's be on our way."

As the driver eased the heavily laden vehicle into motion with a whine from its electric power pack, he asked, "What about the others?"

"They'll be along. They first have to load everything useful at the reaction force camp. Another group hit it at the same time we took this place. They had plenty of flitterbugs, with orders to let the defenders see them and be given a chance to surrender before they used them. I'm willing to bet that's just what they did."

The driver shivered. "In their shoes, I'd do the same. Those damned bugs have killed a hell of a lot of our people."

"Yes, but any killing these ones do in future will be on our side."

"I can live with that – even if the Bactrians can't!"

Laughter floated from the cab as the transporter turned out of the camp onto the road.

Laredo: December 20 2851 GSC

MILITARY HEADQUARTERS, TAPURIA

Brigadier-General Khan stared down at the operations table from the elevated vantage point of the visitors' gallery. Five red stars marked known incidents. Even as he watched, a sixth star was placed over the icon identifying the garrison at Ligarda. He allowed no change of expression to cross his face, but he knew it was yet another nail in the coffin of his hopes for promotion to Major-General... unless – *unless* – he could find a way to manage this crisis in a way that pleased the Satrap. If he did, even the censure of his superior officers might perhaps be offset. After all, that's what had happened the previous year following the Battle of Tapuria. The Satrap had promoted him to his present rank despite the poor performance of his regiment, because he'd seen the way the Royal wind was blowing and set his sails accordingly. *The fact that almost every one of our units performed just as poorly probably helped*, he thought cynically to himself. *The rebels wrong-footed us all.*

An aide entered behind him and coughed to attract his attention. "The Staff are ready with their preliminary assessments, Sir."

"Thank you. I'll come."

He walked into the conference room to find the atmosphere so tense it felt as if it could be cut with a knife. Looking around, he noted that several of his staff had red, angry faces. Clearly they had been arguing among themselves. *Almost certainly trying to point fingers at everyone else*, he mused as he sat down. *That's what most staff officers do best, after all. It's never their fault!*

"Very well, let's start with an overall appreciation of what's happened. Lieutenant-Colonel Oxus?"

His G-2 Staff Intelligence Officer strode to a map on the wall. She referred to it as she made her points.

"We've been hit hard, Sir. Both prison camps have been emptied. Both reaction force bases, intended to protect them against any rebel attempt to rescue the prisoners of war, were hit at the same time. The auxiliary supply depot at Colosio was raided, and the garrison at Ligarda. We've had no reports of any other incidents as of five minutes ago."

"I imagine those six are more than enough to be going on with," the General observed sardonically. "Go into more detail, please."

"Yes, Sir. Both prison camps were equipped with sensors to monitor the area above ground inside the camps and on likely avenues of approach, plus anti-tunneling sensors buried around the perimeter to detect any attempt by the prisoners of war to dig their way out. Unfortunately, in both cases rebel forces appear to have dug their way *in,* at a deep enough level to avoid the sensors. We've found what appear to be large, well-constructed tunnels that must start well outside the area. They come to the surface halfway between the prison camps and their reaction force bases, out of sight and earshot of both locations, where their sensors didn't provide coverage. From the freshly disturbed earth around their exits, it appears they weren't opened until just before the assaults, so as not to give any warning to the bases. We'll know more once we can get into them and explore them, but that won't be for some time."

"Why not?" demanded a black-uniformed SS colonel in a cold voice.

"Because, Sir, the rebels booby-trapped the hell out of them, and were kind enough to warn us about that," she said flatly.

"They *warned* you? And you believed them?"

"They posted signs at the exits to both tunnels, Sir, warning they were guarded by flitterbugs, nanobugs, and explosive and other booby-traps. The Commanding Officer at Camp Three had the sense to heed the warnings and wait for specialists to investigate. The Commanding Officer at Camp Two did not, and sent scouts down the tunnel. A short while later there were screams from inside, then silence. None of the scouts have communicated or returned. The commander has been ordered not to send any more scouts underground until specialists arrive."

"And they'll go underground?"

"I can't say, Sir. They'll make that decision based on their on-scene assessment."

"I don't think they will, Colonel," Khan observed. "We've already lost half a dozen soldiers at Camp Two. I see no point in losing more. We know our flitterbugs and nanobugs can remain active for a week to ten days on a single battery charge. We'll wait at least that long before sending anyone else down; and even then we'll have to move very slowly and carefully to find and disarm booby-traps or demolition charges. I should think it'll take us at least a month to investigate the tunnels."

"But we might glean vital intelligence from them!" the SS officer protested. "If we wait that long, it'll lose much of its value!"

"What intelligence do you expect to gain from a hole in the ground, Colonel?"

"I – ah… How can I answer that when I don't know what the tunnels contain or where they lead, Sir?"

"Precisely. However, I don't think the answers are likely to be worth good soldiers' lives. I'm sure the rebels will have removed anything that might provide us with useful information. That's what you or I would do in their shoes, after all." He turned back at his G-2. "Carry on, please."

"Yes, Sir. We presume two assault parties came out of each tunnel, one going to each of the nearby bases. They carried conventional weapons and flitterbugs. They neutralized the sentries on guard duty, secured vital installations such as armories and communication centers, then used the flitterbugs to intimidate our soldiers in their barracks. The troops were given a choice: surrender or die. Since they weren't allowed to have weapons with them in their barracks and they had no protection against flitterbugs, they had no option but to surrender. At that stage or later, all our troops were warned that the black bands around the bugs' bodies indicated they'd been captured from SS Headquarters in Tapuria last year, and that their darts carried lethal poison."

The SS colonel expostulated, "But there were no flitterbugs at our headquarters! They were kept at our technical workshops!"

"We know that now, Colonel, but our troops in the field did not. It was a clever bluff, and it worked."

"*Bah!* It gave those troops something to blame for their cowardice!"

"That's *enough*, Colonel!" Khan surged angrily to his feet. "You weren't on this planet last year. I was! After the Battle of Tapuria I walked through installations where our personnel had come under nanobug and flitterbug attack. I saw their bodies, and the agony etched forever on their faces as the poison took effect. Most of our experienced troops did too. You may be sure they've shared their memories with those who've joined their units since then. I assure you, if I'd been in one of those barracks and heard that threat, I'd have surrendered too! That's not cowardice. It's common sense!"

The man in black glared at him, but remained defiantly silent. Khan waited a moment, then nodded to his G-2. "Go on." He sat down to listen.

"Thank you, Sir. The supply depot at Colosio was handled differently. Perhaps Major Hadda could speak to that, as logistics are his responsibility. He's been investigating what happened there."

"Thank you, Colonel." The tall, gaunt G-4 staff officer turned towards the General. "Sir, yesterday a convoy delivered a number of containers to Colosio. They were stacked in a corner of the depot, ready to be unloaded into transporters for local distribution. Our main depot in Tapuria is adamant that they were checked and sealed before they left there. However, rebels managed to get into at least some of them. They may have taken advantage of one or more rest stops to infiltrate the convoy.

"They broke out at about twenty-two and followed the same pattern as the attacks on the prison camps: neutralized the sentries, secured important buildings, then produced flitterbugs and gave the staff a choice between surrendering and dying. They then opened the gates to admit an unknown number of their compatriots driving a fleet of transporters. At least some of them were stolen from a nearby trucking firm, possibly with the collusion of some of its staff who are now missing. They spent the night loading them with everything they wanted. The last vehicle left just before dawn."

"How much did they get?"

"Sir, they appear to have stripped the depot of almost everything of value. They got weapons – including heavy weapons – and ammunition; field gear; ration packs; electronics, including sensors and night vision equipment; nanobugs and flitterbugs and their control consoles;

reconnaissance hoversats; basically, everything needed to support a regiment in the field for an extended period of operations. The ration packs alone were enough to feed that many troops for three months."

"How were they able to load so much, so quickly?"

"The stores were containerized and palletized, Sir, and the loading process is automated. It takes no more than ten minutes to load a transporter. I presume they made return trips to get more after offloading the first shipments."

"But that implies their destination was close enough to allow them to do that. Was there no sign of where they took it all? No tire marks on the road? No tracks where they turned off?"

"No, Sir. The rescue force sent up drones to search the vicinity, but found no tracks or other indications of a nearby rebel base."

"Hmm... that's strange." The Brigadier-General got up and crossed to the map on the wall, peering at it. His finger came to rest on an icon. "What's this? A mine?"

There was a flurry as staff officers hurried to look up the information. At last the G-5, responsible for civil-military cooperation, reported, "Yes, Sir, it's a mine, tunneling into the mountainside. It was shut down last year after the Satrap ordered the release of all slave laborers, because no other workforce was available. Its equipment was mothballed pending re-opening as soon as replacement labor could be found, but that hasn't happened yet."

"A-*ha!* And it's only five kilometers from the depot! Ten will get you one we'll find the answers to two questions when we get in there. First, where did the rebels get so much tunneling equipment, and how did they learn to use it? It's a very specialized skill. I'm willing to bet that all the mine's mothballed gear will be gone, including laser rock cutters. Some of the former slave laborers who used to operate it probably told the rebels about it and offered to use it in their service. Next –" He snapped his fingers. "Quick, bring up a satellite image of the area."

Another bustle, and a picture was displayed on a large wall screen.

"Zoom in on the area between the road and the mine." The operator did so. "There you are! There's a hardtop connection between the main road and the mine, less than a kilometer away, ending in a hard surface of compacted mine tailings around the buildings and mine entrance. Those transporters could turn off and drive right into the mine without leaving any tracks or other traces. I bet the rebels drove their first loads into the mine, stacked them in buildings or even underground – there's sure to have been loading equipment there – then came back for more. By dawn they were safely hidden with their loot. While our reaction force was moving in, they were probably taking everything out through a new tunnel. It'll come out far enough away to be clear of local surveillance, perhaps on the far side of the mountain. From there, they'll have gone on to their destination."

"We must send troops there at once!" the SS Colonel said eagerly.

Khan sighed. "We'll send them, Colonel, but by the time they get there the rebels will be long gone. They've done extremely well in all their other operations. I don't expect them to have fallen down on the job here. Besides, if there's a new tunnel as I expect, they'll booby-trap it once they finish using it. Our forces will have to proceed very slowly and carefully." He turned back to his G-2. "Go on, please. What about Ligarda?"

She grimaced. "That was disgraceful, Sir. There's no other word for it. The half-company there are supposed to be fighting troops, but due to the drawdown of combat regiments returning to Bactria we had to take them from a lower-quality support unit instead. It seems yesterday afternoon a transporter carrying a cargo of illegally distilled liquor was stopped in Ligarda. The local police discovered the moonshine and arrested the driver. It was already late, giving them no time to arrange secure storage for something that big, so they asked our garrison if they could park it inside the base overnight. I'm sure you can guess the rest, Sir."

Khan nodded. "The troops broke into the moonshine and had themselves one hell of a party, right?"

"Yes, Sir. The rebels struck at about twenty-two, by which time most of the garrison were paralytic drunk. Those remaining on their feet, even those on guard duty, were in no condition to resist. The rebels rounded them up, flex-cuffed everybody and locked them in a barracks to sleep it off. They then loaded everything they wanted onto transporters and disappeared into the hills, taking with them a dozen armored cars stationed there for convoy escort duties. Even worse, Sir, there were two assault shuttles at Ligarda. The rebels stole both, presumably after loading them to max capacity with supplies, weapons and reactor fuel cartridges. What's more, townspeople report hearing three more assault shuttles arrive at the garrison late last night. We know three rebel shuttles escaped from Tapuria

137

after the big assault last year. I presume they were the late arrivals. The rebels probably refueled and rearmed them, loaded them with the rest of the spares and support equipment, then flew them out again."

"Oh, that's just *wonderful.*" Khan shook his head slowly. "Let me guess. On their way out, the rebels stopped at the police station and released the transporter driver?"

"Er… yes, Sir, they did. In fact, they released all the prisoners and locked the police in their cells instead."

The SS Colonel sniffed. "At least we have the driver's mugshot, fingerprints and DNA profile. We'll catch up with him sooner or later."

"No, Sir, we don't. The rebels took the police station computer and everything in the evidence locker, including all records of those arrested yesterday. They hadn't yet been uploaded to the central database."

The SS man glared at her incredulously. He opened his mouth to say something, but caught sight of the Brigadier-General's expression and wisely decided to remain silent.

Khan observed bitterly, "So the rebels now have five fully fueled, fully armed, operational assault shuttles and a dozen armored cars." He looked at his G-4. "Major Hadda, based on the weapons and equipment the rebels seized last night, what sort of force can they now equip?"

"A big one, Sir. Preliminary checks indicate they took at least two and a half thousand rifles, several dozen shoulder-fired multi-sensor missiles, rocket launchers, mortars, grenades, and plenty of ammunition for everything. Combined with what they may have had in storage from previous operations, it would be enough to equip at least two thousand men – two battalions, or a full infantry regiment. They may even have enough for a third battalion. Their units will have plenty of light weapons, but not as many heavy weapons or vehicles or as much support equipment as ours."

"True. On the other hand, they've managed to get by like that for years. I see no reason why they can't carry on like that. They may be able to equip that many troops, but where will they recruit them? They were down to only a few hundred last year, as far as we know."

The SS Colonel snapped, "I'll tell you where, Sir. The Satrap most unwisely ordered the release of all slave laborers after the Battle of Tapuria last year. They had no reason to love us after the way they'd been treated. That wouldn't have mattered if we'd worked them to death as we did before, but instead they were freed. They had a strong motivation to seek revenge, and the example of Tapuria was fresh in their minds. I expect many of them joined the rebels. After weeding out those unsuitable or unfit, they could easily have two to three thousand recruits by now – perhaps more."

"But how could they have trained them without bases and equipment?"

"Perhaps I can answer that, Sir," his G-1 said.

"Go ahead, Major Shadba. Our personnel are your responsibility, after all, so I'll be interested to hear your views about the enemy's."

"Yes, Sir. I think the rebels wouldn't even have tried to train their new recruits as we train ours. After all, we put them through three months' basic training, plus three months' advanced training for infantry and longer than that for specialized units. We typically don't regard a soldier as combat-ready until he's had a year's service. However, the rebels didn't need that intensity of training. They had a core of a couple of hundred veterans, all combat-hardened and very experienced. Each of those people could take several recruits, perhaps in one or two groups, and teach them the equivalent of our basic training course over six to nine months. They wouldn't have bothered with parade-ground drill or other outward trappings. They'd have concentrated on tactical and fighting skills. After all, they've had plenty of opportunity to learn what's useful and discard what's not.

"After that training they'd have prepared them, not for general operations, but for last night's missions. It's a lot of work to train a soldier to handle whatever combat may throw at him. It's a lot simpler to train him to tackle one specific operation at one specific installation under a specific set of circumstances, with experienced leaders to supervise every step. They've had almost eighteen months since the slave laborers were released, Sir. I think that's more than long enough to conduct a training program like that on a part-time basis. Now that they've freed even more of their experienced combatants and leaders and got their hands on much more equipment, they'll be able to expand the training of their new recruits and prepare them for general military operations."

Khan nodded thoughtfully. "I daresay you're right, Major."

"Thank you, Sir. There's another thing. I've no doubt the rebels could have fought if they'd had to, but they deliberately struck at places, times and targets where they were sure to find few of our troops equipped or ready to resist. They hit them with surprise and overwhelming force, enough to ensure that any attempt to put up a fight would have been tantamount to suicide. They then subdued off-duty personnel using the threat of flitterbugs rather than attacking them with rifles and grenades. In fact, one wonders whether they deliberately bent over backwards to *avoid* causing casualties to our personnel, Sir – and if so, why?"

Khan looked at him, startled. "Now *that* is a *very* interesting observation, Major."

"I wish I could claim credit for it, Sir, but it was suggested by Lieutenant Sangin, one of my assistants." He gestured to a young officer standing against the wall. "She has some more thoughts about it that may interest you."

Mentally the Brigadier-General put a positive check mark against his G-1's name. Not all officers would willingly share credit with their subordinates like that. The Lieutenant flushed as she realized that everyone was looking at her.

"What could a wet-behind-the-ears Lieutenant have to contribute to a high-level discussion like this?" the SS Colonel snapped.

Khan suppressed the urge to blast him for his rudeness. Instead he said mildly, "May I remind you, Colonel, that Her Majesty was also a 'wet-behind-the-ears Lieutenant', as you put it, during the Battle of Tapuria? She certainly made an outstanding contribution there. The late Satrap awarded her the Star of Bactria for valor in action, and I had the honor of granting her a battlefield promotion to the rank of Captain immediately afterwards." He carefully didn't add aloud, *after watching her shoot an SS officer for daring to question the Crown Prince's authority, and after he'd asked me to promote her.* Such details would only confuse the point he was trying to make. "Perhaps I should advise Her Majesty about your opinion of junior officers. I'm sure she – and her husband – would find it interesting. They might even wish to discuss the matter with you."

The Colonel's mouth opened, then hung there as he suddenly realized the trap into which he'd walked. He ultimately managed to say, "I… ah… that won't be necessary, Sir." He half-bowed to the Lieutenant. "I apologize, Lieutenant. I spoke thoughtlessly." His voice was curt, clipped, angry… but cautious.

"Thank you, Colonel," Khan answered on her behalf. "Lieutenant, tell us more, please."

"Th – thank you, Sir." She straightened her shoulders. "I believe the rebels may be trying to send us a message, Sir. They could have killed up to a thousand of our troops last night, but they chose not to. In fact, our only fatalities seem likely to have been caused by our own error of judgment at Prison Camp Two. What's more, the rebels warned their prisoners not to come after them, and to disobey any orders to do so, on pain of death. That made me wonder why, Sir.

"They've got their imprisoned leaders back now, plus enough equipment and supplies to reconstitute two or three battalions. That means both sides are at a stalemate, Sir. We no longer have enough combat troops on this planet to overcome two or three rebel battalions without suffering horrendous losses; but they can't defeat us without themselves suffering losses on the same scale. In so many words, Sir, I think they're offering us an armed truce. They're showing us by example that if we leave them alone, they'll leave us alone. I think they expect the conflict over this planet to be resolved at the United Planets and by whatever their Government-in-Exile is doing. I think they don't want to do anything locally that will interfere with external plans and activities."

The G-2 nodded vigorously. "Lieutenant, that's a very interesting theory. I think it may be supported by the discovery earlier this year of communications modules hidden inside the prisoners' book readers. Clearly, leaders in both camps were able to talk to contacts outside. They were probably informed about at least some interplanetary developments, and probably coordinated last night's operations with those outside."

"How could they?" the SS Colonel asked. "They haven't had any book readers for the past six months."

"There are other ways to communicate, Colonel," the General reminded him. "They may have signaled with lights, or used semaphore, or smuggled messages in and out in other ways. We'll probably never know. I agree with Lieutenant-Colonel Oxus. The likelihood of coordination of last night's attacks is so high as to approach certainty."

"But how could they have learned what's happened off-planet? We've deliberately restricted communication, censored news bulletins, and done everything we can to prevent the locals learning of our difficulties at the United Planets and the actions of their Government-in-Exile. I don't see how the rebel prisoners could have found out about them."

"Neither do I, Colonel, but I won't be at all surprised to find out that they have. We didn't think they could threaten the Satrap's parade last year, but they destroyed it and killed him, not to mention wiping out most of our infrastructure in Tapuria. We didn't think they had nuclear warheads, but they used one to destroy the Space Station – and we still don't know whether they have any more. Don't underestimate them. Every time we do, they surprise us. I think we'll all do well to keep that in mind." Unanimous nods and very serious expressions on the faces of his Planetary Staff showed that they agreed with him.

"We're going to do three things in the short term. First, the Ministry of War and the Satrap must be informed of the latest developments. All of you are to prepare detailed reports covering your areas of responsibility. I want first drafts ready by tomorrow morning. Second, I have an appointment with Mrs. Aldred this afternoon. We've been instructed to help her set up a local political party to counterbalance the rebels. I think that under the present circumstances, I'll ask her to speed up her efforts. If we're going to have a *de facto* truce, let's take advantage of it to pursue non-military options. After all, that's what the Satrap had in mind when he sent her back here.

"Finally, I want to examine how we can use a truce, formal or informal, to improve our military position. For example, the rebels have resupplied themselves at our expense for years. What if we pull back our outlying garrisons and concentrate our forces in larger bases closer to Tapuria? The rebels will find it much more difficult to raid them, and they'll no longer be able to waylay convoys to more distant units. That might cripple them almost as badly as a military defeat."

"But that would mean abandoning large areas of the continent to their control," the SS officer objected.

"Yes, it would, Colonel; but what would the rebels do with those areas? They aren't of any particular importance, economically speaking. They aren't even politically important, because most potential voters live in larger centers that would now also have larger garrisons, making it more difficult for the rebels to disrupt Mrs. Aldred's plans. Do the advantages of concentrating our forces in fewer centers outweigh the disadvantages? That decision will have to be taken on Bactria. I want to offer the Satrap a range – a list – of options. I want all of you to work together to make that list as comprehensive as possible, then evaluate every option and make recommendations."

He turned to Lieutenant Sangin. "Lieutenant, I'm going to send you to Bactria as my personal messenger to deliver our report to the Satrap. I'll suggest that he listen to your ideas in person. I hope they, and you, will receive the recognition I think they deserve."

She blushed scarlet. "Th – thank you, Sir."

He rose to his feet, and his Staff stood in automatic response. He strode to the door, then turned around and looked at them. "The war memorial for Bactrian forces and officials on the hillside outside Tapuria has almost twenty-nine thousand gravestones around it. Let's make sure that we don't push that total any higher than we absolutely have to. As far as I'm concerned, this planet isn't worth even one more Bactrian life, and I shall so advise the Satrap."

There was a deafening silence as they all stared at him.

~ ~ ~

Khan rose from his desk as his aide ushered Gloria Aldred into his office. He walked around the desk to meet her, holding out his hand. "Mrs. Aldred, how nice to see you again."

"And you, General Khan." She returned his grasp firmly. "What's this I hear about trouble at the prison camp?"

"Ah... yes, there were some problems last night. Sit down and I'll tell you about them."

Giving as few details as possible, he explained that all the former prisoners-of-war were now at large, and that the Resistance appeared to have been reconstituted and re-equipped. "I don't know what that's going to mean for us in the short term, Mrs. Aldred, but I don't think it can be good. I'm hoping your efforts will help to keep things from deteriorating into open hostilities once more."

143

She nodded vehemently. "I'll do my very best to help, General, but it's difficult. I've managed to recruit a dozen or so helpers, but none of them are particularly influential in the community. We've all had enough of violence and bloodshed, and we all want peace, but we're very much in a minority among the residents of Laredo. Too many of them remember the invasion and the evil years that followed – just as I'm sure many of your peoples' attitudes are conditioned by the same memories."

"That's true, I'm afraid. Has the security we've provided been adequate?"

"Well, I'm still alive, if that's what you mean!" They smiled wryly at each other. "It hasn't stopped a whispering campaign against all of us, particularly me. I thought my description of how the Resistance tried to kill me would help to open people's eyes, but I'm afraid it hasn't. Most of them believe the Resistance's claim that it had nothing to do with shooting down that cutter, even though it's a matter of public record. I wanted to ask for your help in answering an argument that was thrown at me at our latest public meeting. A heckler stood up and shouted that if the Resistance had shot down that cutter, there would have been casualties; but he claimed that none had been admitted to hospital that day, and none had been buried as a result of the crash. He said the whole thing was a set-up by the Security Service. Could we check your records? There must have been at least a list of the names of those involved."

"Yes, of course. I'll take you to our Records section as soon as we've finished our other business. They maintain a centralized database of all our records, including those from the spaceport, the hospital and the War Memorial. All three departments should have the information you need to counter such allegations."

Ten minutes later they walked down the corridor together. The General showed her into the Records section ahead of him, and led her to the counter where a clerk snapped to attention.

"Mrs. Aldred is looking for some information," Khan told him. "Get her what she needs at once, please."

"Yessir!"

"I'll leave you to it, Mrs. Aldred."

"Thank you, General. I'll put the information to good use in debunking our critics."

144

She explained to the clerk what she needed, and he tapped in a series of queries. He frowned. "Ma'am, are you sure of the date of that crash? We have no injuries or fatalities recorded at all from the spaceport on that day – in fact, not for a week on either side of it."

Her face went blank for a moment. "Yes, I'm certain. It must have been in the news, surely?"

He checked. "Yes, Ma'am, it's reported that a cutter was shot down on that date, but no deaths or injuries were reported. Let me pull up more information about the crash… that's odd. The record's locked, with a notation that it can't be unsealed without authorization from the Security Service."

Gloria felt a chill run down her spine. Almost desperately she asked, "Is there any record of a platoon sergeant, her husband and their two children being buried anytime within a few weeks after the crash, and perhaps a pilot too?"

"I'll check… no, Ma'am. The only funerals reported that month were those of the Commandant of a prison camp, his pilot and two guards who were killed in the crash of an airvan on their way to Tapuria. The other occupant was a prisoner, a rebel Lieutenant-Colonel. His body was buried at the prison camp."

She froze, horror roaring through her. "What was the Lieutenant-Colonel's name? Why was he on the way to Tapuria with the others?"

The clerk tapped in another query. "He was Lieutenant-Colonel Jake Carson, Ma'am. It seems the Security Service called the camp on the same morning as the incident at the spaceport, telling them to bring him in for interrogation. According to the camp records, the SS said he'd been using another name and they'd just found out who he really was. The airvan bringing him here crashed soon after takeoff. Everyone aboard was killed."

"I… I see," she said automatically, blankly. "Th – thank you."

"My pleasure, Ma'am. Do you want printouts of these records?"

"N – no, thank you. That won't be necessary."

She just managed to hold down the bitter bile rising in her throat until she reached the restroom and bolted a stall door behind her; then she vomited endlessly, retching and heaving until she was sure her stomach would follow its contents up her throat and out of her mouth. When the dry heaves subsided at last she slumped down on the toilet seat, wiping her mouth with a handful of paper, weeping bitterly. Three sentences chased each other through her mind in an endless, incessant yammering.

It really was *a Security Service setup.*

I betrayed Jake Carson.

Jake always swore he'd never allow them to use him as a lever against his son.

She sat for what seemed like a timeless age, listening to the accusatory voices in her head. At last she managed to stand and flush the toilet, then crossed to the basins. She rinsed out her mouth and washed her face with cold water, patting it dry with more toilet tissue.

As she drove numbly back to her apartment, another line added itself to the three already repeating themselves in her head.

When Dave finds out . . . he's going to kill me.

Neue Helvetica: February 11 2852 GSC

Dave scrolled through the last few lines of the report, his head whirling with the pain and sorrow of loss, shock at the latest developments, and a growing sense of excitement.

Is this it? he wondered. *Is this what we've been waiting for? It may be... it could just possibly be that Dad's final orders have precipitated a crisis on Laredo that's tailor-made for us if – if – we can react in time... but how do we respond? We're nowhere near ready, but if we don't seize this opportunity it'll be a hell of a poor memorial to Dad and a tragedy for Laredo. We've got to seize the moment... but how? Is it worth risking everything on a single roll of the dice?*

He thrust back his chair from the desk and began pacing back and forth, mulling over the implications of what he'd just read. The news was totally unexpected. The death of his father had rocked him to the core of his being, particularly coming so soon after learning that against all expectations, he'd survived the Battle of Banka. However, it was no less than he'd have expected of him under the circumstances. Even though he was proud of his courage and self-sacrifice, he couldn't help weeping for his own loss. *I hope Mom and Timmy and Janet were there to meet you, Dad. I hope you gave them a hug for me. If this whole thing doesn't work, I might be joining you a whole lot sooner than any of us expected... but I hope not. Tamsin and I have started our own family now. I'd like as many years with them as I can get before I see you again.*

He paced far into the night and early into the morning. At three Tamsin put her head around the door of the study. She was bleary-eyed and tousle-haired with sleep. "I woke up and you weren't in bed," she complained. "What's wrong?" Her eyes focused on his face, and suddenly she wasn't sleepy any more. "You've been crying!"

He took her gently in his arms as she hurried over. "I'm sorry, love. Dad's dead."

Her eyes widened with shock and sorrow. "Oh, *no!*"

"He died a hero, just like you'd expect from a man like him. I'll mourn him properly when I have time. The reason he died is that everything's breaking loose – and he helped that happen with his final orders."

"What do you mean?"

"I enlisted the Dragon Tong's help on Marano to put one of Manuel's people aboard the ferry that went to Laredo in December to collect the hulks of the two corvettes we damaged last year. He contacted the Resistance through the back door Mac installed in the satellite network – it's still operational. He got back to Marano last month, then headed for New Brisbane, where Manuel wrote up his report and sent it aboard the first available express courier. It hit my mail queue yesterday evening. We're facing a crisis that's blown up with no warning at all. It might offer us a golden opportunity, or it might cost us everything we've been working for. I've been trying to figure out how to handle it."

She was wide awake now. "Need any help?"

He hugged her. "From you? Always. I'll make tea while you read the report, then we'll talk."

"Thanks. You'd better take a stim-tab, too, if you haven't got any sleep yet. Bring one for me while you're at it, because from the sound of it I won't be getting any more!"

"Will do."

He indicated the document on his desktop monitor. She sat down and reached for the control unit as he headed for the kitchen.

~ ~ ~

Captain Deacon was breathing heavily as he hurried into the conference room, looking around. "Looks like we're the last ones to get here."

Dave nodded as Elisabeta came in after him. She was moving slowly thanks to the infant at her breast. She nodded to them all with a cheery smile, and sat down at the rear of the room to continue feeding her baby.

Dave stood up. "The reason I called you in before first light is that we're facing a crisis. If we handle this right, we might hurt Bactria worse than it's ever been hurt before. If we don't, it could mean really serious trouble for the Resistance on Laredo. Let me tell you what's been happening."

He began with Gloria Aldred's seeming betrayal, particularly the confiscation of the book readers and his father's unmasking. There were exclamations of sorrow and anger as he told them of Jake's death, but he shook his head. "I simply don't know what part, if any, Gloria may have played in that. She's clearly at least partly aligned with the enemy now – more about that later – but I can't believe she'd deliberately betray Dad. They'd worked together for far too long.

"The important thing is that Dad gave two critical orders before his death. First, as soon as he made contact with the survivors of the Resistance on the outside, he ordered them to start Operation Phoenix. By the middle of last year almost three thousand new recruits – most of them former slave laborers – had been given at least rudimentary basic training. The Resistance had been reborn. His second order, his last before he died, was to implement what he called Operation Delve: to dig tunnels into the prison camp areas from outside, much deeper than anything the POW's could do themselves. The Resistance recruited former slave miners to do the job, using laser rock cutters. They hit both prison camps in December and freed every single POW without loss."

The room erupted in cheering. Dave let them celebrate for a moment, then held up his hand. "That's not all. They also hit the two reaction force bases near the camps, plus an auxiliary supply depot and the garrison at Ligarda."

"That's the second time Ligarda's been attacked," Deacon observed with a laugh. "It was one of the places we hit to get assault shuttles before the Battle of Banka."

"That's right. They've just lost two more shuttles there, and the Resistance used the garrison's supplies to refuel and rearm the three that escaped from Banka after the big fight. The condensed version is, they now have enough weapons, ammo and other supplies to equip three thousand people. The Resistance is back in a big way."

More cheers broke out, but Dave held up his hand again. "There's a lot more, so keep it quiet until I finish." He told them of the *de facto* truce that had existed on Laredo since the escape. "It looks like the Bactrians got the message. They haven't tried to go after the Resistance, so our people have left them in peace. Trouble is, the Bactrians are using the truce in ways they hadn't expected. First, Gloria's stomping around in our cities and towns, accusing the Resistance of prolonging everyone's suffering and demanding local elections so that 'ordinary people' can have a say in what happens on their planet. It looks like the Bactrians are encouraging her."

"That's treason!" Staff Sergeant Bujold spat. "Why hasn't the Resistance shot her?"

"Because they daren't make her a martyr. She claims they've already tried to kill her." Dave explained about the cutter incident at the spaceport. "The Resistance adamantly denies it had anything to do with that. I believe them. I'm pretty sure it was a Bactrian deception operation. It looks like it succeeded, because she blames the Resistance. In order not to make things worse, Major Tredegar and his new Council have told their people to back off and wait." He held up his hand to silence a rebellious murmur. "I agree with him. She'll have to be dealt with, but let it be by a jury of her peers. She's not your ordinary low-level collaborator who can be used as a lesson to others. She's too visible, too well-known. Let's not paint ourselves as the big, bad boys who kill anyone who gets crossways with us. We want to liberate our planet and our people, not enslave them again! Besides, if we kill her, the Bactrians will be forced to respond – just what we don't want at present.

"The next thing is that the Bactrians are pulling back as fast as they can. They've already abandoned almost all their outlying garrisons. They're concentrating their forces in and around the capital, within a radius of about a hundred kilometers. They're taking everything with them. They aren't even providing food to more distant settlements any more. They're being left to fend for themselves. If they want anything from the bigger towns, they have to go there in their own transport to get it."

"But that's got to be hurting the Resistance as much as civilians!" Deacon exclaimed. "We always used to feed ourselves on captured rations. Now there won't be any to capture!"

"I think that's precisely what they're aiming for. This Brigadier-General Khan seems to have his head on straighter than some of his predecessors. Very fortunately, the Resistance captured enough ration packs to keep itself going for three to four months during their recent operations. They've also hit a few convoys taking supplies back to the larger towns as part of the withdrawal, and captured more. However, they're now having to share their rations with people in the smaller settlements. That means they're *all* going to run out of food by the end of March, at normal rates of consumption. They've gone to two-thirds rations, but that'll only give them until the end of April, even though they're supplementing their packaged food by hunting wild game and slaughtering cattle. We're very fortunate that so many wild cattle are out on the range. Without them people would already be in serious trouble."

"Can't they grow more?" Rusty Higgs asked. "After all, if the Bactrians have abandoned the outlying areas, surely the farms there can now divert all their produce to helping our people?"

"Nice theory, Rusty, but it doesn't work that way. There aren't enough farmers left on the land. Many are dead; others joined the Resistance. If they release them to go back to their farms, the Bactrians might learn about it and hit them there to stop food at its source."

Higgs frowned. "So where the hell are they going to get food?"

Dave grinned. "We're going to take it to them."

"*WHAT?*" Everyone around the table was suddenly sitting bolt upright, shocked looks on their faces. Rusty added, "That's suicide! They'll blow out of space any freighter we send!"

"No, they won't – because we're going to blow them out of space first."

There was a stunned silence in the room as everyone stared at him.

At last Deacon stirred. "You know our ships won't be fully armed until the fourth quarter of this year – and that's only if everything goes according to plan?"

"Yes."

"And yet you're talking about blowing the Bactrians out of space – at least, Laredo's space?"

"Yes."

He heaved a long-suffering sigh. "I guess you'd better tell us what you have in mind."

"Sit back and listen. This is going to take a while."

It did. Dave talked for over half an hour, handing over to Tamsin to discuss some issues. The expressions on the faces of his audience changed from doubt, to deep thought, to a growing understanding, to enthusiasm.

At last he concluded, "We'll be taking a heck of a chance, but I honestly don't see any other way of solving this problem and turning it to our advantage. If it works, the war won't be over, not by a long way. We'll still have to deal with Bactria, because if we don't it'll undoubtedly deal with us. Even so, if we get this right, we'll be halfway home. What do you say?"

Another very long silence ensued. It was again Bill Deacon who broke it.

"Aw, what the hell!" He laughed suddenly. "We're just taking the biggest gamble any of us have ever heard of. Well, why not? Let's go for broke!"

There was a chorus of agreement around the table, except for Rusty Higgs, who looked concerned. Dave knew at once what was worrying him. "Rusty, don't worry. You've made it clear you want to return to civilian life, and we all respect that. Like I said when we got here, you've earned that right. I've got a vitally important job for you. I can't give it to anyone else, because we'll all be tied up. I want you to take over as our Ambassador to the United Planets until we can find a professional to handle it."

'*Me*, Boss? Hell, I'm no diplomat!"

"That's what I said two years ago," Deacon reminded him. "Did they listen to me? Like hell they did!" Everyone laughed.

"No, we didn't," Dave agreed, chuckling, "and we're not going to listen to Rusty either. I'm leaving three people here to handle Laredo's international affairs. Tamsin will be Vice-President Pro Tem and head of our Government-in-Exile while I'm with our fighting forces. Elisabeta will remain our Press Secretary and handle communications with the media. If this works out she'll be busier than ever, because every news organization in the settled galaxy will be screaming for press credentials, news releases and anything else they can get their hands on."

Elisabeta grinned from her place in the rear. "Sounds like I'd better breast-feed Junior here while I've got the chance. He'll have to rely on bottles if I get that busy!" Another laugh ran around the table.

"We'll subsidize his formula," Dave promised, drawing another chuckle. "Rusty, you'll be the third person looking after our international affairs, focusing on the UP. Don't forget, the inquiry into Bactria's actions on Laredo will release its report next month. Its findings are pretty much a foregone conclusion after the latest evidence we provided, but you'll have to steer them through the General Assembly and work for a resolution imposing sanctions on Bactria. Obviously you'll liaise with Tamsin and Elisabeta about that, plus the consultants we've hired, but I daren't give that job to anyone we can't trust one hundred per cent. You're it."

"Well… when you put it like that, I guess I don't have much choice, do I?"

"No," Dave agreed cheerfully. "However, look on the bright side. I'll demobilize you to take the job. You'll be *Mister* Ambassador Higgs."

"Mister *Civilian* Ambassador Higgs, thank you very much!" More laughter.

"What about the rest of us, Sir?" Deacon asked.

"We'll all be busier than one-legged men in an ass-kicking contest. To start with, I'm commissioning everyone who's not yet an officer – including you, Rusty. You'll all be appointed as Lieutenants, and I'll assign higher temporary or acting rank depending on your mission. For example, everyone aboard one of our ships as a planetary representative will be an acting Lieutenant-Colonel or Colonel, to put them in the same grade as the Commanding Officer of that ship."

There was a stunned silence for a moment as they absorbed the news, then Bujold asked, "And you, Sir?"

Dave shrugged. "I'm the *de facto* Admiral of our Fleet, but we've never had an Admiral on Laredo before. You all remember my orders from the Council of the Resistance?" Everyone nodded. "They give me the authority to commission and promote anyone in our off-planet forces, including myself. I've also inherited the authority of the President Pro Tem of our Government-in-Exile. I'm therefore going to retain my substantive rank of

Major, but give myself the acting rank of Brigadier-General. We'll let a new, freely elected Laredo government decide whether to make the higher ranks permanent. If it doesn't, we'll all revert to our substantive ranks if we decide to stay in the military. If we don't, we'll be civilians and our ranks won't matter."

There was a murmur of satisfaction around the table. Dave knew they were all worried about doing anything that might be seen as taking advantage of their – hopefully temporary – position as the involuntary custodians of their planet's political authority. It was why he'd always taken great care to operate within the – admittedly generous – boundaries laid out by his orders from the now-defunct Council of the Resistance, and by the emergency act establishing the Presidency Pro Tem filed by Laredo with the United Planets before the Bactrian invasion. By awarding acting rank rather than permanent promotions, he'd eliminated a possible source of concern.

"Next, most of us will be leaving the planet very soon, so start packing your travel gear. I'll go into more detail later, but here are the most critical assignments. Bill, pick two people to help you. I want you to work with brokers and agents to track down very large quantities of decent ration packs as quickly as possible. Note that I said *decent* ration packs. I don't want stuff that tastes like wet cardboard!" Laughter. "Get good-tasting, nutritious rations, even if they're more expensive. It's for Laredo, after all.

"Remember, we can't just cater for the present situation. If things go as we hope, there'll be no more food coming in from Bactria at all. We may have to feed up to a quarter of a million people for up to six months – and that may be just the beginning. You'll have to look for up to fifty million 24-hour ration packs."

Deacon whistled in astonishment. *'Fifty million?* Where the hell am I going to find that many?"

"All over the settled galaxy," Dave told him unsympathetically. "I don't care how you do it – just do it! It's absolutely critical. It's the primary reason we're jumping the gun like this, after all."

"OK. I'll do my best."

"I know you will. That's why I gave you the hardest job." Chuckles. "You don't have to buy them all at once. If you can find five to ten million available for short-term collection, that'll be a good start. You can offer larger, longer-term orders to suppliers who come through for you, to give them an incentive to ramp up production as fast as they can.

"Rusty, while he's doing that, your first job is going to be to talk to ship brokers on Neue Helvetica. I want to charter a couple of half-million-ton general-purpose freighters and two communications vessels – fast courier boats. Wet-lease them; in other words, charter them with crews, operating expenses and insurance all provided by their owners. That's the most expensive form of charter, but we don't have time for anything else. The initial term should be for six Galactic Standard months, with an option to extend for up to six more.

"While you're doing that, Bill will set up the first food purchases. As soon as he's done that, work out routing with the brokers and send the freighters to collect the ration packs and take them to Rolla, where they'll be transshipped to our two tramp freighters."

Rusty nodded as he scribbled notes. "Can do, but why transship them at all? Why not send the chartered freighters to Laredo?"

"It's a war zone, remember? Last year we issued a formal advisory through the Interplanetary Transportation Union that as of January first this year, any space traffic in either the Laredo or Bactria systems might be subject to attack without warning. No-one's paid much attention to it yet – they probably think we're grandstanding, because we haven't told anyone about our ships – but standard charters include clauses that forbid taking the ships into zones of conflict. Some allow it, but only at much higher rates and insurance premiums. We're going to get around that by not taking the chartered ships into Laredo or Bactrian space at all. Instead, we'll use our own."

"I get it. How will ours know when it's safe to head for Laredo?"

"I'll tell them."

"OK. What about the communications vessels?"

"One is for me. Charter that first, and very urgently, because I'm got a lot of travel to do in a very short time and I'll need speed like never before. The other is for you and Tamsin. Either of you may need to make a rapid trip in connection with political developments, or to warn us about something that might affect our operations. You might not be able to charter a fast ship at short notice, so we're just going to have to suck up the expense and keep one at your beck and call, even if you never need it.

Charter all the ships from large, reliable companies with proven track records, who'll put up a bond to guarantee the performance of the vessels and their crews. That'll cost more, but we can't afford fly-by-night operators who'll take our money and run, leaving us stranded."

"I'll get right on it, Sir."

"Good man." Dave stretched wearily and yawned. "Sorry – I didn't get any sleep last night. Tamsin and I are existing on stim-tabs right now."

Tamsin said thoughtfully, "There's one point we haven't addressed. What's the Resistance going to do when it looks like they may run out of food? They won't know we're coming, or that we're bringing food with us. What if they try a desperation raid on the Bactrians' supply depots?"

"Dammit, I hadn't thought about that!" Dave tried to cudgel his tired brain into action. "I think it'll be possible to send them a message, but only at the risk of compromising the satellite backdoor communications channel. What do you think? Is it worth that risk?"

"I think so. After all, how will they feel if they take casualties – maybe lots of casualties – to steal food, only to have us arrive a few weeks later bringing plenty of it? They'll resent the hell out of us for making them lose a lot of good people for no good reason. The satellite backdoor's not as important as that. Besides, if things work out as we hope, soon we may not need it anymore."

"All right. Here's what we'll do." He explained his plan. "What do you think?"

"Will that work?" Bill Deacon asked doubtfully. "I've never heard of anything like it before."

"That Lancastrian officer, Steve Maxwell, mentioned it. He didn't go into detail, but said it was a common tactic in space warfare. If that's the case, I'm sure I can find out more from the former Fleet officers we've recruited for our ships. If they confirm it, I'll pick the most operationally ready ship to deliver the message. The next two in line can go to Vesta to be modified."

"OK, but if you can get a ship close to Laredo like that, why bother using the satellite backdoor channel at all? Why not broadcast a signal direct to the surface? It won't matter if the Bactrians pick it up, because the ship will be out of range before they can do anything about it."

"Maybe, but that depends where their ships are. If they're in position to intercept, that would be too risky."

"So give the ship two options. If there are no Bactrians within range to intercept, broadcast the signal and save the backdoor channel. If the enemy's positions won't allow that, have the ship get close enough to the planet to hit the satellites with a tight-beam laser without being detected."

"Good point, Bill. I'll speak to the captain of the ship I send and work it out with him." He stretched again. "I'll leave for Vesta within two to three days. I'll try to buy some more used cargo shuttles there and have them serviced and refurbished, then sent to Rolla. I'll ask the dockyard's technical experts to prepare modifications to our ships' armament. At Rolla I'll select the ships and crews most ready for operations and send one to Laredo with the message and two to Vesta; then it's off to Marano to collect our laser cannon. I promised the broker a ten per cent bonus if everything went smoothly and on time. If I'm not there to give it to him, I daresay our lasers won't get loaded. After that it's back to Vesta, where I'll supervise the final preparation of our ships."

"And after that, Sir?" Bill Deacon asked.

"After that, it's showtime."

They grinned hungrily at him.

Laredo: March 12 2852 GSC

Laredo Ship *Freedom* crossed the system boundary at a quarter of light speed in utter electronic silence, every possible emission shut down. Even those that could not be completely eliminated were dialed back to the minimum level consistent with safety. "She's like a fast-moving hole in space right now," her Commanding Officer, retired Lancastrian Commonwealth Fleet Commander Andrews, explained to his Laredo liaison officer.

Newly-promoted acting Lieutenant-Colonel Hein (substantive Lieutenant, until recently Staff Sergeant) nodded, his fascinated eyes glued to the Plot display. "I'm real glad you guys know what you're doing. I feel like I'm in some kind of fourth or fifth dimension, completely out of my depth. I've had basic Spacer training and I've read the theory, but I'm a ground-pounder. Put a rifle in my hands and an enemy out there in the bush and I'll know exactly what to do about him. Speeding like this with millions upon millions of cubic kilometers of vacuum all around me... it feels weird."

Andrews nodded, smiling sympathetically. "I suppose it does, but if you put me in the middle of the bush with a rifle in my hand and told me someone, somewhere nearby, was trying to kill me, I'd be terrified! No sensors, no missiles, no laser cannon, nothing except the old Mark I Eyeball and my other senses... no, thank you. I'll pass!"

"Why are we altering course?" Hein asked.

"We're taking up our final trajectory to broadcast the signal as we pass Laredo. We couldn't steer accurately enough from our point of arrival, because the distances were too great for the sort of precision we need."

Hein sighed. "That was sixteen days ago. *Damn,* it's been frustrating just sitting here, twiddling our thumbs, not able to do anything except creep closer to Laredo. I know a quarter of light speed isn't exactly 'creeping', but that's what it felt like."

"Yes, but it was necessary. A hyper-jump signature isn't easily detected at over two light-days' distance. At four light-days it's lost in the background radiation of space, as far as shipborne sensors are concerned. The Bactrians don't have wide-array sensors here, so their ships are all we have to worry about. We made our final hyper-jump to a point four light-days from Laredo, accelerated to max cruise speed, then shut everything down while we were still too far away for them to detect our gravitic drive emissions. On a ballistic trajectory like this we only need to use our drive now and then at very low power to change course, so they shouldn't have detected us at all."

"Yeah. The long transit time's been useful, too. I've learned a lot, and I saw you were constantly running classes for the Gurkha spacers. I bet my boss has been using his time on board that courier ship in the same way. He should be arriving at Marano any day now, along with our freighter."

"He's a remarkable man. You're all remarkable people. For a team of only fourteen to have accomplished all this, starting from a background of guerrilla warfare with virtually no experience in geopolitics or strategy, is nothing short of amazing."

Hein grinned. "Hey, we know our limitations. Once we'd raised enough money, we used it to hire the expertise we needed. That's where people like you come in. We're just along for the ride at this stage."

Andrews shook his head. "I think you're underestimating your accomplishment. This is unprecedented, as far as I know. Military strategists will be studying Laredo's fight for freedom for generations to come, to learn what really determined guerrillas can do if they're given the resources to take the fight to the enemy."

Hein's face sobered. "It's not only determination. Remember, you're looking at people who've been winnowed by war. Those of us who've survived this long aren't the brightest or strongest or most patriotic. We've just managed – God only knows how! – to survive more than three years of brutal, almost non-stop fighting that killed well over half our planet's population and seven-eighths of our armed forces. We've learned to be ruthless, to kill our enemies without a second thought whenever and wherever possible. Working like we have for the past two years is easy for people forged in that kind of crucible. It's just preparing for the next round of killing in a different way."

"I hadn't thought of it like that, but I take your point."

"Yeah." He gave a short, humorless laugh. "Before we left Laredo, the head of the Council of the Resistance – she was a psychiatrist – asked us to talk to people in her field when we reached safety. She reckoned we'd need help to cope with what we'd been through. I guess they did help – they gave us some new tools to deal with some of the memories, that sort of thing – but in the end, *they* were worse affected by our experiences than *we* were, especially when we showed 'em some of the vid that went into that documentary on what the Bactrians did to Laredo. A lot of 'em got real stressed. They had nightmares for months. They're writing a report that they reckon will blow the socks off their profession when they present it in a couple of years' time."

"That's one way to get academics out of their ivory towers, I suppose." They chuckled softly together.

"It sure was! OK. You were telling me why we're changing course now."

"Yes. Let's look at the Plot." They crossed to the three-dimensional holographic display, and the Captain pointed out icons and features as he spoke. "We know where the Bactrian ships are because they're all broadcasting identifying beacons. Even if they weren't, they're using their gravitic drives at power levels sufficient for us to detect them. Their Orbital Control Center is an old freighter in orbit around Laredo – that red flashing icon there. The blue one next to it is a corvette, also in powered orbit. The green icon about one light-hour away from the far side of the planet is an armed merchant cruiser on routine patrol. It looks like it's making a wide circle around Laredo every day, moving slowly and scanning carefully."

"Why would they have their weakest ship doing that? It's more vulnerable to attack way out there. I thought their corvettes were much more powerful than their converted freighters?"

"They are, but they don't have enough of either right now. Remember, they've got that big order in at Marano for more ships. When those arrive they'll be able to have more on patrol, but for now they're doing the best they can with what they've got. It's not a very good best, fortunately for us, because it means we can get in and out before they can do anything about us.

"That armed merchant cruiser on outer patrol is a tripwire as much as anything else. If we were coming in to launch an attack in a similar ship, we couldn't afford to leave her behind us. We'd have to attack or neutralize her before approaching the planet. That's what the corvette is waiting for. They expect us to be using a ship or ships of the same basic type as their AMC. If we were, and we fought their AMC, the corvette would get early warning of our approach and be able to interdict us. As it is, they don't know we've got a much more powerful ship than either of theirs – or, rather, we will have when we get proper offensive missiles, not to mention defensive missiles and laser cannon, of which we have none right now."

"That's why we're sneaking in like this – because we're defenseless?"

"Not exactly; on this mission, our speed and stealthy hull are our defenses. The Bactrians won't know we're here until it's too late for them to do anything about it. We're altering course now to pass within one light-hour of the planet. When we're in position we're going to broadcast the message three times, on each of three different frequencies, beamed directly at the planet on full power. It'll get there an hour later, by which time we'll already be past the planet and on our way out of the system. That corvette will be an hour late before it even begins to accelerate out of orbit, and it can't go any faster than we can. Besides, as soon as the signal has been sent we'll change course by five to ten degrees, and do that again an hour later. That'll make impossible for the Bactrians to predict our course by following the line from which the signals were broadcast."

"And their missiles?"

"Their main battery missiles have a similar top speed to their ships – point two five Cee. Fired from rest, in orbit around the planet, they could never catch up to us because we're already moving that fast. If the corvette could close in on us – which it can't, given our relative positions – it could launch them while traveling at its own max speed, so that their starting velocity would already be that high and they could build on it. They'd get up to a little less than half of light speed under those circumstances, but their powered range is no more than six million kilometers. That means they'd run out of fuel to maneuver after us if we changed course. They couldn't close in on us."

"So this course, our distance from the enemy, and our speed work together to make us immune to attack?"

"This time, yes. They wouldn't necessarily do so in a more heavily defended system, you understand. The Bactrian system has more warships, a better command and control setup, and probably orbital mines and planetary defense missiles as well. They might be able to set up an ambush if they knew we were coming. Out here, we don't think they have any of that. One purpose of this visit is to listen with all our sensors to find out exactly what they *do* have. When they detect our message they'll almost certainly use everything they've got to look for us. We'll record all their transmissions for later analysis, to use what we learn against them when we come back."

Hein smiled unpleasantly. "Which will hopefully be a whole lot sooner than they expect. How long until we transmit?"

"It'll be another couple of hours."

"And how will we know whether our people received the message?"

"They probably won't be able to acknowledge it, but your boss seemed pretty sure that if we used those three frequencies and repeated the message three times, someone would hear it."

"Let's hope he's right!"

"He's been right a damn sight more often than he's been wrong, if you ask me. Given a track record like that, I'll trust his judgment."

~ ~ ~

Brigadier-General Khan had just settled his head on his pillow when his bedside comm unit trilled urgently. His eyes flew open. It trilled again. With a growl of anger he reached a hand out from under the warm, comfortable covers and grabbed it.

"This had better be good!"

"Sir, this is the Officer of the Watch in the Operations Center. We've just picked up a radio transmission in clear from an unknown station one light-hour from the planet. It repeated a message three times on three different frequencies before shutting down. We tracked it during the transmission period, and it appears to have been moving at one-quarter of the speed of light, Sir."

Suddenly the warm covers couldn't compensate for the icy chill in the General's guts. "What was it?"

"We don't know, Sir. The only emissions it produced were radio transmissions, and they were live for a very short time. It can only have been either a message drone or a spaceship."

"What was the message?"

"I'll read it verbatim, Sir. 'BOLUS calling TANTO, personal for DIVOT. Be advised negative RAPID under any circumstances. MEADOW and DIGEST will be the winning margin of DIVOT's last blackjack hand with BOLUS, units UPFIELD, plus or minus two. Alert will be PEACOCK. All callsigns and codewords used in this message are now compromised due to transmission in clear. Do not reuse. BOLUS out.' That's all, Sir."

"And what the devil does that mean?"

"I have no idea, Sir. I've passed it to your G-2."

"Good. Tell her I'll be in the OpCen in ten minutes. What's the Navy doing?"

"OrbCon has ordered the corvette to pursue whatever it was, Sir, but her Commanding Officer is saying it won't do any good. They're still discussing it."

Bloody fools! he thought resentfully. *This is no time to argue!* "Very well. I'm on my way."

"Yessir!"

~ ~ ~

Major Tredegar was in a large office attached lean-to style to a warehouse wall. He and a group of officers and senior NCO's were sitting at a round table, pondering a series of maps and charts. They all looked up as a hammering knock came at the door and it burst open.

"Sorry to interrupt, Sir. This just came in. The sending station didn't identify itself, and the message uses two-year-old code words. It was addressed to you personally." The speaker, a grizzled Sergeant, thrust a message form at the Major.

Tredegar took it, read rapidly, and bounced to his feet, grinning from ear to ear as his chair clattered to the floor behind him. *"Yeah!"* He pumped his arm up and down in triumph. "Cancel our plans for the attack!"

Everyone was on their feet now. "What do you mean, Sir?" Captain Barger asked eagerly.

"I'll translate this on the fly. It's from Dave Carson. He says, 'Be advised, don't attack under any circumstances. Relief and rations will be there in ten weeks, plus or minus two weeks. Alert will be hours. The callsigns and codewords I used are now compromised, because they were transmitted over a non-secure frequency. Don't reuse them.' He's coming, boys! He's coming!"

Jubilation erupted in the room. At last they knew they truly were not alone. The realization was heady.

The Major gave them a few minutes to enjoy the celebration, then called them to order. "All our plans to attack the Bactrians to get more food are now on hold. Instead, we need to figure out how to get our people ready for anything when Dave moves in. I think that's what he meant when he said that the alert will be hours – we won't have much prior warning. We have to be ready to support whatever he has in mind. I need you to switch mental gears and start thinking about how to get the word to our units as fast as possible when it arrives, and get them into action if necessary."

"We'd also better start planning to economize on rations even more than we already are, Sir," Sergeant-Major O'Connor warned. "That won't be popular, but we've got no choice. Even at half-rations, we've got barely enough to last that long."

"You're right. We'll also put cattle roundups on a more organized footing and send out more hunting parties. The country boys will love that. It may denude the back country herds, but at least they'll help us avoid starvation while we wait."

~ ~ ~

Khan looked grimly at his G-2. "All right. We don't know what the message means, but it's pretty clear it was a heads-up of some kind to the rebels. My best guess would be that it told them relief was on the way, using a timeline we can't identify. We also don't know what sort of relief – food, an invasion, whatever."

"That's about it, Sir. What's more, I'm really worried about whatever it was that transmitted the message. It was moving at a quarter of light speed. That's the same as our corvettes' maximum speed. If it was able to move at warship speeds, have the rebels got their hands on genuine warships instead of armed merchant cruisers? If so, where? What type? How are they armed?"

"The corvette Commanding Officer thinks this may have been a civilian courier ship," the Brigadier-General pointed out. "He says if it had been a warship, they could have made a firing pass and destroyed OrbCon and his ship before anyone knew it was there, or done the same to the cruiser on outer patrol. The fact that it didn't makes him think it was unarmed."

"Yes, Sir, but with respect, courier ships – at least, the ones I've seen at Bactria – are a lot faster than one-quarter Cee. Most of them can do one-third Cee or slightly better. Why would one come in at a slower speed when it knew it would be facing armed opposition?"

Khan shrugged. "If it knew the fastest our ships could move was that speed, it might have reckoned it didn't need to go any faster. Still, there's no point in arguing about it. We don't know enough to make an informed judgment. The question is, what are we going to do about it?"

"What *can* we do, Sir? If we send word about this to Bactria right away, it'll mean using either the corvette or the armed merchant cruiser, leaving us only one vessel to defend the approaches to the planet. That's not enough if a relief ship may be coming, much less a full-scale relief expedition. On the other hand, if we wait to send word by the next monthly freighter, it won't be here until three weeks from now. It'll take another two weeks to get back. Given the time it'll take for Bactria to get things organized after hearing the news, we probably won't get any reinforcements in less than ten to twelve weeks from now. What if something happens in the interim?"

"We'll have to deal with it using the resources we have on hand. I'm not prepared to send one of our two armed ships – we may need them both – so we'll have to wait for the monthly freighter. What worries me is, what if Bactria doesn't reinforce us at all? They've been drawing down our forces, particularly combat units and heavy weapons, for almost two years. They may not want to send them back, and until our new warships arrive they may not be able to spare a second corvette. What if we're left to fend for ourselves?"

They stared unhappily at each other.

Marano: March 13-14 2852 GSC

"What do you mean, there's a problem?" Dave's voice went dangerously quiet.

The freighter captain's voice sounded worried, even over the digitally smoothed radio connection. "I don't know, Sir. That's all the cargo shuttle operator would say. We've loaded sixteen out of the twenty lasers, but he says the rest won't be coming until we sort out whatever the problem is. He says you'll have to contact the broker for more information."

Dave thought for a moment. "Very well. Secure what you have, then wait for further instructions. I'll get hold of the broker right away."

"Aye aye, Sir."

Dave placed another call through the orbital communications system. A few clicks, beeps and buzzes later, it reached its destination on the surface of the planet.

"Salvatore Brokerage," a crisp, efficient female voice answered.

"This is Mr. Young," Dave introduced himself, using the false identity he'd adopted for his visits to Murano. "I need to speak with Mr. Salvatore, please. It's in connection with problems concerning the loading of my order."

"Yes, Sir. Just a minute, please."

A short wait, then, "Mr. Young, this is Guiseppe Salvatore. How are you, my friend?" The voice was oily, unctuous.

"I'm not happy, Mr. Salvatore. What's this I hear about problems with our order?"

"Ah, yes. There is a little bird down here who wants to dip his beak into our transaction, you understand me? It will be necessary to accommodate him, I fear."

"That's your problem, Mr. Salvatore. You guaranteed that in return for the sum we agreed, our order would go through with no delays and no issues. Are you going back on your word?"

"That's a hard line to take, Mr. Young. You must understand, in this line of business... *complications*... can arise from time to time. You're a man of the world. I'm sure you understand."

"I do understand, but you're supposed to deal with those complications on your dime. We're paying you enough as it is, including a contingency allowance for that sort of thing."

"This contingency is larger than I'm able to cover, Mr. Young. I'll need you to come planetside to deal with it yourself."

Alarm bells rang in Dave's mind. "Surely that's not necessary? Even if I agree to cover the contingency – which I haven't, at least not yet – I can cash a bearer bank draft at the Elevator terminal and transfer the funds to your account for distribution planetside."

"Ah... I'm sorry, Mr. Young, but in this case that won't do. I need you to be physically present to help resolve this situation. The other party insists on it."

Dave thought fast. "I've first got to finish working on a project up here, then there's the delay in processing through Customs and catching a personnel pod down the Planetary Elevator. I can be at your office by... let's see... fourteen tomorrow afternoon. Will that do?"

He thought he could detect a glimmer of relief in the broker's voice. "I'll advise the other party of that time, Mr. Young. He'll look forward to seeing you here. Thank you for understanding."

"Very well, Mr. Salvatore. Until tomorrow."

Dave put down the handset, frowning. All his warning senses were tingling. If he'd been in the bush on Laredo, they'd have been screaming to him that an ambush lay somewhere ahead. This wasn't Laredo, but he'd bet his life on this sort of intuition too many times to doubt it.

He looked up a code he'd noted on his previous visit, and placed a call to the Elevator Terminus. The person who answered did so only with a monosyllabic "Yes?"

"I'd like to speak to Mr. Marciano, please."

"May I ask who's calling?"

"It's Mr. Young."

"I'm afraid Mr. Marciano isn't available right now. Where may he reach you?"

"At this code, or on a courier vessel in planetary orbit, the Neue Helvetica ship *Weissenbach*. For reasons of confidentiality, it might be best for his representative to visit me aboard her. I'll cover all expenses, of course."

"I'll tell Mr. Marciano. Expect a visitor within two hours."

"Thank you."

~ ~ ~

To Dave's relief, the promised visitor proved to be the same person he'd met during his last visit.

"Good morning, Mr. Feng. It's good to see you again. Thank you for coming at such short notice."

Feng smiled genially. "Someone who can afford to pay the Dragon Tong so much money up front, and whose project holds out the prospect of an even more lucrative return for us, may be sure of our interest when he calls. What can we do for you?"

"Let's go to my cabin."

Once they were alone, Dave explained his concerns about the broker. "I'm sure there's something wrong. I haven't survived three and a half years of guerrilla warfare to ignore premonitions this strong. Do you have any ideas?"

"We don't deal with Mr. Salvatore in the normal course of events, but he does have a reputation for being... slippery. He sells himself and his goods to the highest bidder, but doesn't always stay bought. Do you have enemies who might wish to do you harm?"

Dave laughed aloud. "Only the entire Satrapy of Bactria, and possibly their suppliers on this planet as well."

Feng had to laugh with him. "Of course. That was a silly question. Let's assume some of those enemies have 'persuaded' Mr. Salvatore to bring you planetside, where they can get at you. How thoroughly do you want them discouraged?"

"The more permanently the better, as far as I'm concerned. If you'll kindly arrange for me to be given a silenced pulser when I get planetside, I'll do some of the discouraging myself. This isn't my first rodeo."

"So I understand. Your combat record speaks for itself." There was real respect in the Tong man's voice. "However, I'm not sure it would be wise for you to go planetside yourself. If anything happened to you, what would happen to our deal later this year?"

"I take your point. Unfortunately, if I don't go planetside I can't see any other way of getting the last of our shipment released."

"Let me think." Feng was silent for a few minutes as he pondered. "With your permission, I'd like to borrow your passport. I'll have it digitally cloned at our facilities on the Elevator Terminal, then return it to you. Your DNA and other identifying characteristics have never been recorded here, have they?"

"Not officially. Whenever I've met anyone from Marano for business purposes, it's been in the free trade zone of the Terminal without having to go through Immigration and Customs controls."

"Excellent! That means we can digitally substitute the details of one of our operatives, and have him go planetside using your name. That will put Mr. Salvatore at ease, as well as any others watching for your name on the passenger manifest. By the time our man gets to the ground, we'll have made the necessary arrangements to deal with them."

"And what will I be doing while this is going on?"

"Stay aboard this ship. The Tong will use its influence at the orbital warehouse patronized by Mr. Salvatore to ensure that the last four laser cannon are sent to your freighter within the next hour or two. They won't appear on any manifest. Once they're aboard, we'll get your freighter and this ship clearance for departure without it being recorded in the public database, so that Mr. Salvatore won't see it and grow suspicious. The freighter can be on her way by early evening. I suggest you stay in orbit until tomorrow morning, by which time she'll be well over halfway to the system boundary; then have your ship leave orbit without mentioning your name. If her Captain's asked, you've gone down to the planet – the authorities will show you in their records as having done that, of course – and you'll make your own arrangements for onward travel. Your ship will reach the system boundary at the same time as your freighter."

"And whatever you have in mind for Mr. Salvatore and any others won't impact that?"

"I think the authorities won't make the connection until after you've hyper-jumped away from the system, and perhaps not even then. However, if you ever need to come back to Marano a different ID will be advisable, and possibly an effective disguise as well."

Dave laughed. "I hear you. I think that can be arranged. You won't need me here in June?"

"No. We'll take care of that mission. We'll see you at the rendezvous in space afterwards."

"Good. What additional costs will be involved for helping me like this?"

Feng pretended to think. "I daresay three million Neue Helvetica francs should cover them."

Dave had to fight hard not to wince… but he knew that if you hired the best in the business, you had to pay the going rate. "I can give you a bearer bank draft for five million francs. Will you please credit the balance to my account with your organization? We can settle up later."

"That will be very satisfactory, thank you."

Stifling a sigh of resignation, Dave reached for his briefcase. As he handed over the draft, a thought struck him. "Since you're here, there's another project I've been considering. Do you think the Dragon Tong would be open to a longer-term intelligence-gathering project on behalf of my Government-in-Exile?"

"Possibly. What do you have in mind?"

"We need to know what's going on in Bactria – not so much on the planet itself as what its Navy is doing in orbit and in the star system. What ships are at work in the asteroid belt? What space stations are there, what satellites, what depot ships, what orbital facilities? What are their orbits? How busy are they? How often, if at all, do they change position? We need an initial comprehensive survey, including detailed electronic signature profiles of every emitter and ship and platform in the system. After that we'll need updates at one- to two-month intervals – the more regular, the better – highlighting changes and new developments. I suppose whoever does the job for me will need to send a ship, or their representative aboard another ship, to conduct each survey. Can your organization undertake such a task, and what would it cost me? I have other options, of course, including a detective agency that's done intelligence work for us before, but since you people run several space freight lines it might be easier and quicker for you to do the work."

"It might. I'll have to consult with my superiors, and they'll probably have to send your request to higher authority for approval. If they do, I expect you'll have to pay twenty to thirty million Neue Helvetica francs for an initial, comprehensive report, plus another five to ten million for each update. Spaceships are expensive to operate, after all, and the kind of sensors needed for such a survey are specialized equipment not normally carried by merchant freighters. Then there's the risk involved. We'd have to develop cover stories for each voyage, including competing for contracts to collect or deliver cargoes there, which may not be easy to arrange at short notice. Bribes will probably have to be paid."

Dave nodded. "If you provide what I need, in the level of detail and at the frequency I want, I'm willing to pay for it. Please ask your superiors to expedite the matter. They can reach me care of our Embassy to the United Planets. If they approve, I'd like to ask that you proceed with the initial survey as quickly as possible, even in advance of payment. You know I'm good for the money."

"Yes, based on our previous dealings I believe they'll trust you to pay us on delivery." Feng rose. "Thank you, Mr. President. We'll be in touch."

~ ~ ~

The call reached the Bactrian Ambassador just as he was putting away his papers and preparing to go home. Annoyed, he picked up the handset. "What is it? I was just leaving."

His secretary answered, "Inspector Giolitti of the Marano Police Service is on the line, Sir. He says it's urgent."

The diplomat sobered. The Embassy paid a sizable monthly retainer to the Inspector for his official and unofficial assistance. "Very well, put him through."

There was a click on the line. "Good afternoon, Inspector. What can I do for you?"

"It's the other way around, Mr. Ambassador." The policeman's voice sounded... different, the Ambassador thought... almost queasy. "You remember the six men you asked me to assist as and when necessary, a few months ago?"

"Yes, I do." *That's the Security Service team,* the Ambassador thought to himself.

"They're dead."

"What?"

"They're dead. I'm standing in front of a passenger van that went off the edge of the Tiorano Pass just outside the city. There were seven people inside; your six, and a well-known weapons broker by the name of Giuseppe Salvatore. The van rolled down a steep mountainside, crashed into a nest of rocks and burst into flames. They've all been burned to a crisp."

The Ambassador swallowed hard. "How... how were you able to identify them, if they're so badly burned?"

"That's the funny thing, Mr. Ambassador. Their ID documents – all seven of them – were in a single plastic bag that somehow got thrown clear of the van as it hit the rocks. It was lying in the open ten meters from the wreckage, in plain sight, almost as if Divine Providence wanted it to be found intact. Funny how these things happen, isn't it? What's even funnier is that there are no fingerprints or other forensic evidence on that bag at all."

Funny, hell! the Ambassador wanted to scream, but didn't. *This was no accident, and you damn well know it! That bag's a message... but who's sending it?*

"Do you think you can keep things quiet?"

"I can try, Mr. Ambassador, but other cops got here first. I might be able to persuade them to forget they saw that bag, but it won't be cheap."

"I'll guarantee your expenses, and pay a bonus on top. Can you bring me the bag and its contents, intact?"

"You mean lose it from the evidence room?"

It hasn't got there yet, you greedy bastard! the Ambassador thought savagely. "Yes, I suppose that's what I mean."

"That'll be tricky."

"Charge me for it."

"Oh, well, if you put it like that, I'll see what I can do. A little palm-crossing with silver goes a long way when it comes to evidence clerks. This will be more expensive – after all, Mr. Salvatore was a well-known and respected businessman – but I think something can be arranged."

Bull! He was as crooked as they come! "Thank you, Inspector. I'll wait for you at the Embassy."

"I'll be there in about two hours, Mr. Ambassador. You'll be able to take care of me? I mean, I'll have immediate expenses to cover."

"I'll have funds available."

"Thank you, Mr. Ambassador. I'm sure you'll live up to your reputation as a generous man. See you soon."

The diplomat broke the connection, then dialed his secretary's code. "Please call my wife. I'm unavoidably detained at the office. I won't be home until late tonight."

"Of course, Sir. Will you be needing my... services?" There was a wealth of suggestion in her voice.

Why not? he thought resignedly to himself. *If I'm going to have to bribe a local Inspector to the tune of most of my emergency fund, there's no reason not to spend the rest on a willing and compliant secretary to keep me entertained until he gets here. I can always charge it to his account on the books.* "Yes, thank you. Please come to my office."

"I'll be right there, Sir." He could hear the anticipation in her voice. He knew she'd pause to pat a little perfume behind her ears and between her breasts, tug at her shirt and open a couple of its buttons to better display her bountiful assets... she knew all the tricks.

As he sat down to wait for her, he thought bitterly, *Damn those SS thugs for getting caught off guard like that! Now I've got to tell General Gedrosia that he's lost an entire team to unknown enemies. I don't even know who his people were tailing, or why! I presume it had something to do with that weapons broker, but the SS doesn't tell me a damn thing. Oh, well. I'll pay off the Inspector, then they can sort it out. I'm just a diplomat. I wash my hands of the whole damn affair!*

Bactria: April 17 2852 GSC

MINISTRY OF WAR, SODIA

"But what can the Foreign Ministry actually *do*, Your Majesty?" General Demetrias expostulated. "So far they seem to be merely making excuses for their inability to actually accomplish anything!"

"I'm afraid there's more truth to that than any of us would like to acknowledge," the Satrap replied ruefully. "The findings of the Commission of Inquiry into events on Termaz were so damning that I don't think there's any chance at all of avoiding sanctions against us. All we can hope to do – and it's not a very big hope – is to mitigate their severity. Believe me, I'm driving the diplomats hard on that, and there are some strings we can pull; a few bureaucrats among those responsible for preparing the resolution, a few Ambassadors who'll have to vote on it, and so on. They might be persuaded to be more helpful and reasonable in return for a not-so-small consideration. However, the Ministry doesn't want to throw good money after bad. We tried everything we could to obtain a better result from the Inquiry, at great expense, and failed miserably. I agree with them that we shouldn't waste time or resources on the General Assembly debate if failure is a foregone conclusion. Right now there doesn't appear to be much hope for anything else."

"Might that not be described as a dangerously defeatist attitude on the part of the Foreign Ministry, Your Majesty?" General Gedrosia asked in a silky-smooth tone. He very carefully did not say – but everyone nevertheless caught the unspoken implication – that the Satrap's attitude might be described in the same terms.

"It might, by someone who was blind to the realities of the situation," Rostam replied with a smile on his face and steel in his eyes and voice. "Defeatism is to be avoided at all costs. So are over-confidence, arrogance and overweening pride. We're in this mess precisely because the latter dominated policymaking in previous Administrations. I'm not going to allow them to dominate mine. We're going to face facts and act accordingly."

He looked around the table. "Now, let's turn to the situation on Bactria. We've already agreed that we can't afford to send more troops and equipment there. The Navy doesn't have the shipping capacity to spare, the Army doesn't have the budget or the manpower, and more mouths would only make the current food crisis on Termaz worse. Admiral, what's the result of the Navy's investigation into that message that seemingly came out of nowhere?"

Rear-Admiral Stasanor made a wry face. "I'm afraid we have so little to go on that we can't add much, Your Majesty. However, I'm inclined to think it was probably sent from a military vessel. You see, to come in like that with no signature to warn of their presence, they'd have had to exit their final hyper-jump about four light-days from the planet, accelerate to cruising speed, then shut down their gravitic drive and coast on a ballistic trajectory. If they were moving at a quarter of light speed, they'd take sixteen days to cover the distance. Add to that however long they took to travel from wherever they started to the Termaz system, plus the time taken to return to a friendly planet after they hyper-jumped away, and you're looking at thirty days or more in space. No courier vessel in my experience carries that much in the way of stores and supplies, particularly rations. They don't need to, because they can hyper-jump twice as far each day as conventional spaceships. I therefore submit that a courier ship wouldn't have had the crew endurance for a round trip of that duration."

The Satrap frowned. "I suppose that makes sense; but if it was a warship, what kind of warship? The Security Service hasn't found any record of interstellar warships being sold to unknown purchasers, much less the Termaz rebels and their Government-in-Exile."

General Gedrosia nodded. "It's as His Majesty says. It would be hard to hide a transaction like that. Warship sales are closely monitored and recorded by the United Planets."

Commodore Eschate shook his head. "With the greatest respect, General, I fear the SS may have been looking in the wrong place. I don't blame you, of course; this is something only a professional spacer would know to look for. Perhaps we should consider seconding some of our officers to you, to help with the analysis of Naval and Fleet intelligence. Anyway, I've been looking into the sale of fleet transports and auxiliaries. How much do you know about such ships?"

"Not much," the SS officer admitted.

"They're designed to keep up with warships and maneuver in formation with them. As a result, their construction is much stronger and stiffer than a conventional freighter's, and they have warship-grade gravitic drives, fusion reactors and other systems. We don't have any, because they're almost as expensive to build and operate as warships. If you recall, when we invaded Termaz we had to charter eight merchant freighters and install personnel pods in them so that each could carry a battalion of troops plus its heavy equipment. A military assault transport has all the necessary capability built in."

"I see. And have some of these military transports been sold recently?"

"As a matter of fact, yes. The Bismarck Cluster sold off eight of its old *Bavaria* class assault transports last year; three hundred thousand tons capacity, with stealthy hulls and capable of cruising at point two five Cee, the same speed as our corvettes – or the ship that transmitted that message in the Termaz system. They were sold for scrap, but I haven't been able to find any record of a shipyard dismantling them. They seem to have dropped out of space."

"What about weapons for them?" the Satrap demanded.

"I have no idea, Your Majesty. Again, the SS haven't been able to find any record of missiles being sold to unknown buyers. However, they did trace the rebel leader to Marano some months ago, where he apparently ordered twenty laser cannon turrets. Each *Bavaria* class ship had four such turrets while in service, although they were removed before the ships were sold. Our engineers tell me there's no reason why the Marano cannon couldn't be fitted in their place."

"So he has enough to outfit five ships?"

"More likely four, Your Majesty, with one spare unit for each ship. That's the way we'd do it if we'd bought them."

"I see. And how many missiles could ships like that carry, if he can get them?"

"That's a very worrying thought, Your Majesty. Each *Bavaria* is a little larger than a typical cruiser. In theory they could each carry two hundred or more main battery missiles, plus the same number of defensive weapons."

There was an audible intake of breath around the table. General Demetrias' voice was, for once, neither sarcastic nor belittling when he observed, "So one of them might bring almost as much firepower to a fight as all our remaining corvettes put together?"

"Precisely, General."

"Then let's hope they haven't got any missiles yet!"

Rear-Admiral Stasanor reassured him, "It's not just the weapons, General. The rebels will require the services of a military dockyard to convert the ships to accommodate so many missile cells or tubes. They'll also need fire control systems capable of handling that many weapons, plus radar, lidar and other sensors to identify and track their targets. Those are very expensive and hard to come by – even more so than missiles – and so are the skilled operators needed to use them. If the rebels have, indeed, bought those ships, I daresay they're still a long way from combat-ready. However, they do have stealthy hulls. There's no reason why one of them, even unarmed, couldn't have made a fast run through the Termaz system to deliver that message without being detected."

"But if that's the case, couldn't they make a run through this system as well?"

"I see you're thinking along the same lines as ourselves, General. Yes, they certainly could. They can use such a ship to scan everything we're doing, and possibly lay space mines – nuclear warheads with limited mobility – between our planet and our asteroid mining facilities. If that happens, they'll interdict much of our space-based economy. Space mines are a lot easier to get hold of, or make, than missiles. They're basically just warheads in housings with detection and detonation mechanisms. What's more, last year the rebels warned through the Interplanetary Transportation Union that the Bactrian and Termaz systems would be under interdiction from the beginning of this year. Space mines would be a legitimate tactic in terms of that declaration."

"What can we do to prevent that?" the Satrap demanded, sitting bolt upright in his chair.

"We've already increased the frequency of our patrols, Your Majesty. Unfortunately it's going to put enormous strain on our corvettes until our new patrol craft get here, because they're the only ships we have that are fast enough to be able to close with the rebels if we detect one of their ships. In fact, I'm seriously considering bringing back the corvette presently at Termaz and sending all our armed merchant cruisers out there instead. They're no use to us here against that sort of threat."

"But they won't be much use there, either, if the rebels come calling."

"I'm afraid not, Your Majesty; but let's face facts. Our space-based economy is far more important to us than the entire Termaz system. The former is a net economic contributor. Hundreds of thousands of Bactrian jobs and many of our industries depend on it, directly and indirectly. The latter is a net economic drain. We're pouring billions of bezants a year into what's become essentially a bottomless pit. I submit we have to allocate our present, very limited resources according to economic reality. Bactria's economy can, if necessary, survive the loss of Termaz. It can't survive the loss of our space-based commerce and industry. It's as simple as that."

Major-General Pamir erupted from his chair, face suffused with fury. "You denigrate the sacrifice of thousands – no, *tens* of thousands – of our faithful troops! How *dare* you insinuate they died in vain! I –"

"*SIT DOWN!*" The Satrap was also on his feet.

Pamir stood his ground. "Your Majesty, this insult is not to be borne!"

"I heard no insult. I heard only common sense!"

Grimly Rostam stared down the rebellious General. At last Pamir resumed his seat, lips still pursed in outrage. After standing for a moment longer, emphasizing his authority and dominance of proceedings, the Satrap said, "I take second place to no-one in my admiration for the courage and self-sacrifice displayed by so many of our armed forces on Termaz. Furthermore, I remind you that the Navy has taken casualties there too. Two transports were lost with all hands during the invasion, and the Space Station, the Satrap's yacht, two corvettes and an armed merchant cruiser were destroyed or damaged during the Battle of Tapuria with the loss of hundreds of lives. I'm sure the Admiral meant no insult." He looked at the Navy representatives as he sat down once more.

"Of course not, Your Majesty," Stasanor agreed. "General Pamir, I apologize if for any reason you gained that impression. It was not my intention."

Pamir gave a grudging nod, but said nothing.

"As a matter of fact, Admiral, your idea of sending all of our armed merchant cruisers to Termaz gives us an opportunity for a public relations coup that will be very useful at the United Planets," the Satrap said thoughtfully. "We've heard from General Demetrias that the food situation on the planet is becoming critical. In one sense that's good news for us, because we can supply our own forces while starving the rebels. However, the civilian population will starve as well. We're legally responsible for them. How would it appear if we mounted a major 'humanitarian effort' to relieve hunger after what we'll call the 'failure of the harvest' on Termaz?"

"It would help, Your Majesty," Demetrias agreed dubiously. "Unfortunately, the failure of the harvest was largely due to our seizing many farmers for slave labor, then pulling back from the agricultural areas before crops could be sown for the current season. That should be happening now, but it isn't, so things are going to get a lot worse before they get better."

"Yes, but we needn't admit that to the United Planets. We can even blame the rebels by claiming the unrest they foment makes it impossible for farmers to till their fields." The Army and SS officers cheered up noticeably at the thought of the enemy being the whipping boy for once.

"How many ration packs are stockpiled on Termaz and in our orbital warehouse there?"

Demetrias glanced at his subordinate. "General Pamir?"

"Sir, there are approximately eight million ration packs in orbital storage – just over three hundred days' supply for our armed forces there, at one pack per person per day. There are a few hundred thousand planetside. We send more down each week aboard cargo shuttles, and replenish our orbital stocks via the monthly freighter."

"But the planetary population in total, including our forces and administration personnel, is a little under two hundred thousand, right?" the Satrap asked.

"I believe so, Your Majesty."

"So eight million ration packs will feed that many for only about forty days. That's not nearly good enough. Of course, we normally expect the planet to be self-sufficient in food production, but the earliest they could bring in a harvest would be four or five months from now, right?"

"Yes, Your Majesty, provided they plant by not later than next month."

"All right. We'll tell Brigadier-General Khan to encourage farmers to return to their land to do that. We'll authorize him to declare a truce in the farming areas, and ask the rebels to allow farmers to work undisturbed and his techs to help repair farm machinery and infrastructure. We'll publicize all that as ways in which our armed forces are benevolently helping the local people, despite difficulties placed in their path by the rebels." The Army men smiled and nodded.

"Another thing we can do is publicize a buildup of rations for emergency use. Admiral Stasanor, how many ration packs can we load aboard the two armed merchant cruisers still in this system?"

"If we stuff every hold to overflowing, probably three to four million apiece, Your Majesty."

"And how many ration packs do we have available?"

General Demetrias frowned. "We have only ten million in our planetary reserve, Your Majesty. Sending that many to Termaz will render it useless in case of emergency."

"But we're not facing an emergency, are we? The food emergency is on Termaz. What's more, our farmers are reporting that this year should see bumper harvests across the board, so we can start to replenish our stock of ration packs within a few months. Imagine the headlines, General: 'Bactria succors Termaz'- although we'd better refer to it as Laredo for external consumption. Cargo shuttles are filled with tens of thousands of ration packs by uniformed Army working parties – also with sacks of seed for sowing. Those same shuttles load the rations into Navy transports, which head for Termaz and offload their cargoes into our orbital facility under the eyes of journalists, who then accompany some of it planetside aboard cargo shuttles delivering rations to residents and seed to farmers – all visibly protected by your troops, of course, and visibly grateful for it. I think that would go a long way towards defusing some of the more hate-filled propaganda against us at the United Planets. At the same time, it would portray our Armed Forces in a humanitarian light rather than as an occupying power."

Demetrias nodded thoughtfully. "I must admit, Your Majesty makes a compelling case. However, what if those journalists stay on the planet long enough for the rebels to give them a different picture?"

"We'll take care of that by whisking them away as fast as possible. Admiral, you want to bring back your corvette. We'll leave it at Termaz until the two armed merchant cruisers arrive. Within a day of their settling into orbit, your corvette will leave, taking with it the journalists who arrived aboard the AMC's. That'll get them out of the way quickly, and enable them to file their stories faster as well. After they've gone, the propaganda flights can be suspended and the ration packs offloaded into orbital storage for later distribution. Needless to say, our armed forces will get priority in that."

"That sounds like an excellent plan, Your Majesty. I foresee no difficulty."

"Very well. I invite the War Council to vote on that proposal. All those in favor?"

For once, every hand around the table was raised.

"I'm grateful for your unanimous support. Very well, the proposal is approved. We'll begin implementing it at once. General Demetrias, please start making arrangements to load the ration packs onto cargo shuttles. Admiral Stasanor, please start planning the movement of ships between the planets and any transfers of personnel involved. I know you'll both liaise with each other."

~ ~ ~

In the darkness she could hear his breathing. It wasn't the deep, even rhythm of sleep. Every now and then he'd toss, turn or twist in bed. She could imagine him frowning in the darkness.

At last she turned to face him. "What's wrong, Rostam? You've been doing an imitation of a whirling dervish ever since we went to bed."

He started. "Oh! I'm sorry, darling. I've just got a lot on my mind."

"I can see that. Can I help you carry the load?"

He rearranged himself, wordlessly inviting her to lie closer against him. She did so, snuggling into his warmth with a small sigh of satisfaction, and felt his left arm close around her.

"I... I'm not sure how to put this," her husband said slowly. "Today's meeting of the War Council went relatively well, all things considered. We only had one explosion of anger, two vehement disagreements and half a dozen minor conflicts to paper over." She chuckled. "Trouble is, I'm getting the feeling that we're not actually achieving anything of value. It seems as if we're just... pushing things around, rearranging problems without really solving them. Even the so-called 'truths' in which we were raised – the superiority of Bactrian culture, our historical destiny, the greatness of our forefathers, all that sort of thing – somehow they seem... less than truthful, these days."

"Why not come right out and say it? They were lies from beginning to end. We were raised in a lie, and we're perpetuating that lie rather than dealing with it."

He froze alongside her for a moment, then relaxed slowly. "Zeba, if you said that to anyone but me, in our private quarters like this, there are plenty of people who'd scream 'Treason!' and demand your head for it."

"Yes, I know. That's why I'd only say it in here like this. That doesn't stop it being true, does it?"

He slowly shook his head in the darkness. "I can't argue with you. That's the hell of it. I *want* to argue with you. All the instincts nurtured by my parents and grandparents tell me I should be screaming 'Treason!' and committing you for immediate trial... but I can't, because I know you're speaking the truth. That truth is biting us in the ass right now at the United Planets. If the rebels ever get their hands on a meaningful space warfare capability, it's going to bite us on the ass on the battlefield as well. I just can't see any good ending to all this."

"And meanwhile the Army and SS Generals, and the conservatives among the nobles, make common cause together and conspire against you because you're not fully committed to the same false dream that inspires them."

"That's right. They're still trapped in the framework in which they were raised – in which everyone on this planet was raised, come to that. What's going to happen to all of us when that framework collapses?"

"Will it collapse?"

"I'm afraid it might. I'm seeing all sorts of stresses here, strains there. We – the whole edifice of pride we've built for ourselves as a nation – took a hammer-blow at Tapuria two years ago. We saw the myth of our military invincibility shattered. My father's head was sent rolling around the floor by a rebel hit squad using our own captured equipment against him. Our occupation of Termaz has never recovered, because we couldn't afford to replace most of the troops and equipment we lost; and the thousands of dead listed in the news media, and the thousands of injured – a lot of them maimed for life – who came trickling home to tell their families about the disaster, did an immense amount of damage to the reputation of our armed forces. They've never recovered from it."

She nodded beside him. "I know. Enlistments are still way down, and the numbers trying to dodge military conscription – even at the cost of a jail sentence if they're caught – are way up. The House of the People flat turned down our request for an increase in the defense budget last year, on the grounds that we hadn't made the best use of what we'd already been given. They'd been bled dry by the war establishment for years. For the first time they cracked under the pressure and said, 'No more'. I couldn't blame them, quite frankly."

"Yes. Shakespeare would say that the worm turned at last."

She sighed. "If you want to get all literary about it – not to mention religious, in this case – I can't help but be reminded of a line from one of the ancient Jewish prophets. It was something like 'They have sown the wind, so they'll reap the whirlwind'. Scary."

"It's not a bad way of putting it. The whirlwind's getting closer all the time, both inside our society and externally at the United Planets."

"And militarily?"

"I don't know. None of us do. We don't know what the rebels have been doing or what their capabilities are."

"I guess by the time we find out, it'll be too late to take cover from the whirlwind in the storm cellar."

"I hope you're wrong. I really, *really* hope you're wrong, darling... Whatever happens, all we can do is hang on and try to ride the whirlwind wherever it takes us. It's going to be a bumpy ride."

Bactria: April 18 2852 GSC

SATRAP'S GUARD RESEARCH CENTER, OUTSIDE SODIA

The guard on duty at the console stiffened as a red light began to flash. He pulled his chair closer, peering at a screen. It showed a lidar image of something very small approaching the corner of the flat roof. He reached for a microphone.

"Security Center to roof sentry, looks like a flitterbug approaching the south corner, over."

"Roof to SecCen, understood, I'm scanning, wait one."

Silence for a few moments.

"Roof here, I see it. Do you want me to take it down? Over."

"SecCen to roof, take it intact for analysis if you can. Over."

"Roof to SecCen, stand by." Silence again, then, "Got it! It's in the nets. It seemed to be coming in a straight line from the Weapons Center, from what I could see. Over."

"SecCen to Roof, I agree – the lidar track indicates that too. Don't pick it up. Wait for the Sergeant-Major. I'm going to alert Security to check the Weapons Center roof. Stand by."

~ ~ ~

Sergeant-Major Indic watched as the security vid ran its course. "And you've no idea who that is, Sir?" he asked.

"None," Major Daria replied curtly. "He's all bundled up, he's wearing dark glasses and his face is wrapped. Our facial recognition software can't pick up enough features to function."

"With respect, Sir, that won't do."

The officer flared up at once. "Who the hell do you think you are to tell me what will or won't do? I'm a Major, dammit! You're just an NCO! Wait – what do you think you're doing?" Indic had picked up the officer's handset from the desk.

"Just a moment, please, Sir." Indic's voice was curt, unforgiving as he entered a code. He waited until a voice responded, then said, "Sergeant-Major Indic requests to speak to the Colonel urgently."

"Wait one," a crisp voice responded.

"The *Colonel?*" Major Daria's voice was suddenly an octave higher, panicky. "Look, there's no need to –"

Indic ignored him as another voice came on the line. "Good morning, Sir. Sergeant-Major Indic here... Fine, thank you, Sir. I regret to have to report a lack of performance, initiative and support from Major Daria of the Security Desk at the Research Center, Sir. He's just blown me off after we detected an attempted intrusion into our project... Yes, Sir, I'm in his office at present... Here he is, Sir."

He handed the handset to the stunned Major. "The Colonel wishes to speak to you, Sir." Without waiting for a reply, he turned on his heel and walked out.

Chief Sergeant Traxiane was waiting patiently outside. She smiled at him as he emerged. "Sorted?"

"No, but it will be soon. I reckon we'll have a new Security CO within the hour." They began walking down the corridor towards the elevators.

"So that top-level access they promised you really does work?"

"I reckon so. If the Colonel doesn't come through, the next call goes to Her Majesty. I figure the Colonel knows that."

She gave a low, throaty chuckle. "That'll concentrate his mind, all right!"

"I hope so. Did you look at the vid?"

"Yeah. I ran it three times. Hard to identify a bulky figure coming downstairs in a hurry carrying a console, but I noticed two things. He was wearing old-fashioned brown leather shoes, not our issue synthetics; and the console looked to be off-white or gray instead of our standard white flitterbug control units."

"Good work!" He clapped his deputy on the back. "I hadn't had time to watch it more than once. You've just saved me the effort. Let's get a couple more people here and stand by. We should have permission to proceed within a few minutes. Oh – and be prepared for trouble. If we find this guy, he may not come quietly."

"Got it."

As soon as they reached the entrance lobby Indic asked the Sergeant in charge at the security desk, "OK if I use your comm unit?"

"Anything at all, Sergeant-Major." The man offered him the handset with almost exaggerated respect. Indic's reputation had acquired legendary proportions in the Satrap's Guard since his recruitment on Turmaz and the savage, no-nonsense, no-holds-barred combat training he'd put them through after his return to Bactria. His recent two-step promotion and appointment to command a team of the toughest, most experienced NCO's and troops in the Guard, protecting a top-secret 'research project' about which nobody knew anything, had done nothing to diminish his status.

The Sergeant-Major entered the code for the main entrance to the secure Research Center compound. "Sergeant-Major Indic speaking. I need the Officer of the Watch, please... Hello, Lieutenant. Sergeant-Major Indic here. Sir, I respectfully request that your guards stop anyone leaving who's wearing old-fashioned brown leather shoes instead of our issue synthetics, or who's carrying a control console in off-white or light gray color instead of standard white... Yes, Sir, I know that means they'll have to look inside briefcases and other containers... Yes, Sir, please feel free to confirm this with Major Daria. I'm sure he's finished his conversation with the Colonel by now... Thank you, Sir. Please keep me informed if you find anything. Here's my personal comm code." He read off the digits. "Thank you, Sir."

He returned the handset to the NCO behind the counter. "Thank you, Sergeant. I'm going to bring in a few of my people. As soon as we hear from Major Daria, we'll be splitting up to search every floor of this building."

The Sergeant's eyebrows flew up, but he didn't hesitate. "Is something wrong, Sergeant-Major? Would you like the help of any of my team? Take whoever you need."

Indic grinned at him. "Thanks for your co-operation. I won't forget it; but I think we can manage. I –"

He was interrupted by the crackle of shots from the main entrance to the compound, a hundred meters away. The sergeant could only gape as Indic and his deputy spun on their heels and disappeared through the door like greyhounds leaving the starting gate, drawing their pulsers as they sprinted towards the sound of the guns.

~ ~ ~

The ornate car, flying the Satrap's personal flag, drew up outside the entrance to the compound. A half-shouted, half-screamed "At-*ten*-SHUN!" from the nearest Guardsman slammed everyone into a rigid brace.

The rear window of the limousine rolled down, and the face of the Satrap's wife appeared. "Sergeant-Major Indic!"

"Coming, Ma'am!" He hurried over to the car.

"I just heard. Is…?"

He lowered his voice. "Everything's fine, Ma'am. Someone tried to snoop on our… project. We saw his flitterbug coming and caught it. He tried to get away, but my deputy had noticed a couple of clues in his appearance on security vid. I notified the gate, and they spotted him. He tried to fight his way clear and they shot him. One of the gate guards was injured, but not badly."

"Is he dead?"

"Yes, Ma'am."

"Who was he?"

"We don't know yet, Ma'am. He was using a fake Guard ID. However, we have the flitterbug he used, the console from which he controlled it, and his pulser. They all have serial numbers. We should be able to trace who bought them, when and where. That'll give us a starting point for further investigations."

"Good. Call your deputy over and get in. I need to talk with both of you privately."

"Yes, Ma'am."

He looked around, spotted Chief Sergeant Traxiane and waved her over, then walked around to the other side of the vehicle. He ushered her into the back seat, then opened the front door and sat down beside the driver, a uniformed guard from the Satrap's hand-picked personal security detachment. He'd chosen them personally, discretion being among their most important attributes; but even such hand-picked guards didn't need to be part of a conversation like this. "Go get a cup of coffee in the guardhouse," he told him. "I'll call you when we finish."

"Yes, Sergeant-Major!" The driver let himself out of the vehicle and closed the door.

"Thank you both for your alertness this morning," Zeba began with a sigh. "I was petrified when I heard there was trouble. I didn't know everything was OK until I got here. You're not just saying that to reassure me, are you?"

"No, Ma'am," Traxiane said briskly, shaking her head. "He never got his flitterbug inside, and he didn't enter our building at all."

"D'you think it's still safe to hide in plain sight like this?"

"Why not, Ma'am?" Indic asked reasonably. "Here we're just one high-security building in a compound full of them, each one busy with a different project. There's nothing to make us stand out. I reckon whoever that was that tried to snoop couldn't have known anything about... our special project." Even in the presence of the person responsible for his being here, he couldn't bring himself to identify what they were guarding.

He went on, "He probably wanted to check all the buildings, and we were just the next on his list. We'll know more when we check the records on the data chip in his pocket. They're also checking every building's roof to see whether any of them have possible entry points for flitterbugs. If they do, he may have infiltrated more than one project. They'll work through the night if necessary to track them down."

"All right." She was silent for a moment, clearly collecting her thoughts. "If it turns out to be an attempt to infiltrate all the Guard's secret projects, you know as well as I do who's likely to be behind it."

"Yes, Ma'am. That'll be just like the SS. They never trust anybody, and suspect even their own side." He spat out the name in disgust. No combat veteran had anything but contempt for the Security Service. On Termaz it had often arrested soldiers suspected of 'defeatism', tortured them in the name of 'interrogation', and more often than not returned the innocent ones to their units so broken in spirit as to be useless for further soldiering.

"If they suspect what you're really doing here, that makes it even more important to keep this secret, even after the baby's born."

"I understand, Ma'am. I hope you're taking extra precautions with your firstborn?"

"Yes, we are." Her face broke into a soft, warm smile despite the worry on her features. "He's being well guarded, and we've vetted all his nurses and caretakers more strictly than ever before. Some of those who were turned down are livid about it, because their families had traditionally provided such services, but my husband's been absolutely ruthless about it."

"As well he should, Ma'am!" Traxiane agreed vehemently.

"According to the grapevine, I understand that you two are becoming an item. Is that right?" Zeba asked, looking back and forth between them.

Indic blushed. "Er... well... ah, yes, Ma'am. We're talking about it."

Traxiane grinned wickedly. "Doing something about it, too, now and again." She nudged Indic with her elbow, and Zeba laughed aloud.

"I'm very glad to hear it. It makes it easier for me to ask you to do more. I know we said that when this child was born, she'd join her brother in the Royal Nursery. Now... now I'm not so sure that's a good idea, at least not right away. There are undercurrents that I really don't like. I may ask you to keep her secure in the country for a while longer – not here, of course, but somewhere else that's secure. I'll visit when I can, but it may be several months before we dare have both of our children in the same location. Will you do your best to care for her until we can do that? As far as the rest of the planet's concerned, she'll be your own child."

Indic rolled his eyes heavenwards. "What was that ancient ditty from Old Home Earth? I think it began, 'Kiss me goodnight, Sergeant-Major'. I never dreamed it'd come true!"

The ladies broke into delighted laughter. "I've never heard of that one," Zeba said, chuckling. "I'll have to look it up. Yes, Sergeant-Major, I want you to kiss my daughter goodnight in my stead. You do the same, please, Chief Sergeant. With luck it'll only be for a few months, then we can get back to normal."

"We'll do it, Ma'am," Traxiane assured her. "It'll be good practice for someone I know before his own kids begin to pop out."

As the others laughed again, Indic could only grit his teeth. He couldn't remember blushing this much since he'd wandered into the wrong changing-room at school in his pre-teen years.

~ ~ ~

ENTERTAINMENT DISTRICT, SODIA

A uniformed waiter knocked at the door of the private dining room, entered, walked swiftly and silently to Wazir Khanoum at the head of the table and handed him a note. The Wazir unfolded and read it as the waiter left the room.

"It seems Major Kadeh is unavoidably detained. He asks that we start without him, but not leave until he gets here, as he has news that affects all of us."

"Hmm. Wonder what's going on?" General Demetrias pondered aloud as he reached for his glass. "Oh, well, I suppose we'll find out soon enough."

"Yes. I'm glad we can get down to business, because my first issue concerns the Army in particular, my dear General."

"Oh? Is something wrong?"

"Let's just say I'm concerned. Are you aware of the growing tide of resentment against the military among the common people?"

Major-General Pamir snorted. "We can hardly *not* be aware of it, Wazir! Ever since the House of the People turned down the Satrap's request for an increased defense budget last year, they've been getting uppity. I can't understand why the Satrap didn't do what his father and grandfather used to do; arrest some of the recalcitrant ones and call for another vote while they were safely locked up. By the time they got out, loyal delegates would have passed whatever the Satrap wanted and further opposition usually proved pointless. If they didn't learn the first time, they learned the next – if they were ever released after their second arrest, that is."

"I agree, General. Unfortunately the present Satrap has more patience than his predecessors in office with 'the recalcitrant ones', as you called them. He really seems to believe that they have the right to vote as they see fit. That's not a problem in the House of Nobles, fortunately." The Wazir snorted in disdain. "If the junior nobles don't vote as we Wazirs tell them to, they soon hear about it from us! We'll have no independent thinking in *our* House, thank you very much!"

"I only wish you could apply the same discipline to the House of the People," General Gedrosia of the SS assured him fervently.

"Perhaps one day we will. Anyway, let's get back to the point. It seems to me that as more and more troops come back from Termaz and share their stories with their families and friends, that's spreading greater resentment, even disaffection, among the people. Would you agree?"

"I fear you're right, Wazir," Demetrias admitted. "I'd much rather not have brought those units back until we'd been able to stiffen their spines after the calamity at Tapuria. Unfortunately, the Satrap didn't listen to my arguments against reducing our forces on Termaz. He made decisions based solely on what he believed we could afford. That's very hard to argue against, of course; but to my mind, military priorities should override mere bezants and bean-counters and budgets. In the past we always found money for them from somewhere, even if we had to squeeze the people a little harder or reduce state subsidies for other things."

Colonel Fergan added, "Failures to report for conscripted service are thirty per cent higher this year than last year, Wazir, and last year they were twenty per cent higher than the year before. It's becoming a serious drain on our infantry strength. What's more, re-enlistments are down by almost half. We used to be able to offer bonuses to those with skills in areas of high demand to encourage their retention, but now we can't afford that; so commerce and industry are poaching our best, most highly trained, most skilled soldiers from us in ever-increasing numbers."

Khanoum sat forward, frowning. "All you say confirms my impression. What I'm most concerned about is the internal security environment. We seem to be getting into a pressure-cooker situation, where all sorts of issues are occupying our peoples' minds and keeping them agitated and worked up. At present we're able to keep a lid on the situation, and we can continue to do that for the foreseeable future; but what about factors we *can't* foresee? What if the rebels launch new attacks on Termaz and inflict severe casualties? Even worse, what if they use some of their newly-acquired ships – which appear, at least in theory, to be more capable than first thought – to launch attacks in this, our home system? What would that do to the peoples' willingness to trust us to run Bactria as we've always done? Would it lead to a serious challenge to our authority?"

SS Colonel Arachosia said quietly, "That's a growing concern of ours, Wazir. We see the same developments you've noted. We're able to keep things under control at their present levels, but if they get worse, we'll have to rely on the Army to provide troops for internal security."

"We won't be able to provide as many as you'd like," Demetrias warned bluntly. "We can't send conscripts into such situations. They'd be far too likely to side with their families and friends in the mob. We can only rely on our regulars, and as Colonel Fergan has pointed out, we don't have enough of them anymore. About half of them are on Termaz, with the rest spread thin across our forces here to train new recruits and conscripts. They're not concentrated in reliable units we can dispatch to a trouble spot."

"That's the nub of my concern," the Wazir sighed. "In the past nobles could raise their own troops of guards, who were available to deal with local or regional security issues. However, after a series of conflicts with the nobles, Satrap Alexandros terminated that right three centuries ago. I know we daren't start raising our own units again in defiance of the Satrap, but what if we were to make our country estates available to the Army to gather reservists into small 'volunteer' units, General? If we selected trustworthy individuals, we might be able to build up small, select security forces who would answer directly to the nobles when the time came. They wouldn't be the equal of the regular Army, of course, but they wouldn't have to be. We could use them to control unrest and whip the people back into line if necessary. What do you think?"

"The idea has possibilities," Demetrias said slowly. "General Pamir, what do you think?"

"I see no reason not to do it," his deputy affirmed stoutly. "We can form platoon- or company-size units under the auspices of existing Reserve formations, and issue them uniforms, weapons and transport on the same basis. They won't be in full-time service and won't be quartered in our regular bases, so they won't require barracks and won't be on our ration strength. By using existing units as cover for them, we can conceal the fact that they exist and operate independently."

"That would be very useful," his superior officer agreed. "Very well, Wazir. We'll see what can be done, and get back to you within the week with concrete proposals."

"Thank you, gentlemen. That will be –"

He was interrupted by a knock at the door. Major Kadeh slipped into the room. His uniform was disheveled, as if he'd been out of doors, and he was breathing hard like a man who'd been running.

"I'm sorry I'm late," he said brusquely, "but there's a crisis to deal with. It may affect all of us." He crossed to his seat as he glared at General Gedrosia. "May I ask what the *hell* the SS thinks it's playing at?"

The General sat bolt upright in shock, which rapidly changed to anger. "How dare you address a superior officer like that?"

"I dare because the SS has just precipitated a crisis, General! I repeat – what the hell does your organization think it's playing at?"

"What are you talking about?"

"Oh, come *on!* Don't tell me you didn't know that one of your people was shot dead trying to infiltrate the Satrap's Guard research facility this morning?"

"What?" The General goggled at him. "You can't be serious!"

"You mean you *didn't* know?"

"How could I? I never ordered anything of the kind!" He glanced at Colonel Arachosia. "Did you?"

"No, of course not, Sir!"

Kadeh sank into his seat. "In that case, Sir, I apologize for my rudeness; but I must also tell you that you have some sort of rogue element in the SS that you need to straighten out *right now*. A man wearing Guard uniform, with the correct ID, entered the Research Center this morning. It seems he sent spy flitterbugs into half a dozen buildings there, infiltrating via the roof or open windows. They were found in nooks and crannies, recording whatever they could for later transmission. We found out about them from a data chip on his body. He was detected while trying to do the same at a special project building. The security team there sounded the alert, and he was stopped at the gate. He tried to shoot his way out, and was killed."

Everyone had listened with shocked, disbelieving expressions on their faces. "But this is *madness!*" the Wazir exclaimed. "How – why – I... I just don't understand!"

"It gets worse, Wazir," Kadeh said grimly. "His vehicle was found in the parking lot. It contained an SS identification wallet. What's more, he carried a pulser and had several flitterbugs and a control console in his possession. I'm informed by my sources in the Guard that they've already traced the serial numbers on all that equipment to the SS. By tomorrow morning – maybe even later tonight – they're going to be knocking on your door, wanting answers."

General Gedrosia sat in stunned silence, shaking his head. Colonel Arachosia snapped, "Any such operation would have originated in our Central Bureau, but that's *my* unit. I've never authorized anything of the kind. I don't know what the devil's going on here, but I think we're being set up."

Gedrosia shook his head violently, as if to clear it. "That would fit with other recent events. The first team we sent to Neue Helvetica were all killed in a so-called 'vehicle accident'. We didn't find out about it for some time, thanks to the closure of our Consulate there. We sent another team a few months ago, but they've vanished into thin air. We haven't heard a word from them. Is it possible they're dead too? Then there's that report last month from our Ambassador to Marano. Our entire six-person team there was found dead in a burned-out van, along with a weapons broker, with all their ID's carefully packed into a plastic bag and left on the ground, clear of the wreckage and fire, where the police could find them. It was clearly an assassination, but we've no idea who was behind it. Now there's this – an intrusion we didn't order, but which implicates us. The fallout is bound to disrupt our operations, not to mention cause further distrust of us in official circles. Put all that together, and what have you got?"

"Someone's infiltrated us, Sir," the Colonel said slowly, nodding as his eyes narrowed. "I don't see any other possibility. Could it be the rebel Government-in-Exile?"

"*How?* They never displayed any such capability before their escape, and I don't see how they could have developed it since then. More to the point, they've never had any operatives on Bactria as far as we know. No, I think this is internal. It's got to come from another government agency;

someone or some group that doesn't like our influence. Remember, we used to be an independent Cabinet-level office. After Tapuria we were reduced to department level under the Ministry of War. Are these incidents designed to set us up to lose even more credibility?"

"But *who,* Sir? Who would have the ability to do that, and the facilities to set up everything?"

Wazir Khanoum snapped, "Isn't it obvious? There's only one possible candidate – the Satrap!"

"What?" Everyone goggled at him.

"His Guard has always had a confidential bureau for covert operations – not so, Major Kadeh?"

"That's right, Wazir. I don't know much about it, because I've never been part of it."

"But it's staffed by competent people, right?"

"I assume so, Wazir."

"Very well then. The Satrap has his own spy service at his beck and call. He was responsible for subordinating the SS to the Ministry of War, and he's refused to replace the equipment and agents you lost on Termaz, citing budgetary pressures as an excuse. It would suit him to reduce your status even further. Even your failures on other planets may not be so much failures as betrayals. After all, he benefits from them, because he can use them to undermine and discredit your leadership." He looked directly at the two SS officers.

Dawning understanding crept across the faces of his listeners. General Demetrias gurgled, "But the intruder this morning was killed! How could the Satrap persuade an agent to accept death, merely to discredit the SS? No sane man would do that!"

Major Kadeh shook his head. "The man might not have known the Satrap was involved, Sir. He might have received his orders from a source he believed had the right to give them – perhaps someone pretending to be an SS officer, or even a genuine SS officer who's been suborned and is working in secret for another agency – without being aware that he was being set up for death."

Gedrosia cursed aloud. "That must be it! I'm going to…" He suddenly hesitated. "No. We can't make accusations against the Satrap without overwhelmingly strong evidence, and we have none."

"I'm afraid you're right, Sir," Colonel Arachosia agreed unhappily. "The Satrap can simply deny everything. In fact, if we tried to make a fuss, he could cite that as evidence that we were completely out of touch with reality, and use it as an excuse to remove us from our posts."

"I fear you're right, Colonel," the Wazir agreed, his mouth tight. "This has been masterfully done. The SS is caught in a no-win situation – at least for now. I suspect the only possibility in the short term is for you to brazen it out and play for time."

"But how much time do we have?" General Demetrias' voice was plaintive. "You said yourself that pressures are building up in our society. They're building externally, too. There's that intruder ship reported from Termaz. Other rebel ships may come here in the same way – Rear-Admiral Stasanor spoke just yesterday of the danger from space mines."

Khanoum sighed. "The situation might deteriorate drastically at any moment. We may not have the luxury of waiting a few years for the crisis to unfold, because neither the Satrap nor the rebels on Termaz may give us that much time. We must be prepared for anything."

He rose to his feet. "I won't detain you any longer, my friends. Our SS colleagues have much to do to prepare themselves for the inquiry that's about to hit them. I suggest we leave Major Kadeh to enjoy a well-earned supper, and get back to our responsibilities. I'll send in a waiter with food for you, Major. Thank you very much for bringing us advance warning of this crisis. You've given us more time to prepare a response."

There was a murmur of assent as the others stood. The Wazir escorted them to the lobby of the restaurant as a waiter wheeled in a trolley with a three-course meal for Kadeh. He was hungrily devouring a meat soup when his host returned.

Khanoum closed the door behind him and sat down. "That was exceptionally well done, my young friend," he said quietly and very approvingly. "We've got all of them chasing their own tails, worrying that there may be traitors within their departments. All very satisfactory."

Kadeh swallowed a mouthful of soup and grinned. "Yes, and they'll look to you to be the steadying hand of experience, to provide leadership while their heads are spinning with the implications of unknown dangers."

"Precisely. You've done everything and more that I asked you to do. You had no trouble convincing your man?"

"None at all, Sir. He really is – or, rather, was – an SS agent, one I'd worked with on another operation. I was able to persuade him to help me test the security of the Satrap's Guard. He thought his pulser and the guards' weapons were loaded with practice rounds for exercise purposes. The funds you provided helped, of course. I paid him lavishly for his assistance. He suspected nothing."

"And now it's too late for him to suspect anything." They chuckled softly together. "What would you have done if he'd succeeded in his mission without being detected?"

"I'd have made sure he was detected, Wazir. If necessary he'd have 'been killed while attempting to escape'. Fortunately, I didn't have to intervene. A security team in another building spotted him first."

"Very good. What about his pulser, flitterbugs and other equipment?"

"He provided everything from SS stocks, Wazir, even his pulser. I provided a charger of training ammo with which to load it for what he assumed to be an 'exercise'. However, unknown to him I filled the charger with the real thing, so when he opened fire on the guards he injured one of them. Seeing that, of course, the other guards killed him, ensuring he could never talk."

"You're an uncommonly inventive, efficient and competent officer, my dear Major. I'm glad I decided to approach you privately to ask for assistance. I promise you, on the day our coup succeeds, you'll wear General's stars. I'll need a strong right-hand man when I rule as Vizier, to control our Army and the SS while I direct our figurehead on the Satrap's throne."

Vesta: April 20-21 2852 GSC

"Plot to Command. Target Lima-One bearing 272:271, range one-zero-two kilometers, Sir."

"Command to Plot, thank you. Break. Command to Navigation. Bring the ship to rest with Lima-One bearing precisely 270:270 from us at a range of one hundred kilometers."

"Navigation to Command, aye aye, Sir."

As the Navigating Officer began making tiny, precise adjustments to Laredo Ship *Liberty*'s position, her Commanding Officer glanced over his shoulder to where Dave was sitting in the Operation Center's visitors' chairs. "So far, so good, Sir."

"So I see. I'm impressed by the way your crew's come together. You're satisfied they're all performing at a suitable level for combat conditions?"

"Yes, Sir." Captain Cullew grinned. "I'd have liked a couple more months to knock them into shape, but I suspect that's been said by every warship captain since long before Nelson's time."

Dave couldn't help smiling. "The missile cells?"

"All tubes tested correctly just before you arrived from Marano, Sir. They've put a second cell into another cargo hold aboard both this ship and LS *Independence*, Sir, so we each have a hundred target missiles. Fortunately that wasn't a problem, given the number of cells they removed from the old *Legion* class battleships. We still don't have any defensive missiles, unfortunately."

"Yes, but I hope we can get by without them for this mission. We expect to have some by the third quarter, if another project goes well. Once we've calibrated your new laser turrets they'll give you at least some defensive capability, and our stealth features and systems should enable us to imitate a hole in space long enough to duck out of the path of incoming fire. What's more, our target missiles used to be battleship main battery missiles. They're much longer-ranged than the smaller missiles used by Bactrian corvettes, and they're faster, too. That means we can fire an initial salvo a long way out, before the enemy can realistically shoot back."

"Yes, Sir, although that gives the enemy more time to dodge our fire."

"But our missiles have enough speed and range to change course and follow them. It's a complex equation, I know. We'll run simulations on the way to Laredo. Fortunately we have a battleship's fire control system, so we're likely to have better electronics than they do."

"Yes, Sir. The *Legion* class may have been obsolete by Lancastrian Commonwealth Fleet standards, but that's close to state-of-the-art as far as the warships of minor powers are concerned."

"I'm not complaining! What happens when we're in position?"

"We'll begin by firing three rounds from each laser cannon, Sir, aiming at a target at point-blank range. That'll allow us to calculate the calibration error of each turret. Our artificers will correct that, then we'll fire another three rounds from each, and so on until every turret is spot-on at a range of one hundred kilometers. We'll then repeat that at a thousand, ten thousand and one hundred thousand kilometers. Finally we'll move half a million kilometers out and do it for the last time. At that range our lasers can't deliver enough energy for a kill shot, of course, but they can blind the sensors on an incoming missile so it can't see its target anymore."

"It can still close in on a ballistic trajectory, can't it?"

"Yes, Sir, it can, but you aren't exactly going to hang around waiting for it to reach you."

"I take your point. How long will the entire process last?"

"About a week, Sir. We'll end it by going into deep space and having another ship fire a few training missiles set to pass close to us, to give our laser cannon a workout under combat conditions. Our sister ship, LS *Independence,* is doing that right now. After that it's back to the dockyard for final adjustments; then we load ourselves to the max with stores and supplies, to give ourselves four months' operational endurance."

"Yes, I've arranged for everything to be ready to load. Cargo shuttles will be standing by. There's a last-minute item to load into one of your smaller unused holds; a hundred empty plasfiber garbage compactor containers – the kind you use to offload your garbage or toss it into the nearest star if there are no processing facilities – plus some large plastic balls, glue, paint and stencils. Make sure the containers are evenly spaced to fill the hold and secured upside-down so their access hatches can't be seen. During the voyage I want your crew to cut the balls carefully in half, cap each container with half a ball, then paint them all gray and stencil letters and symbols on them. I'll give you photographs to serve as a guide."

The Captain's voice was mystified. "But, Sir, by convention garbage containers are supposed to be bright yellow with waste identifiers on them."

"These won't be garbage containers any more by the time we're finished with them. I'll say no more about that right now. Once you've painted them, I want them covered with transparent plaswrap to make it look as if they're sensitive cargo."

"Ah… very well, Sir. You're the boss."

"Thank you. When will both ships be ready to leave?"

"If all goes well, by the first of next month, Sir."

"And how long will it take us to reach Laredo?"

"Twelve days, Sir."

"The twelfth of May, then. *God*, I hope they can hold out that long!" Dave spoke the last words *sotto voce*, almost afraid to verbalize his fears. He knew his compatriots would be eking out their rations as carefully as they could, to make them last until the promised relief came. At least he'd get there a little before his promised deadline.

"Will you be staying with us for the duration of the laser trials, Sir?"

"No, I'm afraid I have a great deal to do before we leave. I'll get you to drop me at the range control ship after we finish this first series of shots. I'll take the shuttle back to the dockyard from there this evening, and return aboard when you get back."

"Very well, Sir. Thanks for taking the time out of your schedule to be with us yesterday and today. I know the crew appreciated it very much, particularly when you took the time to go round the ship with me and inspect every compartment."

"It's my pleasure, Captain. After all, we'll be going into action together. The least I can do is make sure you're all good enough to keep my favorite butt attached to my favorite body!"

~ ~ ~

The next morning found Dave hard at work in his office aboard the courier ship. He'd appropriated two of its small passenger cabins, one as sleeping quarters and one for work.

He frowned as he scrolled through sheets of figures. Warfare in space was proving to be an extraordinarily expensive business. If he'd had to pay full rate for his ships, the modifications to them, their weapons and systems, and his crews, the Resistance would have been bankrupt long ago. As it was, they had less than a billion Neue Helvetica francs left in their main account, and it was flowing like water under the impact of ship charters, purchases of ration packs, and the operating expenses of three – soon to be four – warships and two freighters in commission. He still had a couple of hundred million in his secret account for special projects, but he wanted to hold on to that as an emergency reserve.

He pulled out a recorder next to his terminal, which he was using to note instructions to Tamsin and Rusty as he thought of them. Activating it and looking into the lens, he said, "Our finances are taking a beating. If we continue to buy food for Laredo at the present rate and ship it aboard chartered freighters, whilst still funding limited military operations, we'll go broke in less than six months. Rusty, plan to return the freighters to their owners after present shipments are delivered. I'll send word to Rolla for one of our freighters to report to you at Neue Helvetica ASAP, so you can use it to collect future shipments. Rations arriving at Rolla will have to be stored aboard one of our inactive assault transports until a freighter's available to make the run to Laredo.

"I'm going to ask the broker we used before to look for two more tramp freighters. We can buy them in good condition for twenty to twenty-five million apiece. We'll get that back when we sell them. The running costs are much lower than a wet-leased freighter or our military-grade transports, so we'll save money by using our own ships. We have enough trained spacers to crew them now. It looks like each combat ship will need one hundred and fifty to two hundred Spacers, and the freighters need thirty to forty each; so with four combat ships and four freighters, we'll use all of the thousand Gurkhas we've trained. We desperately need a couple of our own communications ships to replace the chartered courier vessels, but we can't afford them right now. That'll have to wait until we have more funds.

"Tamsin, it's going to be absolutely critical for us to get more money from UP donors. We can't realistically launch a new appeal until we prove that previous donations have been well spent. I think our present operation ought to do that, if all goes well. I want you to prepare a huge public relations blitz. I'll send you as much vid and other material as I can, plus a few eye-witnesses for media interviews. Meanwhile, have Elisabeta set up a program to swamp the news media with that material, and prepare some tear-jerking appeals to 'help the people of Laredo fight off continued Bactrian aggression'. With any luck, that'll bring in a billion or two in cash within a few months, which will keep our heads above water.

"Food aid will be a big part of that. If planets don't want to give us money or weapons, ask them to give us food. If we can persuade a couple of dozen planets to each send us a freighter loaded with food, we'll be OK. Also, ask whether anyone's willing to sponsor orbital farm units at Laredo for a year or so. They can produce food in orbit while planetary farms recover and get back into production. It'll be a lot more expensive to ferry it down from orbit than grow it planetside, but that'll still be much cheaper than bringing it from all over the settled galaxy! Also, ask for donations of seed, farm implements, fertilized cattle embryos and breeder pods, and so on."

He switched off the recorder with a grimace. That request might be premature. After all, if they didn't control the Laredo system, there was no guarantee the Bactrians would allow food shipments or orbital farms at all. However, the need was critical. Better to have a potential solution at hand rather than have no solution at all. They could figure out how to implement it when the time came.

He'd never anticipated just how many issues had to be managed in running a Government-in-Exile while fighting a war. So many problems reared their heads that if they were all given the attention they demanded – if not rightfully deserved – no-one would ever have time to fight, much less win. Only by being ruthless about priorities, making decisions as quickly as possible and acting on them – even if they weren't necessarily the best decisions – could operations be kept going. That was the leader's job, thereby freeing his subordinates to get on with their jobs.

If this operation succeeds, it's going to beget a swarm of new problems, he reminded himself as he sat back, fingers rubbing at his jaw. *Bactria's going to hit back at us just as soon as they can manage it. They daren't leave us alone. If they do, all those lives their armed forces lost on Laredo will have been in vain. Their people won't stand for it. More to the point, the nobles who've staked their reputation on Bactrian superiority won't stand for it. They can't, because the people will revolt against them if they do. They've whipped up popular sentiment with their propaganda, but if they're not careful it'll make a noose for their own necks.*

We can't invade Bactria, and I wouldn't want to even if we could. Why get bogged down on another planet when we won't have enough people to properly rebuild our own? We may have to launch an appeal for immigrants after we free Laredo – and that's going to open a whole new can of worms. What if we succeed in attracting new people, but they want to live in their kind of society rather than what we had before the war?

To end the threat from Bactria we're ultimately going to have to hit them so hard they bleed – and do it in their own system, not at Laredo. Sanctions are part of that, so they can't replenish their stocks of weapons or build up their economy in a hurry. Tamsin's running with that ball already. Then, we've got to make sure we do enough damage that they lose the ability to threaten us until we're strong enough to resist them on our own turf. How do we do that? How can we afford to take the fight to them when we can't even afford enough food to ensure our people's survival? No. Let it lie for now. That's tomorrow's problem. I've already got more than enough to deal with today!

~ ~ ~

That night, after supper, he called the courier boat's skipper into a meeting on the bridge. "I'll be leaving the ship tomorrow morning," he told him. "I'm sending you off on your own. First, you'll head for Rolla. There should be a freighter there already, almost fully loaded with rations and other essential supplies. You must pass a message to her giving details of a rendezvous. It'll be here." He pointed to the three-dimensional Plot display, which was zoomed in on a hundred-light-year sphere surrounding the Laredo system. A red icon flashed nine light years from Laredo. "That's an unnamed star system."

The captain looked it up on the Navigation console. "It's a white dwarf star with only a single dead planet orbiting it, far out. There's nothing and no-one there."

"That's right. I want you to tell our freighter to depart for that system at once. She needs to get there by not later than the twelfth of May. She must wait in orbit around its planet until she hears from me."

"OK. Next?"

"Our other freighter is to head for Neue Helvetica and report to our Ambassador to the United Planets for orders. I want you to do the same, taking with you messages I'll give you for our Vice-President Pro Tem and Ambassador. When you get there, pass the messages, then stock up with as many supplies and stores as you can load and wait to be joined by some of our people who'll take passage with you. As soon as they're aboard and our Vice-President and Ambassador have given you any messages for the rest of us, head for that white dwarf system. Join our freighter in orbit around the planet, also by not later than the twelfth of May. Transfer your passengers and messages to her, then both vessels are to wait there for further orders."

The captain hesitated. "I'm not supposed to take this ship into a conflict zone, Sir."

"That system isn't in a conflict zone. It's nine light years from Laredo. That's why I'm sending you there. Once our operations have concluded I'll send one of my ships to meet you. She'll transfer messages and passengers to you to take back to Neue Helvetica. She'll also have orders for the freighter."

"I see. I guess that'll be OK, Sir."

"Good. After you get back to Neue Helvetica, I'm not sure whether we'll renew the charter for your ship or not. That'll depend on events as they unfold. You'll be told more at the rendezvous."

"Very well, Sir."

"Thanks." Dave stretched, groaning. "I'm exhausted! Too many hours bent over a desk with no exercise tires me almost as much as a good workout. I'm going to hit the gym for half an hour to raise a sweat, then shower and hit the sack. I'll need transport to the dockyard at six tomorrow morning, please."

"I'll have our gig standing by, Sir." He hesitated. "I know I'm just a civilian skipper, Sir, and I don't have a dog in your fight: but I hope you win. I watched that documentary. It was… some of it was hideous beyond speech, Sir. I hope you make them pay for that." He held out his hand.

Dave took it. "We'll do our best. Keep your fingers crossed for us."

Laredo: May 12 2852 GSC, 05:00

In the dim half-light before the dawn, Major Tredegar cradled a cup of coffee in his hands and breathed in deeply of the fresh, cool air. *The hot months aren't far away now,* he reminded himself. *Better make the most of the late spring weather while it's here.*

A rustling in the room behind him made him look around. The tall, craggy figure of Sergeant-Major O'Connor walked carefully through the cluttered living-room of the farmhouse and joined him on the porch. "Morning, Sir," the NCO said grumpily, raising his coffee mug to his lips and sipping. *"Aaah!* That's what a man needs to get the sleep out of his eyes!"

"What time did you get in?"

"I left as soon as I got your message, Sir. I got here in the small hours. I figured you'd be up early – you always are – so I set my alarm to catch you before anyone else did."

"Thanks. What do you think the Bactrians are up to?"

O'Connor shrugged. "I reckon it's three things at once, Sir. If they're bringing in as many rations as they promise, it'll ward off starvation – but only if they distribute them. Who's going to get them? I'm willing to bet they won't send any to areas where they might end up in our hands."

"Neither would I, in their shoes. Next?"

"It'll be a propaganda exercise, Sir. They'll have journalists filming the food arriving. They may even bring some down to the surface right away and show families lining up to receive it. Last, it'll be a morale-booster for their armed forces and colonial administration, reassuring them that Bactria hasn't forgotten them."

"True enough. Most of them don't want to be here, particularly after so many have been rotated home since the Battle of Banka. The rest can't wait for their turn to come around." Tredegar sipped his coffee again. "How's the planting going?"

"Not real well, Sir. We don't have enough seed or tractors or plows or other implements, but we're doing the best we can with what we have. If we get enough rain and avoid the worst of the heat in the farming areas, we may get between a third and a half of the usual crop by harvest time."

"That may be enough to scrape by. Don't forget, we have less than half our pre-war planetary population now, and more than half of them are behind Bactrian lines. Technically, it's their responsibility to feed them."

"Y'know, I hadn't thought about that, but you're right, Sir – and given all the cattle we've been slaughtering and eating, we'll need a lot less hay and grain for them too. Even if we raise less food than usual, we might be able to last until next year. Hopefully we'll be able to plant more by then."

"If Dave Carson comes through for us, yes."

"I'm crossing everything I can for that, Sir, and tying knots in what I can't cross! We've only food enough for another month at half a ration pack per day. After that, we either fight the Bactrians for more, or we starve."

"You heard his message: 'Don't attack under any circumstances.' That's why I asked all our farmers to return to their farms and plant crops, and put you in charge of it, even though I really couldn't spare you. I needed the right person to ramrod the project, and I didn't dare settle for second best over something so important to our future."

"Gee, Sir, you'll make me blush if you're not careful!" They chuckled.

"You told them to stay put if Dave arrives?"

"Yes, Sir. Even if all our units mobilize for action, they'll carry on with their farming. They know the whole planet's depending on them."

"Truer words were never spoken. It won't do us any good to win a fight, then starve to death."

"That's what I told them, Sir. Some of 'em were a bit grumpy about it, but they got the point."

Tredegar glanced up at the lightening sky. "I wonder when those Bactrian ships will enter orbit?"

"If the messages we picked up yesterday evening are accurate, Sir, they'll be here any time now."

~ ~ ~

Tension sang intangibly in the Operating Center of LS *Liberty* like an over-tightened violin string, vibrating out of key and torturing the ear. Dave sat in the visitors' chairs once more, looking down at the scene as the well-trained OpCen crew made their final preparations.

Captain Cullew glanced at the Plot again. LS *Independence* was two thousand kilometers away to port, a very tight formation at warship velocities, even though both vessels were currently ambling along at only five per cent of light speed.

"All OpCen consoles, report in sequence."

"Plot ready, Sir."

"Communications ready, Sir."

"Electronic warfare ready, Sir."

"Weapons ready, Sir."

"Navigation ready, Sir."

"Command console is ready. Exec, call the roll from Damage Control."

Far aft in the ship, beyond the docking bay, the Executive Officer manned the Damage Control Center, which was also a backup OpCen with a limited crew. If battle damage took out the main OpCen, they'd take over and get the ship to safety. "Damage Control is ready, Sir. Engineering?"

"Engineering ready, Sir."

"Docking bay?"

"Docking bay ready, Sir."

"Damage control to Opcen, all ready, Sir."

"Good. All stations stand by." He turned to look at Dave. "We're ready, Sir. We're just waiting to hear from *Independence.*"

"Thank you." He shook his head. "It seems odd to be sitting only half a light year from Laredo, knowing that in a few minutes we'll be fighting for our lives."

"It won't be that fast, I'm sure, Sir. I reckon the Bactrian ships will be closer to the planet. We'll have time to assess the situation and make detailed plans. We'll jump at General Quarters anyway, just in case. Wouldn't do to find ourselves on top of a Bactrian corvette doing distant patrol and be unable to swat her before she swats us."

"That wouldn't be a good start to our relief mission, would it?"

"Not at all. That's also why we'll make our final hyper-jump from such short range, and so close together. Given normal margins of error, no matter how tightly we calculate things we're going to be tens of thousands of kilometers above or below, left or right, or in front of or behind our target position for arrival. We'll also be much further apart than we are now, given that both ships will have different margins of error. Of course, when you're dealing with distances measured in whole or even partial light years, such errors are tiny in comparison to the whole. We'll close up again as quickly as we can to maneuver in formation."

"What if the margin of error puts you right on top of each other? It wouldn't help if we collided."

Cullew gave a short, humorless laugh. "Don't even *think* about it, Sir! That's a very remote possibility given the millions upon millions of cubic kilometers of space that surround our arrival point, but yes, there's always that chance. I haven't heard of it actually happening yet, but in my years in the Lancastrian Commonwealth Fleet I can recall a couple of close shaves during large-scale maneuvers. It's a risk one simply has to accept when maneuvering in Fleet-size formations."

"You'll have to tell me about them sometime."

"With pleasure, Sir, but if you please, not just before we make our arrival jump!"

"I'll give you a pass until this is over."

Their mutual laughter was interrupted. "Communications to Command. Signal from *Independence:* 'Ready when you are,' Sir."

"Command to Communications, thank you. Make to *Independence,* 'We jump as planned at 05:30 precisely.' Let me know when they acknowledge."

"Communications to Command, aye aye, Sir."

~ ~ ~

Brigadier-General Khan strode into the Orbital Control Center's operations room, which had been converted from the bridge of the old freighter. He was followed by his aide, a young Lieutenant. The watch commander jumped up from behind the command console.

"Good morning, Sir."

"Morning," Khan said shortly, grumpily. "Got any coffee up here?"

"Yes, Sir. The duty watch galley is through that door there, Sir. I'm sorry we don't have a steward on duty, but –"

"Not to worry. I'll get it myself."

As he headed towards the door, the watch commander glanced at the Lieutenant. "Is he always this grumpy in the mornings?" he asked very quietly, winking.

The aide returned the wink. "We had to leave the planet very early this morning, to reach orbit in time to meet the ships," she replied equally softly. "He's not used to getting up at three-thirty."

"It must be hard being a General."

"I hope to find out for myself one day!" Shared soft laughter.

Khan returned holding a mug of coffee. "That's better! Now, where are they?"

"The armed merchant cruisers are less than thirty minutes from orbit, Sir." The watch commander indicated the Plot display. "Commodore Eschate's gig will be docking with us in about fifteen minutes."

"It's a good thing I got here early, then. It wouldn't do to have a visiting Flag Officer beat the General Officer in Command to the punch! Where's our AMC?"

"She was on the far side of the planet when the other two arrived at the system boundary, Sir, but she circled round to meet them. They're all inbound in formation. I understand it's a public relations thing, Sir; they wanted images of all three ships in tight formation to take back to Bactria with them. They launched a cutter to get vid of them together."

"I see. Where's the monthly freighter?"

"In orbit behind us, Sir. She's finished disembarking her cargo, and is cleaning out her personnel pods, sanitary tanks and environmental systems before loading passengers for the return trip to Bactria."

"And the corvette?"

"In orbit ahead of us, Sir, preparing to depart this evening. She'll take the journalists aboard as soon as they have their stories and vid from planetside."

"Good. The less time they spend here, the better!"

Khan thought moodily to himself as he sipped his coffee and stared at the Plot display. *All we need are interfering busybody journalists running all over the planet asking damn fool questions! We didn't publicly announce that we've pulled back our forces to Tapuria and nearby towns. If they aren't here for long, we can hide that; but if they stay, they'll be sure to figure it out in due course. The Satrap will be furious if I allow that to become public knowledge. He let me keep my post — and my head — after the debacle at the prison camps, but I won't get away with another screw-up. I wonder what new orders this Commodore is bringing for me?*

He endured the formal, official welcoming ceremony for the Commodore in the docking bay and their long trek up the automated walkway from the rear of the ship to the bridge in the forward third of her spine. After a brief inspection of the bridge crew, he invited the Commodore to join him in the adjoining conference room. His aide and a couple of crew members served coffee and a tray of sweet rolls, then withdrew.

"So, what's the word from Bactria?" he asked as they closed the door, trying to sound offhand.

"It's fair to middling," his visitor replied, taking a pastry from his plate and biting into it. He waited until he'd chewed and swallowed, then went on, "As the Satrap told you in his last message, we can't reinforce Termaz with more troops right now. We're facing too many demands and challenges back home. By the way, your statement last year that Termaz wasn't worth one more Bactrian life almost cost you your job. General Demetrias accused you of defeatism and wanted you relieved, and General Gedrosia of the SS wanted you court-martialed. The Satrap overruled them both, you'll be pleased to hear. Rear-Admiral Stasanor and I supported you, as did the Minister of War and his deputy. It came down to a 5-4 vote by the War Council in the end."

Brigadier-General Khan grimaced. "I'm very grateful for your support, Commodore. I wanted to put the matter as plainly as possible. With a rejuvenated Resistance to deal with, and far too few combat units to do so decisively, we face the prospect of heavy casualties if hostilities are renewed.

I'm mindful of the impact on Bactria of our losses during the big fight in Tapuria two years ago. I don't know whether we dare risk another blow to morale like that, whether in the armed forces or the general public. That's one reason why I've tacitly accepted the unspoken truce offered by the rebels, at least so far. I suppose they don't want heavy casualties any more than we do."

"Agreed. However, General Gedrosia pointed out that while they were being 'left in peace', as he put it, they were training their new recruits, arming them with the weapons and equipment they stole from us, and getting more battle-ready by the day."

Khan shrugged. "That's true, of course. We could have interrupted it, but after the escape they had several hundred battle-hardened veterans to oppose us. It would have cost us multiple casualties for every one we managed to inflict on them, just as it's always been since we invaded. If the Satrap was prepared to countenance such a cost, I'd have gone ahead; but that's why I waited, to give him a chance to assess wider priorities and make a decision in Bactria's best interests overall. It seems he agreed with my assessment, even if only tacitly."

"He did. He said as much privately to Admiral Stasanor and myself during our planning for this exchange of ships."

The Brigadier-General exhaled with relief. "I can't tell you how happy it makes me to hear that. I'd been wondering how securely my head was attached to my shoulders."

"Not very securely at all if the SS had its way, but I don't think you need worry about them at present. They've screwed up horribly." He explained the actions of the dead SS agent at the research facility of the Satrap's Guard. "No-one seems to know who ordered it, or authorized it, or knew anything about it. General Gedrosia went so far as to offer to undergo truth-tester examination, along with all his senior officers, to prove none of them were involved. For a moment I thought the Satrap was going to accept his offer, even though that would have been a terminal insult to them. I've never seen him so angry before. It's almost as if he had a personal stake in the place or something. Anyway, the repercussions are still going on. The SS is making like a tortoise, pulling its head back into its shell until the shouting and tumult are over."

Khan was grinning from ear to ear. "Just between the two of us, Commodore, I trust you'll forgive me if I indulge in a moment of *schadenfreude* over this."

"Just between the two of us, General, Admiral Stasanor and I have already done that; but I'll be delighted to join you in another one."

They were still chuckling when a knock came at the door. The General's aide opened it. "Sir, the three AMC's have all entered orbit. The journalists will come here to witness the first shipments being transferred to OrbCon's holds. They'll arrive in about twenty minutes, if you want to meet them in the docking bay, Sir. They'll then accompany some shipments planetside aboard cargo shuttles to witness the start of distribution."

"Very good. Thank you, Lieutenant."

As the door closed he remarked, "I suppose I must get back to the docking bay. Can't have those pesky journalists think they're not important enough for the Commanding General to meet them, you know."

The Commodore nodded ruefully. "Why they have such an inflated opinion of themselves I don't know."

"We'll just have to cater to their sensibilities. Hopefully we'll get some good publicity in return." He glanced at the time display on the wall. "It's 06:27. We've just time for another cup of coffee."

"Thank you. I don't mind if I do."

The Commodore reached for the coffee pot – and froze in his seat for a shocked, unbelieving moment as a harsh buzzer sounded an alert in the OpCen outside. He thrust himself to his feet and lunged for the door, ignoring his chair as it clattered to the floor behind him. He heard the astonished Brigadier-General ask, "What the...?", but he didn't bother to reply.

He found the duty watch staring in bewilderment at the Plot display. The operator looked up to see him bearing down on the console, and stammered, "S – Sir, two unknown contacts detected at the system boundary. We aren't expecting any traffic except your ships, and the new arrivals' drive signatures don't match anything in our database."

"What are they doing? *Quick*, man! Pull yourself together!"

The operator bent over his console, fingers flying across the controls as he analyzed the inputs from OrbCon's sensors. "Ah... they're moving to join up with each other, Sir, and accelerating towards the planet. They're...

I don't believe it, Sir! They're already at point zero five Cee! No merchant ship can accelerate that fast!"

"They carried most of that velocity into their final hyper-jump, Spacer," the Commodore reminded him, eyes riveted to the Plot. "Designate targets as Alpha and Bravo, and classify them as bogeys – potentially hostile, but not yet certain. I want their rate of acceleration as soon as you can give it to me."

"Aye aye, Sir!"

He spun around to the Communications console, vaguely aware that the Brigadier was standing in the door to the conference room, watching him, mouth agape. "Communications, get me an open circuit to all ships right away. Fast as you can!"

"Aye aye, Sir! Everyone should be monitoring Guard channel." He tapped in a series of instructions. "I've alerted them all, Sir." He offered a microphone.

"Thank you. Attention all vessels! Attention all vessels! This is Commodore Eschate. You should all have seen on your Plot displays that two unidentified ships have arrived at the system boundary. No traffic was expected. They may be harmless visitors, or they may be ships operated by the rebels. Be ready for anything. Preliminary orders are as follows. Armed merchant cruisers are to remain in orbit and continue offloading supplies, but be ready to go to General Quarters at short notice. Freighter is to stay put. Corvette is to go to General Quarters at once and stand by for my arrival. All vessels, listen for further orders on this frequency. Eschate out."

He turned, to find the Brigadier at his side. "You think they're the enemy?"

"I can't say yet, Brigadier, but I'll be surprised if they're not. We weren't expecting even one ship, let alone two. We'll know more as soon as we can calculate their speed."

"Why are you going aboard the corvette?"

"If it's the enemy I'll take her out to intercept them. If they look like simple armed merchant cruisers, similar to ours, I'll have our AMC's follow me; but if they show the same kind of performance as the mystery ship that sent that radio message a few months ago, our AMC's will be hopelessly outclassed in terms of performance. In that case, I'll leave them in orbit to provide what point defense they can to OrbCon and the planet. After the destruction of the space station, there's nothing else available to do that."

"What should I do?"

"Let's wait until we're more certain what they are. If they're the enemy, you'll –"

He was interrupted by the Plot operator. "Sir, they're accelerating very fast. They're already up to point-zero-eight Cee. They're heading straight for us, and closing up into tighter formation."

"That settles it! With acceleration like that, it's got to be the rebels, Brigadier. They're already almost an hour closer to us than the Plot indicates – don't forget, light speed delay is affecting our sensors. By now they're almost a third of the way in from the system boundary. I suggest you take your shuttle back down to the planet right away and prepare your defenses."

"You're right. I'll –"

Another interruption. "Communications to Commodore. Sir, a message has just come through in clear over multiple radio frequencies. It reads, 'Carson to Tredegar. Stand by for action.' It's repeated over and over, Sir."

Khan grimaced. "That'll be their President Pro Tem. I'm not surprised he's here himself. He was a soldier – and, by all accounts, a good one – before he became a politician."

"I venture to doubt he's a politician at all, General. He may be acting as one now because circumstances forced it upon him, but a leopard can't change its spots, to quote the Old Home Earth proverb. He's coming for a fight."

"Then I hope and trust you'll give him one, Commodore."

"I'll... come into the conference room again for a moment."

They hurried back into the soundproof room, and Eschate closed the door. "Brigadier, they're already moving faster than any merchant ship. I think they're operating former military transports converted to carry weapons." He hurriedly explained about the eight assault transports sold by the Bismarck Cluster the year before.

"They know we've got a fully-fledged warship here, yet they're still coming in at full bore. That means they're confident they can handle anything we throw at them, and probably throw some pretty good punches themselves. I'll do my best, but my best may not be good enough. If it's not, the defense of the planet will fall on your shoulders alone." He hesitated. "If worse comes to worst, please tell my wife and children how I died, will you?"

Khan stared at him, gulped, and offered his hand. "I'll do that, but remember what I said. I don't think Termaz is worth another Bactrian life – particularly not yours!"

"That can't be helped now. There's another reason to fight. We don't know what weapons the rebels have. I'll order the AMC's to monitor the engagement using their sensors and record as much information as possible, and tell them to obey your orders if my ship's destroyed. It'll be up to you to find a way to get the information back to Bactria. That'll help the rest of the Navy prepare for what may come their way in due course. It's *essential* that the information gets to them. I'm relying on you."

"I'll do my best. I hope and pray you survive and triumph. If not, and if I'm spared, I'll make sure the Satrap hears of your courage and determination. May the Gods protect you and strengthen your arm!"

"I hope they hear you. You'd better head back to the planet. You can't command ground forces very easily from up here."

~ ~ ~

"They'll have seen our arrival by now, Sir, and intercepted our message to Major Tredegar and your compatriots on Laredo," Captain Cullew advised from the command console.

"Thank you. I wonder what they'll do about us?"

"It'll be interesting to see, Sir. We've already covered a third of the distance to the planet from the system boundary, but they've only just detected our arrival. They can't see what we've done since then. Light speed delay is working in our favor. Now it's going to start working in theirs, too, because we won't see their movements for thirty-five minutes after they make them."

"What would you do in their shoes?"

"I'm not sure, Sir. The fact that we're coming in at such high speed will tell them we're military vessels, but they won't know if we're warships or fleet auxiliaries. Our confidence in steering straight for them must also indicate that we have weapons of our own, and we think we can handle theirs. Given that they've only one real warship there, plus those three armed merchant cruisers – if they're all AMC's, which we don't yet know for sure; some may be merchant freighters – I'd expect them to be cautious. I'd have the corvette intercept us while the AMC's head away from us on the far side of the planet, in the hope that the corvette can either destroy or damage us, or delay us enough for them to escape. Alternatively, I'd leave the AMC's in orbit to provide local defense and stop us entering orbit ourselves, or taking out OrbCon. I guess it's a toss-up, Sir."

"You reckon we can deal with the corvette?"

"Definitely, Sir. We loaded the heaviest and longest-ranged target missiles for this mission. They were all formerly battleship main battery missiles, which means they're much faster than a corvette's missiles and have two to three times the range. They may lack warheads, but we'll launch enough of them to swamp her defenses. After that, all we need is one good solid contact hit."

"What about any missiles that run past her? The planet will be in their line of fire. We daren't risk them hitting it."

"No, Sir. Their self-destruct sequence still works. It'll cut off the mag bottle containing the fusion reaction in their propulsion systems, but not the reactor itself. The reaction will go out of control and expand outwards until it's consumed all the fuel available, in the process reducing the missile to its component atoms. In effect, it'll be a small thermonuclear explosion in its own right. Any missiles damaged, but not destroyed, by enemy defensive fire will do the same thing."

"Sounds like you've put a lot of thought into their self-destruct systems."

"Yes, Sir. The Fleet tries to make them as foolproof as possible. No-one wants to run into a drifting, derelict missile that can't be detected in time to avoid it. There are more than enough hazards to space navigation without adding to them."

"Well, those Bactrian ships are about to run head-on into the biggest hazard to space navigation they've ever encountered – namely, us!"

Laredo: May 12 2852 GSC, 07:30

"Turnover, Sir! Both enemy ships have turned end-for-end and begun braking."

"Right on time." Commodore Eschate peered into the Plot display from his seat behind the Command console. "That'll let them come to a stop relative to Laredo before they get into range of any missiles fired from orbit."

"They seem pretty confident, Sir," Commander Stater observed. "They're braking even before they've passed us. If I'd been in their shoes, I'd have wanted to keep my speed and kinetic energy high until after the initial exchange of fire was over."

"Enemy formation is changing, Sir!" the Plot operator exclaimed. As they watched, the two icons in the plot identifying Targets Alpha and Bravo began to split, moving apart.

Eschate nodded. "Pincer movement, to prevent us concentrating our fire on them while forcing us to divide our defensive fire. I'm surer than ever that it's not rebels in command of those ships. They've hired experienced Spacer officers from somewhere."

Stater looked around at his superior officer. "Sir, they're approaching one hundred million kilometers range. We're doing a quarter of light speed, same as them, so our closing velocity is point five Cee. I plan to launch our missiles at a distance of twelve million kilometers, because that closing velocity will have the effect of more than doubling their useful range to target. I'll launch ten missiles at each of the enemy ships. Let's see what their defenses are like."

"I agree, Commander. That'll use half your main battery missiles, and keep half in reserve in case a second pass is needed – although it'll take us hours to come around after we pass them, of course. What are your plans for defensive fire?"

"I don't know yet, Sir," the corvette's Commanding Officer admitted frankly. "It depends what they throw at us. All forty defensive missiles are on standby, and our three laser cannon turrets as well. I'll keep the rest of my main battery missiles on standby too, just in case, even though they're not primarily defensive weapons."

The tension in the corvette's OpCen ratcheted even higher as the range dropped below one hundred million kilometers, the ships streaking towards to each other at the unimaginable closing velocity of almost one hundred and fifty thousand kilometers per second. The ship's electronic systems struggled to cope with the added complications of relativistic motion and Lorentz transformation as they plotted firing solutions for the main battery missiles. The defensive missiles alongside them were on standby, ready to deal with any incoming fire.

~ ~ ~

"Weapons to Command. They're still coming, Sir," the Weapons Officer reported, eyes glued to his console as he ran constant checks and updates on his firing solution. "No course change."

"Command to Weapons, very well." Captain Cullew glanced back at Dave. "They can't do much else, Sir. Now that we're splitting our formation, they've basically got to go right down the middle between us if they want their missiles to have an equal chance of hitting both ships."

"But you don't think they'll fire before we do?"

"They can't, Sir. Their relatively small missiles will have a range from rest of six to seven million kilometers. You can double that as a range to target because of our closing velocity, but even so, I doubt they can fire further out than about twelve million kilometers. Our missiles are former battleship weapons. They may be only kinetic weapons now, with no warheads, but we have three different models in our tubes with effective

220

ranges of fifteen to eighteen million clicks from rest. Our closing velocity doubles that, too, so we're going to fire our salvos at a range of thirty million kilometers from them."

"And they don't know what's coming?"

"I don't see how they can, Sir."

"Will they have time to shoot back?"

"That depends what they decide to do, Sir. Corvette fire control systems are smaller and more limited than those of larger warships. Basically, they can control an offensive salvo or a defensive barrage, but not both at once. In their shoes I'd put up a defensive barrage with every missile I had, offensive or defensive, then dodge to try to avoid whatever gets through it. However, they might decide to fire at us at extreme range in the hope of getting a lucky hit, and only then switch to defensive missile control. We'll be taking evasive action, of course, in case they do that."

"I understand. Will they try to evade as well?"

"I'm sure they will, Sir, but they won't have much time after firing. They'll be able to make one, perhaps two changes of course, but after that they'll have to rely on their point defense to take out anything that gets close enough to threaten them."

The Plot operator interrupted them. "Plot to Command, range to enemy one hundred million kilometers, Sir."

"Command to Plot, thank you. Break. Command to Electronic Warfare. Launch a drone now in silent mode. As soon as the salvo has been fired, activate its program and put the ship in silent mode without waiting for further orders."

"EW to Command, launching drone now, activating automated programming, Sir."

"Command to Weapons. You are cleared to engage as previously authorized at thirty million kilometers range without waiting for further orders. Weapons free."

"Weapons to Command, weapons free, activating automated programming, Sir."

"Command to Navigation. As soon as our salvo has been launched and the drone is activated, implement Duck-And-Dive without waiting for further orders."

"Navigation to Command, Duck-And-Dive programmed, Sir."

Captain Cullew turned back to the Plot display. In a voice so quiet Dave could barely hear him, he whispered, "May God have mercy on their souls… and on ours." He looked around at Dave. "It's in the hands of the computers now, Sir. Humans react too slowly at space warfare speeds, so we leave it to electronic brains instead."

~ ~ ~

A long, narrow hatch opened on the port side of LS *Liberty*, ejecting an electronic warfare drone. Already moving at the same speed as its mother ship, it drifted slowly away, paralleling its trajectory. Its internal fusion reactor spooled up, providing power to its gravitic drive and electronic systems. It twisted in space, aligning itself with the ship's direction of travel, then started forward under minimum thrust, its low power levels emitting a signal so weak as to be undetectable at anything but close range. The drone moved to a point between its mother ship and the enemy, then held that position as it waited to be activated.

Two cells containing fifty missiles each had been installed in *Liberty*'s holds. Once battleship main battery weapons, then repurposed as targets, they were now deadly kinetic energy threats even though they lacked warheads. The ship's massive reactors had kept them warmed up and ready for action during the approach. Now forty missiles, twenty in each cell, spaced evenly across its length and width, came to life as their internal fusion reactors were started. Their gravitic drives came to standby mode as their sensors and navigation systems received information from the ship's fire control system. Their electronic brains and artificial intelligence software ran self-checks as they absorbed the data, fed it as input to their control programs, and waited.

Around the bow massive maneuvering reaction thrusters swiveled out of their housings, pointing straight up. Others did likewise at the stern.

A hundred thousand kilometers to port, the same sequence of events took place aboard LS *Independence* as she sped along on the same course at the same speed. An automated self-test of one of her missiles indicated a possible malfunction. Instantly it was powered down and flagged for the attention of a maintenance crew at a more appropriate time. An alternate missile was selected, brought online, tested, and incorporated into the firing pattern.

Aboard both ships, their Weapons Officers locked in an automated firing program. The battle computers would take their cue from the ships' passive sensors, which were counting down the rapidly decreasing range as they focused on the Bactrian corvette's gravitic drive emissions. The active sensors – radar and lidar – were silent. At this range they would be worse than useless; in fact, if switched on, their emissions would only indicate the ships' positions more clearly to the enemy. They had no place in such long-range missile combat. Nevertheless, they were on standby, ready to assist with the defense of the ship if needed.

At fifty million kilometers' range from their target, the caps over the selected missile tubes in each ship slid back into the framework of their missile cells. Simultaneously the vessels' reactors spooled up to maximum output. Just over half a minute later, at forty-five million kilometers' range, the fire control computers energized the powerful electromagnetic mass drivers in the selected tubes. The missiles quivered on their launch rails as final system checks were performed. Aboard *Liberty* a tube's mass driver malfunctioned. At once it was dropped from the attack roster and the missile it contained was flagged as unavailable. A backup missile and tube were activated, brought to a ready state and their systems checked, then slotted into the ship's firing pattern.

The ships hurtled onward through the vacuum of space. At such speeds, the effects of relativity rendered raw sensor data unreliable. The battle computers used complex algorithms to allow for space-time distortion and make the data usable. Their ultra-powerful processors made billions of calculations every second, refining the missiles' targeting information so that their less powerful onboard sensors and processors would have the best possible data at launch. After that, it would be up to them to home on the enemy's gravitic drive and other emissions as the range closed.

At forty million kilometers the battle computers signaled the fusion reactors on board every missile. They came to life, spooling up to maximum power, preparing to funnel their output to the gravitic drives that would send the weapons streaking to destruction – their own, and hopefully the enemy's as well.

At thirty-one million kilometers the battle computers sent the last updates to the missiles' own computers, then cut their links. From now on it would be up to the weapons to guide themselves.

At thirty million kilometers everything seemed to happen at once. The missile cells began vomiting their lethal cargoes, three missiles every second spearing outwards, using the mass drivers in their tubes to get clear of the gravitic drive fields of their launching vessels as quickly as possible. As each reached a distance of two to three kilometers from the hull its own gravitic drive sprang to life, turning the missile sharply ahead, aiming at the calculated position where it would intercept the enemy ship at the end of its run. Already moving at one-quarter of the speed of light, the drives thrust the missiles forward, accelerating hard, their sensors searching for the enemy's emissions to home on them.

Three missiles experienced malfunctions that prevented launch, and one weapon's gravitic drive failed to engage as it thrust outward. Its onboard systems tried again, then a third time, but without success. As soon as the missile's control system calculated it had traveled fifty kilometers from the point where it was launched, it deactivated the magnetic 'bottle' enclosing and containing the fusion reaction that powered it. The resulting eruption of superheated thermonuclear plasma reduced the errant missile to its component molecules, eliminating any threat to navigation from a derelict drifting in vacuum.

The remaining missiles disappeared into the blackness of space. As the last one leapt from its tube, the electronic warfare drones began spooling up their output over a carefully calculated space of three seconds. Over the same period, the ships' own gravitic drives and other emitters spooled down until they were silent, inactive. Because the drones were positioned precisely between the ships and their target, sensors on the latter vessel didn't detect the change. Now they were tracking the drones, which proceeded to curve upward and outward, imitating an evasive maneuver.

Behind them, the ships activated their upward-aimed reaction thrusters. They gave off no electromagnetic radiation at all, and at so great a range the light emitted from their throats was as good as invisible. They thrust the ships bodily downward, dropping them below their existing trajectory. As soon as the desired change was established the thrusters were cut off, their angle was altered, then they were reactivated at low power to roll the ships onto their backs, exposing the four laser cannon turrets set into their sides and bellies. The turrets swiveled towards the direction from which enemy missiles would approach, but the radar and lidar systems that would guide their fire remained silent for the time being. They would be activated only if needed. The maneuver completed, the thrusters turned to face in the direction of travel and went to full power once more, braking the ship, slowing her progress, allowing the drone to pull ahead of her. The thrusters couldn't provide anything like as much braking energy as the gravitic drive, but unlike the drive they emitted no radiation onto which enemy missiles could home.

The two groups of missiles bore down on the Bactrian corvette at ever-increasing, mind-boggling velocity. They spread out in space in accordance with their pre-programmed trajectories, offering a multitude of targets to the enemy's countermeasures, avoiding clumping together so that a single defensive missile couldn't take out more than one or two of them.

~ ~ ~

The team in the corvette's OpCen froze. Time seemed to stand still for an endless moment as the torrent of missiles shown in the Plot display grew... and grew... and grew. Commodore Eschate realized with a sort of detached bemusement that he wasn't breathing. His heart was pounding furiously within his chest. He tried to cudgel his brain into action, but all he could hear was a shrill voice yammering in an echoing silence inside his head. *They've launched twice as many offensive missiles as we have defensive missiles – and from far outside our range! Where the hell did they get weapons like that?*

The Plot operator reported, "S – Seventy-six missiles inbound, closing speed point-five-five Cee and climbing, time to arrival estimated one hundred fifty-two seconds!" He sounded incredulous, as if he couldn't believe the evidence offered to his eyes by his own display.

Commander Stater was the first to snap out of his astonishment. *"Attention!* Weapons, use all forty main battery missiles, not half as previously planned. We'll only have time for one salvo, twenty missiles to each enemy ship. Aim ten at their emissions signature, but they might be using drones, so aim ten more in a wide circle around the interception point where they would have been if they'd continued on the same course and speed as before they fired. Those ten are to use their active sensors to search for a target. As soon as the main battery missiles have gone, use our defensive missiles on the leading incoming weapons. If you have time, concentrate on those that maintain a constant bearing on us. They're the biggest threat. EW, launch both drones, one to head for each group of incoming missiles. They'll distract some of them. Helm, stand by for an emergency course change, climbing to starboard as soon as the main battery missiles and drones have launched, then – if we have time – a second change diving to port as soon as the defensive missiles have been fired."

A rush of replies, interspersed with scattered, muffled curses and muttered oaths, greeted his commands. The Commodore found time to be proud of the OpCen crew as they swung into action. Even staring almost certain death in the face, they were responding like professionals.

Commander Stater spun his command chair to face him. His face was deathly white, beads of sweat clinging to his forehead, but his eyes were steady. "Sir, there's just time for you to abandon ship. If you take the lifeboat abaft the bridge and direct it straight downward the instant you launch, you'll be clear of our present trajectory by the time the missiles arrive."

Eschate shook his head. "I…" He had to clear his throat. "I can't do that, Commander. We're in this together, whatever happens."

"Thank you, Sir," Stater said simply. He held out his hand, and the Commodore leaned forward to squeeze it hard.

"Fight the enemy, Commander. Don't worry about me. I've got to send an urgent message to the ships in orbit around the planet."

"Go ahead, Sir."

Eschate thrust himself to his feet and crossed to the Communications console, forcing himself to control legs that suddenly felt weak and shaky. "Give me a microphone and put me on Guard channel, so all the ships in orbit will hear me. We're a long way from the planet, so use full power on your transmitter."

"Y – Yessir!" The operator handed him a microphone, his hand visibly trembling, and pressed a couple of controls. "Live, Sir."

He hesitated for a moment, knowing that the rebel ships would hear this transmission too and take full advantage of it. Even so, he could not honorably condemn more of his spacers to a pointless death. He took a deep breath.

"This is Commodore Eschate calling all ships. The enemy has launched twice as many missiles at us as we're carrying. Their effective range appears to be at least double that of our weapons, if not more. Furthermore, they won't have emptied their missile cells at us – they're certain to be carrying more of them. Given their overwhelming advantage in performance and weapons, all ships in orbit are hereby ordered to surrender rather than fight. You haven't got the speed to run away from them, and there's no sense in throwing your lives away against an enemy whose paint you can't even scratch with your short-range missiles. Obey their orders and preserve the lives of your crews. Convey my apologies to Brigadier-General Khan. Tell him from me that the orbitals are lost. The surface defense of Termaz is in his hands. Eschate out."

He handed back the microphone, then turned on his heel as the Plot operator announced, "Time to first missile now thirty seconds!"

He didn't bother going back to his seat. He'd meet his fate standing on his own two feet. Numbly he tried to force his mind to pray.

~ ~ ~

The enemy's missiles were approaching at a closing speed of well over six-tenths of light speed. They would have been moving even faster but for the effects of relativity, which increased their mass and hampered their gravitic drives' rate of acceleration – not that it would have made much difference at such already-staggering velocities.

By the time the corvette got within twelve million kilometers' range of the two rebel ships, the first incoming missiles were less than half a minute from impact. The Weapons Officer launched all forty main battery missiles, but by the time the last one left its tube there were fewer than ten seconds left to program the defensive missiles. He barraged all forty of them in a single salvo, abandoning any attempt to guide them individually, trusting to sheer blind chance that their internal systems might be able to home on a target.

The decoys sucked more than a dozen of the first incoming missiles off target, but they were destroyed by the resulting kinetic impacts, removing their distracting influence from follow-up weapons. The first defensive missiles took out the next group of onrushing enemy weapons at desperately close range, their thermonuclear detonations forming a blast front of heat and light in front of the dodging, twisting corvette. That provided a measure of protection from the next few missiles, whose sensors could no longer home on the corvette's emissions through the radiation. They streaked through the blast front, searched for a few moments, found nothing within range, and self-destructed in thermonuclear plasma fireballs.

Unfortunately, the corvette's climb and turn to starboard took her clear of the concealment provided by her detonating defensive missiles. The remaining thirty-plus attacking missiles swerved to meet her, and at such extreme velocities they offered only split seconds for the warship's three laser cannon to target them. Two of the cannon scored hits on onrushing missiles, blinding their sensors and sending them tumbling... but there were too many more screaming in behind them.

Several missiles howled past the little ship, missing by no more than one to two kilometers, but no-one on the corvette ever knew they had come so close. The next incoming missile tracked the Bactrian warship from a long way out by her drive emissions, saw her desperate climbing turn, adjusted its trajectory, and slammed into her head-on at a closing velocity of point six four two Cee. The kinetic energy released by the collision, at that speed, of a two hundred ton battleship main battery missile and a thirty thousand ton corvette, dwarfed the energy of any thermonuclear warhead ever fitted to any missile. The fireball expanded several kilometers in all directions, blinding white at first, fading to yellow, then orange, then crimson, then turning brown and black. The corvette and the missile were reduced to their component atoms, along with every member of the warship's crew.

They didn't live long enough to see their own missiles arrive at the enemy's positions.

~ ~ ~

There was no need to issue commands in the operating centers aboard *Liberty* and *Independence*. All the preparations that could be made, had been made. Now it was up to the console operators and the battle computers.

The missiles aimed at the ships' drones were ignored. They could safely spend their bomb-pumped laser warheads on the harmless decoys. Those making for where the ships would have been had they continued on their original courses and speeds were another matter. Those weapons were actively searching, using onboard sensors to seek out their targets. There were no gravitic drive emissions for them to find, but if one or more of them happened to catch even the most fleeting glimpse of a target...

Two of them spotted *Liberty*. The battle computers, tracking their drive emissions, detected the sudden jink as they changed course to intercept, and automatically activated the immense active electronic scanned arrays paneled around the ship's hull. A torrent of radar and lidar energy bathed the onrushing missiles as the laser cannon turrets spun, locked onto the bearing, and began to fire.

At a third of a million kilometers' range the first of the incoming missiles collected a laser beam full on its nose, followed an instant later by a second. Its sensors blinded, it could no longer figure out where to aim. It rushed past the ship, useless, to self-destruct a few seconds later.

The second missile dodged left as it detected the laser cannon emissions, then dodged right again. It snaked past three laser bolts, swiveled to point its bomb-pumped laser head at the ship, and detonated. Its warhead blasted thirty laser generating rods with megatons of thermonuclear energy, in the instant of their destruction sending a tightly focused cone of laser beams flashing across the twelve thousand kilometers separating the missile from its target.

The laser cone was designed to encompass a target the size of a corvette from stem to stern at that range. Against a much larger vessel like a *Bavaria* class transport it could hardly miss. Twenty-three of its thirty beams struck home. Thanks to *Liberty* having rolled onto her back to unmask the laser cannon, most of them hit cargo holds or utility spaces in the belly of the ship, missing vital installations, inflicting minimal harm and no casualties.

Two beams caused more serious damage. One smashed Laser Cannon Three into scrap metal and electronic slag; but as it was an unmanned barbette design rather than a manned turret, no-one was hurt. Not so the second beam. It ripped into the port docking bay in the rear of the hull, destroying a cutter, blasting through the wreckage and the airlock beyond it into the foyer, venting the local atmosphere to vacuum. The damage control party waiting in the foyer had no warning. Four died instantly as pieces of steel were blasted loose from the hull, slashing through the spaces where they were standing. Two more were injured, one grievously, as their spacesuits were pierced by multiple smaller fragments. The others, further from the impact site, were left stunned and shaken as the air around them rushed out into space with a hissing, moaning sound that quickly died away to leave them standing in vacuum, protected by their spacesuits.

Airtight doors throughout the ship were closed during General Quarters. They confined the loss of atmosphere and prevented it spreading beyond the docking bay. Alarms clanged in the Damage Control Center, where the Executive Officer was manning the backup OpCen. Space-suited rescue parties were instantly dispatched to set up temporary airlocks to give access to the damaged area, help their comrades, assess the situation, and make whatever running repairs were needed to keep the ship fighting.

~ ~ ~

Dave waited tensely in the visitor's area behind the Command console as Captain Cullew and his team responded to the damage, assessed the ship's condition, and confirmed the destruction of the Bactrian corvette. It seemed like hours, but was in reality only a couple of minutes, before the Captain turned to face him.

"All's well, Sir. We've taken moderate damage, but we're still spaceworthy and fighting fit, apart from one laser cannon that'll need to be replaced at a dockyard. Our port docking bay will be out of action until repaired, but our starboard bay is still operational. I don't yet know our casualties, Sir – we're waiting for rescuers to get into the damaged bay – but there are bound to be some. You heard the transmission from the enemy commander to his ships in orbit, Sir. What's next?"

"I want to make sure we capture those ships intact, with all their systems in working order. How do we stop their crews sabotaging them?"

Cullew pursed his lips. "Tricky, Sir. We're an hour away from orbit, and we can't afford to get within range of their missiles until we've neutralized them. We're going to have to come to a halt relative to the planet, about eight to ten million kilometers away, and send over Gurkha boarding parties in assault shuttles to take possession of each ship. They'll have to round up their crews and lock them up, perhaps using the OrbCon freighter as a temporary prison, so that we can send prize crews to take control of every ship. That's going to be a problem in itself – there are three armed merchant cruisers, a freighter, and OrbCon itself. We don't have enough Spacers to provide crews for them all. We'll have to put anchor watches aboard until we figure out what to do next."

"All right. Put me on that circuit the enemy commander used and give me a microphone."

"Aye aye, Sir. Command to Communications, give Brigadier-General Carson a microphone and put him on the planetary Guard channel at full power."

"Communications to Command, aye aye, Sir."

Dave walked over to the console, accepted the offered microphone, and gathered his thoughts as he pressed the 'Transmit' button.

"Attention all Bactrian vessels in orbit around Laredo – or Termaz, as you call our planet. This is Brigadier-General David Carson, President Pro Tem of Laredo's Government-in-Exile and Commanding Officer of her off-planet forces. Listen carefully.

"You heard the orders of your late Commanding Officer. I require you to obey them, and my orders, to the letter. You will shut down all your weapons systems and sensors immediately and withdraw all operators from them and their consoles. You will preserve all your ships' systems, without exception, intact and undamaged. Any deviation will result in your being treated as pirates rather than prisoners of war – and you know the punishment for piracy. It *will* be applied instantly and without mercy. Do not doubt my determination in that regard. Your planet has slaughtered something like two-thirds of the population of mine. I'm not inclined to be any more lenient than interplanetary convention requires me to be, and even that is only on sufferance. Disobey me at your mortal peril.

"Our ships will brake to a halt relative to Laredo, then send over armed boarding parties. You will assemble your crews in central locations to await their arrival, and obey their orders. Once we've confined you aboard a single ship, we'll discuss your future. If you obey my orders and co-operate with my boarding parties, I'll consider sending you all back to Bactria aboard one of your vessels. If you don't, I can arrange many less pleasant alternatives. I suggest you keep that firmly in mind."

He took a deep breath. "Finally, inform Brigadier-General Khan on the surface of the planet that provided his forces remain confined to their bases and make no hostile moves against anyone, I won't attack them until we've had a chance to discuss matters. I'll be in touch with him as soon as we've secured the orbitals. If he does anything other than wait for me to contact him, I will bombard his forces from orbit and wipe them out to the last man. Their deaths will be on his head. That's all. Carson out."

His knees felt weak as he handed back the microphone. He noted that everyone in the OpCen was staring at him, some of them with their mouths open. He'd clearly sounded convincing to them. He thought to himself, *Now, if only I've managed to impress the enemy half as much…*

Captain Cullew nodded to him as he walked back to the Command console. "That was very persuasive, Sir, if I may say so. What will you do if Brigadier-General Khan doesn't listen to you?"

"That's a good question, Captain," Dave admitted with a grin. "We'd better make sure the General gets the message. Please prepare one of our former target missiles."

Cullew's face sobered. "Sir, you know that interplanetary convention forbids bombardment of civilian population centers."

"Oh, don't worry, Captain. I won't do that. After all, there are my own people to consider down there. No, I have something else in mind." He quickly explained.

The Captain began to smile again. "That should do it, Sir."

"I'll ask our forces on the planet to nominate a suitable target. Speaking of them, would you please send Message Two to the Resistance? We won't need the others, of course." Multiple messages had been pre-recorded to cover various degrees of success or failure. The first had been broadcast on arrival in the system. Most of the remainder were now redundant.

"Of course, Sir. Command to Communications. Send Message Two to the Resistance forces on the planet, repeated three times on all designated frequencies."

"Communications to Command, aye aye, Sir."

"How long will it take us to secure the ships in orbit?" Dave asked.

"Plan on up to twenty-four hours, Sir. During that time we'll board and search all their ships, gather up their crews and assemble them in a central location, then enter orbit ourselves."

"Very well. I'm going to think about what I'll say to Brigadier-General Khan. I'll leave you to it."

"Aye aye, Sir. *Attention in the OpCen!*"

Everyone snapped to attention, sitting or standing, as Dave strode to the door. He glanced around, nodding to acknowledge their salute, then walked out. The door slid closed behind him.

"I wonder if he realizes what an incredible achievement this has been, Sir?" the Weapons Officer said softly. "I don't think I've ever heard of a planetary Resistance on its last legs bouncing back like this, to such an extent that it's retaken the orbitals of its own planet from an enemy Fleet."

"I don't think I have either," Cullew admitted. "It's a privilege to be part of it, though. We're making history, ladies and gentlemen. This will be something to tell our grandchildren about – and I have a feeling we haven't seen anything yet."

~ ~ ~

Major Tredegar and Sergeant-Major O'Connor were sitting in the makeshift Operations Room when a Corporal barged through the door, face alight with excitement. "Sir! We've just picked up a transmission on Guard channel! The enemy commander in space has told the ships in orbit to surrender rather than fight! He says they haven't got the performance or the weapons to challenge President Carson!"

The NCO's manning desks and makeshift consoles in the Ops Room erupted in cheers and yells of delight. Tredegar shook his head, grinning from ear to ear. "I don't know how the hell Major Carson managed to do it, but I can't tell you how happy I am to hear it!"

O'Connor observed, "Unless I'm mistaken, that means he'll soon control the orbitals. Isn't the old maxim 'Control the orbitals, control the planet'? What does that mean for us, Sir?"

"I don't know, but I suspect things are about to get very interesting indeed. Corporal, get a radio in here tuned to Guard channel. I suspect the enemy will be hearing more from Major Carson very shortly."

"Yessir!"

A radio was brought in from the adjacent comms room and set up on a table, its speaker burbling gently, No sooner had it been tuned than a familiar voice crackled from its speaker. The operators listened in fascination as Dave delivered his ultimatum to the ships in orbit, and his message for them to relay to the Bactrian commander on the planet.

O'Connor whistled gently. "Does that mean what I think it means, Sir?"

"Yes. It means he's coming down. I don't know what sort of landing force he has, but if he's making demands like that he must have something with which to back them up. He'd better have, because Brigadier-General Khan isn't going to just give up. He'll have to be convinced he can't win. If he surrenders without that, he knows his head will be forfeit the moment he gets back to Bactria. What's more, his own forces will disobey his orders unless they're convinced there's no alternative."

The Sergeant-Major grinned. "I see Major Carson's promoted himself, too, Sir."

"And a good thing he did! For a start, he's now the Commanding Officer of all our off-planet forces, and if they include ships of war, that's a lot bigger than a Major's berth. Also, if he's going to negotiate with Brigadier-General Khan, he'll be of equal rank. That might be very useful."

"True, Sir. What are we going to do?"

"We wait and watch. Let's get messages out to all our units to observe what the Bactrians are doing and let us know the moment any of their units look like leaving their bases. We'll have to get word about that to Dave somehow."

They were in the midst of passing the messages when the Corporal from the communications room came in again. "Sir, this has just been broadcast on the same three frequencies as the first message to us from Major – sorry, Brigadier-General Carson."

He handed a slip of paper to Major Tredegar, who unfolded it and read it aloud. "Carson to Tredegar. These communications are not secure. I want to set up a secure channel. Can you meet my people at the rendezvous you used to meet the General's transports after you escaped from BONAPARTE? If so, put out signal panels at that location observable from orbit. As soon as possible after I see them, I'll send down a comms team. You won't know them, but I'll send a handwritten note with identifying information. Look for an assault shuttle with side panels the same color as your wife's eyes. Expect it to approach from the same direction as Nature intended. Warn your forces not to shoot at it, because it will return fire if fired upon and its weapons are a lot more deadly than those you're used to. If unable to get to that place, you'll have to use the orbital Guard channel to set up a rendezvous. Don't provide any instructions or identify any locations that the enemy might be able to understand. Use incidents from the past that we'll both remember to convey information. Until a secure channel is established, take no action upon any orders purporting to come from me. Carson out."

O'Connor frowned. "That's a bit cryptic, Sir."

"Yes, but it makes sense to me. Let's look at the map." They hurried over to the wall, and the Major pointed at a spot on the banks of the Renosa River. "That's where Brigadier-General Aldred sent transporters to meet us after we escaped from the Matopo Hills base. There's a clearing on the bank where an assault shuttle can land. I guess that bit about 'approaching from the same direction as Nature intended' means it'll come from upstream, following the flow of the river. That'll help to identify it even before we see it, because the sound should come from that direction. We don't have any bases nearby, so I'm going to take one of our captured shuttles and head out there."

"During daylight, Sir? What if the Bactrians see you? They'll be sure to fire on you."

"Now that they've pulled all their forces back they don't have any bases out there anymore. Besides, there's General Carson's message to their Commanding General. If his forces take any action against us, he knows it'll bring retaliation – Dave made that clear."

"OK, Sir, but shouldn't you stay here where you can keep your finger on the pulse of everything? I can go out there instead of you." The Sergeant-Major's voice was hopeful.

"Yes, you can, and yes, I should, dammit! Let's work out a couple of phrases to indicate success or failure, so you can let me know what's happening. Get back here with the comms team as fast as you can, so we can coordinate our actions with General Carson's."

"Yessir!"

Laredo: May 13 2852 GSC, 07:25

MILITARY HEADQUARTERS, TAPURIA

"What d'you think he's going to do, Sir?" the G-1 asked almost plaintively.

Brigadier-General Khan regarded him almost pityingly. "How, precisely, do you expect me to know that, Major Shadba? D'you think I've suddenly become clairvoyant?"

The major flushed as he shook his head. "No, Sir. Sorry, Sir."

"Never mind, Major. We're all on edge right now. None of us have had any sleep since the night before last. Stim-tabs are all very well to keep us functioning, but they don't do a damn thing to reduce stress levels – and we've all got more than enough to be stressed about." Around the table his assembled staff exchanged rueful nods and sighs.

The large display screen at the foot of the table suddenly flickered to life. It showed a mountain peak standing proud of the surrounding hills, tip gleaming in the morning sunlight. It was a peaceful scene, almost idyllic, like something out of a tourist advertisement.

"I see the feed from Camp Seven has been activated," Lieutenant-Colonel Oxus observed unnecessarily. "Mount Sinclair looks just as it's always done."

"Yes, but they wouldn't have told us to watch its peak between 07:30 and 07:45 if they weren't planning on doing something fairly spectacular," the General pointed out. He glanced at the time display on the wall of the conference room. "It's 07:28. We won't have long to wait." He pushed back his chair and stood, carrying his coffee cup to the sideboard where he refilled it. Several of his staff did likewise, some taking more breakfast pastries before resuming their seats.

Khan picked up the handset at his place and dialed a code. "Communications, confirm that all units are displaying the feed from Camp Seven on all their public displays."

The duty operator's voice came over the line. "Confirmed, Sir. We're pushing the feed to all units as you ordered."

"Thank you."

As he replaced the handset, he thought grimly, *I can guess why General Carson told me to have all my units watching. He's going to give all of us a demonstration of why continued resistance would be stupid.* He glanced at the SS Colonel across the table. He knew the man had brought a full platoon of black-uniformed SS guards with him this morning. He'd expected something like that, and had taken precautions.

"Holy *shit!*" The exclamation burst from Major Hadda as he stared at the screen. Everyone swiveled in their chairs to look, and gasped in disbelief to see the entire peak of Mount Sinclair vanish in an eruption of dust and black smoke. There was no sound on the vid feed, so the column of debris towered into the air in utter silence, roiling upwards until it was thousands of meters high, looking not unlike the mushroom cloud left by a nuclear explosion. A huge curtain-like pall of dust and debris showered down around the peak, obscuring the entire mountain, drifting westward with the strong prevailing winds for which the area was infamous.

They watched for ten minutes in awestruck silence until the outlines of the peak became visible once more – only there was no peak as such any longer. Mount Sinclair was now at least a hundred meters shorter than it had been. The steep triangle that had surmounted it now resembled a saddle carved out between two smaller and much lower peaks. Debris flows had covered the once uneven, rocky upper slopes of the mountain in a thick layer of dust, dirt, gravel and rocks. The new surface was still very unstable, small avalanches starting almost at random across its surface as they watched, sliding a few hundred meters then petering out.

Brigadier-General Khan rose from his seat, crossed to a window, and peered out. The immense black cloud of dust and dirt over Mount Sinclair was visible as a faint dark stain on the horizon. He nodded slowly to himself as he turned back to his chair – and the comm unit rang sharply. He picked it up.

"Khan."

"Sir, CommCen here. We have a direct call for you from the enemy General."

"Put it over the conference room speaker system and activate the central microphone. Make sure all units receive the feed as well, so they can listen in."

"Yes, Sir."

As he sat down he told the others, "The rebel commander wants to speak to me again. I think we all know what's coming." Grim nods and dark looks of foreboding showed they understood.

The SS Colonel snorted, "How *dare* he style himself a Brigadier-General? He was a Captain when he left here!"

"He's also now the President of their Government-in-Exile," Khan pointed out. "I've no doubt his orders when he left here, and the office he later assumed, are more than sufficient authority for him to promote anyone he wishes, including himself."

The rebel commander's face appeared on the big vid screen. He hesitated for a moment as the return feed showed him that General Khan was surrounded by other officers, then nodded. "Good morning, General. I see you have your staff with you."

"Yes, General. I felt it would be best to have them all aware of what we discuss, and provide input if necessary. I'm also sharing this feed with all our units."

He saw what he thought was a flicker of understanding in his enemy's eyes. "As you wish, General Khan. You saw the demonstration we've just provided?"

"We could hardly miss it. May I remind you that interplanetary conventions prohibit using weapons of mass destruction, including kinetic weapons, against the surface of a planet without providing adequate warning and sufficient time for those nearby to be moved to a place of safety?"

The rebel officer grinned. "First of all, those conventions apply to an *enemy* planet. Laredo is *my* planet. I'm President Pro Tem of its legitimate government, which is recognized as such by the United Planets. The conventions say nothing about a government bombarding its own planet. Secondly, the few inhabitants near the mountain were all evacuated last night by local forces. Some of them didn't want to leave, but we can be very persuasive when we have to be. That ends the problem as far as I'm concerned. I'm pretty sure the United Planets will see it that way too.

"Let's cut to the chase. There are three fully armed, equipped and trained battalions of the Resistance around your occupation area on Laredo as we speak. They're ready, willing and able to stop your forces going anywhere we don't want them to go. I brought with me another battalion of Gurkha mercenaries." He gestured to one side, and a short, wiry, brown-skinned officer wearing a dark green uniform stepped into view of the camera, coming to attention. "This is Lieutenant-Colonel Gurung, their commanding officer. The Gurkhas use assault shuttles and weapons far more modern and capable than anything in Bactria's arsenal. If you make it necessary, I'll land them to spearhead our assault on your positions. However, there won't be much left for them to assault, because if you continue to resist I'll destroy your positions from orbit with more kinetic weapons. All our forces will have to do is bury the bodies of your soldiers – what's left of them."

The Gurkha officer moved out of view of the camera as Carson continued, "On the other hand, if you're willing to be sensible and surrender, handing over all your equipment, weapons and installations in good working order without sabotaging them, I'm willing to be reasonable. We'll arrange to have you returned to Bactria as soon as your home planet can provide transportation. I'll send you and your officers back aboard one of your ships currently in orbit, all of which we've captured intact. While you're organizing transport at Bactria, your troops will be held in makeshift tented prisoner-of-war camps in remote areas of the interior. They won't be comfortable during the hot season, but they'll survive. If Bactria provides the necessary shipping, they'll all be home within a matter of months. What do you say?"

"What about Bactrian civilians? There are thousands of them here – colonial administrators and bureaucrats, military support personnel, even some settlers."

"They'll all be imprisoned with your soldiers, and return to Bactria with you. You'll have to send sufficient transport for them as well. I'll probably send back each ship with a mixed complement of passengers, half military and half civilian, until they've all been repatriated."

"And their possessions?"

"They can take what they can carry with them, to a size and weight limit to be determined. They'll lose everything else. They can claim compensation from your government, since it sent them here in the first place."

"What if some of them want to stay here – the settlers, for example?"

"No. They can't. They'll all go, whether they like it or not."

"And if they refuse? What if they won't obey when we order them to assemble?"

"Then I'll hold back some of your prisoners of war until they do, and if necessary tell local forces to round them up the hard way, whether they want to come or not. There will be no Bactrians left on Laredo, and that's final."

"What about the bodies of our dead? There are tens of thousands of them buried here."

Carson hesitated a moment. "That will have to be worked out between the governments of Bactria and Laredo at a future date."

"What about Laredans who've cooperated with us?"

"The fate of collaborators will be decided by juries of their peers through the court system once we've re-established it."

Khan hesitated. "General Carson, I have a moral responsibility to them. What if they want to return to Bactria with us, for fear of retaliation if they stay here? Will you allow that?"

Now it was the rebel leader's turn to hesitate. "I'll have to consult with planetary commanders about that," he said at last.

"I understand. How long do we have to decide whether or not to accept your ultimatum?"

"I'll give you until noon today, local time, provided your forces don't leave their present positions or make obvious preparations to do so. If they do, I'll destroy them without further warning. While you're making up your mind, I'll talk to local commanders about the collaborator problem."

"Very well. I'll call you at noon on this circuit."

"Thank you, General." The screen blinked out as Carson's image disappeared.

Khan looked around at his staff. "Well?"

The SS Colonel erupted from his seat. "How *dare* you even *consider* his demands? They're outrageous! We'll fight to the death rather than surrender! I'll –"

His eyes bulged as a shot sounded. He clutched his chest, red blood appearing on his fingers even though it was invisible on his black uniform, then collapsed forward onto the table, sliding off it to the floor. On the other side of the table, Major Hadda laid his pulser on the mat in front of him. He looked at the General. "Terribly sorry about that, Sir. Accidental discharge."

"That was very careless of you, Major. Consider yourself formally reprimanded. What about his escort?"

"With your permission, Sir, I'll go and see to their needs right away."

"Thank you, Major. Please return here once you've done so. Take your pulser with you. Who knows? You might need another accidental discharge or two." The others grinned.

"Yes, Sir." Holstering his weapon, Hadda headed for the door.

As it closed behind him, Khan asked, "Does anyone disagree that surrender is our only realistic option?"

Everyone shook their heads. Lieutenant-Colonel Oxus said, "Sir, we can't fight orbital kinetic weapons even if we wanted to. Besides, our troops have all seen that demonstration, just as we did. After that, how many of them will obey an order to fight?"

"None of them with any sense, I should think."

"Yes, Sir. There's another thing. Remember Commodore Eschate's last instructions? He said we had to get word back to Bactria about the rebel ships and their weapons. The only way we can do that is to surrender. If this General Carson keeps his word and sends us back ahead of the others, we can at least give our Navy early warning, and more time to make what preparations they can to intercept any attack on our home system. I don't see any other way to do that, Sir."

"Neither do I. However, I'll try to remain on Termaz until the last of our forces have been repatriated. I'll leave with them aboard the final ship.

I'll send all of you ahead of me with news of our surrender, and to make the necessary arrangements."

"What if the rebels won't allow you to do that, Sir?"

"I think General Carson will understand. At any rate, all I can do is ask. Begin drafting orders for our units to preserve all their equipment and installations intact, return all their weapons – and I do mean *all* weapons, without exception – to armories or secure storage, and stand by for further instructions. Include the information that if they offer no resistance and make no trouble, they'll all be repatriated to Bactria as soon as we can arrange it. Give me the draft for my approval by not later than eleven. Meanwhile, I'll work out points for an agreement of surrender to discuss with General Carson. I suspect he's going to be hard-nosed about them, but I'll do my best to get the least bad deal we can out of him."

~ ~ ~

REBEL HEADQUARTERS, IN THE FIELD, LAREDO

The assault shuttle, oddly shaped to eyes that had only known those brought to Laredo by the Bactrian forces, touched down in a cloud of dust. Its rear ramp whined down, and Dave strode down it to touch the soil of his native planet for the first time in over two years. He had to swallow a lump in his throat as he smelled long-familiar scents.

Major Tredegar was waiting for him ahead of his assembled staff. He snapped to attention and saluted, grinning hugely. "Welcome home, Sir!"

Dave laughed as he returned his salute, then hugged him. "It's good to be back at last. I recognize some of your staff, but not others."

"Let me introduce you." Handshakes and mutual congratulations occupied the next few minutes.

At last Dave held up his hand. "Reunions are all very well, but we've got a hell of a lot to do. Let's go somewhere we can talk. I'll lay it out for you, then give you time to discuss things from your perspective."

They gathered in the makeshift Operations Center. Everyone helped themselves to coffee, then sat down as Dave began to speak.

"Before anything else, let me congratulate all of you on your achievements here while I've been off-planet. Frankly, I'm astonished at how much you've accomplished, all without any outside assistance. When I left here two years ago the Resistance was on its last legs, with only a few hundred fighters left and virtually no reserve supplies. I've come back to three full battalions of soldiers, well equipped, and well on the way to becoming as capable as we were at the start of this war. I don't think anyone else could have done even half as well as you have.

"General Khan has agreed to formally surrender all Bactrian forces on Laredo at noon tomorrow. I'll accept his surrender in what was once Parliament Square in the center of Banka. After that we have an enormous amount to do. I'm going to lay out the high points alone, and leave it to you to decide how to implement them.

"First and foremost, for better or for worse, I'm the President Pro Tem of Laredo's Government-in-Exile. Our planetary Government no longer exists. It was wiped out by the enemy, all except for Gloria Aldred who, I understand, is no longer trustworthy. Am I right?"

"Yes, Sir," Tredegar replied, frowning. "Did General Khan say anything about her when he discussed local collaborators?"

"He did, and I've agreed in principle to his suggestion. He wants to send her and all her principal collaborators to Bactria with the first shipload of his officers. He says it's the only way he can be sure they'll be safe, because no matter what official guarantees we give, there'll be those among our forces who'll want to shoot them out of hand as traitors, the first chance they get. I couldn't argue with him. After all this is over, an elected government can consider whether and on what terms to allow them to return."

"That works for me, Sir."

"Good. Next, there's the question of running this planet until we can organize elections. I'm going to insist that we wait at least one year from the surrender before doing that. There are two reasons. One is that we have an immense amount to do, interning and repatriating Bactrian prisoners, arranging food and other necessary supplies for our people from across the settled galaxy, preparing our defenses against any Bactrian counterstrike, and planning what to do if they won't make a lasting peace. There's also a complete lack of local infrastructure to conduct elections. We'll have to set it all up from scratch, including registering eligible voters.

"I therefore propose that all of you, as the *de facto* Council of the Resistance, should constitute a temporary Administration for the planet under my interim authority, with the right to co-opt further members as and when you need them. I'll make that a decree of the Government-in-Exile in my capacity as President Pro Tem if you agree, and promote all of you to appropriate ranks on a temporary, acting basis, just as my present rank is temporary and acting. All promotions will be subject to ratification by our first elected government. If they do, great; if they don't, we'll all revert to our substantive ranks, or become civilians again if we so choose."

He paused, looking around. "You don't have to give me an immediate answer. I'll give you a day to think this over, along with all my other proposals. However, we've got to move fast, so don't delay unduly.

"Next, I've been arranging food supplies from across the settled galaxy ever since we heard about the situation here. With what they just delivered, there are enough Bactrian supplies to last everyone on the planet for up to three months, but I'm sure you're all tired of them by now." Groans and nodding heads showed he was right. "I've got a ship only a few light years away, waiting for a message. She'll bring fresh and much better-tasting ration packs, and more will follow. We'll let the Bactrian prisoners eat what their planet has provided." Cheers ran around the table. Dave couldn't help smiling.

"Another vessel at the rendezvous will take orders to our other ships, and news of our success to our Embassy at the United Planets. I want you to select one or two of your number to go to Neue Helvetica aboard the courier ship. They'll brief our Ambassador – Rusty Higgs, whom some of you will remember – and the Vice-President – my wife, Tamsin – about what's happened here over the two years since we left, and make themselves available for press conferences in due course. Thereafter they'll assist our Ambassador until we can get them back here. Pick articulate, presentable people who'll make a good impression. I'll send a couple of my people with them to describe the space combat that took back the system.

"I'll send most of the officers of the Bactrian forces back there aboard the first ship, along with General Khan's staff. That'll deprive their units of most of their leaders. Their NCO's can maintain order until they're repatriated. I'll allow General Khan and a small staff to stay here until the majority of them have left, at his request. We'll begin setting up tented prison camps immediately, using the prisoners as a labor force. You'll have to provide guards and a transport unit to shuttle supplies to and from the camps as needed. I'll leave it to you to arrange that."

"What about our own structure, Sir?" Tredegar asked. "Will you take over Brigadier-General Aldred's position as Commanding Officer of Laredo's armed forces?"

"No. We're going to need three commanders. Vice-President Johns appointed me her successor as President Pro Tem before she died. I'll retain that office, and also command our space defenses. In the latter capacity I'll change my rank to acting Commodore, the Fleet equivalent of my present rank of acting Brigadier-General. I'll promote you to acting Brigadier-General with immediate effect, reporting to the office of the President Pro Tem. You'll command our armed forces planetside, continue their training, take over all the Bactrians' equipment, and supervise the prisoners until they've been repatriated. We'll need a third person to begin to re-establish our civil planetary administration, keeping whatever's worth keeping from the Bactrians and discarding the rest, then deciding what parts of our pre-invasion infrastructure should be rebuilt right away and what can be left until later. I nominate former Sergeant-Major Deacon for that job. He's been my strong right arm in setting up the administrative side of our Government-in-Exile, and more recently he's ramrodded the purchase and shipping of food for Laredo from across the settled galaxy. He's now a substantive Captain and acting Colonel. He'll join us in a few days." A rustle of recognition and amusement ran around the table.

"I want to begin training at least two thousand members of the Resistance as Spacers, up to five hundred at once, the rest over the remainder of this year and early next year. We're not finished with Bactria, not by a long way. I don't believe for a moment they'll let matters rest as they are now. We're going to have to discourage them the hard way from ever bothering us again." A growl of angry, determined agreement came from his listeners.

"I think I have a way to keep them from interfering for the next few months, but as soon as the repatriation of prisoners has been completed they'll be spoiling for a fight. We have to train our own people to first augment, then eventually replace the Gurkha spacers I've used up till now. I want you to ask for volunteers among your people. It'll be brutally hard work under very high pressure. We can't afford to cut them any slack.

They'll have to work faster, harder and smarter than ever before. I'm sure we'll have more volunteers than we need, so choose the best among them with that in mind."

"What about those Gurkhas, Sir?" Tredegar asked curiously. "You said you had a battalion with you."

"I have a battalion of Gurkhas, but they're all serving as Spacers. Most of them aren't even here. That was a bluff, to give General Khan another reason to give up without a fight." Another laugh ran around the table.

"It seems to have worked, Sir."

"Yes – so far. In due course volunteer spacers from other planets may join us as well, but I can't say for sure yet. Is there anything of immediate importance from your side?"

Those around the table shook their heads. Tredegar observed, "As you said, Sir, there's going to be a mammoth amount of work for all of us for the next year or so, just to keep our heads above water. We'll have to work out most of it as we go along. Let's get the Bactrian prisoners sorted out, then we'll take it from there."

"Yes, we will. Let me have nominations for promotion as quickly as possible. We need proper command structures for your three battalions, under Brigadier-General Tredegar as the Laredo Army's new General Officer in Command. All ranks will be temporary and in an acting capacity until confirmed – or otherwise – by our first elected Government. We'll also have to account to that Government for our stewardship of the planet and its resources. Keep that firmly in mind at all times."

~ ~ ~

Late that night Dave emerged from the temporary command center in a cluster of farm buildings, looked up at the stars, and breathed a long sigh. "There were times I thought I'd never see Laredo's stars again," he remarked.

"I guess it must have been difficult for you," Tredegar said.

"Not half as difficult as it was for you here. Still, we've had our fair share of adventures off-planet. One day we'll have to write a book about the Laredo War. There'll be a lot to tell our children and grandchildren, to make sure they don't forget what happened."

"Probably more than one book. Your adventures off-planet are a story in themselves, judging by all you've told us."

"Oh, you haven't heard the half of it yet! We've been blessed with some powerful friends who helped us with a lot of money and even more technical help, but we've basically had to grab for the brass ring whenever we saw it and hope for the best."

He looked soberly at his companion. "Be real clear about this, Paul. We're on our beam ends financially. We took in close to two billion Neue Helvetica francs after Vice-President Johns was assassinated, and another half-billion or so in donations since we published the documentary and book about what Bactria did to Laredo. We've spent just about all of that, or committed it, to buy and equip our warships, train their crews, and buy the rations we need to keep this planet going for the next year or so. When word gets out about our success here, I expect another one to two billion francs in further donations over the next six months, but we can't spend it all on fighting a war. We need as much as possible to help rebuild things here.

"What that means is that we have to finish this war within the next year, or find ourselves too broke to fight on. I'll try to buy us short-term immunity from attack by bluffing Bactria about our capabilities. After that, once the prisoners are gone, we're going to have to hit them as hard as we can. It'll be a one-off, all-or-nothing strike. If we succeed, we'll smash their threat and win the war. If we lose, it'll drag on and they'll likely be back with another invasion force in a few years. I don't think we'll be able to resist them at that point."

Tredegar nodded slowly. "I hear you. I didn't think about the financial side before, but I guess warships are a very expensive proposition."

"You've no idea. Every missile they fire is like shooting thirty to forty million francs out of the tube. So far we've been very lucky to get our hands on a lower-cost solution, and I hope to get more soon at Bactria's expense, but we can't afford to replace what we fire if we have to pay market prices. Same goes for our ships. We got a lot of help from the Lancastrian Commonwealth because they really want us to succeed, then form a defensive alliance with other small planets worried about facing something like a Bactrian invasion themselves. They've spent a lot of money and lives on United Planets missions to places like that. They reckon if we succeed,

247

it'll help reduce that burden in future, so they're helping us out of their own self-interest. If we don't succeed, that won't continue – and without that sort of engineering and technical backup, we may as well give up right now. We could never afford to pay for it at commercial rates."

"So how do you plan to hit Bactria?"

"I've got some ideas. I'll refine them in consultation with some of the experts we've hired, then prepare a plan. It'll be three to four months before we'll have something we can discuss in detail. Meanwhile, there's more than enough to do getting things sorted out here. You and Bill Deacon can focus on that. That'll free me to worry about the space side of the fight."

"Sooner you than me!"

Bactria: June 1 2852 GSC

MINISTRY OF WAR, SODIA

The War Council sat in stunned, incredulous silence as Lieutenant-Colonel Oxus gave her report. She concluded, "Brigadier-General Khan felt it his duty to remain with his troops on Termaz to do all he could for their well-being until the last of them is repatriated. He's submitted a personal, eyes-only report to you, Your Majesty." She took a data chip from her pocket and placed it on the table in front of the Satrap. "I don't know what's in it – he said it was confidential."

"Thank you, Lieutenant-Colonel," Rostam said automatically, face pale. "I'll read it later."

"There's one more thing, Your Majesty. I don't know enough about space warfare to be sure of what we saw, but before General Khan's staff were put aboard the freighter, we were taken to Brigadier-General Carson's flagship. He showed us a cargo hold that contained a lot of big gray boxes with a sort of dome on top. He claimed they were nuclear space mines, and warned that if Bactria made any attempt to reinvade Termaz, or our ships entered its space without permission, or we failed to repatriate all of our prisoners within six months, he'd send some of his ships to sow them throughout our system and shut down our space-based industries. He could see that we didn't understand, so he told us to ask our Navy. He said they'd know what he was talking about."

The Satrap glanced at Rear-Admiral Stasanor. "Admiral?"

The Admiral was tapping rapidly at a keyboard. "Just a moment, please, Your Majesty…" A holographic display came to life at the bottom of the conference table. "Look at that, please, Lieutenant-Colonel Oxus. Is that what you saw aboard his flagship?"

She peered at the display. It showed a tall rectangular structure topped with a hemisphere. "Yes, Sir – that, or something almost identical to it. The stenciled letters on the side seem to be very similar as well."

Stasanor's mouth twisted bitterly. "Your Majesty, it looks as if laser cannon weren't all that the rebels bought from Marano. That's an image from their catalog of weapons for sale. It's their standard model of nuclear space mine. We use some of them ourselves in our orbital defenses. How many do you think you saw, Colonel?"

"I'd say probably a hundred or thereabouts, Sir."

"And that's aboard only one ship. We know he's got at least two operational, and probably more that haven't reached Termaz yet. If each of them has the same number of mines, they can cripple us with a single pass through our system. Those things are stealthy, almost impossible to pick up by radar or lidar except at point-blank range, and they have their own gravitic drive units to move slowly from one point to another. No matter how hard we tried, we could never be sure we'd swept them all up – and we'd lose many of our minesweeping ships to them in the process."

"But our agents didn't uncover any record of such a sale," SS Lieutenant-General Gedrosia objected. "As far as we know, the rebels only bought laser cannon – defensive weapons. I don't see how Marano could have sold them offensive weapons they'd be sure to use against us. I mean, we're a much bigger customer than the rebels. They wouldn't want to offend us."

"Which may be why your agents found no trace of the transaction," Stasanor pointed out. "Marano would have done its utmost to keep it under wraps, to prevent us finding out about it. Even if we challenge them about it, they'll just deny it; and without one of those mines in our hands, with its serial numbers intact, we've got no hard evidence. What's more, those mines are much more affordable than missiles – no more than a couple of million Neue Helvetica francs apiece. They're well within the rebels' budget, if the figures we've discussed for that are correct."

The Satrap suddenly slapped his forehead in anguished realization. "Oh, *hell!* What about our big weapons order from Marano? We were going to pay for it in part with an exclusive ten-year asteroid mining concession in the Termaz system. Will Marano find out about this disaster in time to stop the shipment before it leaves?"

There was an even more agonized silence for a moment, broken by the Rear-Admiral. "I don't think so, Your Majesty. Their timetable was to have everything loaded by today. There may be a couple of days' delay – there often is with a big order like this – but the ship's due to leave by not later than the seventh. I don't see how news of the loss of Termaz can reach them before then. For a start, where would they learn about it? We haven't announced anything yet, and according to Lieutenant-Colonel Oxus, General Khan ordered the freighter's crew and everyone aboard to say nothing and release no information until she'd reported to you. The rebels will no doubt announce it at the United Planets, but they can't do that until they send word there. That'll take them another week or two from now, I should think."

"Yes, thank heaven! We're going to keep everyone aboard that ship and clamp down on any release of information until we can figure out how to handle this."

Stasanor nodded. "Once the Marano delivery ship is in deep space, it'll be out of communication. As long as we clamp down on the news here until it arrives, so it doesn't hear anything on our news broadcasts or from our people, we can take delivery of the shipment and sign the concessions as if nothing had happened. Those in the Termaz system will be worthless until we take it back, of course, but we can worry about that later. The important thing is to get our hands on those patrol craft and missiles. Without them, we'll have a much harder time stopping the rebels if they come to call."

"Very well. Lieutenant-Colonel Oxus, please wait outside in the anteroom. I'll have orders for you in a short while."

"Yes, Your Majesty." She snapped to attention, held her brace for a moment, then walked to the door and let herself out.

As soon as she'd gone Lieutenant-General Demetrias growled, "That fool Khan should have fought, dammit! He'd have taken heavy casualties, sure enough, but he had the best part of four thousand combat troops to

251

face three thousand rebels and a Gurkha battalion – if that actually exists; we've seen no evidence yet to prove that it does. He could have fought a force like that on even terms."

"And what about the kinetic weapons the rebels threatened to deploy from orbit?" Rear-Admiral Stasanor asked acidly. "You saw the vid of the destruction of Mount Sinclair. If I'd been there, that would have been more than enough to convince me that there was no point in resistance. He had no way of avoiding or evading them except to keep moving incessantly. The moment one of his units stopped to rest or eat or refuel, it would have been destroyed."

"Then he should have done that! Better to lose his army than allow it to be captured without firing a shot! He's disgraced us!"

"Enough, gentlemen." The Satrap's voice was suddenly very tired. "There's no point in arguing about what might have happened or should have happened. We've got to deal with what *did* happen, and the problems facing us as a result. Admiral, can we repatriate that many people within six months?"

"I'll have to run it past our logistics people, Your Majesty. We've lost our three armed merchant cruisers, which will make it difficult, but the rebels sent back our freighter, which helps. If we charter three or four merchant freighters and fit personnel pods in a couple of their holds, I think we can do it. We still have most of the pods we used to invade Termaz several years ago – they're in orbital storage, and can be reactivated. Brigadier-General Khan estimated that we'd have to lift up to forty thousand people. If we hot-bunk every berth, and cram in as many as possible sleeping on mattresses on the floor, we can lift three to four thousand in a single trip; so ten to twelve trips ought to do it. They won't be comfortable, but that's not our priority right now."

"Very well. Begin making preparations, please, and find out what ships are available for charter. If our space freight lines won't cooperate, I'll issue requisition orders for them." He rubbed his eyes. He'd been woken in the small hours of the morning with the news of the ship's arrival, and hadn't had any sleep since then.

"Gentlemen, we face an unprecedented crisis. I'm not going to put forward proposals on how to deal with it yet, because the implications are so staggering I don't think any of us have any idea what the long-term

252

effects are likely to be. Please begin that assessment in terms of your own areas of responsibility. We'll reconvene this meeting tomorrow morning, at which time you should each be prepared to offer preliminary proposals for action. Meanwhile, the news of the loss of Termaz is strictly embargoed. You may not discuss it with *anyone,* even your staff members. If you require their assistance to develop your proposals, use as few as possible and put it to them as if this is a snap war game scenario. Admiral Stasanor, please ensure that the freighter maintains radio silence and doesn't allow any of her passengers to communicate with anyone."

"Yes, Sir."

"Very well. This meeting of the War Council is adjourned until ten tomorrow morning. Admiral, please remain behind for a moment."

Stasanor waited until the others had left, then approached the Satrap as he sat slumped in his seat, staring at the tabletop as if he expected it to suddenly light up with answers to the crisis that had blown up out of nowhere. "Yes, Your Majesty?"

Rostam looked up, shaking himself free of his reverie. "Admiral, my condolences on the loss of Commodore Eschate, as well as another corvette and its crew. If we need to make any special arrangements for their family members, please let me know. Meanwhile, you'll need another officer to assume the Commodore's responsibilities. I know that promotions to Flag rank must be approved by the legislature, but due to the magnitude of the present crisis I'll accept your nominee as an acting member of the War Council, with the right to vote in Commodore Eschate's stead, until such approval can be arranged. Do you have anyone in mind?"

The Admiral blinked sudden moisture from his eyes. He and Commodore Eschate had developed a close personal friendship over the years, over and above their professional relationship, and his death had hit him hard. He forced himself to be gruffly professional. "Yes, Your Majesty; Captain Kabhara, my Chief of Staff. Our succession plans had included my retiring in two years, upon which the Commodore would have succeeded to my position and the Captain to his."

"Very well. You may tell him only, in the strictest confidence, about what's happened. He's to attend meetings of the War Council with you from now on, including tomorrow morning's session."

"Yes, Your Majesty."

"Thank you, Admiral. I'll see you tomorrow."

~ ~ ~

SATRAP'S PALACE, SODIA

Zeba gazed at Rostam in horror as he summarized the events of the morning. "It looks like we've lost Termaz for good," he concluded bitterly. "I don't see any way we can afford to mount another invasion – not after all we've spent on that damned planet already."

"But what's that going to do domestically? Won't our people revolt at the thought of so many wasted lives and so much wasted money?"

"They may," he admitted grimly, "and if they do I can't blame them at all! If I were a commoner, groaning under the burden of war taxes on top of the normal demands of the Treasury, I'd be ready to revolt too. The fact that neither of us had anything to do with starting the war is neither here nor there. We're the people at the top of the pyramid. We're going to be blamed."

She nodded soberly. "And the more reactionary nobles, who bear most of the real guilt for the invasion of Termaz, will make sure to deflect as much of the blame as possible onto us in order to save their own skins."

"They'll try; but I think I can nip that in the bud. I've already got a couple of people collecting information. After we found so many records had been sanitized, I made sure to get copies of the remaining databases in case it happened again. My grandfather may have taken care to remove the most incriminating evidence against the military, but he didn't do the same for the nobles who urged the invasion in the first place and colluded in plans to reduce Termaz' population to slavery. I've already begun to drop hints in certain ears, through trusted sources, that I've got a little list and a file of evidence. If they try to use the current situation to bring me down, I'll take them down with me."

"Do you think they'll try?"

"They'll never have a better opportunity than the coming year, if that's what they want. This is going to hit our people like a hammer-blow, and then we're certain to face United Planets sanctions before the end of the year. That'll be a second major blow right after the first. Two crises like that are going to stretch us to the limits of our resilience as a society. We're already too fragile, too over-stressed as a nation."

She looked at him in worried silence for a moment, then asked, "In that case, shouldn't we at least pretend that we're planning to take back Termaz at some stage? If the hardline nobles and the Army believe that, they may back off the pressure and give us time to reorganize."

He looked at her with startled respect. "You know, that's a really good idea! I'll call General Demetrias at once and ask him to start preparing plans along those lines. I'll mention it to the War Council tomorrow as well. I'll tell them we won't take immediate action against Termaz – we can't, due to the more immediate priority of repatriating our troops – but once they're back here we can re-equip and retrain them and organize another invasion. That'll keep the Army busy, and divert the attention of the nobles whose industries will benefit from big orders for new equipment. The windfall profits will keep them occupied. Later, once the immediate pressure's off, we can make a more rational assessment of the situation and try to make the case that it's not worth the risks or the costs involved."

"They're still going to want to pin the blame on someone for losing Termaz. If not you, who?"

"General Khan foresaw that. He sent me a private, personal report. He's basically offered himself as a scapegoat. He foresaw the impact this may have on our people, and told me in so many words that if I have to pin the blame on anyone, to do so on him. He says he's a lifelong bachelor and has no family to worry about, so no-one else will suffer but him."

"That's very... noble of him. Are you going to do as he suggests?"

"Yes and no. I'll use him as a scapegoat if I have to, but I'm going to send a private message to the rebel leader aboard the first transport, probably by personal courier to ensure its security. I'll ask him to give asylum to General Khan if necessary, or allow him to leave for another planet if he so chooses, rather than force him to return here. I'll also send him funds from the secret account to make a fresh start somewhere else. I think we owe him that."

"I agree."

"He also told me he's put Gloria Aldred and a dozen of her main collaborators aboard the freighter. He said they would have been in real danger if they'd stayed on Termaz, not so much from the rebel leadership as from rank and file members who regard them as traitors for working with us. They probably wouldn't have waited for legal proceedings against them, but shot them out of hand. He made their repatriation to Bactria a condition of his surrender. What are we going to do with them? We can't just let them run around freely. As soon as our people learn that we've lost Termaz, any of its citizens will be automatic targets for the anger of the mob."

She nodded, eyes wide. "General Khan is right – yet another reason to give him a way out of this, rather than a show trial and a public execution. I'll ask Sergeant-Major Indic to suggest a safe place where we can confine them – for their protection rather than as a jail – and how best to arrange their security. Perhaps he can integrate that with Elislis' security as well, so the same team can look after them all." Her eyes softened as she mentioned their daughter.

"That's not a bad idea, and it'd provide cover for her. For public consumption, we can let it be known in due course that he's in charge of the security of the Termaz 'prisoners'. Everyone will be so nosy about them they won't think to ask questions about his new wife and their 'daughter'."

"I'll see the Sergeant-Major this afternoon to arrange that. Can I tell him about Termaz?"

Her husband thought for a moment, then sighed. "I suppose you'll have to under the circumstances, but only him and his second-in-command. Thank heaven she's now his wife, so any pillow talk won't be an indiscretion! Make sure they know to keep it secret from everyone else."

~ ~ ~

KHOTAN ESTATE

Indic wrinkled his brow in thought. "It could work, Ma'am. The walls around this estate were built to be decorative, but they'll serve to keep people in or out as well. That's one reason I chose it as our base. How many prisoners are there?"

"I understand there's a dozen or so, but don't think of them as prisoners. They're more like refugees."

"So they won't have to be closely guarded?"

"I shouldn't think so. They'll be confined here more for their security than ours. This estate's fifty kilometers out of town. There aren't many people nearby to see them and not much of a local threat if it comes to unrest or mob violence."

His eyebrows shot up. "Mob violence? You really expect that, Ma'am?"

Zeba sighed. "Think about it, Sergeant-Major. We've lost something like thirty thousand people on that damned planet. Their relatives and friends have never forgotten them, and many have never forgiven those who killed them – or those who sent them there. Our people and our economy are laboring under a war tax burden that's half again as high as it should be. The news of the loss of Termaz is going to be a body blow to our entire society. Add to that the near-certainty of economic sanctions from the United Planets later this year, and who knows what might happen?"

"Sanctions? Ma'am, this is the first I've heard of that." For the first time, she heard worry in his voice.

"We've kept it under wraps for as long as possible, but that can't last much longer. Have you heard rumors about a documentary and book put out by the rebels, alleging Bactrian atrocities on Termaz?"

"Yes, I have, Ma'am, but they've been pretty wild and confused. No-one seems to know exactly what's going on."

"I'll arrange to have a copy of the documentary sent to you and your wife. It's for your eyes only, under pain of death if you tell others – and I mean that literally. It's sickening stuff, and the greatest tragedy is that much of it appears to be the exact and literal truth. Our Army and former Administrations deliberately deceived us all. Those chickens are going to come home to roost real soon now, and we're all going to pay the price. The rebels laid all their evidence before the United Planets. It's ensured that we're going to be the pariahs of the settled galaxy before long."

He was silent for a moment, then asked, "What about the Satrap and yourself, Ma'am? If there's a backlash, both of you are going to be targets. You're the most likely to be blamed. What's more, if the nobles are looking for a scapegoat to escape blame themselves, they'll combine against you."

"I understand some of them already are. We've heard rumors of at least three cabals plotting against the Satrap. One of them is said to involve senior officers from the Army and the Security Service, but we've not been able to penetrate it to any depth as yet. There was even a whisper that it might have been behind the intrusion into the Satrap's Guard Research Center, although why they'd have done that I have no idea."

"They couldn't have found out about your daughter, Ma'am?"

"I don't think so, but it's impossible to be sure. That's why we're passing her off as your child for the time being. People are only too willing to believe that you and Chief Sergeant Traxiane enjoyed the honeymoon before the wedding, so to speak, and that Elislis was the result."

He grinned. "Well, we did, and people know it, so that helps to make the cover story more believable. Still, Ma'am, if things are going to get as bad as you say, I'd be making plans to get out of Sodia quickly and quietly if necessary. Don't rely on assault shuttles or anything like that – they're too easily targeted, particularly if traitors from the Army have provided the opposition with missiles and plasma cannon. You need a low-profile exit plan, just in case. Tell as few people as possible about it. After all, you don't know who might be plotting against you."

"I'll see what can be done. Can you nominate a few absolutely trustworthy NCO's to form a small, very private security team for us, over and above our regular guards? If worse comes to worst we can have the regulars hold the Satrap's Palace while the smaller team gets us clear."

"I'll start digging through the records and asking my team for recommendations, without telling them what it's all about. I reckon I can come up with half a dozen names within a month. I'll probably send a couple of my people from here to command your team."

"Thank you, Sergeant-Major. Oh – one more thing. If things look like they're about to go bad, there may not be time to co-ordinate our movements with you. I want you to plan on hunkering down here and waiting for us to join you. I'm not going to abandon my daughter! However, have a backup plan to get away from here, with or without us, just in case, and set up a couple of rendezvouses where we can meet you. If you need any more equipment to make that possible, let me know and I'll arrange to have it sent to you."

He nodded firmly. "Thanks, Ma'am. One thing you can get for us right away is a couple of assault shuttles. I know I just said they're vulnerable to missiles and plasma cannon, but out here we're not as likely to face those weapons as you are in Sodia. Airvans simply won't cut it against even lightly armed opposition – a standard rifle will shoot through them from end to end. We need armor to protect those inside, and our own missiles and plasma cannon to carve our way out if it comes to that. I won't keep the shuttles here, but at the farm attached to the estate. They can be concealed in one of the barns. We'll fly them in at night, when no-one's likely to see them arrive."

"I'll see what I can do – or, rather, what my husband can do. Let me have the names of crew members you trust to operate them. I'll have them assigned to you as well."

"Thanks, Ma'am. Another thing. We're on the coast, and there's a fishing and leisure craft harbor below the bluff. I'd like to have a couple of fast boats there, big enough to accommodate everyone. They'll be another string to our bow, just in case. If they can be armed with a concealed plasma cannon and a couple of missiles, so much the better, but they need to look like regular civilian craft, not military patrol vessels. We'll need trustworthy crews for them as well."

"I'll ask Rostam to fix that up. Now, let's go and see Elislis. I'm not coming all the way out here without hugging my baby!"

~ ~ ~

ENTERTAINMENT DISTRICT, SODIA

"So you think the Satrap will try to retake Termaz?" The Wazir's voice was thoughtful.

"It certainly sounds like it," General Demetrias replied. "He was angry and frustrated when we spoke this afternoon. He says he'll raise the issue at tomorrow morning's continuation of the War Council meeting. We can't do much while our forces are effectively held hostage on Termaz, of course, but we can re-train and re-equip them as they return, and begin preparing for a new invasion next year. He's asked me to put my staff to work drawing up the necessary plans."

"I'm surprised," SS General Gedrosia said with a frown. "I'd have thought he'd seize the opportunity to declare it more trouble and expense than it was worth to try to retake Termaz."

"I was too," Demetrias agreed. "Who knows? Perhaps the experience of governing is beginning to knock some of the youthful foolishness out of his head."

"I wouldn't be too sure about that," Khanoum warned. "We haven't seen any sign of it in other areas. This may be a diversionary maneuver, designed to make us think one thing while he does another behind our backs. However, it may also work to our advantage. Don't forget, the news is going to have an enormous impact when it's eventually released. If we can channel the anger and frustration of the mob into a national determination to retake Termaz, we can stop it spilling over into their blaming the Army or pointing fingers at the House of Nobles, which was the driving force behind the invasion in the first place."

"What about sanctions?" Major-General Pamir asked. "We're expecting the United Planets to vote on a resolution within three to six months. If they impose them, where will we get the heavy weapons we need to retake Termaz? Don't forget, the rebels there captured everything intact – that was part of the terms of surrender. They now have over a hundred assault shuttles, as many armored cars, artillery, guided weapons, plasma and laser cannon – far more than they had when we first invaded. We'll need to build up much larger stocks before we reinvade, so as to have big enough reserves to grind down all they have and still have sufficient to win."

"True, very true," the Wazir observed. "I've… let's just say I've been taking steps to make sure we have hard currency available when we take over. I don't expect the Satrap to release enough from the national budget to buy all the weapons we need. However, I own three of the five refinery ships that process the output from our asteroid mines. Last year, after we began meeting like this, I took steps to put trustworthy people into positions where they could program some of the digger units to increase the ratio of precious metals mined in relation to industrial minerals. I've had them divert a large proportion of that output into what I might call an 'orbital reserve fund', for want of a better term. It's stored in secret compartments aboard a couple of my ships, off the company's books and unknown to the authorities. By the end of this year it should amount to almost a thousand tons of gold, plus several hundred tons of platinum, five to ten tons of rhodium, and other metals."

His listeners blinked as they heard the figures. "But... but that's..." Major Kadeh's voice trailed away as he tried to mentally compute the value of the hoard.

"It'll be worth between sixty and seventy billion Neue Helvetica francs, which is one of the standard currency for conversion of gold in interplanetary trade. That makes it almost as much as this planet's annual budget." The Wazir smiled. "When we take over, particularly if it's through... less peaceful means, I expect there to be a temporary shortfall in government revenue due to the political upheaval. I therefore felt it best to ensure that we'll have enough money to make up for that, so we can spend what we need to solidify our grasp on power before any rivals can organize themselves. I think there'll be enough for us to buy the weapons we need as well. There are arms dealers and brokers all across the settled galaxy who'll sell their own grandmothers for the right amount in cash or hard assets."

Smiles dawned on the faces of the military and SS officers. "That was very far-sighted of you, Wazir," SS Colonel Arachosia declared. "I'm glad we have someone with your vision at the helm of our enterprise. I'd never have thought of that."

"My family has helped rule Bactria for many generations. It's not surprising that we've learned some of the pitfalls to power. On Old Home Earth, some centuries before the Space Age, a man named Machiavelli wrote a treatise on how to rule for the princes of his city-state. I sometimes think that I could produce a much more useful and realistic – not to mention ruthless – book using extracts from the journals of my ancestors. They had valuable lessons to impart, and I've done my best to take them to heart and apply them."

"What about those nuclear space mines?" Major Kadeh asked. "If the rebels release them into our system, won't it cripple our economy no matter how much you've stashed away in hidden reserves?"

Khanoum made a dismissive gesture. "Yes, it certainly will; but two can play at that game. We have some of the same mines in our orbital defenses. If we let the rebels know that any attempt to mine our system will meet an equal response from us, crippling their space-based economy and interplanetary commerce as surely as our own, I think they'll see reason."

"Should I suggest that to the Satrap at tomorrow's War Council meeting?" Demetrias asked.

"Why not? In fact, it might be amusing to have the suggestion come from the Army rather than the Navy. You can score points off Rear-Admiral Stasanor in the process."

The Wazir courteously escorted his guests to the door of the restaurant, exchanging polite goodbyes as they went out into the night. He lingered near the door until Major Kadeh slipped back inside, ten minutes later, and led him to his private office.

"Do you think the others suspect that we're a conspiracy within a conspiracy?" the Major asked as he accepted a glass of the Wazir's private brand of liqueur.

"I doubt it. They accept that you're my protégé, of course – that's been clear for some time now – but I think they assume I'm grooming you for promotion in our service after the coup. After all, what threat can a middle-ranking field officer in the Satrap's Guard conceivably pose to the top commanders of the Army and the SS?" They grinned at each other.

"Let's hope they go on thinking that way."

"We'll do our best to make sure that happens. Now, what do you have to report?"

"I've been making a nuisance of myself conducting snap inspections of security teams in the Satrap's Palace. They hate me, but they've sharpened up a lot. More to the point, when they see me sneaking around they now assume I'm trying to catch another team being slack, so they no longer suspect I might be up to no good. That's come in handy a few times already. Even better, the Colonel's commended me for my 'drive and initiative' in improving Palace security." They chuckled. "I don't yet have enough time in grade to be promoted to command one of our two battalions, but think I might be in line to become the next Executive Officer of the Regiment, if I keep this up and play my cards right."

'Excellent! That will be even more useful to us than commanding a battalion, because in an emergency you can give orders to both battalions in the Colonel's name. They won't find that strange. You'll also be able to monitor all their activities, so you can keep us informed." The Wazir shifted in his comfortable chair. "How are you enjoying your new estate?"

"Very much, thank you, Wazir. It's far nicer than any home I've ever been able to afford before. My wife absolutely loves it, and it's wonderful to be able to play with our children in such extensive grounds. We've only lived in apartments before. We're all very grateful to you."

"You've earned it, my dear Major. I'm very pleased to hear it's to your liking."

After Kadeh took his leave for the second time, the nobleman sat late into the night, thinking over the many threads in the web he was weaving, trying to assess how each of them was progressing, how it contributed to the overall plan, whether any of them needed to be strengthened or cut short in the light of changing circumstances. Major Kadeh was an indispensable part of his plans, but even so he'd made sure to assign many essential elements to others. There was no sense in allowing any individual – except himself – to understand the whole picture. That way, no one person could betray everything, and every critical component of the plan could have a backup.

In the small hours of the morning he came to a conclusion. *The impact of United Planets sanctions is going to be worse than these officers suspect,* he thought to himself. *Our economy's going to be shaken to its roots, and a lot of people will be thrown out of work. Add that to popular anger and resentment over the loss of Termaz, and I won't be surprised to see rioting in the streets. We may have no choice but to strike swiftly to restore order, particularly if the Satrap won't rule with the iron hand it'll take to keep things under control. If so, we need him off-balance, unable to cope. How best to ensure that? Hmmm... yes... his son. We need to remove his spawn anyway, so there's no-one to later challenge the successor we install. Losing him at the critical moment will render the Satrap grief-stricken, emotionally unstable, easier to deal with. I think I'll have a word with General Gedrosia about that. He's a man who understands the necessity for strong measures, even though they may be distasteful at times; and he's convinced the Satrap backed the SS into a corner over that 'rogue operator' a few months ago. He'll be willing to do what needs to be done.*

Laredo: June 1 2852 GSC

The stars were fading in the half-light before dawn as Dave walked out of the farmhouse, carrying a briefcase. Brigadier-General Tredegar and Colonel Deacon walked with him.

"How long will you be gone, Sir?" Bill Deacon asked.

"Probably two months or more. I've got that rendezvous in deep space next week. After that I'm heading for Vesta, where our other two warships are waiting. They should have been converted by now to handle a hundred target missiles each. I'm going to send *Freedom* here right away to join *Independence* and bolster our local defenses. I'll leave *Liberty* with *Liberation* at the dockyard to have her battle damage repaired, and for both ships to be equipped with our new missiles if all goes well. As soon as they're ready, they'll relieve *Freedom* and *Independence* to return to Vesta for re-equipping in their turn. I'm also going to ask our contacts at the Fleet dockyard to find us half a dozen personnel pods to fit one of our freighters. We'll need to rig up at least one of them as an accommodation ship in orbit to help train all our new Spacers."

Tredegar asked, "What about our three newly-acquired AMC's?"

"They're older ships and not in very good shape. If I can persuade the Lancastrians to refit and update them as part of their deal with us, I'll do that, but in their original freighter configuration. We're going to need transports very badly to get our space industries up and running. We didn't have much in that line before, but given the devastation the war's left behind on our planet we're going to have to turn to our asteroids to reboot our economy. That means mining, interstellar freight and everything that goes with it. If the AMC's can be refitted at reasonable cost, and not at our expense, I'm not going to turn down three free ships, that's for sure! If they can't, we'll sell them for what they can fetch, and use the money to buy others more suitable for what we need."

"Sounds logical. Where are you bound from Vesta?"

"I'll head for Rolla to make sure our freight line is on the ball with all the shipments of food and ration packs that should be coming in from all over the settled galaxy. You did a great job there, Bill. If everything comes in as the vendors promised, we'll be set fair until early next year; and I hope food donations from other planets will extend that by another six months at least. Hopefully the harvest this year will be enough to start building up local reserves, although I realize it won't be nearly as good as before the invasion."

Deacon nodded. "By the end of summer next year we should be able to produce enough food to support ourselves. I know Tamsin's planning to ask for donations of machinery, fertilizer and other necessities to help us expand our farms."

"With the help of a couple of orbital farms, yes, I think we'll be all right. In case I've never told you, we couldn't have got this far without you. You've been a tower of strength to me, and to all of us, in handling these infrastructure issues. I couldn't possibly have gone running around as I have without knowing that you were backstopping me all the way on the administration and logistics side. If anyone deserves a medal for our liberation, you do."

The Colonel actually blushed. "Hey, we all did our part. I'm just one of the cogs in the machine."

"You're a bloody big cog, and the machine wouldn't work without you. However, I'll stop embarrassing you."

"Good!" They all laughed.

"I'll tell our freight line to begin planning to move their operations here next year," Dave continued. "I don't want them to come until our warships have all been converted and we're fairly sure we can protect our system from intruders. I'll have *Reliance* – our fifth assault transport, the one we're using as a depot ship for the four warships – come here right away, along with enough spares and supplies to keep them operational for the next year. The Lancastrians will send a number of their people aboard her to keep training our technicians. I hope there'll also be a few patrol craft available soon, to carry out local patrols while our larger warships are busy elsewhere.

"From Rolla I'll head for Neue Helvetica. The news media are sure to be screaming to talk to me. You'll have some here by then, I'm sure, wanting the inside story of the Resistance over the past couple of years. I'll leave you to deal with them as you see fit."

Tredegar asked, "What are you going to do about the Government-in-Exile now that we've re-established an interim government here?"

"I'll have to talk to them about that. Part of me wants to keep the Government-in-Exile going as a backup, in case the Bactrians have something nasty up their sleeve. On the other hand, that's an expense I'm not sure we can afford. If Tamsin's fund-raising efforts after our victory have been as successful as we hoped, I'll leave her there to continue them. We desperately need as much money as we can get, and we can't talk to donors from here. If she hasn't raised much, I'll shut down the Government-in-Exile and bring everyone back here except for our Embassy to the United Planets. I guess I'm saying 'It depends'. I can't say for sure right now what's going to happen there."

"That's understandable."

Bill said, longing in his voice, "Part of me really hopes you'll shut it down, because then I'll see Elisabeta and our kid sooner. On the other hand, I know she's doing a really important job there. Just tell her I love her, please, and I'll see her as soon as we can arrange it."

"I'll do that. I'm in the same boat with Tamsin and our children. I guess we're going to have that problem until we settle our account with Bactria once and for all."

"And when will we do that?" Tredegar asked.

Dave's face turned grim. "It's as I said to you after General Khan surrendered. We can only afford to continue this fight for another year at most, and that only by pinching every penny until it screams for mercy. Once the prisoners have been repatriated, there won't be anything to stop Bactria getting feisty again if they want to – unless we shut them down once and for all.

266

"We fought a war to the knife on Laredo up to the Battle of Banka. By then our old blade – the Resistance – had been ground down to a nub. Since then we've forged a new blade, with a reborn Resistance here on Laredo and our warships and Government-in-Exile off-planet. That new blade's just been tested and proven. Now we're going to use our knife to the hilt – sink it into Bactria as deep as it can go. We're going to hurt them so badly in their own system that they'll never dare bother us again. We're going to hit them so hard that Bactrian mothers will use Laredo as a threat to keep their children in line for generations to come. 'Do as I say, or the Laredans will get you!' That's how badly I want them to fear us by the time we finish with them. It may cost us every warship we have, and everyone aboard them, but that's a price I'm willing to pay if necessary."

Tredegar and Deacon watched as Dave's assault shuttle took flight, climbing steeply as it vanished into the lightening sky, heading for orbit. As the thunder of its reaction thrusters died away slowly, the newly-promoted Brigadier-General said softly, "Knife to the hilt, eh? I suppose that says it all."

"It does, Sir," Deacon confirmed soberly. "We didn't start this war… but next year we're going to finish it, or die trying!"

ABOUT THE AUTHOR

Peter Grant was born and raised in Cape Town, South Africa. Between military service, the IT industry and humanitarian involvement, he traveled throughout sub-Saharan Africa before being ordained as a pastor. He later immigrated to the USA, where he worked as a pastor and prison chaplain until an injury forced his retirement. He is now a full-time writer, and married to a pilot from Alaska. They currently live in Tennessee.

See all of Peter's books at his Amazon.com author page, or visit him at his blog, Bayou Renaissance Man, where you can also sign up for his mailing list to receive a monthly newsletter and be kept informed of upcoming books.